North
Atlantic
Ocean

THE BAHAMAS

CUBA

CAMAGÜEY

GUANTÁNAMO

SANTIAGO
DE CUBA

Caribbean Sea

HAITI

JAMAICA

Cold Havana Ground

A NOVEL BY
ARNALDO CORREA

TRANSLATION BY MARJORIE MOORE

Akashic Books
New York

Published by Akashic Books
©2003 Arnaldo Correa

Cover design by Keith Campbell
Cover photo by Miriam Berkley
Cuba map and inside layout by Sohrab Habibion

ISBN: 1-888451-52-1
Library of Congress Control Number: 2003109535
First printing

Printed in Canada

Akashic Books
PO Box 1456
New York, NY 10009
Akashic7@aol.com
www.akashicbooks.com

This novel is dedicated to my wife María Julia, my children Sonia, Arnaldo,
and Aramís, and my grandchildren, Claudia and Aramisito;
from whom I stole all the time dedicated to this project.

ACKNOWLEDGMENTS

First, I wish to express my deep gratitude to Marjorie Moore and her husband Luis Ríos for their prolonged effort in translating this difficult book. Unfortunately, Marjorie did not live long enough to see it published. My thanks to Natalia Bolívar, one of the top authorities in Afro-Cuban religions, for carefully reviewing this key aspect of the novel.

I would also like to thank Colonel Benjamín of the DTI, who put the police files in my hands on which a previous television program and this novel are based. My recognition to the Guanabacoa Police for all their help, and particularly for facilitating a memorable meeting with the heads of the main Abakuá chapters.

My special thanks to Enrique "Enriquito" Armenteros, an authority in *Regla Mayombe (Palo Monte)*, for his teachings and wise advise; to the memory of my great friend and teacher *Tata Nkisi* Planta Firme, who, loyal to his beliefs, asked to be cremated to ensure that his corpse would not be stolen and put into an unknown *nganga*; to Ana Vinent, a true daughter of Oshún and a very knowledgeable *Iyalosha*; to the priests and believers in these religions from whom I have been able to extract my characters and give them life in this story; to Dacio, a sharp reviewer of my first drafts; to Agenor Martí for the valuable information he gave me; and, last but not least, to Akashic Books for their fine editing.

NASAKÓ

SEVEN SMALL PILES OF gunpowder blazed up simultaneously, illuminating the entranced face of the *Nasakó*—accentuating the white of his eyes—and the surprised expressions of the three men standing behind him. "Everything will be fine," he said with absolute assurance, flashing his coconut-white teeth. The faces behind him grinned in relief at the good omen of the flames on the machete blade.

The *Nasakó*, who had been crouched before his *nganga* until that moment, shirtless and barefoot and breathing deeply, moved now to a stool so low it was almost flush with the floor. He removed the purple rag tied around his head and wiped sweat from his forehead and neck. From the bottle of *aguardiente* next to the *nganga*, he filled three cups made of güira shell. He served one to each of those present, linking hands with them as was required, and took a long swig directly from the bottle. Then, with surprising care, he set the bottle in its place beside the large pot that held his *nganga*, an offering to Zarabanda, the vengeful *mpungo* governing all iron.

The *Nasakó* turned suddenly toward the men. "Do *exactly* as I tell you!" he exclaimed, slapping his hand on the floor so sharply that it sounded like a small-caliber pistol shot.

"I have it all written down," Adrián said.

"Written, no, *coño*! Here! Here!" shouted the *Nasakó*, tapping his forehead with his fingers.

Adrián nodded obediently. He raised his cup to drink, then visibly repressed an urge to retch, repelled by the sweet, pungent aroma of the *aguardiente* mixed with all the other odors of the place: the soothing smell of the burnt gunpowder; the rancid stench emerging from the *nganga* recently sprinkled with blood from two roosters and a black goat; the sour vapor wafting up from the half-rotted fruit in the corner; the mild rankness of four buzzard feathers strung together on a gourd hanging from the ceiling; the omnipresent dry smell circulating with the dust that never seemed to settle but floated from place to place; and the acidic, penetrating reek from the sweat of the *Nasakó*.

The *Nasakó* observed Adrián with suspicion and disdain, thinking that he had brought disturbing spirits that might hinder his work and his communication with the enormous power contained in the *nganga*. He smiled with a grimace.

Pedro shuddered as the *aguardiente* ran down his throat—like lye down the drain of a stopped-up toilet—till it reached his stomach, spreading heat through his body. He looked longingly toward the bottle. The *Nasakó*, usually so perspicacious, seemed unaware that Pedro was asking for another drink.

Mulo, far in the rear, outside the circle illuminated by the candles, sipped his drink slowly, moving like a cold-blooded animal poised for action. He was the first to leap toward the door upon hearing the noise. The other two followed closely. Pedro pulled out his gun.

"Mice, it's only mice!" shouted the *Nasakó*, ordering them back inside with a brusque movement of his arms. "No stranger would dare come in here! And you!" He pointed to Pedro. "Don't ever pull out a gun before a *nganga*. Not even a little knife! Do you hear me?"

On his feet, the *Nasakó* almost brushed the ceiling with the top of his head. The others hunched down slightly, fearing the giant mind reader.

Lorenzo Bantú, *Nasakó* of an Abakuá chapter, opened the door and filled his lungs with deep satisfaction as he stepped out, letting a waft of fresh air into the room. He walked toward a damp hollow where grass and trees grew riotously: the woodland of his ancestors. In the daytime, it was a large blotch of dark green surrounding an ancient *ceiba* that embraced a young palm almost lustfully amidst a clutter of gray shacks piled in disorder as if thrown there by someone in a drunken frenzy. He walked in the darkness toward the silent and mysterious shadows, a microworld separated from the lights, the noises, the voices, and the singing and beating of drums from the La Jata neighborhood in Guanabacoa.

The fourth Lorenzo Bantú moved directly to the foot of the royal palm tree, feeling he finally had the right to do something he had never done before. His stream of urine pattered musically against the thin walls of a metallic container, just like the urine of his great-grandfather and his grandfather, the second and the third Lorenzo Bantús, in ages past.

AUTHOR'S WARNING TO THE READER

This novel is based on events that occurred in the recent past in Cuba. The characters are real, the names fictitious. Descriptions of the Afro-Cuban religious practices are authentic. A glossary is provided at the back of this novel with explanations and definitions of some of the religious words and concepts found in the story.

Several years ago, I was given access to the police files of a case that was deeply tied to believers in the three African-rooted religions practiced in Cuba: Regla de Osha, also called Santería; Regla Mayombe, usually called Palo Monte; and the Abakuá Secret Society. Weeks of research on the case and on these religions resulted in a one-hour television program for a police series watched by most Cubans.

I became convinced that the story warranted a book focused on the complex world of the believers in these religions, whose behavior is very influenced by the oracles they consult. For several years I continued conducting field research for a novel that would someday be written. During this time, extraordinary facts about the case were unveiled, which drew me in even further.

As time passed, this increasingly became a search for some of the basic clues to the idiosyncrasies of the Cuban people, and in many ways a search for keys to self-understanding. During this quest, I witnessed incidents and events that could not yet be explained by science.

I strongly discourage the reader from using, on your own, any of the conjurations, curses, magic work, maledictions, or divination methods found in this book. I also want to state that I cannot be held responsible in any way for the results that may ensue from such use. This should be made clear to anyone who reads this book.

Yours truly,
Arnaldo Correa
Havana, August 2003

IN THE FIRST PLACE, THE SENSATION
OF THE MARVELOUS PRESUPPOSES FAITH.
THOSE WHO DON'T BELIEVE IN SAINTS
CANNOT BE CURED BY REMEDIES OF SAINTS.

ALEJO CARPENTIER

THE CHINESE CEMETERY

ENTERING THROUGH A PORTAL with Chinese inscriptions, a visitor finds a road some eighty yards long that divides Havana's Chinese cemetery into two equal parts. Occupying scarcely a quarter of a city block, the entire graveyard can be captured in a single glance, including the surrounding greenish-gray wall, intensely cracked and seemingly about to crumble. The wall is shoulder-high, and passersby peering over it often notice something odd about the crosses, aligned in accordance with the sun's movement across the sky, each with its back to another. The Chinese cemetery lies alongside the broad Calle 26, always agitated with vehicles and noise, in the heart of Vedado, a neighborhood inhabited by over one hundred thousand people; but anyone entering the cemetery immediately feels that he or she has escaped from the city.

The grave digger slowed his movements to regulate the sweat streaming down his face, clouding his thick eyeglasses. He paused in his work hoeing weeds around a tomb to observe a tall, blond, bearded visitor who had just arrived. The newcomer stopped a few meters inside the gate, glancing about until he sighted the inquiring gaze of the grave digger, who dropped his hoe and walked toward him with alacrity, relieved for the excuse to interrupt his exhausting labor.

"You're Cancio!" the visitor exclaimed, smiling, showing strong white teeth. He then jabbed the grave digger in the center of the chest with a forefinger at the same time that he threw an arm over his shoulders, seemingly impervious to the stench of sweat and the vapor rising from the laborer's body, hot from the sun and physical activity.

Trapped in the embrace, the grave digger responded: "At your orders!"

"Cancio, I heard about the theft of the Chinaman from a friend of yours here in the neighborhood—Pepe Pérez. He said, 'You've got to hear Cancio's story. Go see him, and tell him I sent you.'" The visitor winked broadly. "You know the guy I mean?"

"Pepe Pérez?"

"That's the one!"

Cancio led the tall visitor along the road toward the rear of the cemetery. Small houses shaped like pagodas held the ossuaries—the bones of the dead—and each dwelling belonged to a Chinese society. The grave digger pointed to a tomb in which another Chinaman had been buried for over twenty years. "And he's still in perfect condition," he said, "except where the cockroaches've eaten him around the ears and nose."

As they arrived at a back entrance to the cemetery, sealed by an iron gate, Cancio reached his arm through the bars and pointed to a spot just outside the grounds. "They left the truck parked there, beside that pile of grass. There wasn't any moon that night. They arrived near dawn. They cut the padlock with a fretsaw. The lock wasn't very big, but it was a good one. The next mornin' I saw it lyin' there on the ground, but I didn't touch it. The police took it as evidence of burglary . . . that's what the technician called it . . . and to see if it had any fingerprints. The chain had disappeared, and it was a good chain, too . . . been there Lord knows how long. They still haven't brought me another padlock and chain, so I had to use that piece of barbed wire to seal the gate."

The grave digger spoke in short spurts interspersed with asthmatic wheezing, occasionally spitting out a sticky, greenish fluid onto the grass.

"A veteran two-pack-a-day smoker!" exclaimed the visitor, giving him three smart blows on the back. The grave digger, left breathless for several seconds, merely nodded.

"Where was the stolen Chinaman buried?"

"In the niches." The grave digger turned and pointed a finger toward another area, coughing up ammunition for another shot of phlegm.

The blond man stared at the still-pointing finger of the grave digger, extraordinarily thick and curved. "What happened to that finger, Cancio?"

"The lid of a tomb fell on it. Anyway, they carried off that Chinaman still fresh in the ground, you might say. The cement hadn't even hardened. When the burial procession arrived here, it was pourin' rain. In summer, they should bury everyone early in the mornin', since it always rains in the afternoon. I waited awhile for it to clear up a little, but it was still comin' down pretty hard when I started to close the tomb. I covered it with a piece of nylon afterwards, but the mixture of sand and cement must've stayed pretty wet."

They walked on to the niche where Rafael Cuan had been interred. The tall, blond man knelt down to look inside the empty enclosure, then confirmed with a gesture that the coffin was not there. The grave digger used the time to pull a large, dirty handkerchief from his pocket and pass it over his face and the lenses of his glasses, managing to smear them uniformly.

"The night watchman said he didn't see or hear anyone. But after things calmed down a little, the administration transferred him to Colón cemetery. I guess the police figured that this is just a little place and no matter how dark it was that night, he had to've seen or heard somethin'. A deaf person would've heard the ruckus of them takin' the coffin out of the niche and cuttin' that padlock . . . I think the poor guy lost his nerve. This place is pretty spooky at night, 'specially with the bats."

"Bats?" The visitor raised his eyebrows.

"They scare the pants off you all night long. They say the tormented souls of the *chinos* buried here take possession of those critters and use 'em to fly from one side to another, like ridin' horseback. I don't put much store in that, but I respect it. That watchman was a good *compañero*. The one they've put in his place now . . ." The grave digger shook his head and tipped an imaginary bottle to his lips. "The binges he goes on ev'ry night with cookin' alcohol!"

As they walked back toward the entrance, the blond man noted that the crosses were wider toward the ends, the cause of the strange impression he had received upon his first glance at the place.

"Me, now, I'm always alert," Cancio continued. "As soon as anyone arrives, I ask who he is, what his business here is, and what he wants. You can spot family members a mile away. That's the advantage of workin' in the Chinese cemetery. But other kinds of people come here, too. The worst are the ones that hang around to see if they can carry off bones."

"Bones?"

Cancio nodded solemnly. "They're *Paleros,* or come sent by 'em. They use 'em for their witchcraft. I don't let 'em out of my sight when they come pretendin' to be lookin' for a certain tomb. The first funny move and I throw 'em out. Some of 'em ask me for permission to take earth from the four corners of the cemetery, and I let 'em do that. But bones, no way!"

"Where did they enter from?"

"Climbed over that wall. Since the ground was still wet, the police had a party makin' molds of their footprints. There were three of 'em."

"Why did they climb over the wall if they cut the padlock and opened the gate?"

Cancio opened his mouth, then closed it again, but the visitor didn't allow him time for much consideration of the question.

"Have you personally seen anything suspicious?"

"Well, I didn't remember it that day because you get confused with all the hullabaloo all of a sudden . . . the police in here with their cars . . . dogs smelling around everywhere and everybody askin' the same thing . . . Anyway, about a week later, I remembered somethin' and called the police right away. A big young fella came. A lieutenant, he said. He asked me a lot of questions, like he was tryin' to catch me up. You know how some of these young fellas are nowadays . . . think everythin' has to be learned from books."

"Tell me what you remembered."

"About two weeks before they stole the Chinaman, I was workin' over there on that side when a guy entered on a bicycle—a young white guy. He stopped in front of me and said, '*Tío,* every time I pass by here, I think of visiting this cemetery, but I never have time.' Then he asked if it was true that *chinos* are buried standin' up. I told him in this cemetery we bury 'em lyin' down and face up. He stood there awhile, watchin' me work, then he asked if they still bring many *legitimate* Chinamen to be buried here. That smelled sort of funny to me, and I asked what a *legitimate* Chinaman was. He said, '*Tío*, a Chinaman from China, one of the original ones, the real ones, not one crossed with a black.' Then I stopped what I was doin' and asked him straight out, 'Just what are you lookin' for, anyway?' Then he got on his bicycle and said, 'Nothing, *tío*, don't get your hack up, I'm just leavin',' and he went pedallin' away."

"Cancio, did you notice anything unusual about that man?"

"Really, I don't remember very well what he looked like. Young, white— well, Cuban-white—you know how they say, the one not mixed with Congolese is mixed with Carabalí! Now that I think of it, he had a matchstick in his mouth with the head outside and he talked to me like this, with his mouth closed." The grave digger imitated the unknown man's way of speaking. "I told the lieutenant, but he didn't pay any attention. He thinks he knows everythin' and that I invented the guy. What good would that do me? You tell me, what would I gain with that?"

"With the match head outside?"

"*Sí*, with the match's head outside." He repeated the imitation.

"You haven't seen him again?"

"A few days ago, a man walked past on the sidewalk outside and, I don't know why, but I had an idea that it was that same fella. But no, I don't really remember him well enough to say for sure that it was him."

The visitor and the grave digger had almost reached the entrance portico and stopped before the cemetery office, a small building with a flat, thick concrete roof.

"Cancio, how did you let them build this ugly office in such a pretty cemetery?"

The grave digger grinned, uncertain how to answer, still perturbed by the visitor's instant familiarity from the moment he had entered the cemetery.

"They ought to dynamite this junk pile with whoever built it inside . . . and whoever ordered it built, too." The man's tone gave the impression that he was about to set to work on the project at that very moment. Hands on hips, he turned suddenly to the grave digger. "And couldn't it have been a family member that took him away?"

Cancio shook his head. "These people are really respectful of their dead. Why would they take him away?"

"Why not?"

"You don't know 'em. They even bring 'em food on the Chinese All Souls' Day." He smiled, having found a convincing argument. "They bring 'em what they most liked: chop suey, chilied shrimp, even roast pork. These *Chinos* really know how to cook!" Cancio swallowed, as if his mouth was watering. "They used to leave the food there, and some people from around here would come and eat it. Now, they just leave it awhile and then take it away. I guess these ain't times to be sharin' food with the dead."

"How do you know they entered near dawn? The watchman swore he didn't hear or see anything. Did he tell you that? Come on, Cancio, just between you and me."

After a moment of doubt, the grave digger nodded guiltily, as if revealing something improper. He accompanied the visitor out to the sidewalk, eager to continue being interrogated, to keep talking about the theft of the Chinese cadaver, the most important event in his life at the moment.

The grave digger asked the visitor's name, but the blond man didn't answer, seemingly lost in thought. He cast a last glance back into the cemetery and, after patting Cancio on the shoulder absentmindedly, walked off in the direction of Calle 23, leaving the grave digger perplexed. From his first gesture, when he had entered and beckoned with an air of authority, Cancio had taken him for a policeman, one of the many that had made him repeat the story. After speaking with the man for a bit, he had figured the man was just a friend of someone from the neighborhood, maybe one of those whose gardens he took care of after finishing his work shift at the cemetery. Now he realized that he should have asked who the man was before he told him anything. Maybe that was a mistake. And to top it all off, he was now quite sure he'd never heard of anyone named Pepe Pérez!

Just in case, he decided that he should report the visit to the police, since it suddenly seemed very suspicious. And that would probably provoke more questioning, a search for fingerprints on anything the man might have touched and footprints in the places where he walked. There would also be another horrible session with the technician who made the verbal portraits, tormenting him with questions—if the chin was more pointed, the forehead wider or narrower, the mouth this way or that way—until his head was swimming and he couldn't sleep for several nights, trying to remember . . . remember . . . remember.

Anguished, the grave digger watched the man as he walked away, trying to engrave the face in his memory. Almost a block away, the tall, blond man with the blue eyes turned, smiled like a child who had just played a prank, and lifted an arm in a farewell gesture, as if reading the thoughts of the grave digger, who was now completely destabilized and convinced that he had committed a grave error. The incident could even cost him a transfer to the Colón cemetery, where many people are buried every day—not like the peaceful Chinese cemetery, where a cadaver is brought in only every now and then. His gaze remained fixed on the stranger to see if he got into a vehicle, with the idea of describing it to the police. But the man continued on foot until he disappeared, turning on Calle 25 toward Marianao. Disconsolate, the grave digger went back to weeding the tombs.

THE SANTERA

SHE AWAKENED STARTLED. She resisted the temptation to leave her bed and turn on the light. Instead, without opening her eyes, she remained taut, listening. She could hear only the hum of the air conditioner, isolating her from other nocturnal sounds. Gradually, she identified the cause of her sudden awakening: A *presence* was moving about the house, something indefinable but surely malignant.

She sat up on the right side of her bed and finally opened her eyes to look at the doll dressed in pink in the small castle resting on a shelf built into the wall at shoulder height. She stood up to observe her *orisha madre* more closely. At times, she detected slight variations in Yewá's expression; this time, Yewá seemed to avoid her gaze. The crown of *cauris*, the symbol of Yewá Binoyé's status as a princess in her human existence, was slightly askew. The pink necklaces shone strangely in the light of the permanently lit candle before her. The *Santera* detected no changes in the attributes of the *orisha*: neither in the small earthen jar where her nine smooth pebbles were kept nor in the human tibia wrapped with pink ribbons recalling that Yewá is the queen of cemeteries.

From a small plate in front of the little castle—similar to the one in which the *orisha* had lived, jealously guarded by her father before Shangó won the bet to seduce her—the *Santera* took four pieces of coconut meat. She passed her fingers over the floor and kissed the bit of dust collected on her fingertips. Then she prayed briefly, consulting Yewá: She wanted to know the nature of the *presence* in the house. She asked the question, rolled the pieces of coconut between her hands, and threw them from the height of her knees. They all fell with the meat upwards: *Alafia*, a letter indicating something positive and good. But she would have to repeat the throw. *Alafia* was not conclusive. She threw the pieces again and this time *Eyife* came out: two face down and two face up—the most definitive letter of the coconut oracles, an emphatic *yes*, confirming the first letter. There was nothing to fear.

In any event, she decided, she would look through the house and, while she was at it, urinate. The hall enveloped her in a kind of hot breath, full of emanations accumulated in the closed house. There the *presence* was much stronger. It came from the rear, from the kitchen, or, perhaps, the patio. It was not a sensation created by the spirit of an ordinary dead person. Nor did she feel that exalted sense that announced the arrival of the *orishas*. It was something different, a strange and threatening and, at the same time, very strong being with the power to penetrate the formidable defenses of the house.

Uncertain what to do, she stood in the hall outside her room. She glanced to her left and peered at the main entrance of the house and the living room, which was connected to a corridor from which other rooms branched out. The first of these, devoted to *Regla de Osha*, was where she held consultations for her godchildren and clients, surrounded by the altar presided over by Yemayá and by the basket with the soup tureens where she kept the essentials of Obatalá, Shangó, Yemayá, and Oshún. Before the altar, beside the *chequerés* and the *agogó* for summoning the *orishas* and asking for health and good luck, was a good supply of fruit and homemade sweets brought by her godchildren as offerings. Behind the door stood a small house of the warriors Elégguá, Oggún, and Ochosi. Safely placed, at head height, was her Osún, in the form of a bird.

The second room down the hall was her bedroom, where she kept her secret cult to Yewá. Five years before, she had installed an air conditioner that, even after it was turned off, kept the air fresh in the corners, in the wardrobe, and between the sheets. Next to her room was a bathroom, used only by her and her brother, and occasionally by close relatives and special friends. Everyone else used the toilet installed in the patio in place of the latrine from the times of their great-grandfather and grandfather.

Next to the bathroom was a big kitchen where huge quantities of food were prepared on feast days, when fowls, goats, and sheep were sacrificed. The kitchen was followed by a dining room, also spacious, which served as a waiting area for those who came to consult her brother. And this was the edge of the new section of the house—built with brick walls, tiled floors, and a wooden, red-tiled roof—that had replaced the old thatched wooden dwelling constructed early in the century by their great-grandfather, the second Lorenzo Bantú.

Beyond the dining room, two rooms from the original house had been preserved: a bedroom with a pale blue door where her brother slept, and the *mumanso*, the room of the *nganga*, that could only be entered from the patio. Here, her brother gave consultations, in the same spot where their grandfather and great-grandfather had done the same. This part of the house was constructed with the hardest wood from the Zapata swamp forests and lined with boards of royal palm. Only the roof had been altered. Under the rigorous supervision of the grandfather, the original palm-leaf thatch had been replaced by galvanized zinc, and below that had been built a false ceiling of exquisitely finished, tightly dovetailed wood, in strong contrast to the coarseness of the original construction.

Between the zinc roof and the false ceiling, a space remained in which the grandfather had kept many of his *Palo Monte* possessions and other relics inherited from his ancestors. The *Santera* had never figured out how to enter that secret place, although she was sure her brother Lorenzo knew. At times, late at night, she heard sounds coming from the secret room and drew near, trying to surprise Lorenzo. But no matter how silently she approached, the sounds ceased until she moved away again. This was one of three enigmas the old man had left his two grandchildren.

In the kitchen, she found an unwashed cup and felt extremely annoyed. Later she would recall that, at that moment, she had experienced a kind of fury difficult to contain. Why did Lorenzo do that? How much effort did it take to clean a cup? "Washing dishes is for women," he would say, ignoring his sister's need for cleanliness and order.

From a plastic container holding the henequen juice she used as a detergent, she withdrew a pad made of threads from the same plant and cleaned the cup carefully in the sink, rinsing it afterwards. As she set it aside, she saw that it was still not clean; something remained stuck to it. She took a little charcoal ash from a jar and scrubbed the cup again until she was satisfied.

As she entered the dining room, the *presence* felt stronger and nearer. What was it? With slight trepidation, she walked slowly to the pale blue door. Then she had no doubt; it was inside her brother's room. Alarmed, she pressed her ear to the door. At first, she heard only Lorenzo's evenly spaced snores. Then she perceived subtle changes, small gasps, until an almost imperceptible moaning began. Suddenly, she heard a piercing scream and the sound of the heavyset man, frightened and half-asleep, bolting up on the bed made of woven-wire springs and a thin mattress.

Startled, Lorenzo opened his eyes. He looked about him, momentarily bewildered, then saw the shadow of two feet under his door against a thin line of light from the lamp in the dining room that his sister insisted always remain lit.

"Who's there?"

No response.

"Is it you?"

Silence.

Finally a calm voice answered: "You were saying something in your sleep. Is anything wrong?"

"Nothing's wrong. Go back to bed."

The shadow remained under the door awhile longer, then disappeared silently, letting the strip of light from the dining room bulb pass freely under the door again, exercising, as always, a hypnotic effect on him. The *Nasakó's* eyelids closed and he immediately fell back to sleep.

Now that she knew her brother was being visited in his sleep by *something*, she returned to her room and sat down on the bed. It was definitely not the spirit of one of their ancestors; their *presence* never upset sleep unless they wanted to warn them of something important. Then she remembered how tenaciously the dirt had remained on the cup. That detail had some significance, she thought, but she couldn't figure out what it might be.

Her brother's scream was not a good omen. It had indicated surprise, fear. *A foreign spirit—a malevolent one—was definitely working on her brother's dreams.* How was that possible, with all the protection he and the house had?

She closed her eyes and again saw the four pieces of coconut as they had fallen, two of them face up with the white meat palely reflected in the penumbra of her room, where the candlelight was fading rapidly. *What was happening? Why those comforting letters? What was the significance of the coconut oracle's deception? Why was Yewá avoiding her gaze?*

She remained seated, puzzling out the situation. There were two factors, perhaps related, perhaps not: On the one hand, there was the misleading information of the oracle; on the other, the danger to her brother. Could this have something to do with the work he had done for Adrián, Pedro, and Mulo earlier that night? That work had to have been unusual because Lorenzo had waited until she was asleep. Her brother almost never worked with *Palo* outside of his regular hours. Whenever, very occasionally, he had to do something after midnight, he always warned her that strangers would be coming. So far, he had never dared to do anything important without first consulting her.

She suspected this was the explanation. That work had surely provoked an adverse reaction from some *nkisi* or *nfumbe mayor* which was now working on him. *Palo Monte* was like that. "*Kindambazo* goes, *kindambazo* comes," their grandfather had repeatedly warned them, so that they would never lower their guard.

Her brother overestimated his knowledge of *Palo Monte*. He had been very young, almost a child, when their grandfather died, and he'd had no one, really, to teach him since. He'd had to guide himself by the fading copybooks the old man had dictated when his memory was already slipping.

There was no getting around it. That work late at night had to be the cause of the strange *presence* in the house. A piece of work turned backwards is always a serious problem. She had to find out what work her brother had done for Adrián; that was the key.

ADRIÁN

HE ALWAYS ARRIVED JUST as the afternoon was dying and would go directly to the kitchen for a cup of coffee. He would tell her the latest jokes from the street and always managed to extract information about her prettiest clients and goddaughters. He also always touched her with one pretext or another, adjusting something on her clothing or removing a loose thread, real or imagined. Those moments of contact, for her, were like high-voltage sparks.

She recalled the first time he had come to their house. Night was falling. She had finished her consultations and gone to the kitchen when she heard someone pounding on the door. Their godchildren and clients always entered without knocking, whether visiting her or her brother. Those who visited the house for the first time always rang the doorbell. Why the loud knocking?

Peering through the peephole in the door, she saw Adrián standing on the porch with a red-billed cap in his hand, looking down at the floor. Sensing himself spied upon, he raised his head. Her heartbeat quickened at the sight of his green eyes and handsome face. Instinctively, she smoothed her hair and unbuttoned the top of her blouse. Then she opened the door.

Adrián had asked a half-question: "Is the . . . ?" He stopped, not knowing the name of her brother or daring to call him "*el Palero.*" She asked if he had an appointment to see Lorenzo. No, he only wanted to know if he could set up an appointment for later. Instead of leading him to the dining room, she offered him a seat in the living room. Observing the fine shape of his body under his faded blue jeans, she felt almost suffocated, and her heart began pounding wildly as she became aware of his cologne and bodily scent. Why had Adrián had such an immediate effect on her?

"You're going to have to wait a little," she said primly.

Adrián looked up at her from his sprawled position in the beat-up old armchair. His eyes seemed to scintillate as they slid sensuously over her body. "I'm not in a hurry," he drawled lazily. She was a stunning creature: tall, high-breasted and wide-hipped, with large, almond-shaped eyes, clear, chocolate-brown skin, and full, sensuous lips. But there was nothing sexy about her dress, which resembled a nun's frock.

Aware of his scrutiny, she turned and walked toward the rear of the house, deliberately swaying her butt. "I'll bring you some coffee," she said.

On Adrián's first visit, she had used her own cup for his coffee, passing her tongue over the entire rim before taking it to him. Now she reproached herself for having acted so irresponsibly. Why had she provoked him? What had brought on that burning lust?

A horrible dilemma confronted her every time she met a man like Adrián. The restrictions she lived under made her feel worse than if she were imprisoned. Rebelling would be useless, she well knew. Everything had been defined in the *Bajada de Orula* made by four *babalawos*, and in the *Registro de Itá*, in which Yewá was revealed as her *orisha madre* and her life-long regime was established. Undoubtedly, her behavior with Adrián was the cause of Yewá's attitude and the strange response she had received from her throw of the cocos in the morning. Yewá was so severe that even inno-cent flirting was considered evil. But there was no need to give so much weight to a simple throw of cocos; on other occasions, her *orisha madre* had been angry with her at first, but had later forgiven her.

Suddenly, she was consumed by a great doubt: *What if Yewá was actually telling her, through the cocos, that the malignant presence was necessary, that this turn of events was for the best?* She pushed these strange thoughts out of her mind.

She had spied on Adrián's first consultation with Lorenzo. He said he was sure that somebody had hexed him. He had nightmares in which he saw a dark, half-dead cock vomiting up a small, bloody ball with his name written on it in India ink. Other times a woman, always the same one, suddenly hacked off his penis with a Sevillian knife while he was making love with her in the middle of a canefield.

Lorenzo listened closely to the new client. To free him of these ills, Lorenzo sprinkled Adrián with tobacco smoke and *chamba,* the liturgical brew of *Palo Monte* made from *aguardiente*, pepper, gunpowder, bone shavings, and other powerful ingredients. He also whipped Adrián with branches from trees with great powers of their own as he moved from side to side to the rhythm of his own chanting.

It seemed to her, as she watched, that Adrián was amused, barely able to suppress laughter, despite the ferocious appearance of the witch doctor. Adrián, nevertheless, returned several times for consultations with Lorenzo, explaining that he felt better but was not entirely cured.

During the consultations, Lorenzo threw seven seashells in the air, which he then "read" with astonishment, or he sat absorbed, staring at the *mpaca mensu*, a bull's horn filled with magic materials, and recommended baths and infusions for Adrián. It nonetheless seemed like her brother wasn't taking the new client very seriously. He had always said that his treatments were primarily for safety, for precaution. But the shells' letters were very favorable; they hadn't indicated any need for caution.

Early on, when Lorenzo noticed his sister interacting with Adrián, he drew her aside and warned: "That guy is a *fiana*; I'm nearly certain he works for the police. Never trust him and don't chat with him while he's waiting for me."

But one night Lorenzo changed his attitude completely. She had never forgotten that visit. It was February 14 of that same year. Adrián arrived at almost midnight. He brought several packages in a box and a briefcase. He handed her a tiny flower, plucked from the hedge in front of their house, and, looking deeply into her eyes, wished her a happy St. Valentine's Day. Something inside her vibrated, though she knew he had come on other business. Without speaking further with her, he sat down in the living room to watch television while waiting for Lorenzo.

She waited a short time, then, yawning and pretending to be sleepy, announced that she was headed to bed. Instead of going to her bedroom, however, she waited in the next room until she heard Adrián and her brother pass into the dining room. To be able to follow their conversation, she quietly moved outside and huddled below a window. Seated face to face, Adrián and her brother proceeded to drink nearly two whole bottles of rum. Adrián spoke nonstop, relating a far-flung set of experiences, until after two o'clock in the morning. Then they headed to the room of the *nganga*, where evidently they intended to close some kind of deal.

She realized that Adrián was the indirect cause of both situations that were worrying her: It was clear that he had induced her brother to perform some works that had been turned against Lorenzo, and that the attraction he exerted on her had angered Yewá. She felt stunned for a moment by the implications of this. Then she immediately dismissed the thoughts; she had to be objective and practical. The most pressing issue was to find a way to neutralize the force that was working against her brother, whatever the cause.

She decided to prepare a *rogación de cabeza* for very early the next morning. That was the best way to renew and strengthen her brother's *eleda*, his guardian angel. This was the most important *ebbó* of all. She had to hurry to gather the necessary ingredients: coco, eggshells, cacao butter, snail, cotton . . . *Caramba!* If necessary, she should be ready to perform the *rogación* according to *Palo Monte* instead of *Regla de Osha*. Where could she get white pigeons at this hour?

LORENZO BANTÚ

WHY ARE YOU standing in the doorway with that pack of witches? Get them out of here! Dark and skinny, dressed all in white—they look like a flock of albino vultures! . . . *You* stay put! I have plenty to say to you. How many times have I told you to stay out of my life and not try to control me? You're as hardheaded as Granddad—exactly alike, the two of you. No wonder you hated each other so much . . . Don't look at me like that, I'm not crazy! . . . You know what I'm talking about. You've always treated me like the family idiot, your stupid little brother, while you're the smart one, the clever one, the one who knows everything . . . I used to believe that. My big sister, raised in a rich household like a *señorita*, an uppity Negress, instead of the maid's daughter. Even studied at the university! But I've come to see how you envy me . . . Yes, yes, envy! Don't give me that little laugh of yours. I can't stand that smirk anymore! You're jealous because I've gotten ahead of you. People respect me. In *Palo Monte*, my balls are as big as anyone else's! And I earned that by myself, using my own head! If I'd gone on listening to you, I'd have hung myself a long time ago . . . You, always advising me to do things I couldn't do—to get me out of the way. You wanted to fuck me up! You're a real bitch . . . You're the one who's stayed behind. Nobody comes to consult you anymore because you only look for the dark side. Nobody except that band of old weirdos you just had here, and four or five queers. Well, that's your business. The only thing I care about is that you stay out of my business! . . . Tell me, what the hell were you doing last night standing there at the door of my room? Of course I have nightmares with an evil shadow like you hanging over my sleep! And earlier, when I was doing a special invocation for Adrián? You came as silent as death. You climbed on the stool in my room and peeked through the hole in the wall. Well I've sealed it now, so that you'll never spy on me again . . . Ah! You thought I didn't know? I saw it in the *mpaca mensu*, which tells me everything that happens. And the candles flickered every time air came through that hole . . . Mice? You know very well who I am referring to—to a certain big female mouse that messes with my things every day. You know there haven't been any mice in this house since the old man croaked. I couldn't live any longer with those damned vermin in here. I couldn't stand them running all over the place, climbing everywhere, looking at me with their little round eyes gleaming in the dark . . . When I was a kid, they always woke me up with their racing around in the roof thatch, with that squeaky laughter that sounds just like you. I couldn't fall back to sleep, afraid that they might fall on me and nibble my lips off. So I would stay awake until dawn, trembling under my blanket, sweating, until sleep finally knocked me out . . . After the old man died, I spread all the poison I could get hold of into every corner of the house. That's how all the vermin in the neighborhood disappeared: chickens, dogs, cats, lizards, cockroaches, ants, everything . . . You didn't know that, did you? . . . Even a big goat the old man had been preparing for feeding the *nganga*. When the owner of the *nganga* arrived that night, he freaked out when he saw his goat with its legs stiff up in the air, just like the old man laid out in the living room. That man went flying out of here and I've never heard from him again. He left his *nganga*, which must have cost a small fortune . . . I know you've been spying on me through that hole in the wall in the *nganga* room. Spying so that you could make me think you know everything, that nothing can be hidden from you, that without you I'm a dead duck! . . . Don't shake your head. I've tried to reason with you, to wake you up. Well I won't take it anymore! . . . Do you hear me? Do you understand? It's over! Finished! Don't stick your nose into my business or try to find out what I'm doing. From now on, my cases are *my* cases, and my clients are *my* clients . . . Don't even dream that I'm going to let you in on what I'm doing. And if there's anything I don't want you nosing around in, it's what I'm doing for Adrián. I'm warning you! . . . What you need is a *macho*. That's what has you so wrong, wrong, wrong! And don't run away as if you're speaking to the devil himself! . . . I've wanted to tell you this for a long time because I can't stand it anymore. Don't even show your face back here, I don't want your evil shadow spoiling my work! . . . That's what you are, an evil shadow . . ."

This was not her brother! Lorenzo was stubborn, quick-tempered, capricious, yes, but he had always been kind and considerate, incapable of saying such awful things to her. He'd never before dared to address her like that—much less in the presence of her goddaughters. What was happening to him?

OBATALÁ

I
T SEEMED IMPOSSIBLE THAT all this hate could suddenly come to the surface, as if all his life he'd harbored jealousy and twisted thoughts. Her poor little brother—well, hardly *little*, but she still thought of him that way—hadn't been himself since that *thing* took control of him, dominating him. As soon as it saw that she had prepared everything for a *rogación de cabeza*, it went wild, knowing what was in store for it. Obviously, the *thing* was also doing everything in its power to push her into having sexual relations. Her brother had said she needed a *macho*, but nobody knew better than Lorenzo that a daughter of Yewá can never lie with a man without going mad or dying. Four *babaloshas* had agreed that the goddess of the cemeteries claimed her. If she wanted to live in peace and quiet, she was obliged to live in strictest conformity with the rules laid down by that deity for her daughters! No one and nothing could change that destiny.

She would appeal to Obatalá for help. As the god of everything white and pure, creator of the Earth, entrusted by his father, the supreme god Olofí, with the forming of men, Obatalá is the ruler of heads, the controller of dreams and ideas. His name says it all: *Obba*, meaning *king*, and *talá*, meaning *of everything*, the only god capable of placating his vengeful and violent son, Oggún. And her brother Lorenzo was, precisely, a son of Oggún. For the moment, it was best to ignore Yewá until she could set things right with her.

She bathed and then dressed entirely in white. She went to the *Ilé Osha* and prostrated herself before the basket in front of Obatalá's porcelain soup tureen, where the god's four *otá* were kept carefully wrapped in *ceiba* cotton beside white necklaces, two ivory eggs, and a silver hand.

Straightening from her obeisance, she performed all of the actions indicated by the liturgy to favor the attention of the gods before she laid out her eighteen shells needed to consult Obatalá. She then took the silver *agogó* used exclusively to call Obatalá and swung it from side to side, making it ring softly, before offering up the god's favorite prayer:

Orishanlá, okenrin ati obinrini laiye eleda ni gbogbo na daradara ati burukú oba ati ayaba afin oga ni talá ati gbogbo na cheche baba aliya alobo mi ati mi gbogbo na ejun daradara, babá wa afin alano kekua badami. Modupué . . . (Great saint man and woman, world creator of all of the good, healthy, and ill, king and queen, albino ruler of purity and of all the righteous, father, summit of the entire world, my protector and protector of all good things, our pure father, compassionate albino, my living father. Thank you . . .)

At that moment, she heard knocking at the door. She felt her heart leap violently. Something important was about to happen! With trembling hands, she lit her last beeswax candle, bought last year in the city of Trinidad and saved for a special occasion such as this one. The knocks sounded again, this time stronger and more urgent. She stood and walked quickly to the door, ready for what might come.

Opening the door, she stared incredulously. A wrinkled old lady, dressed in white, wavered precariously before her, moved by a strong wind that seemed to have arisen spontaneously and threatened to blow the woman away.

"Come in, come in, señora," she said hastily, extending her hand.

As the visitor passed into the living room, the *Santera* immediately recognized Obanlá, one of the sixteen paths of Obatalá, eight males and eight females. The *Santera* first hugged herself, then embraced the visitor, crossing heads with her after the embrace, as required in the presence of that god.

"May I take a sprig from your tree of paradise?" the visitor asked.

A less knowledgeable person would have believed that the visitor was Doña Concha, a neighbor who visited the *Santera* frequently to borrow things. Concha was very old and no longer clear in her head, sometimes forgetting why she had come. She was obviously a daughter of Obatalá because she always dressed in white, in contrast to the daughters and sons of other saints who wore white only on the first year after their initiation and on the anniversaries of the initiation. But this time everything was different, beginning with that strange wind and the harsh radiance that had surrounded the woman as she entered.

This had to be a direct answer to her invocation, something that had only happened to her once before. As a child, she had called Babalú Ayé three times, and a beggar had appeared immediately, followed by a one-eyed black dog. The *orisha* had kissed her hands after she gave him the candy she had been licking. Since then, she had never had problems of any kind with her skin, which was still smooth and unwrinkled, and her legs and feet had remained healthy, without varicose veins or other blemishes.

As if unaware of the disguise, she pretended that the visitor was her neighbor. "Doña Concha, take whatever you like, but don't forget to pay the fee."

Obanlá looked at her roguishly. "How could I forget?" She held out her palm, displaying a coin. *Whoever doesn't pay the* monte—*forest—can take anything he likes, but it will have no power whatsoever.*

The visitor disappeared down the hall, seeming to float a few centimeters above the floor, wrapped in a strange luminosity that contrasted sharply with her intensely black face. In an instant, she was back with a sprig of paradise in one hand. No one could possibly have gone to the patio and returned so quickly.

"What is your problem?" Obanlá said, cocking her head to one side.

"I prepared a *rogación de cabeza* for my brother, but he insulted the *Iyaloshas* that were going to help me and threw them out; then he said even worse things to me. He isn't like that. Some dark spirit must have stolen his head."

The saint took the *Santera*'s hands and shook her head with a tired look, as if worn out from struggling against so much evil. "Don't worry," she said, looking at her fixedly. "Listen to me carefully. *Everything is going to be resolved in a way that you least expect. You'll see.*"

Then something extraordinary occurred. The false Concha burst into raucous laughter, turned to leave, and continued laughing uproariously as she whirled toward the door.

The *Santera* felt frightened. That could not be Obatalá! Alarmed, her heart pounding, she realized that she had not completed her invocation. She hadn't had time to throw her shells and receive the answers to her questions. Neither had she received instructions about the *ebbó* she should offer. This had to be a trick!

The old woman threw the door open, allowing the radiance from the street to inundate the living room. The bad weather had yielded a small hurricane. Drops of water flew in all directions like fine dust, each drop reflecting the sun. When the *Santera* reached the door to close it, the street was deserted. Then the wind died down abruptly and the rain ceased.

Thoroughly frightened after the false Obatalá had abandoned her house, the *Santera* returned to her room and threw herself on her bed. The problem was extremely complex and was becoming more so with each step she took to try to solve it. There was no longer any doubt: A very powerful evil spirit was taking possession of Lorenzo. She needed to take her time to figure out what to do before she made a fatal mistake.

THE HUNTER

AFTER SIGNALING FAREWELL to the grave digger, the tall blond man continued walking toward the bridge over the Almendares River. As almost always occurred when he passed this way, his thoughts flew back in time. Five centuries earlier, Christopher Columbus had anchored his ships a little further downstream, at the outlet to the sea, to repair their hulls with tar from an outflow discovered among the corals on the shore. At the same time, he and his crew took aboard supplies of crystalline fresh water from a short distance upstream beyond the farthest reach of the tide.

The English fleet had done the same during the siege and capture of Havana in 1762, choosing this site as its principal camp because of the abundance of pure drinking water. At that time, all of the surroundings were virginal woods. Now the river was contaminated by the industries that had developed along its shores during the first half of the twentieth century, taking water from it and returning an unending flow of toxins and feces.

If the admiral of the Ocean Sea or the British fleet came back today, they'd be annihilated by diarrhea, he told himself as he crossed over to the other side of the bridge, evading a swarm of bicycles whizzing past.

Coming to the far end of the bridge, he turned right and walked down the steps cut into the steep bank. He reached a road that bordered the river and wound through a small patch of trees reminiscent of the forest that had once covered the entire island. As usual when passing en route to his parents' house, he amused himself by contemplating the gigantic trees and wondering if any of them had been witness to the epoch he liked to imagine. His mind's eye saw the painted faces of a band of fierce Carib warriors, crouched among the branches of an enormous *jagüey* and gaping bewildered at the fabulous dimensions of the boats anchored at the river's mouth. A group of strange beings came out of the astonishing canoes carrying large round pots and began moving upstream into the thickest part of the forest. The band of Caribs was soon in pursuit of them, anticipating the flavor of the strangers' flesh.

Fifteen minutes later, the tall man reached his parents' home, where he had returned to live two years earlier. He was forty-five years old, although his thick mat of blond hair, with almost no gray in it, gave him a younger look. Six months before, after having worked for twenty-five years in criminal investigation, he had given his life a complete turnabout by requesting retirement. The abrupt decision surprised his superiors, his colleagues, and, perhaps more than anyone else, himself. His reasons had been clear: He had completed the length of service required to qualify for a pension; his health was no longer as good as it had been; and he was an only son—his father had recently died and his mother needed his care now.

But he knew that all of this was only his *apparent* motive. The real causes lay deeper inside him and had grown imperceptibly over the years, finally pushing him to make the decision. Since then, he had tried to explain it all to himself. Some reasons he had figured out, but the survey, he felt, had not yet been exhausted. Perhaps even the most important reason remained to be discovered.

For one thing, the work of police investigation was hard on him. His stubborn character obliged him to immerse himself profoundly in each case with a bulldog-like tenacity that his colleagues secretly admired but neither envied nor had any wish to imitate. For them, working the required hours, then getting together in their homes for Saturday beers and games of dominoes, cheating occasionally on their wives, and watching baseball games religiously at the stadium or on television helped to erase the unsavory aspects of their work. He, however, like a hopelessly addicted smoker fully aware of the damage inflicted by tobacco, was incapable of leaving his profession merely because of duress.

Certainly, he had no lack of projects. For one thing, he firmly intended to employ his mind reading the hundreds of books in his family's library. His work on the police force had virtually liquidated his boyhood habit of reading literature. He felt a need to recover that lost custom. He didn't want to reach the end of his existence without devouring the long list of essential books he carried in his wallet and to which he added, every now and then, a new title. He felt sure that this old hunger was one of the reasons for his decision.

Since making peace with his father ten years before, he'd also had the idea of transforming the area surrounding his parents' house—that at the moment only had lawn, flowers, and a few fruit trees—into a useful food-producing plot. It had originally been a project for the future, for the time when he, too, was old and had plenty of free time. As years went by, though, he had slowly arrived at the conclusion that making the Earth produce was man's only truly worthwhile labor. Gradually, that parcel called out to him more and more strongly each time he looked at it. And the moment had come. The year was 1993, and the country was going through the "Special Period," which included a great food shortage, following the collapse of the socialist bloc to which its economy had been tied. If he could demonstrate that one person could produce, on about three hundred square yards of soil, double or triple the amount of food needed to live, he could contribute to solving a national problem. This was another reason for leaving his job, he told himself.

It had seemed to him that getting rid of the lawn and so much useless vegetation around the house, then harvesting nourishing plants and raising livestock, would be a simple matter for which no great amount of preparation would be needed. He found himself stunned, however, by the quantity of agricultural knowledge required to confront the task successfully. He thus devoted his days to conditioning the soil and planting crops and his evenings to reading technical manuals and documents, postponing the start of a serious attack on his list of books. In the last six months, all of his energy had been employed in his agricultural project with a meticulousness and zeal that were simultaneously his greatest strengths and weaknesses.

He had exactly 310 square yards of soil to work with, excluding the front lawn—the domain of his mother, who would defend every inch of that area with her life if need be. The land at his disposal, with the exception of a quarter of the plot that was either too rocky or refilled terrain, was deep and fertile, according to tests he conducted. The area was divided into two blocks, two-thirds of the land to the north of the house and the rest to the south. Since the south side received less sunlight, he had already planted forty coffee bushes there with about a yard of separation between each. The first harvest in approximately twelve months should yield no fewer than twelve pounds of coffee after toasting and grinding. That volume would be duplicated the following year and increase thereafter until they reached self-sufficiency, abundance, and even superabundance. Among the coffee bushes, he also planted two grafted avocado trees that would bear fruit in the winter, much later than the single tree already there in the backyard. He allowed twelve yards distance between them, less than the recommended separation, but he trusted that the upper branches would seek sunlight by inclining over the roof of the house, thus increasing the space available and shading the house in summer. In due time, the three avocado trees would yield over three hundred pounds of salad, rich in vitamins and oil without cholesterol. In the future, he would plant more coffee under these trees or, perhaps, cacao.

In an area of a hundred square yards on the north side, he planted twenty banana and plantain trees, which, together with twenty square yards of cassava and sweet potato, should provide at least nine hundred pounds per year of food rich in carbohydrates. Following the instructions of Emilio Farrés, a neighbor knowledgeable in horticulture, he also planted five dwarf guava trees on eighteen square yards in places with shallow and rocky soil. These guava trees, that would begin to bear fruit six months after planting and would reach full production three years later, might produce over seventy pounds of fruit per tree. That meant 350 pounds of raw material. Emilio assured him that guava contained five times more vitamin C than citrus fruits.

In the best and sunniest parts of the terrain, he laid out four plots, each one yard wide and twelve to thirteen yards long, and, after enhancing the soil with organic fertilizer, planted vegetables. His first harvest from these fifty square yards had yielded nearly 250 pounds of vegetables, including all of the garlic and onion needed in the house for the entire year. In one corner, he already had several hot and sweet pepper plants to assure a variety of seasonings. Now he was preparing the plots for the summer planting of squash, cucumber, and green beans, the only vegetables, as far as he knew, capable of resisting the Cuban heat and the pests of that season. According to what he had been informed, each of those fifty square yards could provide up to thirty pounds of fresh vegetables, a total of 1500 pounds per year—more than enough for two people.

On the remaining area, in the shade of two already existing Mexican lime trees that bore fruit all year, he built cages for hens and a roofed pen for a milking goat. The animals would provide most of the protein, in addition to organic fertilizer. He anticipated that, once in full production, the animals would get sufficient feed from the leftovers of garden produce. And by then, perhaps, he could think of raising a hog, since the production of adequate amounts of fat and meat was still an unsolved problem. At the same time, the hog's feces together with vegetable waste would serve to produce compost—organic fertilizer rich in nitrogen, phosphorus, and potassium.

Finally, he acquired a German shepherd pup to guard the place at night. The dog barked frenziedly by day at everyone who passed by the house, then slumbered as if comatose all night.

This whole picture passed through his mind as he changed into work clothes to tend to his "farm." The search for excellence in the cultivation of animals, trees, and seeds; the battle with pests that attacked his treasures; the implacable struggle against the weeds that multiplied like Hydras; the watering of thirsty plants, always in danger of perishing in the persistent drought; the training of the dim-witted and playful dog that refused to take its mission seriously—all of this had helped pave the way for his acceptance of the proposal from his former chief and good friend.

* * *

Carrillo had arrived in work clothes and immediately begun to weed a plantain patch at his side with the extra hoe that was always kept on hand to discourage unwanted visitors. They had worked thus in silence the rest of the afternoon. No other visitor had done this, much less an official with the rank of colonel. Finally, as the sun began to sink below the horizon, they sat down on the back porch, admiring the results of their work and the gorgeous sunset, and drank banana milkshakes—made from store-bought bananas, but giving a taste of future afternoons when the farm would be in full production.

"So, what brings you here?"

"Came to see your farm."

The retired policeman shook his head slightly at his visitor, a massively built man of roughly fifty with a clear, intelligent, and penetrating gaze.

"What's the real reason, Carrillo?"

"I'm worried."

"Worried?"

Carrillo drank the rest of his milkshake before answering. "Alvarito, you've lost weight. You're taking this thing too seriously."

"I've never felt better. I stopped smoking. I don't have a trace of high blood pressure. The goat's milk has cured my ulcer."

Carrillo grimaced at the mention of the goat and its milk. He tipped his glass to drink the last drops of the milkshake while he searched for the best way to approach what he had come to say. "I think if you stay stuck in this garden, you're going to go nuts . . . Look at you! With that beard and long hair, you look like Jesus Christ. You know it damned well. Of course, I know you like that. Admit it! You love looking like Jesus."

"I know others who wear beards, and just try to give *them* any crap!" The blue-eyed man laughed at his own joke, but it sounded forced.

Carrillo went on: "Everyone's talking about it. Whenever anyone comes to see you, the only thing you talk about is how many pounds of coffee you should get the first year, the second year, and so on, or the production you expect from each square inch of this farm . . . You have everything calculated down to a thousandth of an inch. These four or five plants of yours have become an obsession . . . Is it true that you spend your nights killing cutter ants?"

The blond man stroked his beard. Maybe Carrillo was right. As his plants had grown, his concern for them had also increased, together with his impatience to achieve nutritional self-sufficiency.

"Alvaro, why haven't you remarried?" Carrillo continued. "That would give you the equilibrium you need. That's the thing, equilibrium. Everything in life—hell, in life, no . . . in the universe—functions with equilibrium. Look what's happening to the world's climate because the equilibrium's been destroyed. We're running out of ozone; we're all going to suffocate and roast in the hothouse that's being created with the excess of carbon dioxide. You don't have a sense of balance either."

"No woman will put up with me. Two marriages are enough . . . That doesn't mean I don't sleep with one occasionally."

Carrillo was silent for a moment. Suddenly, he smiled enigmatically. "Maybe I can help you. Maybe I'll let you handle a case now and then . . . something that would occupy your afternoons only, but it would help your equilibrium. You'd have to cut that hair and get rid of that beard. That should help, too."

The bearded man leaned his head back and closed his eyes. The absence of protest suggested to Carrillo that he was making progress.

Carrillo stood up and paused a moment, feeling a creaking like that of rusty gear teeth in his knees. He went to his car and returned with four thick files that he dropped beside the blender on a small table, then he sat down again. "I'm going to give you a fabulous case, like you've never had before: the theft of a cadaver from the Chinese cemetery—a case to make any police investigator green with envy. I was able to photocopy all the important details. In the first file, I put what we might call the basic elements: the technicians' report on the work at the cemetery, foot and tire prints, data on the dead man, etc. The second file contains the medical and family reports related to the hypothesis of poisoning. This hypothesis is complete with conclusions—subject to your revision, of course."

As he identified each file, Carrillo handed them over, securely bound in colorful plastic binders, to the astonished retired policeman. His previous experience of official archives had been, in the best of cases, bundles of papers precariously clipped together and enclosed in cheap file folders that had almost invariably been used several times before.

"This file has all the work done so far in following up the hypothesis of Chinese vengeance. Rafael Cuan, the missing man, had a long life. The majority of the enemies he might have made must be buried by now in that same cemetery from which he's disappeared. But, since feuds between Chinese families can last for generations, it's possible that the removal of the body could be a case of vengeance, especially since it happened immediately after his burial, thus keeping his family and friends from offering a tribute on the customary third and ninth days. That's information we received from our best investigator at the police station covering the Chinese quarter, Lieutenant Colonel Francisco Lin, who is of Chinese descent, very professional and efficient, but a little touchy, persnickety. He should be winding up his work on this hypothesis very soon, so that part is well covered. Wait until he's finished to see if anything else shows up there."

Alvaro flipped through the files. From time to time, he raised his eyes to glance, surprised, at Carrillo. So many resources devoted to a crime that, although certainly out of the ordinary, was hardly monumental. How important could one less cadaver in the Chinese cemetery be? In a country where it was difficult to find a working photocopy machine in the office of a government minister, these hundreds of photocopies struck him as little short of scandalous.

"We're in an embarrassing position with the leaders of the Chinese community. We need to find this cadaver quickly. Just concentrate your work on this objective."

The retired policeman stared at Carrillo incredulously. It was clear to him that this was not the real reason for his being invited to participate in the case, any more than the alleged concern for his health. Such an extraordinary use of resources not available for more important matters, the haste to recover the cadaver, and the last-minute decision to recruit him indicated a much more substantial motive. At the same time, Carrillo was letting him know with his choice of words and an evasive expression that the real significance of the case was not being revealed to him.

"I trust I'll be able to work without interference."

Carrillo measured him carefully with his gaze before replying, thinking that his friend's lack of equilibrium was matched by his lack of limits. "Well, of course, without interference," he said with a nod.

Alvaro gave his former chief a long skeptical look as he collected the files and brought them into the house. Carrillo took advantage of his departure to serve himself half of the milkshake left in the blender.

Carrillo wondered briefly whether or not he should be more forthcoming, but discarded the idea immediately; his experience told him that the only incentive required for this master investigator to sink his teeth, bulldog-like, into a case was the pure mystery of the case itself. He hadn't planned to return so soon to the best investigator he had known in his long tenure on the police force and who, over the years, had become a valued personal friend. It was better, he had thought, to leave him in peace for a time—at least until he got bored with his gardening project. But he had made the decision to bring him back into the fray prematurely, convinced that the normal channels were not going to help him find the missing body.

Carrillo knew that he was playing a dangerous card. He had set in motion a thinking machine animated by an almost superhuman will and determination, capable of persisting to incredible extremes. But this time, he needed to impose a limit.

"The hypothesis of Chinese vengeance is intriguing," he said aloud to himself as he straightened and paused from the hard work of hoeing to prepare a cucumber patch. Then his thoughts returned to the path that his life had taken.

In 1961, at the age of thirteen, he had joined the country's Literacy Campaign, teaching people in the eastern mountains of the country to read and write. He had made the decision against the fierce opposition of his father, and, as a result, had not returned to live in the large and comfortable family home until very recently. For many years, he had been sure of his role in his country's struggle and had sought a frontline position in it.

Now, six months after leaving that trench, his ideals were still the same; he felt internally pure, firm, and still believed that his fellow countrymen deserved a better society. But *something* had changed.

In police work, the progress or regression of a society can be best appreciated, he told himself. Roughly one year after the death of Che Guevara in Bolivia, he had made his first arrests, almost all hardened criminals, individuals without the slightest social conscience, detritus of the old society that sought by any means to poison the new creature that was being born and developed against enormous odds. The vast majority of people gave themselves unsparingly to the new ideas, collaborating with the police in the suppression of delinquency, and the country became a safe, tranquil place with a minimal index of crime. A new society was arising little by little, based on great transformations. There was no just cause in the world that did not find thousands of supporters in the country. The innumerable blood donations in response to a severe earthquake in Peru exhausted the reserves of empty receptacles in Cuban blood banks. To help quell the threat of the racist regime of South Africa to the hard-won independence of Angola, thousands of Cubans volunteered to fight and, in many cases, die in far-off Africa. Each year, hundreds of thousands of city workers abandoned their homes for an entire season to cut sugar cane or harvest potatoes and tobacco under rural conditions lacking any comforts. The "new man" of Che's dreams was arising amidst the roughest challenges in the heat of battle. Like forged steel, the harder and hotter the treatment, the stronger and more flexible the product.

After the Socialist Bloc fell in 1990 and the unique economic ties Cuba had with it disappeared, the equality that had been achieved in so many aspects of national life was being overshadowed by a new phenomenon, the "dollar economy." The spirit of "one for all and all for one" was rapidly becoming "each man for himself." For Alvaro, the magic of the early years of the Revolution had vanished. He no longer felt a part of what was being created and decided that it was time for him to step aside. Why, then, had he now agreed to take on a new case?

THE DEAL

I T ALL STARTED *with the relationship between her brother and Adrián. It was also clear that the* thing *didn't want her to know what kind of work Lorenzo was doing for Adrián—the key to everything lay there.*

It had been almost midnight when he arrived. She herself had let him into the house, but Lorenzo, who was watching *The Maltese Falcon* on television, didn't greet him or move from his chair, continuing to watch the film with a grim face. Everybody knew his consultation hours, and the rest of his time was sacred. No one had a right to come at this hour without being invited, except of course in an emergency, and this visit had no appearance of an emergency. When the film ended, Lorenzo switched off the TV and started to leave the room without even asking the visitor the reason for his untimely visit. Adrián rose from his seat and cut off Lorenzo's retreat, saying he had brought a gift that couldn't be refused. Without asking permission or waiting for an answer, he walked quickly down the hall to the dining room, leaning slightly to one side from the weight of a bulky leather suitcase and a red traveling bag slung over his left shoulder. Lorenzo followed reluctantly, curious in spite of himself. He never accepted gifts, and Adrián knew it. Two months earlier, Adrián had tried to give him a wristwatch, and Lorenzo had refused coldly, saying he already had one. He charged only the going rate for his work. If anyone wanted to show special gratitude, as often happened, his sister attended to such matters.

In the dining room, Adrián extracted a large cardboard box from the suitcase and set it on the table. Then, from the red bag he produced a bottle of Matusalem *añejo* rum, followed by a medium-sized leg of smoked roast pork.

"You don't see this rum anymore. They must be exporting all of it," Adrián said cheerily, fetching a platter from the sideboard as if he were a member of the family. He expertly cut off several slices of the ham, then returned to the sideboard for two glasses, opened the bottle with an almost imperceptible movement of his wrist, and served the rum. After a moment of doubt, Lorenzo sat down, but he didn't touch the liquor or the ham. He merely swirled the rum in his glass briefly, then remained still, waiting for an explanation.

Adrián began to speak enthusiastically of many things: of Cuban baseball, of which they were both fans; of boxing; and then of his adventures in the German Democratic Republic, where he had gone to work in a motor factory. His funniest experience had been when he and three other apprentices at the factory ate, on a bet, an ostrich from the local zoo. When the Germans found the huge bones obstructing the drains in the Cubans' dormitory, the First Secretary of the embassy had been summoned, and the four were expelled back to Cuba. Later, a sign was found in the zoo, in German and in Spanish, with the warning: *"Take care of the bear!"* All the remaining Cubans were then sent home.

Lorenzo had not laughed at the story or engaged in any of the topics of conversation, but he eventually began to drink and to eat. Adrián continued to regale him with conversation until both the platter and the bottle stood empty. Then Lorenzo leaned back, looking intently at Adrián, clearly waiting for the real reason for the visit.

Adrián searched Lorenzo's eyes, and, finding them still too cool and unforgiving, said, "What do you think is in this box?"

Lorenzo looked at the box, narrowing his eyes. An inscription in red said: *"Ron Matusalem, 12 botellas, 0.75 litros."* And below, stamped by hand: *"Añejo."*

"Open it, open it," Adrián insisted.

Lorenzo stretched out one of his long arms and pulled the box toward him. Reaching inside, he grabbed one of the bottles and moved as if to open it. Adrián stopped him. "Tonight the treat is on me. This carton is for you only. When it's finished, give me a call; I know where to find others."

Lorenzo Bantú smiled faintly. The gift had been accepted. Adrián breathed deeply in relief. He attacked the remaining ham on the bone with his Sevillian knife and again filled the platter with thick slices, some with abundant fat on the edges, as Lorenzo liked it. Then, leaning back, Adrián continued with his stories, this time of women, his military service, fishing trips, and finally, again, baseball—the topic that he thought most appealed to his listener.

"I really love this house, with that enormous patio full of trees, isolated from other houses in the city, almost as if we are in the country. I grew up in a house like this with my grandparents. The only thing I hated about it was the siesta hour; the old folks always took a siesta and not even a fly could move during that time. The sacred rule of my grandparents was that I had to be quiet, preferably lying down. Imagine! Even now, I can't stay still for a minute. That was real torture. Time never seemed to pass!" As he spoke, Adrián cast his glance over the beams of the ceiling, the walls, and the open door to the patio that admitted the light of a full moon.

In the silence that followed, Lorenzo Bantú raised his eyes toward the ceiling, then began to speak in a deep voice that seemed to reverberate inside a huge steel barrel before emerging from his lips. He always spoke in short phrases, taking a pause after each sentence as if he had finished, then booming again, disconcerting those who had never heard him speak.

"I, too, was raised by my grandparents, here in this house. At that time, the roof was thatched. The walls were palm boards. My grandfather was a famous *Palero*. His cures were magical. People came to him from all over Cuba. Woods and meadow surrounded the house. People camped under the trees for two and three days, waiting to see him. Every morning the old man walked out among them. He looked into their faces and decided who he would see that day, no matter how long they'd been waiting.

"The processions of St. Lazarus on December seventeenth were tremendous. A multitude gathered here, beginning on the sixteenth. In the early evening, everyone started out on foot to reach the lepers' hospital in El

Rincón. We walked all night, carrying lit candles, my grandfather at the head of the procession. His thundering voice could be heard all the way back to the last ranks. It was impressive!

"When I was nine and my grandfather was ninety, my mother brought me to live here. He wanted to teach me *Palo Monte*. I was terrified of him at first. He was so tall and his voice was so powerful. He used to look at me like this." Lorenzo raised his eyebrows high, opened his eyes wide, and stared fixedly at Adrián for several seconds. Lorenzo took another of his pauses, then told Adrián something so personal that the *Santera*, eavesdropping, was outraged. "My sister was another case altogether. She always liked *Palo Monte*. She wasn't afraid of our grandfather and didn't show him proper respect. When he scolded her, she answered back—rudely. Little by little, he gave her up as a lost cause, because she's capable of anything. He lost interest in teaching her, but she managed to spy on everything the old man did."

She was astonished at how much her brother was opening up to Adrián. He had no business talking about her; it was a big mistake. Thank god she was there listening to every word. Adrián surely was an expert at prying out secrets.

With a jolt she realized that she, herself, had given Adrián the clues he needed to work on Lorenzo: his love of fatty ham, his habit of watching films on television late at night when neither godsons nor clients were likely to be about. As for the rum, what Cuban nowadays would refuse a carton of the best rum? That was a luxury obtainable only at a very high price, or in American dollars, which few people had. What was so important for Adrián to make that kind of an investment? He must have decided, she told herself, that the moment had come to show his hand.

"With what you know of *Palo Monte*, you could have all of Havana at your feet. Have you ever thought of that?" Adrián spoke leaning slightly forward, reminding the *Santera* of a snake charmer weaving his spell.

Lorenzo had also leaned forward, to select a piece of fat ham so that the grease would line his stomach wall and absorb less alcohol. He had learned this trick from a Russian colonel famous for being able to drink more vodka than anyone else and remain on his feet. Lorenzo then poured himself more rum and leaned his chair back far enough to bring his eyes level with Adrián's.

She had to smile. Her brother was no fool. What Adrián undoubtedly didn't realize was that the *Nasakó* had also made his inquiries. Convinced at the beginning that Adrián was with the police, he had commissioned José Miguel, his most trusted Abakuá brother, to find out everything about him. All the special courses José Miguel had taken while he was in the army made him well-suited for this task.

"Money is power. Have you thought of that?" asked Adrián.

"Of what?"

"That money is power."

Lorenzo didn't reply, merely peeking with narrowed eyes at Adrián, trying to penetrate his thoughts. So far, almost nothing he had said was true. Adrián told everybody that he had been discharged from military service for medical reasons. In fact, José Miguel had learned, he had come out of prison only a few months earlier. He had no known occupation, though never lacked money, and just keeping an eight-cylinder, automatic-shift '58 Oldsmobile running cost a small fortune.

"Whoever has plenty of money has a lot of power," Adrián affirmed solemnly.

Lorenzo Bantú was now convinced that Adrián had not been sent by the police or by State Security, as he had at first suspected. He and José Miguel had set a trap to test him: José Miguel had offered Adrián fifty thousand pesos for the use of one of the half-ruined warehouses at the rear of his aunt's house. The warehouse would be used to repackage the contents of a twelve-ton container of talcum powder stolen from the docks. After hearing José Miguel's proposal, Adrián had responded: "Too many people in the operation. Sell the container to another organization. You're sure to make two hundred thousand clear, without risks."

Lorenzo and José Miguel had waited. A container of talcum had, in fact, disappeared from the docks and the police were very actively in pursuit of the thieves. If Adrián were an informer, José Miguel would be detained at any moment for questioning about some of the many "operations" in which he was always engaged, and his house would undoubtedly be searched for any sign that could link him to the theft of the missing container. A reasonable time passed and nothing happened. Nothing seemed to link Adrián to the police. But the *Nasakó* was still very mistrustful; he kept feeding him more bait, and Adrián didn't seem to respond, continuing to visit the house persistently, evidently trying to win Lorenzo's friendship. José Miguel's extensive experience with processing personnel when he was an army officer led him to conclude that Adrián was not from the police nor from any State Security branch.

So what the hell is he after? Lorenzo asked himself. His regular clients were of another cut altogether: simple people from believing families; young men eager to acquire a smattering of *Palo* in order to show off, appear tough, and establish an identity of their own within the aggressive milieu in which they had to live; mothers with sons in prison; chronically ill people who had found no cure with physicians or medicines. Now and then, more cultivated people visited them, fascinated by the rites, the dances, the dancers who fell into trances, the work of the witch doctors, the secret of the color code in their necklaces, and—above all—by the divining methods of *Regla de Osha* and *Palo Monte* and the enigmatic *nganga*. Doubting Thomases with problems so overwhelming they could see no other hope also came as a last resort. And if, suddenly, their fortunes changed or they found consolation, they often became, in one way or another, friends of the house, *aleyos*, and tended to maintain occasional contact with Lorenzo and his sister. If their results were positive, they often brought other skeptics.

Adrián fit none of these categories, and Lorenzo on several occasions had expressed his confusion to his sister. Despite the strong physical attraction she felt toward Adrián, she had to admit that an ancestral intuition alerted her that she was confronting a poisonous serpent intent on mesmerizing and seducing her.

Lorenzo finally stopped drinking, covered his glass with his hand, and looked at Adrián with an expression that clearly said, "*What in the hell do you want from me?*"

Adrián hesitated and smiled slightly. Suddenly, all of the effects from the rum seemed to have vanished. Lorenzo lifted his glass and drank until it was empty. He was trembling. To his disgust, Adrián was dominating him.

Then Adrián seemed to relent. "I'm going to speak plainly. I've been hearing about you for a long time. I spent time in the jug with one of your godsons, Pedro Bermúdez. He told me what you're like, but I wanted to check you out for myself because I can't afford to make a mistake with what I'm going to propose.

"I offer you power. Power such as you have never imagined. And power is the only really important thing in life. Without power, life is worth very little. You know that. What you want, what you need, is power. That's where I come into your life."

Lorenzo Bantú stood up abruptly. "Come with me! I want my *nganga* to hear what you have to propose."

That had to have been the night when a deal between them had been sealed. Since then, she now realized, her brother had changed completely. He now spoke and acted arrogantly, as if he were all-powerful.

RAFAEL CUAN'S DEATH

THE CORONER STUDIED the file that the policeman handed him to refresh his memory of the case. After a quick glance, he nodded. "Yes, I was looking for some indication of poisoning—either something that could have weakened him over a long period or something fast-acting in the last days of his life. I interviewed the doctors who attended him in the hospital and reviewed his case history. I also spoke at length with the family doctor who issued the death certificate. I questioned family members and neighbors who saw Cuan in the days leading up to his death, but nothing suspicious appeared. On the day of his death he had begun to feel very tired in the morning. Although it was Saturday, the family doctor visited him three times, and was present at the moment of death."

The coroner returned the file to the policeman and leaned back, awaiting any further questions. Then, changing his mind, he took back the file. "I want to make it clear that, scientifically, it's impossible to affirm that Cuan *wasn't* poisoned. To know that, an autopsy of the cadaver would be necessary. This is merely an expert opinion, based on the available facts. That's what I was asked for, and that's what I gave." He again returned the file to the policeman and added: "I still think that Cuan may have been poisoned. The disappearance of the cadaver eliminated any evidence that a crime had been committed. No *corpus delicti*, no case. And I don't see any other reason for stealing the corpse, but that's just speculation on my part."

* * *

His next step was to interview some of the people closest to Rafael Cuan in search of a motive for his murder that could have escaped the detection of the investigators of the Centro Habana police station. First he questioned Cuan's widow, a middle-aged Indian-featured mulatta. She was younger than Cuan and, although physically fit, a little overweight.

When the widow went into the kitchen to perform the traditional Cuban ritual of brewing coffee for a visitor, the investigator installed himself at the dining room table to take notes and ask questions. Her answers when she returned revealed a long-suffering but patient and affectionate nature.

The widow declared that on the day of his death, Cuan had arisen in the morning feeling much better than usual. Suddenly, however, he had announced that he was feeling very tired and had gone back to bed. He asked her to telephone Pablo Chang, insisting that he had something important to tell him. She forgot to make the long-distance call to Guantánamo in the morning, and when she remembered, late in the afternoon, Chang was not home. When Chang returned the call later that night, he learned that Cuan had just passed away.

"How could I know that he would die that day?" the widow repeated, trying to absolve her conscience of blame for not having been sufficiently diligent with respect to the last wish of her dying husband. "My *chini* must've had a premonition. He must've guessed it."

"Who's Pablo Chang?"

"A good friend of my husband. He used to come and eat lunch with Rafael the first Sunday of each month when he was working near Havana. Then, after he was transferred to Guantánamo, he came to visit him once or twice a year. Pablo is a big chief in the army. A very good man."

Alvaro wrote the name *Pablo Chang* in his notebook and added a question mark.

The Cuans's only child, Mayulí, had recently graduated as an electronic engineer and had started to work on the maintenance of electronic equipment at the Hermanos Amejeiras hospital. It was not the work she had

had in mind, but the hospital was within walking distance of her home. In the last three months of her father's life, she and her mother had alternated nights sleeping on a cot beside his bed to make sure he took his medicine and to attend to him when he woke during the night. Mayulí, like most only daughters of elderly fathers, had been extremely close to her dad, who, in turn, had adored her.

To this circle of people with the best opportunities for poisoning Cuan, one other person had to be added. Rafael Cuan had spent many of his last hours speaking in Cantonese with a friend of many years, José Ming. No one knew anything about these conversations, since José Ming had died one week after Cuan, according to the files Carrillo had given him. A natural death so close to that of Cuan was not impossible, but it seemed suspicious. It was something to dig into, later.

None of the investigators had uncovered the slightest trace of a family conflict likely to have motivated a homicide. No bank account of sufficient size to warrant a dispute existed, nor did any other assets worthy of note, with the exception of the modest apartment where Cuan had lived with his wife and daughter. This, like all dwellings in postrevolutionary Cuba, was subject, upon the death of the owner, to an exhaustive legal procedure that would amply define the rights of each family member, leaving little room for manipulation.

There was nothing else to do regarding the poisoning hypothesis. Alvaro emptied one of the drawers of the mahogany bureau his father had used as a successful businessman in the '50s. He wiped the dust from inside the drawer with a wet cloth, let it dry, then set down the folder with the poisoning hypothesis and his notes on the case.

Alvaro felt good about working on the hypothesis of Chinese vengeance. It was far more interesting than a vulgar case of poisoning. Up to that moment, the target of the inquiry had been the people closest to the dead man; now it was Rafael Cuan himself, along with his friends and foes.

Alvaro again reviewed the file with the investigations of the deceased. A complete list of the mourners at the wake and burial had been compiled, together with an explanation for the presence of each of them. The report concluded with the description of four people who had no known reasons for being classified as friends, business associates, or relatives. One was an old Chinese man no one knew. The second was a good-looking young Caucasian man who had spent almost the whole time sleeping in a corner of the funeral parlor at Zanja and Belascoain Streets. An elderly man had also wandered in after first visiting other chapels, apparently trying to pick which person to mourn. Another had come twice, taken long looks around, and, on both occasions, drank a cup of coffee and then left. Altogether, thirty-eight people had been present at the funeral parlor and only twenty-three at the burial in the cemetery.

Upon first review, it appeared that the officers from the Centro Habana station had done a thorough job of unraveling the biography of Rafael Cuan since his landing in Cuba in 1937 as one more drop of water in the sea of immigrants arriving on the island's coasts since its discovery in 1492. According to the registry of the ship from which he had disembarked and the data on a merchant-marine ID card bearing a stamp authorizing a six-month stay in the country, Cuan was twenty-two years old at the time of his arrival. This information was followed by a list of the jobs he had held, grouped into three periods, and the people close to him in each: from his arrival until 1945, from 1946 until 1964, and from 1965 until his death.

The report seemed to present a complete and painstaking investigation of the people in Cuan's life, but a visit by the retired policeman to the National Library soon revealed it to be merely a carelessly assembled list of names of residents of the Chinese quarter, taken from old telephone directories, practically in alphabetical order. "They didn't even take the trouble to invent a single name!" Alvaro exclaimed, tossing the file into his knapsack.

Why this deception? It appeared that Carrillo did not want him poking his nose into Cuan's past. *"We need to find this cadaver quickly. Just concentrate your work on this objective."* These had been some of Carrillo's last words. He had to figure out what was really going on.

Mayulí stood on the tips of her tennis shoes to grab her card at the time-clock at the Hermanos Amejeiras hospital. A hundredth of a second before she reached the card, another hand grabbed it, marked the hour, and returned it to its place. Turning and looking up, she saw the tall, blond policeman who had so impressed her mother. She giggled at her momentary confusion.

"Are you headed home? I can take you on the backseat of my bicycle. I'm just a poor policeman in the 'Special Period,' but I need to talk to you alone about your father. Are you up for an adventure?"

The girl accepted, somewhat timidly, and in ten minutes they covered the same distance that she had walked that morning in thirty. And she felt perfectly safe during the ride.

Mayulí invited the policeman to her room, which was spacious and cool. A large window overlooked an expanse of dirty brown roofs spread under a ceiling of dark summer clouds presaging rain. The room exhibited the cleanliness and order of a hospital laboratory. Leaving her visitor to peruse a shoebox full of objects, photographs, letters, and cards related to her father, the young woman excused herself to wash up and change clothes.

She returned in a fresh cloud of perfume, bearing a tray with tea and cookies. She was wearing a red kimono with white flowers that permitted brief but tantalizing glimpses of skin while she served the tea.

"My father was very affectionate. He never spoke a harsh word to anyone and never got upset. He seemed to understand everything and always found a way to solve problems, no matter how complicated. He told me that he hadn't always been that way, that when he was young he'd been impetuous and impatient." As she spoke, her hands flitted gracefully, as if accompanying her words with their own discourse. "From the time that I was very small, I loved to hear him speak. He was so different from other fathers. I never got tired of asking him about China and his life there and why he came to Cuba and how he learned Spanish . . . Whenever he returned from a trip, he always came loaded with gifts, most of them for me. Talking with Papá was a way of traveling to exotic and far-off worlds that were, in a way, mine, too.

"One of my favorite pictures is this one." She showed him an old postcard of the San Francisco Bay Bridge dated August 1952. "I found it among his things and he told me about his visit to the city and the history of this bridge."

The daughter continued tracing the image of the structure that Rafael Cuan had wanted to impress on his beloved child. In contrast to the great majority of Chinese migrants to Cuba, Cuan had had university training, although—his daughter explained—he had never graduated. At the university, he belonged to a group of nationalist students implicated in the escape of several political prisoners in 1936. When his participation was discovered, he had to flee, disguised as an assistant to a Buddhist monk— in reality, one of his uncles. After a long and hazardous trip by land, they reached Saigon, in Indochina. There he became a kitchen hand aboard a French ship sailing to Le Havre, France. A year later, he arrived in Cuba. Up to this point, Mayulí's account coincided well with the documents in Alvaro's possession.

"Papá told me what Cuba was like when he arrived, so far away and different from his homeland." Mayulí showed the policeman objects and documents that Cuan had saved: menus from old restaurants and cafés, opera programs, announcements of famous boxing matches and baseball games. What seemed curious to Alvaro, however, was that the young woman offered no information about Cuan's personal life during that period. Her recollections of things her father had told her gave a detailed portrait of Cuba during the economic boom following World War II and, later, all the changes brought by the revolutionary triumph of 1959. But her father's daily life continued to be obscure. When the policeman tried to probe, she only offered: "Papá never liked to talk at home about his work. He always said that it was enough to devote ten hours to it every day."

Mayulí jumped out of her seat when a thunderbolt struck a power line on Zanja Street, then laughed when she realized the cause of the noise. A gust of wind from the north splashed a wave of rain through the open window and she hurried to close it. She turned on the light switch only to find there was no electricity, then rushed to close other doors in the apartment and fetch some clothes that had been hung to dry in a small patio. Minutes later, she returned with an oil lantern and a dish of hot pork cracklings.

"You can't go home on a bicycle in this storm. All the streets will be flooded."

"Thanks a lot for the pork. The storm will stop in a few minutes. I'll be out in a while, before it's too dark."

The heavy downpour began to stabilize, interrupted at times by strong gusts of wind blowing large droplets of water against the wooden windowpanes; the storm was showing no signs of relenting. Night closed in early, and time passed rapidly as Mayulí and Alvaro turned the discussion to their personal lives.

"Dinner is ready," Mayulí's mother announced from the kitchen.

"I must leave now. It's too late," Alvaro said.

Mayulí took his hand and warned, "Don't you dare do that to my mother. She'll come out of the dark and stab you in the back if you try to escape." Alvaro was unsure how to react. "And I'll help her," she added.

They both laughed and she showed him to the bathroom to wash his hands before dinner.

Two hours later, the policeman left, convinced from his conversation with the girl, as he had been from his interview with her mother, that Cuan had been a stranger to his own family. Prolific in describing vividly the panorama that he saw around him, he had nevertheless revealed himself to them only as an undemanding husband and an affectionate and thrifty father, whose only eccentricity had been a horse-leather belt that he had worn every day for the past twenty years and had insisted on being buried with. Before leaving, Alvaro had given Mayulí his phone number in case she came up with something she wanted to tell him.

But Mayulí's memories lingered in Alvaro's mind. "If I were ten years younger, I'd go right back and ask her to marry me," he said aloud, pedalling home while trying to avoid the big pools of water in the street.

The next day Alvaro showed up in the Centro Habana police station, just three blocks away from Cuan's apartment. It was time to meet Lieutenant Colonel Francisco Lin and try to unravel further information about Cuan.

"It is an honor and a pleasure to meet the famous retired police investigator Alvaro Antonio Molinet." Lin received the visitor with apparent courtesy and admiration, but Alvaro sensed a hidden irony in the pompous greeting.

Alvaro started with simple questions about the information he had received from Carrillo: Who was Ming, Cuan's friend? Where had he lived before? What was his connection with Cuan? Why was there no information about Pablo Chang, an army officer Cuan had tried to call the day he died?

The lieutenant colonel took on the attitude of an offended queen when it became clear that his work was being rigorously reviewed by an officer of lower rank—and retired, to boot.

After an hour of questioning, it was evident that Francisco Lin was withholding information. Worse, everything seemed to indicate that an operation of misinformation intended to divert him had been prepared hastily and ineffectively. He decided to attack with some facts he had gathered. "Why did Cuan take those trips to San Francisco?"

"What trips?" Lin feigned ignorance.

Alvaro explained the contradictions he had found between Cuan's apparently modest employment in Cuba and his trips abroad. Lin began to show further signs of discomfort until, finally, his face froze in a neutral expression and he said in a solemn voice, "Colonel Carrillo informed me that your mission is to find the cadaver, and ours is to seek out the motives. The colonel told you that we are still investigating and that you should wait until we finish. Now it appears that you are interfering with our work."

The retired policeman had seen this response coming and answered energetically. "I'm corroborating the investigation of a possible poisoning, prepared by the investigators of Plaza municipality, and no limit has been placed on my field of action. To carry out this task, it's essential that I meet and talk with the family. It's also crucial that I share any important inconsistencies that I find."

Francisco Lin softened his expression and his tone grew condescending. "We know that Rafael Cuan had other businesses. That isn't unusual in the Chinese quarter. It's logical that he kept this dark side of his life hidden from his family. But thanks for advising me." The lieutenant colonel stood up with a wooden smile on his face and held out his hand to the visitor, thus indicating that the interview was over.

Alvaro rose from his seat as well. "Okay, okay, I get it. You're right. Let's do what the colonel said. Please, do me a favor: Tell Carrillo that I will wait until your group has finished its survey."

The brush with Lin annoyed him. Until this point in the investigation, he had felt Carrillo's shadow always behind him, breathing down his neck. It was clear that his superior was monitoring every step he took. It was also clear that he had entered into an area where he wasn't wanted. Another mystery within the mystery of the theft of the cadaver!

WHAT TO DO?

SHE COULD NOT fail again. Before choosing her next step, she had to carefully review everything that had happened without forgetting anything important or letting passion blind her.

Her *Registro de Itá*, performed by four *babalawos*, had revealed that she would have to protect her brother for the rest of her life. A responsibility imposed at birth, it would end only with the death of one of them; thus the *orishas* had ordained. Until recently, she had always managed to track who Lorenzo saw and the places he visited . . . all of his movements. Thanks to her vigilance and care, he had triumphed in life and was no longer a hulking, helpless boy. But new dangers were lurking over him, much more difficult to avoid, and she had to find a solution. She decided to analyze each recent event in chronological order, step by step.

The turning point had been Adrián's entry into their lives. From his first visit, Lorenzo had distrusted him, violently. Then, suddenly, beginning the night of St. Valentine's Day, her brother had become very interested in Adrián, almost to a point of obsession, and his quiet and humble demeanor had changed completely.

If Adrián were a son of Oshún, everything would be clear, because that *orisha* had been her personal enemy since childhood, when she had almost gone insane. That enmity was also a part of the eternal hatred between that goddess-harlot and her own chaste mother, Yewá. But the *Santera* had studied Adrián closely and was absolutely convinced that he was a son of Shangó, not of Oshún. That unmistakable virility appears only in the sons of Shangó, along with high intelligence, prudence, and a total lack of scruples. Everything about him bespoke his powerful father, the controller of lightning. Further proof of Shangó's paternity was the wily way Adrián had dominated her brother, a son of Oggún.

The preceding night, Lorenzo had left the house around eight-thirty to attend a long session with his Abakuá chapter. She had stayed at home watching television until she got tired and went to bed just before ten o'clock. As she was dropping off to sleep, she heard a tapping at her door. The house was locked, and only she and Lorenzo had keys, so she supposed he had returned early. She called out for him to come in, and was astonished to see Adrián enter. Confused, she neither demanded that he leave immediately nor asked how he had entered the house. He sat down on the right side of her bed and said that he needed a quick consultation, just one throw of the cocos, to decide whether or not he should close a business deal that very night.

To avoid offending Yewá, she got out of bed, slipped on a robe, and received him behind a plywood partition that, together with a sofa, divided her room into two sections.

Adrián sat down beside her on the floor before the large wall mirror. As she began her preparations, he started caressing her thigh on the pretext of examining a small scar above her left knee, and he did not remove his hand after she explained its origin. She became so nervous that she wasn't sure she could control her instincts. Adrián proceeded to caress her whole body until, almost fainting, she pushed him away and threw the cocos.

By the time she had completed the consultation, she felt considerably more calm. She rose quickly and asked him to leave. He nodded, took one of her hands and kissed it, thanked her, and left. She felt exhausted by the experience and fell asleep at once. When she woke up, she sensed that she had dreamed about him all night, and she realized that she had not asked how he had entered the house. She was suddenly unsure if he had really been in her room or if it had just been one of her lustful dreams. The uncertainty left her feeling anguished. How was it possible for her dreams to seem so real?

Everything indicated that Adrián was, indeed, a son of Shangó. As such, he had his vulnerable points. If she had to destroy him, she would work on those weaknesses. Her intuition told her that this moment might not be very far off.

The most inexplicable thing was that Yewá had not given her any signal alerting her to the danger. On the contrary, her consultations with the cocos each morning presented only positive signs. Why this cruel deception? Had Yewá decided to punish her for her fantasies about Adrián? Was she still testing her—as if she hadn't already been sufficiently tried? Had Adrián been sent to be her undoing, as could so easily have happened last night? Was this a final punishment for mistakes of which she was unaware, that only the hard heart of her *orisha madre* knew about? Since her initiation in *Osha*, however, Yewá had never failed her, protecting her from all harm.

A new doubt suddenly assaulted her thoughts: What if Yewá was not actually deceiving her? If everything that occurred was really for the best, what was happening to her brother, no matter how bad it seemed, might actually be necessary. The first time that thought had crossed her mind she had rejected it out of hand. Now, however, she was thinking logically and she had to admit that this hypothesis was, in fact, quite possible.

For some time now, an idea had been hovering at the edges of her consciousness: Her brother was reminding her, more and more, of their grandfather. Furthermore, her brother seemed to know about things that had transpired between her and their grandfather *before* Lorenzo had come to live with them—and she was sure the old man had never related the stories while he was alive. Their grandfather had felt intense resentment toward her as the ordained "protectress" of Lorenzo, whom he had considered his exclusive ward. But her designation had been through no fault or initiative of her own. Yewá, her *orisha madre*, knew well that she had tried to make peace with him, but the old man had died without showing any sign of relenting in his resentment of her.

Was it possible that the spirit of their grandfather had taken possession of Lorenzo? She could by no means underestimate the powers of the old man's spirit or the fact that he would be much more formidable dead than alive. That could also explain how the protection of the house and of Lorenzo had been neutralized, and even Lorenzo's recent attitude toward her. And, if that were the case, what was Adrián's role in all of this? Was he the old man's instrument of revenge against her—as a surefire way to destroy her? She had to admit that all of this was possible. And yet, and yet . . . surely their grandfather's spirit wouldn't put Lorenzo in harm's way.

One afternoon she had a clear answer from Oyá: She must immediately visit her godmother, Margarita.

CHINESE VENGEANCE

ON THE THIRD DAY of his reclusion at home, Alvaro got a phone call from Lieutenant Colonel Francisco Lin. His voice, now friendly and frank, revealed the hand of Carrillo loosening the screws. Lin was calling to invite him to an important interview, "critical for solving the case." He should wear civilian clothes and come by bus to avoid the public embarrassment of a police call on the important family they were going to visit.

He was glad to have an excuse not to take his bicycle, thus sparing himself a trip beneath the summer sun and a sweaty arrival. Although he set out with ample time to travel by bus, public transportation was not in its finest period. He covered the last stretch on foot, walking as quickly as possible. As he approached, he saw Lin pacing impatiently. Well, his conscience was clear. He'd done everything he could to arrive on time.

He was preparing an explanation to fend off the anticipated recrimination from Lin for his slight tardiness, but as he reached the corner of Zanja Street, a loud gong sounded and a dozen Chinese cornets set the air vibrating. Startled, he looked to his right and was transfixed by the effigy of a mythological animal, a combination of dragon, lion, and serpent. The animal trainer, his left hand covering his face with a mask of a wise, old man, controlled each movement of the beast with a long pole in his right hand. Following the dragon, a group of beautiful Asian girls of every possible skin color raised and lowered colorful fans in unison with the movements of their bare thighs, dancing in rhythm with the music. Behind them, a company of young males advanced, marking the rhythm with kung fu blows. It was the *comparsa* of the Chinese quarter, rehearsing for the Havana summer carnival.

The charm of the spectacle diluted the acidity of Lin's opening remarks about punctuality and its decisive effect on the fate of both men. Lin then explained their mission, raising his voice above the din of the *comparsa*. They were going to visit Antonio Choy, who had hired Cuan one year after his arrival in Cuba and had been his main employer. Choy had been the president for many years of one of the most important Chinese societies and was an influential figure in that world. He had an encyclopedic knowledge of its history. Before the triumph of the Revolution in 1959, he had been a wealthy importer. On more than one occasion in those days, important people had appealed to his wisdom and tact to solve major conflicts of interest. Choy was the only living person who could help elucidate the hypothesis of vengeance between Chinese families.

"I requested an interview two weeks ago. Yesterday I received a message to be here at four o'clock. We're a half-hour early. Let's take a walk through the Chinese quarter."

"But you told me to be here at three!"

Lin looked at his watch and smiled, as if his diagnosis of his colleague's character had just been proven correct. "I'd like to handle the conversation with Choy," he replied, ignoring Alvaro's comment. "Okay?"

Alvaro didn't feel obliged to promise anything, so he merely inclined his head to one side, letting Lin interpret for himself whether that meant "yes" or "no." They set off to kill time walking through the now shoddy but formerly flourishing Chinese neighborhood.

"Over there was the Shanghai Theater. Its porn show was one of the world's great tourist attractions. You can see it in the second part of the film *The Godfather*. Remember? It isn't actually shown in the film, but a reference is made to a man with an incredibly big penis."

"At the rate we're going, hunting for U.S. dollars, we'll be seeing that theater open again one of these days!" Alvaro replied. "Better find that guy and see if he's still in shape!"

Lin grimaced with distaste for his colleague's humor. Alvaro was the antithesis, in Lin's opinion, of what a policeman should be. But Francisco Lin was a disciplined officer and he had precise instructions about how to handle this character, so he continued describing the Chinese quarter as he remembered it, with a trace of nostalgia in his voice.

"I was very small. I always accompanied my father on the days I didn't go to school. He had a stand on this block where he sold fresh vegetables. There was a shoe shiner's chair in the doorway next to a counter where lottery tickets were sold. I still remember the names of the three prostitutes that worked that corner: Lucy, Daisy, and Dolores. Dolores was black, a really black woman, and the only one of them who used her own name. They were always teasing me; they made me smell between their legs and put my hands on their breasts. I almost died of shame when they touched my pecker and laughed at how small it was. I let them torment me because they always ended up buying me candy."

Lin continued describing all of the business establishments as he recalled them from his vantage point three feet above the ground. They reached the Aguila de Oro movie house, where Chinese-language films and newsreels were still shown. From there, they turned back toward Choy's house.

"That whole world began to disappear when the Revolution wiped out the economic system. The big Chinese merchants returned to San Francisco, where they'd come from originally."

"Do you have any idea how many Chinese immigrants came to Cuba?"

"The first wave of immigrants was calculated at around 150,000 between 1847 and 1875. Almost all of them were contracted as substitutes for the slaves after abolition of the African slave trade, and they were forced to live and work under even worse conditions than the blacks. From 1875 till the end of the nineteenth century, several thousand came from California, many of them with considerable wealth. Finally, in the boom of the 1920s following World War I, some 30,000 Chinese arrived to make up for the shortage of workers.

"The first immigrants of the nineteenth century participated actively in Cuba's wars of independence and left few descendants. But the later migrations have become totally assimilated, dissolving their genes for round eyes, straight hair, and yellowish skin in this enormous *mestizo* river of Cuban society." Lin finished speaking and slapped his hand against his chest.

"Coño, that was real poetic!" Alvaro smirked.

"What was?"

"That river of Chinese semen."

Lin stared at Alvaro. He couldn't stand the man. It was rumored that he had always refused promotion, preferring to remain a simple investigator. He, Francisco Lin, was already a lieutenant colonel, with almost ten fewer years of service. He looked at his wristwatch. "It's time," he said. "Remember to let me handle the conversation."

They found themselves facing an enormous dragon's head with a knocker between its teeth on the imposing front door of the Choy family home on Zanja Street. Lin stood looking at his watch until four o'clock sharp, then knocked.

His companion passed his hands casually behind his back and moved the minute hand of his watch forward. "Look, Francisco," he said, showing him his watch marking 4:10. "Get rid of that Russian watch. This is a Seiko, one of the good ones, bought with U.S. dollars."

Lin's face changed color and he looked stricken. Just then, the door opened and a beautiful almond-eyed young woman appeared. "Are you the policemen? Come in."

The young woman led them through the house that seemed to extend for a whole block. Each of the rooms through which they passed was marked by rich and tasteful furnishings presumably accumulated over generations. A light fragrance permeated the silent rooms. They were finally brought before their elderly host who was seated in the simplest of the rooms, overlooking a small patio replete with puny, somewhat-yellowed vegetable plants.

Wearing wooden sandals and an old pair of pants cut off at the knees, Choy sat in a wicker armchair in front of a small, round wicker table. At their approach, he rose briskly to his feet. It was impossible to guess his age. The blond policeman placed it somewhere between 80 and 120. The old man's granddaughter pulled up two more wicker chairs. Immediately, her double, though younger, entered with a wooden tray holding coffee and cups.

Choy squinted to get a better look at his visitors against the radiant background of the patio. "How many child?" he asked.

"One," said Lin.

The old man made no effort to hide his pity. "And you? How many?"

"Seven," lied the other.

Choy's face lit up. He rose from his chair and held out his hand effusively. Lin's face reflected his profound disgust at having brought this unpredictable companion.

"I always wanted to have a large family. Since that's difficult these days with just one wife, I had them with three," the blond policeman explained, adding to his lie.

"You wise and fortunate man," said Choy.

"How many do you have?" the policeman asked.

Choy gave them a detailed account of his relatives covering three generations. He had had ten children, but only seven still lived. He had twenty-one grandchildren and five great-grandchildren. Lin remained silent while Choy and the blond policeman discussed a range of topics like a pair of old friends meeting after ten years of separation. When the exchange of secrets about caring for vegetables threatened to extend the conversation interminably, Lin cast a furious glance at his *compañero* in an attempt to silence him.

"We don't want to take up too much of your time, Señor Choy. As you know, we want your opinion on the disappearance of Cuan's body. Do you think it could be a case of vengeance?"

Choy shook his head negatively. "No, no. I tell you that vengeance, no."

Lin said nothing more. He took a sip of coffee from the cup that he had hardly touched, then rose and stretched out his hand to Choy, thanking him for his time. The blond policeman remained seated, waiting.

"Let's go!" snapped Lin.

Alvaro had no choice but to rise and say farewell, although he regretted it. He still had a number of questions. Choy had known Cuan since his arrival in Cuba; he was still mentally alert and his memory was intact. He was also an avid and frank conversationalist.

"*Cubano* always in hurry," their host commented as they returned through the house to the front door. Then, turning to the policeman with the seven children, he invited him to return whenever he liked.

"You like Chinese food?"

"I love it. In my last incarnation, I was a cook in a restaurant on the Shanghai docks, I assure you."

"Be sure to come visit me."

"When?"

"Whenever you want to eat good Chinese food."

Out on the street, the two policemen began to argue above the musical background of the *comparsa* in full swing. "You could at least have asked him how he formed that opinion!"

"Look!" Lin was trying to control his seething anger. "I was born in this neighborhood. My father was Chinese; I know how these people think. I asked to see him over two weeks ago. He kept me waiting until the day before yesterday, not for any lack of personal time—that's obvious. He needed to make all of the necessary consultations before talking to the police. Do you understand? When he said no, it meant no."

The blue-eyed policeman slipped his hands into his pockets and took several steps, looking down at the sidewalk. "You're right. I agree with you."

"What will you recommend to Carrillo?" Lin asked finally, after they had walked in silence for some distance.

"To interrupt this investigation. Cuan was apparently not poisoned, but neither is there anything indicating Chinese vengeance. The explanation has to lie somewhere else."

"I agree with you entirely," Lin said coldly.

Alvaro's blue eyes scrutinized Lin's face closely. He had expected a more emotional response to the idea of losing the hundreds of hours of work that Lin and his fellow officers had invested in the case. Instead, he saw the face of someone relieved of a heavy burden. Without saying goodbye, Lin hastened his steps and turned at the next corner.

The policeman with the long blond hair and beard remained standing in the middle of the sidewalk. He felt that he had simultaneously witnessed two spectacles: the dress rehearsal of the Chinese quarter's *comparsa*, bright and tinseled in preparation for the city's carnival, and the end of a tragi-comedy with a poorly written script and even worse actors, but with a title guaranteed to hook its only spectator: *Chinese Vengeance.*

"To hell with all of this!" he shouted.

The kung fu conga dancers paused involuntarily and shot angry glances at the tall man who was now walking rapidly away.

THE IYARÉ MARGARITA

N SPITE OF the years that had passed, *Iyaré* Margarita's temperament had not changed and she was still a bundle of nerves. She came out to meet the *Santera* as soon as she was told of her arrival. "I know an important matter has brought you here, so come with me. Don't feel embarrassed, these are my godchildren and they understand the situation very well." She took the *Santera* by the arm, practically pulling her through a room full of clients who had already been waiting for some time.

A fat woman, whose age was difficult to judge but who was obviously too old to be the mother of the disfigured child sitting next to her, nodded, expressing the approval of all those present. Margarita escorted the *Santera* into the *Ilé Osha*, a tiny, poorly ventilated room in a very small house that was usually filled with grandchildren. The children constituted a strange kind of tribe that played there silently, hardly moving. The *Santera* always brought some homemade candy for them, and she looked around now, but she didn't see any of them. Then she felt a pull on her skirt and discovered one very small child behind a curtain next to her leg.

Margarita, in her stormy way of doing things which age had not managed to subdue, began preparations even before the visitor had found a place to sit. "You don't have to explain anything! Something serious has brought you to this house. I have a feeling I must consult with cocos today. Yes, I will consult with cocos.

"When Obatalá distributed the powers of Olofi, he celebrated *Apeje Orisha* under a coconut tree and gave a dry coconut to each *orisha*. Only Babalú Ayé was uncooperative at first, but he was eventually persuaded. That is why all the *orishas*, death, and the dead, can be consulted with cocos."

Iyaré Margarita used to say that this oracle, so simple in appearance, was as effective as the *Diloggún* and the *Ipkuele*, if the procedure was done right. And after complaining about the current practices surrounding the throwing of cocos, she often insisted on carrying out the rites in the traditional style preserved by families in her native province of Matanzas.

Her assistant brought a gourd containing fresh water, a candle, a small white dish, and a dry coconut. The *Iyaré* lowered herself onto a small stool so that she faced an effigy of Elégguá made of highly polished black stone, with eyes and ears represented by seashells, giving the *orisha* a dreamy, sensual, and very primitive appearance. This was a piece much appreciated by Margarita, who was a daughter of Elégguá, and she worked with this *orisha* whenever she could, together with Eshú, his dark side. "Elégguá is the first and last *orisha*, the one who opens and closes all paths, who determines the destiny, life, and death of human beings," she said, opening her large, bony hands and raising her eyebrows as if asking, *What else could you want?*

Margarita lit the candle, put it on the small white dish, and placed it before the seashell-eyed *orisha*. From a bottle next to the idol, she poured some *aguardiente* into a small glass, but didn't drink it. She looked at her godchild, then sat next to her to make sure she was ready, and began her *moyugba*, prayers.

"*Omi tutú*, Elégguá" (Fresh water, Elégguá).

With one hand, she spilled a little water in front of the god, repeating the movement each time she said something.

"*Ana tutú* (Fresh relations).

"*Tutú Alaroye* (Freshening, Elégguá, master of discords).

"*Obi tutú, Babá*" (Fresh coconut, Father).

She then recited a long prayer to the *orishas*, to her long-dead ancestors, and to her godmother, also dead. To her godfather, still living, she wished health and a long life. She took the dry coconut and presented it to Elégguá, to the other *orishas* on the altar, and to the soup bowls that held their attributes and other essentials. After cracking the coconut on the tiled floor, she selected four pieces of the mass to make the *obís* and began rounding them off with a long nail on her right thumb. The first three cuttings off the *obís, pikutis,* she dropped on Elégguá, then she continued carving the four *obís,* placing the new *pikutis* on the other *orishas.*

Once finished with the *obís,* the *Iyaré* held them in her left hand and began touching the cocos, the floor, and the idol with her right hand while speaking quickly, in a low, intimate tone:

"*Elégguá, ilé mo kú e o*" (Elégguá, I give you my house).

"*A kú e ye*" (We greet you), added her goddaughter.

"*Elégguá, mo ku e o*" (Elégguá, we entrust ourselves to you).

"*A kú e ye,*" the goddaughter responded.

They repeated the prayer three times.

With the cocos still in her left hand, the *Iyaré* touched the floor and the dreamy-eyed idol with her free hand, then moved the *obís* to her right hand and did the same thing.

"*A kú e ye osuó*" (We revere you with our hands).

"*Akuañá*" (Amen), said the goddaughter firmly.

"*A kú e ye, Omá*" (We revere you, Father).

"*Akuañá,*" the godchild repeated.

"*Arikú Babá wa*" (Greetings, Father, come).

"*Akuañá.*"

The old woman stood up, took the four pieces of coco with both hands, raised them high, then turned right, called Elégguá, turned left, called Elégguá again, and returned to her original position. She asked the *Santera's* guardian angel permission to rub her forehead lightly. She touched her on both sides of her bosom and her knees, and slowly recited:

"*Yu soro mo bi* (Go ahead, speak, I'm going to ask).

"*La fo* (Put unexpected evil aside, the losses).

"*Yote obí!*" (The coco is about to be thrown).

Margarita made the sign of the cross with both hands, holding the *obinús* firmly between them, inhaled, then stood still for an instant with her eyes closed for maximum concentration. If at that moment she did not feel something vibrate or experience some other sensation, she would continue her invocation until she felt she had really communicated with the *orishas*.

"What is happening to my godchild?"

The question should have been voiced by the godchild, but the *Iyaré*, as usual, spoke impulsively. She kissed the cocos and, before tossing them, announced: "*Obí Elégguá.*"

The *Iyaré* flexed her knees and threw the cocos onto a floor mat. Three fell with the flesh upward, and one downward.

"*Itawa.*" Margarita took a breath and kept talking. "Shangó, Inlé, Oshún, and Yemayá are speaking. It's a very delicate letter to interpret when it's a first throw. It's the letter that most resembles life: *Everything is possible, but with opposition.* For now, we will do as recommended."

The *Iyaré* put the cocos in the gourd with water to "refresh" them, then removed them, after which the goddaughter threw the water out the door, holding the gourd with both hands. She returned with the gourd full of fresh water. Margarita held the coco pieces in her left hand and with her right hand touched the floor and her left hand four times, murmuring: "*Mo fe lóny unlo tóri aru, oborí, efo, tóri, ore.*"

She remained pensive for an instant and then, in a loud voice, spoke the *súyer* that accompanies *Itawa*: "*Everything in life has its opposite, all things cast a shadow. There is no first without a second, there is no second without a first. You must lure your enemy to your side to increase your own power; if you destroy your enemy, it will not encumber you, but this will diminish your prestige.*"

How had she not realized it before? It was all very clear now. *Itawa* was referring to her and her brother. Scarcely two weeks before, Lorenzo had shouted that he was the better of the two, that she was lagging behind. "*All things cast a shadow . . .*" He himself had called her his evil shadow.

Alarmed by her discovery, she remembered the second part of the *súyer*, still more revealing: "*You must attract your enemy to increase your power . . .*" Her brother had certainly not been trying to attract her. Might he have decided to destroy her? Scared by the implications of this conclusion, she stopped to consider if there were other possible interpretations of the oracle. Not finding any, she told herself she had to be realistic and objective. There was no other logical explanation: *Her brother, flesh of her own flesh, blood of her own blood, had decided to destroy her.*

Margarita turned to her godchild and said, "Dear, as you know, you are facing a difficulty, an opposition. *Itawa* also indicates a hidden enemy. Now, can this opposition be eliminated? Yes, it is possible, depending on the work that you do for the saints, as they demand. We must continue the search to clarify this letter, to find out what that opposition is."

Who could that hidden enemy be? Her brother? Adrián? They could perhaps be enemies pretending to be friends, but they were certainly not hidden. *Hidden* could also mean *unknown.*

Margarita then conducted the same movements of the first rite until she reached the same level of concentration. The four pieces all fell face down this time.

"*Oyékun!*" shouted the goddaughter, her voice fading on the last syllable. She sat rigid, staring at the *obís.* She knew what this letter meant, an ominous turn.

Margarita rushed to put the cocos in the gourd again while she glanced furtively at her godchild, as if wanting to pierce her mind. After a long pause, she continued: "We must search deeply. After *Itawa, Oyékun* complicates the message. There is no clear answer to the question asked. *Oyékun,* as you know, is not necessarily a bad letter. *Oyékun* only means that death, a dead person, or one of the *orishas* that rule over the dead— Oyá, Babalú Ayé, Obbá, Yewá—wants to talk. Until now, Yewá has been silent. Could she want to talk to you? This must be followed up. It must be done by *apere.*"

The goddaughter was again surprised. The *Santeros* and *Santeras* of *Regla de Osha* almost always consulted with sixteen shells, the *Diloggún.* The *obís,* four pieces of coco, were normally used to direct very concrete questions to the *orishas* and to get direct replies—usually yes or no. This time her godmother was going to continue the search with cocos by *apere,* a practice almost forgotten. The usual practice was to continue asking questions with each of the coco throws. What secret knowledge was her godmother going to reveal this time?

As if reading her godchild's mind, Margarita said, "Only one question should be asked through the *obís*. Additional questions should then be asked by *apere*, taking into account the way the *obís* fall: The figure formed by the cocos on each throw indicates which *orisha* is speaking. That way, one can make up to seven throws."

Margarita then began a long invocation to the *orishas* that speak through the cocos in *apere*: Elégguá, Oggún, Ochosi, Babalú Ayé, Aggayú Solá, Shangó, Obatalá, Oyá, Oshún, Yemayá, Orula, Obbá, Naná Burukú, Yewá, Los Ibedji, and Olofí-Osún. In addition, she invoked Biagué, the discoverer of the oracle of the cocos, and Adiatoto, his son, to try and interpret every position, letter, and *orisha* without error.

The cocos soon rolled with the first throw in *apere*. The *obís* formed a crooked line. Again the letter heading the *registro*, *Itawa*, appeared.

"The cocos have fallen in the form of an ocean wave. Yemayá is talking for *Itawa* and commands you to investigate. She says that the enemy enters your house to find out how you live, and sends you evil thoughts. Every Friday, before breakfast, pour some seawater on yourself."

Yemayá had been the first one to speak by *apere*, and she had been lucid and direct: ". . . *the enemy enters your house to find out how you live* . . ." That was Adrián: *the enemy*. She had not been mistaken. Yemayá's oracle confirmed her suspicions. There could be no further doubt. This explained her erotic dreams and the bewitching effect of Adrián's cologne.

The desire of this formidable *orisha* to help her was logical. Yemayá presided over her altar at home and the *Santera* and her godchildren always kept her amply supplied with fruit and sweets. Yemayá was now repaying her years of devotion, giving her support—the first ray of hope in a desperate situation. This discovery gave her fresh strength.

Margarita kept her eyes almost closed, as if absent from this world. Then, with unexpected deftness, she picked up the cocos and threw them again. This time, three fell in a straight line and the other fell below the middle one. The three top cocos were face down and the last one face up: *Okana*, the worst of the letters, suggesting something gruesome. The goddaughter felt intense fear. The *Iyaré* moved one hand to her breast, frowned, groped with her other hand for the small glass of *aguardiente*, and drank it all down in one gulp.

"Are you all right, godmother?" the goddaughter asked, serving her more *aguardiente*.

With a gesture, the *Iyaré* authorized her to drink, too.

"The figure of the coffin. It is Oyá who will speak. This position means death, disintegration, separation, return, paid-up debt, change in the mode of existence. See how the *obís* have fallen, the same way coffins were placed in the old days, with their center over a base?" Margarita drank another shot of *aguardiente* and couldn't help casting a sad glance at her goddaughter, who was now smiling.

Yes, as she had wished with all her heart, the second one to talk through the *obís* by *apere* was Oyá, one of the rulers of the cemeteries who receives cadavers from Yewá. The queen of lightning had never failed to talk in the oracles. The position of the coconuts resembling a coffin contained an omen related to the world of the dead, over whom Oyá reigned. Margarita had said "*death.*" Was it announcing a death? A death that had already occurred? Could it mean her own death? "*Disintegration.*" That meant something that falls to pieces, that rots and gradually decomposes. "*Debt paid.*" She thought for a moment about anything she might have borrowed and not returned, but she couldn't remember anything of any importance.

She suddenly saw an image of her grandfather, who, without a trace of animosity, told her: "*Don't fool yourself. This could be the announcement of your own death, your disintegration in payment of your debt to Oshún.*"

"Now we will read the letter," announced Margarita, and added, as if her goddaughter were a common client and not an experienced *Santera*: "Always remember that Oyá reigns over the cemetery, owns the lightning and the stormy winds, throws fire from her mouth, the same as her husband Shangó. Through *Okana*, she says that you think that your imagination deceives you when you feel someone at your side, that you have incomprehensible dreams. Those are works of a spirit that you must shun, because it obeys alien wills. Take five baths of ewe, herbs of Oyá, and four with herbs consecrated to Obatalá."

Was the queen of storms affirming that her erotic dreams were produced by a spirit and not by Adrián, as the Yemayá oracle seemed to indicate? That obscured again what had been explained before. She considered this contradiction, and the explanation that came immediately into her mind was simple: Oyá was referring to her brother. That settled it. An alien spirit was disturbing her brother. What a relief to figure out the logical reason for everything, good or bad!

Margarita threw the cocos again and watched them spread over the mat and form a fan, all face down. She remained still, scrutinizing the oracle. A large drop of sweat ran down her forehead and onto the mat.

"Cocos forming a rainbow—Oshún speaks for Eyékun and says that she is claiming your head, and you well know why. You must quickly make her an *ebbó*—*ekú, epó, ejá, agguandó*, colored cloth—and take it all to the cemetery. The *registro* is finished."

With surprising speed, the old woman picked up the cocos and threw them again. This time one fell riding on another—one with the flesh up over the other face down. Margarita scooped them up immediately.

"What does that throw mean, godmother?"

"It speaks only to the *Iyaré*."

But she knew that a coco riding on another like this meant betrayal. *The betrayal of a man by a woman.* That man had to be Lorenzo. He was involved in the entire *registro*, and the only woman who could double-cross him was Miladys, his lover. It could not be otherwise.

She wanted to evoke the face of her brother, but she couldn't. In his place, their grandfather appeared, telling her again as he had on his deathbed: *"Do you think you have won? I will become a snake and will return for you."*

Once more the idea that her grandfather had returned and was now inhabiting the body of Lorenzo terrified her. She could not fool herself. *Itawa* had clearly indicated in the consultation that her brother, flesh of her flesh, blood of her blood, had decided to finish her off. It was all very clear now.

SEVEN DRAGONS

YOU CAN'T QUIT this case just like that," Carrillo said, passing a hand over his recently shaved face. His tone was half-amused, even affectionate. They had worked together closely for twenty years, beginning with Carrillo's promotion to head of special investigations at the Department of Technical Investigations, best known by its abbreviation, DTI. In that time, a rare understanding and unique friendship had developed between them.

"I have to know the reason for all of this searching. Otherwise I can't function—much less by bicycle under this July sun."

"You haven't asked me about transportation. Just request it with a little bit of notice. I can't guarantee it one hundred percent, but something can be done. And, so that you don't dream up any other excuses, I'll tell you what's behind this case. A story that I'm sure you'll forget as soon as I leave. Do I have your promise that you'll stay on if I tell you?"

"Do I have to promise?"

Carrillo leaned back in his chair. "It all started back in Beijing in 1935. In the summer, the imperial capital and its surroundings are among the most beautiful places in the world. I was there once many years ago for almost six months, and even today, when I need to erase my problems so I can sleep at night, I imagine those gardens. I even recall the glorious scents of the cherry blossoms and the humid earth with the first summer rainfalls."

Carrillo was a born narrator. He modulated his voice, changing the tone, rhythm, and register according to the demands of his story. His hands and face, especially his eyes, expressed sentiments that words could not. It was impossible not to be captivated by the magic of his storytelling. Alvaro stretched himself out full-length in his chair, knowing that his time would not be wasted.

Lu Tse Chin quickened his step. The invitation required punctuality. He crossed a small plaza filled with barefoot children engrossed in games, reached an iron railing where colored fish were being sold, and entered a patio where a young boy and an old man were cleaning a fish tank.

"I want to see the exhibition," he told the old man, who, without interrupting his work, looked him up and down, then indicated a door in the basement of a house half-hidden by trees at the end of a stone path. Lu looked at his watch. He still had one minute to spare, so he walked slowly down the path toward a door. As he opened it, a small bell tinkled inside the house, announcing his arrival. He went down two steps and reached a small, poorly illuminated entrance hall. He waited a moment until his pupils adjusted from the brilliant light of the day. In front of him, hanging on a wall, remained two pieces of green silk cloth, meaning that he was the last guest to arrive. The larger piece was a loose tunic that covered him from neck to knees, with long, ample sleeves that hid his arms. The second piece was a hood of the same material, designed to cover the head down to the shoulders, with eyeholes representing the eyes of a dragon head embroidered in black and gold thread.

After donning the disguise, he passed through another door that opened onto a room where the host and other guests waited, all with identical garments in various colors: white, red, yellow, blue, maroon, and black. Lu sat down in the only empty chair, next to the yellow dragon. Immediately, the dragon hooded in white began to speak slowly and clearly, in the same tone with which he always began his unforgettable history classes at the Imperial University of Beijing.

"Welcome. You all know me. This mask is unimportant. What is essential is that you not recognize one another, as you will understand after you hear my proposal. Each one can reject it by not attending the next meeting, or you can accept the cause I present to you. I know none of you will be a traitor. You were all cho-

sen because you are men of honor, so I have no fear of betrayal if you decide not to participate."

The professor offered a brief preamble, explaining in general terms the historical contradictions of China, the only great ancient civilization that survived to the present day. China was the nation most advanced technologically in the first millennium and the beginning of the second in the modern era. China contributed to the world's key inventions that served to awaken the energies of the so-called Western world beginning in the fifteenth century: gunpowder, the compass, the printing press with movable type, and many others.

"What is China now?" The professor paused an instant, peering at those present. "The country with the world's largest population, poor and weak, and one of the most backward nations in the areas of technology and industrial development. Every year, millions of our people die in floods and famines. Our most precious treasures, our millenary integrity as a nation, and our independence are all threatened—for the first time since Genghis Khan—by the inexorable expansion of the Empire of the Rising Sun. They have already installed a government in Manchuria presided over by a puppet emperor, totally dominated by Japan, as an initial step toward enslaving our entire nation."

The White Dragon then presented his proposal: "I have selected you from among the hundreds of students I have had the honor of teaching. I have chosen you on the basis of your fervent patriotism and the social position of your families—all outstandingly influential. And, of primary importance, for your personal qualities of intelligence, astuteness, valor, and an unassailable sense of honor.

"I want you to meditate on the following: The forces that will decide the future of China in the coming years are grouped around three centers of power: General Chiang Kai-shek, leader of the Kuomintang and head of the government of China; Mao Zedong, leader of the Communist Party, who has just led a successful march of the Red Army to Yan'an; and, of course, Japan. I propose that we create an organization to penetrate and influence each of these three centers of power and struggle for a single cause: to save China and raise it to the position it deserves by its history, its culture, and its human resources."

Each of the six guests raised his hand. Thus was founded, on April 17, 1935, the secret society of Seven Dragons, that, in turn, grew into seven secret societies, each headed by one of those present, each becoming a covert action group.

* * *

"The Red Dragon became, in time, one of the most trusted men of Mao Zedong. The Black Dragon became a member of the staff of Chiang Kai-shek and accompanied him in 1949 when the defeated army fled to the island of Taiwan, where today he is the most influential industrialist. The Blue Dragon, born and raised in Japan, went to Manchuria, became a general in the Japanese Army, and has held very high positions in the postwar government administrations. The Maroon Dragon, a leader of the resistance against the Japanese among the large nuclei of industrial workers of Shanghai and other coastal cities, was one of the architects of the Chinese economic miracle.

"The White Dragon, the old history professor and inspiration for the movement, was kidnapped and murdered by the Japanese in 1936 as a part of their efforts to behead any possible opposition to their invasion a year later of ten Chinese provinces. The Yellow Dragon became the head of the *Seven Dragons*, which by then had acquired considerable influence. When his anti-Japanese activities were discovered, he was arrested and condemned to death. During that extreme crisis, the Green Dragon, the son of Beijing's chief of police, singlehandedly rescued the Yellow Dragon the day before his planned execution. The two fugitive dragons fled by different routes. The Yellow Dragon joined the Red Army. The Green Dragon managed to leave China, disguised first as a tow-line laborer on the Yangtse River and later as a Buddhist monk.

"What missions did the Green Dragon carry out in Cuba for more than half a century? Until now, we could only speculate." Carrillo paused, as if wondering how much further to proceed with his story.

Finally, as if he were making a great decision, he continued: "What we do know is that Chinese authorities, with the acquiescence of the family of the dead man, contacted the highest level of the Cuban government to request permission to repatriate the cadaver of Lu Tse Chin, the Green Dragon, known to us as Cuan, to put it to rest in the monumental tomb of the *Seven Dragons* on the outskirts of his native Beijing. The monument stands beside the highway to Suan Hua—on the way to the mountains where the Great Wall is located—in the same place formerly occupied by the country house of the Beijing University history professor, whose family devoted itself to the breeding and sale of colored fish and the cultivation of dwarf trees. The White Dragon, the Maroon, and the Blue already rest in the tomb. Much of what I've just told you is classified information that I only share to let you know the significance of this case. This is very top-level information."

Carrillo remained silent a moment to emphasize what was coming next. "You can imagine the embarrassment of our authorities when the cadaver disappeared, precisely at the moment that an airplane arrived with a refrigerated coffin spectacularly adorned with a green jade dragon and embedded with gold, ivory, and mother-of-pearl."

Silence reigned between them for several more seconds. "So what do you have to say?"

"*Coño*, Carrillo, it sounds like an Akira Kurosawa movie . . . almost like a sequel to *The Seven Samurai*."

Carrillo was not amused. When he spoke again, his voice was filled with the authority of his rank, and it was clear that his patience was diminishing. "I need an answer. Are you going to work on this or not?"

Apparently ignoring the question and the tone of Carrillo's voice, Alvaro asked: "How is it possible that such an important person lived in an apartment in such a run-down building? What was that man doing in Cuba all this time? The Chinese Revolution triumphed half a century ago . . ."

"I told you, we don't know. And it's possible that we'll never know. Maybe the only important feat the Green Dragon performed was to save the life of the Yellow Dragon. Things like that are never forgotten. It may be that simple."

Alvaro Molinet's instinct told him that there was a lot of truth in the story of the *Seven Dragons*. It wasn't likely that Carrillo would invent all of this just to keep him on a case. Besides, this was a case that appeared once in a lifetime. Why had he behaved so childishly, using the first problem he encountered as an excuse to quit? That was not his nature at all.

Carrillo rose from where he was sitting. His face expressed a deep, almost painful worry. He moved to where Alvaro was seated and firmly grasped his friend's shoulder with his strong right hand to emphasize what he was going to say. "Look, old boy. This is the most important case we have ever had, and you'll have to take my word on that. Let's stop fucking around and find that corpse, *coño!*"

Alvaro, hands in his pockets, looked at Carrillo and, in a detached voice he didn't recognize, heard himself say: "Let me think about it. I'll let you know."

WORK WITH COCOS

SHE NEEDED TO USE a method that could not be turned against her and yet was both powerful and reliable. The coconut, the magic fruit par excellence, was the thing. What is done with cocos never angers the *orishas* because it is the prodigious fruit of Eléggua himself.

Her first goal was to rupture the Adrián-Lorenzo relationship. She had come to this conclusion after many sleepless hours. A match without a striking surface will not light; a flame without firewood will not make a bonfire. While each went his own way, everything had been under control, but their union was producing terrible effects. That strange coalition between a son of Oggún and a son of Shangó was extremely powerful. It would be impossible to defeat while they remained together. Once separated, she would find a way to attack and destroy Adrián. Later on, she would take care of Lorenzo, and, after that she would have to definitively liquidate the debt that Oshún was claiming from her again. *Each step at the proper time*, she told herself. *The world was not made in a day. God needed seven.*

She had an abundant repertory of magic recipes to break up relationships, provoke fights over money between partners, create deadly jealousy between lovers, produce endless discord among occupants of a house . . . Some were very effective and reliable; she had used them successfully many times. But now it was different: She was confronting her own brother, *Tata*

Nkisi, a high priest of *Palo Monte*, with many resources at his disposal and the heir to the family *nganga*, of immense strength. Furthermore, she had to work against Adrián, a very special son of Shangó with the power to bewitch her.

When the alarm clock went off at five A.M., she was already awake. She got up and dressed, wrapping her neck to ward off the cold, early-morning air and the hazardous dew. She went to her pantry, where she always kept a good stock of dried coconuts. She chose a large one and carried it to the *Ilé Osha*, where she asked Elégguá for permission to use it to break Adrián and Lorenzo's friendship.

After Eshú—the dark side of Elégguá, the *orisha* governing the paths of life—gave his approval, she put the coconut into a shopping bag and stepped outside. She felt the sudden change from the warm air inside the house to the cool, humid ambience of the early morning. She walked four blocks through a thick fog that hung near the ground, presaging a warm day. On the way, she passed only two people, hurrying to find transportation to distant jobs.

She approached an important intersection of two streets, one of which bordered the outskirts of Guanabacoa until it reached the town's central park, then veered left, entering a more populated area, passed the police station, and finally penetrated the chessboard-like pattern of city blocks that the Spaniards had designed for every one of their colonial settlements. The other street became a highway leading away from town. Farther on, it opened into a traffic circle with three options: east to the Matanzas province; north to the city of Havana; or west to the city of Pinar del Río and the Cape of San Antonio, the westernmost point of the island. She had chosen this crossroads, leading to so many different places and never meeting again, as an ideal place for breaking the association of Lorenzo and Adrián.

A tenuous light began invading the horizon. She hurried toward the rising sun, projecting her shadow behind her. In this type of work, it was imperative to avoid even her own shadow—given what was about to happen—making the location and the hour of utmost importance. At the intersection, night was quickly receding, but it was still not the perfect moment. She smelled coffee brewing in a nearby house and longed for some. She heard someone stop walking behind her, presumably to watch what she was she about to do. She resisted the impulse to turn and send the intruder to hell; if she lost her concentration, her work would have no effect.

To avoid failure, she began repeating in a low voice: "As I break this coconut, let the relationship between Adrián and my brother Lorenzo break. Just as these coconut pieces will go their separate ways, let the lives of Lorenzo and Adrián take different roads. Just as these streets go in different directions and never meet again, let Lorenzo and Adrián never see each other again."

As the first ray of sunlight fell on her face, she threw the coconut with all her strength onto the pavement. It was essential that it break and that its pieces splinter as far as possible. That was why she had chosen a large, heavy coconut—small ones sometimes failed to break, obstructing the spell.

The coconut split into three pieces. One bounced off about two yards in the direction of Guanabacoa and stopped with the flesh side down; another rolled some ten yards down an incline toward a refrigerated warehouse and stopped at the edge of the road, resting also on its fleshy side; the third piece, the smallest, bounced toward her and stopped directly under her skirt, showing its white, wet flesh. This stupefied her. Something like this had never happened to her before. Coconuts almost always break into more than two pieces, but this backward jump of the small portion landing just under her skirt . . . Who did it represent? Was it Miladys seeking her protection?

Careful not to step on any of the coconut pieces or their milk, she turned and started back home by a different route. Streets were beginning to fill with people. A woman who saw her coming abruptly pulled her child back into their house and closed the door. Maybe the woman had seen her doings and was accordingly afraid.

Unsatisfied with her first effort, she again went to her pantry, grabbed several dry coconuts, checked them carefully, and chose a large, dark one and another lighter in color. Elégguá had authorized the use of his coconuts to create a fight between Adrián and Lorenzo. She scraped them with a knife until they were smooth, then grabbed a small pot of cocoa butter she had bought the day before from a godchild at an exorbitant price. She could not do without this marvelous substance, used for so many purposes.

She anointed the large coconut with the cocoa butter, went into the bathroom, wrapped it in a towel used by her brother, and placed it at the rear of the hall closet. She painted the coconut to represent Adrián with a mixture of powdered eggshell and cocoa butter. She now had to put it in contact with some other object that had belonged to Adrián, but she had nothing from him, not even a hair . . . She suddenly thought of the small St. Valentine's Day flower that she had put away in a book, but discarded the idea of using it.

Again her thoughts returned to Adrián. He had not come to see her recently. In the few visits he had made, he had gone directly to Lorenzo, then left as quickly as he had come. "Son of a bitch!" she said aloud, as a thought entered her mind: *Adrián had used her to get to Lorenzo. She had never meant anything to him!*

She went to her wardrobe and fetched a poetry book from which she carefully removed the dry flower. In a bowl, she pounded it into a gray powder with a spoon, then added cocoa butter and spread some of the mixture carefully over the entire surface of the coconut representing Adrián. She put the rest away for future actions.

She then banged the two coconuts against each other several times and put them away separately. This would make them fight, and she would do this again every once in a while to renew the spell.

The main challenge now was confronting Adrián without having the work turned against her. She was in no condition to face a new problem. It was not wise to battle against Adrián directly, since it would unleash the fury of Shangó. After much thought, she decided to do it through Yemayá, the goddess of all waters who let her younger sister, Oshún, reign over the rivers and fresh waters.

She had to provoke a clash between Adrián and someone who could do him much harm. She meditated, wondering who she could use for this purpose. Miladys, perhaps, but she dropped the idea after weighing the advantages and risks. While she continued to think, she decided to begin collecting the ingredients necessary to perform this malediction. She picked up a wash basin and set a candle in the center in hot paraffin before filling it with water. The presence of fire was indispensable in a ceremony with the *orishas*. Now she had to find something to tint the water light blue, similar to the color of shallow seas, the abode of the dreadful Yemayá Okuti, the worst of this *orisha*'s paths. Indigo dye could be used for this purpose, but she had not been able to find any for some time. Searching for a substitute, she went back to the bathroom. On the top shelf of the cabinet, she spotted an old medicine bottle and found it was blue methylene. The saints had undoubtedly guided her hand! She returned to the room with Yemayá's altar, removed the lid of the bottle, and knelt before the wash basin. She momentarily lost her balance and poured too much, making the water dark blue. She headed to the toilet to empty most of the water and refill it with clear water, seeking the right shade of blue, when she suddenly realized that dark blue had a special significance in this case.

"The police!" she cried out. With half-closed eyes, almost in ecstasy, she whispered: "The *orishas* are showing me the way. The sons of Shangó always have problems with the police. *The police will destroy Adrián!*"

POLICE PROCEDURE

SINCE RETIRING FROM the police force, he had begun to leave his bedroom curtains open to let the sun wake him each morning. Gradually, his noctambulist ways had disappeared, and his body had acquired new habits. Now, by ten o'clock each evening a heavy drowsiness came over him, and his light sleep of earlier years gave way to sound slumber from which he awoke alert and rested, the aching muscles with which he'd gone to bed completely refreshed and renewed. Gone, too, was the struggle each morning to open eyelids that fought stubbornly to remain closed for just a few more minutes of sleep, a luxury that had seemed so important to him in an earlier epoch.

That day, he woke before sunrise with a faint sensation of alarm, as if someone had whispered in his ear. He switched on the bedside lamp. Five o'clock—one hour before his usual rising time. He stayed still awhile, trying to go back to sleep, but now his head was full of thoughts about the investigation he had decided to quit in spite of Carrillo's *Seven Dragons* story. Leaving his bed, he went to the bathroom to urinate and wash his face. He suddenly felt a desire to see the sun rise, something he hadn't done since his days in the Literacy Campaign in the mountains of eastern Cuba, back in the '60s. In the *guajiro's* house where he had lived, the day always began in total darkness with the lighting of a wood fire to make the morning coffee.

He climbed the stairs to the roof of the house and saw, to the east, flames shooting up from the oil-refinery towers across Havana Bay, illuminating the dark sky. Slightly south of the refinery towers a tenuous luminosity was beginning to emerge in the direction of Regla and Guanabacoa, towns that greater Havana had long since swallowed up. Within seconds, the light grew stronger, followed by the first rays of sun, spreading with astonishing speed. In a matter of minutes, the soft radiance yielded an opaque, golden disk, growing so swiftly in brilliance that he could no longer look at it directly. He felt the gentle warmth of the early sun rays on his face.

With the arrival of daylight, his mind seemed to clear rapidly, leaving him convinced that both groups of investigators—those of Plaza, the municipality where the Chinese cemetery was located, and those of Centro Habana, where Cuan had lived in the heart of the old Chinese quarter—had let themselves be led astray by the strange nature of the case.

Speaking to the rising sun, he said softly, "You know very well that time is always on the side of the delinquent; it destroys traces, clouds memories, changes things little by little, and eliminates witnesses one by one. Figuring out hypotheses, possible motives, groups of suspects . . . all of these are important and often decisive, but what can under no circumstances be neglected is following the straight and narrow trail marked by physical evidence, real data, concrete facts, no matter how contradictory or absurd they may seem at first."

He began to pace back and forth on the roof, still speaking aloud, a habit he had begun to acquire more and more in recent months. "Concretely, all we have are the shoe prints of three individuals: two with the size and gait of men of medium height, and another with a longer stride and boots size 10-1/2 that sank much deeper into the soft ground of the cemetery, boots of a man nearly six feet tall, weighing over two hundred pounds."

He walked to the far side of the roof, overlooking a broad expanse of rooftops and, below, the Almendares River, but he saw none of this. His mind was busy probing, turning over and minutely examining every aspect of the case. "Therefore, it's easy to deduce from the technical report that the night watchman had to have seen and heard something. His footprints reached up to thirty paces from where the crime was committed and stopped there. It's possible that he got scared, something pardonable in an older man armed only with a three-foot pole and a harmless dog, in a place pretty far from any likely help." He recalled the cemetery and considered what it would be like at night. "A place where the imagination never dismisses the possible intervention of the supernatural behind each sound, each shadow, each event, especially in the solitude of the night. But the night watchman was never questioned in depth.

"What has happened with that investigation? It's been limited to two interrogations without much pressure and a superficial inquiry in the watchman's neighborhood, where he was considered 'an honest man,' 'a good man,' 'a hard worker,' and the head of 'a magnificent family.' And what did any of that have to do with the theft of the Chinaman's body that this bastard had to have witnessed?"

Alvaro Molinet paused, telling himself that he was being harsh with a humble watchman, then continued his monologue with a moderate conclusion: "With a more penetrating interrogation, some key detail might have arisen, at least something to corroborate the technical report." But again the policeman in him returned to the attack: "We also have to think about his possible complicity, under duress at the moment of the crime, or for money or friendship. A painstaking interrogation might have yielded a direct path to the thieves." Shaking his head in dismay, he continued his musing. "The interrogation of the grave digger was even worse. The official investigator decided early on that the man was lying, not realizing that he, himself, had induced him to make erroneous replies. Cancio wears thick eyeglasses, and any idiot knows that people with glasses are visually impaired. And if they are manual laborers, their lenses will almost always be dirty and blurred."

In an imagined confrontation with the lieutenant who had carried out the investigation, Alvaro warned him, almost shouting: "You must never put a witness into a position where he has to invent replies. And that isn't the only foolish mistake you made! You presented him with a collection of photos of movie stars from the '50s to identify the biotype of the man on the bicycle, but you didn't explain what the hell the word *biotype* meant. When the poor grave digger, hoping to please you, pointed out a young Ronald Reagan as 'the cyclist who visited me,' you made him the butt of a big joke. You also had a fine time ridiculing the grave digger's story about the suspicious character on a bicycle who spoke with a matchstick in his mouth. You and your colleagues almost died laughing at your performance, and everyone disqualified the grave digger as a witness.

"*Coño!* If you thought he was lying, why didn't you conduct a full investigation of him? Is he always a liar—with everyone, in relation to everything—or only in this case? That would be worth knowing. What motive could he have in misinforming the police?"

Alvaro paused a moment, ruminating, then continued. "Do you know what I think? Should I tell you? An investigator with such histrionic talent is out of place on the police force. Why not look for work on television or in the theater or, better yet, in a circus?" Alvaro chuckled at his own joke. "Besides, you're lazy. You didn't take the trouble to check the information on the suspicious man reported by the grave digger—including his odd habit of chewing on a matchstick—against the database in the central computer. And you certainly didn't check to see if the information we have on the delinquents in the cemetery agrees with data on other criminal groups. That is so basic, it's the least you should have done."

The previous cases of theft of human bones by *Paleros*, he told himself, had not been wholly neglected. More care had been taken with this aspect, but still had not been exhaustive. The only things checked were the computer database and the memories of some older cops. No specialists on Afro-Cuban religions had been consulted.

"In other words," he announced to himself, "the entire investigation is a load of crap! And the worst thing about it, the most absurd thing, is that I, too, allowed myself to be seduced into following, fascinated, the theories of poisoning and Chinese vengeance. Meanwhile, I've lost ten days!"

Alvaro dashed downstairs, milked the goat, then boiled the milk after adding water to it. He made coffee and prepared a mug of *café con leche* for his breakfast, along with two thin slices of toast from half of his bread quota, enhanced with guava paste made and sold by one of his neighbors. This time next year, he promised himself with satisfaction, they would have their own guavas in abundance!

As he brushed his teeth, it was impossible to avoid seeing himself in the mirror. Several snips of his scissors removed locks of hair that covered his ears. He also cut two hairs growing out of his nose, but left his beard intact. His beard, he thought decidedly, added something to his personality.

His first stop was the police data-processing center. He was aware that much existing information had still not been duly inputted and that, for lack of resources, the Havana police were far from being fully updated on the use of computers. This was nonetheless the best place to start.

Three hours later, he was surprised to stumble upon something interesting: The shoe prints at the cemetery coincided with those of two individuals, members of a band devoted to burglarizing homes. The most interesting aspect of the discovery was a size 10-1/2 boot print, since few Cubans have such large feet. The group was known to rob houses in the more affluent neighborhoods of the capital. Its technique was simple but effective. Operating in broad daylight, the thieves sacked select houses where no one was home during the day. A truck arrived at the front and the driver got out with some papers in his hand. One of the thieves, who had entered the house through a rear window, opened the front door. In a matter of minutes, without the faintest display of nervousness or haste, the delinquents carried off TV sets, radios, tape recorders, electric stoves, and fans. To any casual passerby or neighbor, everything seemed perfectly normal.

Alvaro went to see the technician who had taken the prints in the cemetery, and they compared them with the shoe prints of the house thieves. The prints from the cemetery were very good because they had been taken in wet soil, while the ones from the house thieves were photos of blurred prints on house floors, making it impossible to determine with certainty if they belonged to the same shoes. Even so, it seemed worthwhile to check further.

His next visit was to the Vedado police station, where he interviewed the chief, Lieutenant Colonel Santana. Upon learning the reason for Alvaro's visit, Santana rose from his desk and led him to the staff meeting room. With a wave of his hand, he drew Alvaro's attention to a wall covered with maps and posters and explained a sophisticated plan to trap the house thieves. At Alvaro's nod of approval, Santana shook his head disgustedly and complained about the lack of transportation and fuel that had prevented them from putting their perfect plan into practice.

Alvaro sensed that Santana was offering excuses for something. Perhaps his mention of Colonel Carrillo had led the lieutenant colonel to think he had come on the orders of police headquarters to investigate what had transpired.

"Start from the beginning, as if I knew nothing. I always like to draw my own conclusions with firsthand information."

"I agree!" Santana exclaimed. "I do the same thing. What can I tell you? We almost grabbed them this morning. Lieutenant Camila very bravely managed to detain one of the delinquents, but another son of a bitch attacked her from behind and left her unconscious. The doctors checked her and took X-rays and, fortunately, she's all right, but he could have killed her. Anyway, she'd already managed to alert the mobile unit we'd set up, and they chased the truck and shot in the air several times to get backup. When the thieves saw they were going to be trapped, they blocked the street with the truck and escaped on foot. Our best car crashed into the truck and was left a pile of junk. These thieves are dangerous and very well trained . . . karate, a flight plan . . . At least we recovered everything they'd stolen and the truck. And we won't be seeing any more of them. Now that they know we are aware of their tricks, we won't be bothered with those characters again in this municipality." Santana paused for the reaction of the policeman he believed to have been sent by Colonel Carrillo. "We are preparing a report for the chief with all the details. We already gave out some information by radio. I imagine many of the residents of Nuevo Vedado were alarmed by the shooting and called headquarters. What are they saying 'upstairs'?"

"Colonel Carrillo's messenger" merely raised his eyebrows and smiled.

A good sign, Santana thought.

That same evening, Alvaro visited the officer in charge of the plan to capture the house thieves. He found her already reasonably well recovered from the blows she had received. A graduate of the University of Havana Law School, Camila had worked for a time as a civilian, then decided to enter the School of Police Instructors, from which she had graduated with high honors. A slight woman, very attractive and firmly convinced of the superiority of the female sex, Camila's militant attitude gave the impression that her true purpose in life was to demonstrate this reality. She was blessed at the same time, however, with a rare capacity for self-criticism and a sense of humor impregnated with her exquisite femininity.

The young woman already knew a great deal about her visitor. In school, they had studied several of the dramatic cases he had solved. She considered it an honor to be relaying her account of the morning's adventure to him. Her neck and the lump on her head still hurt, but she was enchanted with the visit. In short, an intellectual love-at-first-sight blossomed between them, each captivated by the experiences of the other in the difficult endeavor of trying to change the world.

He recorded the whole conversation and listened to the tape three times the following morning on his Walkman, a gift from an uncle who had visited Cuba for the first time that year, after thirty years in the U.S. Alvaro finished listening to the tape as he collected every loose blade of grass in his garden, rinsed them, and then fed his goat, who was exceptionally clean and squeamish in her habits. He then telephoned Carrillo, asking him to send for the recording, the grand result of almost two weeks of work on the case.

Carrillo took the cassette home with him, along with the short note that accompanied it: "*As you know, the hypotheses of poisoning and Chinese vengeance have petered out and, with them, the time invested has vanished. Nevertheless, here you have the band of delinquents who stole your Chinaman. One of the tracks they left yesterday in a house in Nuevo Vedado is a perfect match with the big one found in the Chinese cemetery. Good luck capturing them!*"

At the foot of the note was the signature that he had not seen for a long time: a spiral with an almost imperceptible point in the center. He remembered the time he had asked Alvaro the meaning of such a singular identification. "The point in the center is man, and the spiral that opens toward the infinite is time, the only treasure that's been distributed equitably among the creatures of this universe." At the time, Carrillo had suspected that his subordinate had invented the explanation on the spur of the moment. Now he doubted that and told himself that it was, in fact, a good signature for his mysterious friend.

Carrillo decided he would listen to the recording after a cold bath and dinner, while seated in his favorite rocking chair on the balcony in his slippers and shorts. He would wait until his two sons, two daughters-in-law, and two grandchildren had gone to bed and left his wife sleeping in front of the TV. But curiosity got the best of him. Entering his room, he took off his clothes, turned on the electric fan, and settled down to listen.

He wasn't sure if it was the timbre of the young lieutenant's voice or the passion behind each phrase that kept him glued to the recording until it ended.

CLOSE ENCOUNTER

WHEN I WAS ASSIGNED the case, I decided to use the utmost technical rigor, determined to demonstrate that several ounces of brain are worth more than several tons of dashing about with no organization or planning. I enlisted the cooperation of the Institute of Physical Planning through a former university classmate who is now a department head in the Provincial Division of that institute. To convince her, I explained not only the importance of capturing the group of thieves but also the need to modernize our police methods and, incidentally, to prove that women can be as inventive as men. She immediately became enthusiastic and recruited a group of specialists in urban planning, a mathematician, and a 'critic,' a person specialized in detecting where things might go wrong. And she made this whole group available to me.

"In two lively, closed-door sessions before a large map of Nuevo Vedado, we discussed the best way to catch the thieves. We drew up a work plan and put it into effect immediately. We inspected the seven houses that had already been robbed. All were relatively isolated and each had wooden Venetian blinds without the protection of iron grillwork. A subsequent field study revealed 468 other houses with those same characteristics. Finally, we determined the best observation points for houses with a high risk of being robbed. From those points, we could monitor the movement of trucks and suspicious people in the area. Our network of observation points had to be linked by portable radios and backed by a task force of mobile units that could reach any place in the neighborhood in less than five minutes.

"The mathematician made a program simulating the operative situations that gave the optimum locations for the observation points and mobile units, reducing them to nineteen and six, respectively. We ran a series of tests on the computer with all the situations that occurred to us. The efficacy of detection and response in five minutes or less was ninety-six percent! Our plan was practically infallible.

"We managed to work this all out in great detail in just one week, and made three copies of the operation, 'Mortal Trap,' a name we decided on unanimously at three o'clock one morning after discarding two other names, 'Bermuda Triangle' and 'Close Encounter.' We felt certain that we were making history in Cuban criminology.

"I kept the progress on our work secret, justifying my absences from the department with a supposed analysis of the previous robberies and interviews with witnesses. When everything was ready, I told Lieutenant Colonel Santana, the municipal chief of police, that I had a proposal for an operative plan and wanted to submit it for his consideration. Knowing how things often work out, I made it clear that, because of my knowledge of all the work that had been done, if the plan was approved, I should be in charge of it.

"Santana was silent for a while, apparently not thrilled with my flying solo on this, but I wasn't going to give in. He must have seen that in my eyes because he swallowed hard and nodded, as if saying that he accepted the plan, but with reservations. He set the time for a full explanation of the project for the following day. Two hours before the gathering, our group took over the meeting room and covered the walls with maps, time curves of response versus distance, and posters with summaries of our plan. We had an overhead projector to aid the mathematician's exposition and a computer to run the program with some test cases. A real show!

"When Santana and the top officers of the municipality entered, they stood staring, shocked at the display of technology and the strange team accompanying me, seeing with a simple glance the amount of work carried out in such a short time. Nothing like that had ever been done in the history of the department. I felt like I was in heaven, floating five inches above the floor.

"The meeting was a complete success. Without the slightest anxiety, I gave them all the information without reading a single chart. The mathematician was brilliant. As always, two of the officers asked 'innocent' questions that were in reality loaded with poison, hoping to confuse me. With a smile, I simply avoided replying, and Santana, a great chief, came to my aid.

"After an eloquent defense, he proposed that the plan be immediately accepted. He then looked around at all the faces, seeking a consensus. Santana is a natural politician; in another epoch or another country, he could easily have been a city mayor. Pleased, he concluded: 'Good. We can consider the plan approved. We'll begin with five observation points and one mobile unit.'

"I felt as if my heart had stopped. I had emphasized that the mathematical analysis reduced the observation points and the mobile units to an absolute minimum. If we didn't employ the necessary resources, the efficacy of 'Mortal Trap' would be almost zero, with luck as our only aid. Santana must have seen the dismay on my face.

"'I said *to begin.*' He held his hand in the air, pointing at the ceiling, thinking about what else could be done. Then his face lit up. 'When a robbery is detected, we'll announce it by radio with a code word—for example, 'Mortal Trap,' very good . . . perfect. Listen carefully: All patrol cars will rush to block the escape routes at selected points—all of them. What do you think?'

"Thus, our chief began improvising, generating new ideas and changing our plan completely to the delight of the rest of the officers, who seemed very happy to transform our plan into a wild goose chase.

"When we started to collect our posters and maps, Santana told us to leave them there, that this would be the operation's headquarters when all the resources were put to work. So we took only the overhead projector and the computer and went to the home of one of the specialists where we had already collected all the ingredients for a good strong punch, with ninety percent alcohol, that someone had brought from the laboratory where he worked. Everyone contributed something to the celebration of our completely frustrated 'victory.'

"We started. Every morning, the driver of the unmarked car used as a mobile unit dropped four police officers and me near the houses chosen as observation points. The mobile unit was situated at a point equidistant between the observation points. It didn't even have enough gasoline to make a discreet patrol of the neighborhood; that is the plain truth. Santana couldn't give me more personnel and, much less, transportation. Gasoline, once so abundant, is now measured like heroine is in other countries. Meanwhile, time was passing.

"Ten days later, I was on the verge of hysteria, frustrated with the lack of progress on the first case under my direct supervision. During that time, the thieves entered and left the neighborhood, carrying out two burglaries without the slightest difficulty. We always arrived late, having to satisfy ourselves with recording what had been stolen and listening in silence to the complaints about the ineffectiveness of the police. We were too few for an area that big. We could only hope for a lucky strike.

"Today, I arrived a little before eight. The owners always leave the house between seven and seven-thirty. The driver of the mobile unit asked permission to go buy a pack of cigarettes. I hesitated, because we were all supposed to bring whatever was necessary to spend the day on guard. He saw the doubt in my eyes and got an unhappy look, saying he had left his cigarettes in the department in the rush to leave on time. I realized that a day without cigarettes for a smoker, eight or ten hours without his drug, was a hard punishment, so I authorized him to go buy the cigarettes. I crossed the street and, a little farther along, passed a bicycle messenger leaning against a lamppost who was flirting with a young employee of the nearby pharmacy.

"Once inside the house, I opened the blinds. The messenger and his bicycle were gone, and the only thing I could see were the feet of the young woman walking toward the pharmacy. I removed my shoes and put my stuff—my handbag, a package with my lunch, and my portable radio—on top of the TV set. Just then, I heard two loud knocks on the service door in the kitchen.

"Immediately, I recalled the thieves' technique of checking whether or not a house was empty before entering. I thought that the thieves, upon not detecting anyone, would be entering at any moment. I called the mobile unit, giving the emergency signal, but got no response. The driver must have been buying his accursed cigarettes at that very moment. In any event, I thought I should check the house to be sure no one was already inside. I moved to the kitchen with my pistol cocked, then checked downstairs. I repeated the call to the mobile unit, still with no result. The line for cigarettes must have been a long one. I went upstairs. In the hall, clearly marked on the polished surface of the white granite floor, was the trace of a large and dirty boot. As I moved silently toward the bedroom, a white man with black hair and a moustache came out of the boys' room, carrying a tape recorder. I pointed the pistol at his chest and ordered him to stop. He bent down and put the recorder carefully on the floor, then lifted his arms. The last thing I remember after that is the sneer on his face as he looked over my shoulder. At that instant, I felt someone behind me and took a hard blow on my neck. The pistol escaped from my hand as it fired, and a hoarse voice shouted, 'You killed her! You killed her!' I heard the voice like a strong echo that faded away, little by little, leaving only silence and darkness.

"The driver of the mobile unit had managed to hear my last call as he approached the car after having bought coffee. Smokers are apparently incapable of passing up such opportunities; a cigarette before coffee is as inevitable as coffee after a cigarette. He raced to the house and arrived just as the thieves' truck was pulling away at full speed. His duty was to call the department to engage the support mechanisms that Santana had dreamed up, but, instead, he tried to redeem himself by chasing the truck. He followed the truck closely with his lights on, honking to attract the attention of a military unit or patrol car. Suddenly, the truck braked violently and veered sideways, forcing the car to crash into it. The cop was thrown against the steering wheel, taking a blow to the stomach and a gash on his forehead as he was hurled against the windshield. Dazed, he got out of the car and fired his gun in the air, but the delinquents had vanished, leaving the truck and the smashed car blocking the street.

"For months, I have criticized—first in silence and, later, with open exasperation—all of my colleagues' *macho* way of doing things. When I finally had my chance to prove myself, everything began to fall apart, and it wasn't only because of a lack of resources—the patience required for success proved to be too much for the average Cuban policeman. The officers assigned to this task began to show signs of neurosis after a single week. Antonio tripled his consumption of cigarettes; whenever he ran out, he smoked anything he could find. Luis couldn't last long without music on the radio, despite my reprimands and his sincere promises to change. Mariano was overcome with a pernicious sleepiness immediately after entering any silent and dark house. Juan, the driver, was the only one who stayed alert and ready for action the whole time, only to fail miserably at the critical moment.

"I have no right to criticize them, though, since everything went wrong because of my own mistakes. First, I authorized the driver to leave his post; second, I checked the house on my own after suspecting that thieves were going to enter; and third, I advanced along the upstairs hall without first checking out the rooms behind me."

"Has the truck been traced?" Carrillo heard the voice of Alvaro interrupting Camila's taped report.

"The truck was stolen today, early in the morning. Although I'm here at home, I've been following up on that. The truck driver has a perfect alibi. This morning he took his son to the doctor because his wife is a cashier and she couldn't take the boy since today is payday. He had asked for the morning off several days in advance. He left the truck parked in front of his house, as always, since he collects milk from several dairies near Havana and takes it to the bottling plant every morning. When he returned from the visit to the doctor, the truck was gone. He notified his boss several hours later because he couldn't leave the sick child alone to go find a public telephone."

"A perfect alibi for the model father!" Carrillo heard Alvaro's voice again.

"When I examined the files on this gang, I thought that they stole a different truck each time they were going to make a hit. Then I checked the reports of stolen trucks, trying to relate them to the robberies, but they didn't coincide. There are many thefts of cars, motorcycles, and bicycles, but very few trucks. So, I'm now convinced that these thieves have somebody who makes the trucks available to them for just a few hours. If there's no problem, everything follows its normal course. But if a problem arises, they notify the police that the truck has been stolen. What do you think . . . ?"

There was a long silence. Carrillo glanced at the recorder to see if it was still working. Then he heard Alvaro's voice again.

"I'll see that someone follows up on this matter of the trucks . . . Let me ask you a question. You said the only people you saw in the street were a messenger talking to a young woman?"

"Yes. The girl works in the pharmacy."

"A messenger on a bicycle could make a good lookout man, don't you think?"

"Now that you say it, it seems like the most obvious thing in the world. He must be the one who selects the houses and keeps watch while the others break in. Of course! When he saw me enter the house, he left the girl and knocked on the service door to warn the robbers already inside the house. Even with this black eye that makes me look like a pirate, I'm going to go talk to the chick at the pharmacy tomorrow morning. When Santana and the others see that I'm still in the fight, they're going to drop dead. I don't know how to thank you . . . It makes me feel like kissing you!"

"No one's stopping you."

WHAT WENT WRONG?

WHEN LORENZO HEARD loud knocks on the door of the *nganga* room and the voice of Pedro calling him urgently, he was sure an emergency had arisen. He quickly finished his consultation and went out to the patio, signaling Pedro not to say anything. He led him to the trunk of the *ceiba*, protected by the benevolent influence of Iroko, then let him speak.

"The police almost caught us!" Pedro's confession verged on a shout, as he clapped his hands to his head to emphasize the gravity of his words. Lorenzo frowned and told him to lower his voice. Pedro jammed his hands into his pockets to calm himself and spoke in a lower tone.

"We had to scramble out of there with a *fiana* behind us shooting all over Nuevo Vedado. It was like a Wild West movie! I was driving the truck, and I didn't give 'em a chance to pass us. When we'd almost reached the zoo, I made a quick turn to block the street and the police car crashed into us. Mulo and I beat it out of there on foot, but we had to leave all of the loot behind."

Lorenzo listened, nodding his head the whole time as if nothing Pedro was reporting was news to him.

"*Padrino*, let me tell you what happened first. We'd been in the house less than ten minutes when we heard Adrián's danger signal, two hard knocks on a door. I came out of a room with a tape recorder in my hands and met a woman, barefoot, with a gun leveled at me. I put the recorder down on the floor and raised my hands and, just then, Mulo surprised her from behind with a vicious blow to her neck. A shot escaped from the woman's pistol and flew past my ear, just grazing it, and she dropped like a rock."

"Dead?"

"Sure. Mulo doesn't know his own strength."

The *Palero* remained silent. This information, at least, seemed to be new to him, Pedro thought, so he decided to go on explaining. "We dashed out to the truck parked in front of the garage behind the house with the few things that we had already loaded. In less than a minute, we had a police car honking away like crazy behind us. Naturally—"

Lorenzo stopped Pedro with a hand gesture and in a deep, solemn voice said, "I'm going to speak with the *nganga* to find out which of you is at fault. That's the problem. One of the three of you is to blame."

Pedro raised his eyebrows, surprised and confused, then nodded slowly. He took two steps in the direction of the patio through which he had arrived, then turned back toward Lorenzo. "Why us? Couldn't it be the Chinaman?"

With a look of disgust on his face, Lorenzo shook his head from side to side. "How much proof do you need? The three of you get into a mess, you don't do things as planned, and the police still couldn't catch you. How much more proof of the Chinaman's powers do you need? Tell me that."

Pedro considered the *Nasakó's* answer. Then he smiled, convinced. With a wave of his hand, he disappeared behind a line of clothing hung out to dry in the patio.

Nevertheless, Lorenzo still had his own doubts. He began to walk slowly around the trunk of the *ceiba* to absorb the positive influence of the *orisha* Iroko, who never failed to help. He was certain that this encounter with the police was a sign that something wasn't functioning right. Besides, his sister had been acting strange in recent weeks, sticking her nose into everything much more than usual. She knew a lot of *Palo Monte*. Could she be interfering with his work in spite of his warnings to her? To make matters worse, he had noticed that lately the *nganga* seemed to be working sulkily. He must have done something wrong or left something undone. There could no longer be any doubt about that.

Lorenzo continued walking around the *ceiba* until the shadows of the afternoon grew longer and night fell. He looked toward the half-open door of the *nganga* room. He saw the silhouette of his shirtless and barefoot grandfather leaning on his cane. The old man slowly drew near until he had passed beyond the illuminated space next to the house. Then, under the moonlight, he seemed to walk quickly and steadily until he disappeared into the dense shadows of the *ceiba*, where the darkness was complete. Lorenzo suddenly felt the old man's cane almost touch his nose, as it had when he was a child. Again he heard the familiar, thundering voice: "*I told you, young man, that when the moment arrives, don't make any important decision without knowing who the spirit in the* nganga *is. And you didn't obey me!*"

He should never have closed the deal with Adrián without having identified the spirit in the *nganga*. That had to be the problem!

THE SPIRIT OF THE NGANGA

THE MOMENT HAD COME, and he hadn't realized it. Before accepting Adrián's proposal, he should have identified the spirit who gave life and strength to the powerful *nganga* inherited from his grandfather, he from his father, and he, in turn, from *his* father, the first Lorenzo Bantú, born in Africa and brought to Cuba as a slave at the end of the eighteenth century. That must have been the reason Pedro and Mulo had problems with the police, a warning the *nganga* was giving him. Now, as evening fell, he returned to the house, convinced that he must identify the spirit of his *nganga*, whose origin was probably lost in the mists of time.

For the past week, his sister, who rarely left the house, had been going out every day without explanation. Lorenzo was grateful for the moments of quiet and solitude. All day today, he had been feeling the presence of his grandfather.

As he stood in the hallway, his grandfather appeared to him again, outlined against the light from the patio, and he heard his hoarse and trembling voice: "*In the old days, the* nganga *wasn't kept in an iron pot; it was held in a canvas knapsack in the highest place in the* bohío." The old man looked toward the darkness of the ceiling, where he saw something that Lorenzo couldn't. "*When you work with it, you have to be sure the place it touches is very clean.*"

His grandfather suddenly kicked off his wooden flip-flops and, brandishing an imaginary broom, began to dance and sing as he painstakingly cleaned the spot where the *nganga* would rest:

Sweep, sweep, sweep up waste,
Sweep, sweep up waste,
Simbico

The cleaning complete, he withdrew a piece of chalk from his pocket and traced a *Palo Monte* signature, three bows with their arrows, on the spot.

As father ordered,
Lower it, bring down my mama,
Lower it, bring down my mama,
Down, my nganga

He went on singing and dancing with an agility impossible for a man almost one hundred years old. With all his strength, he carefully lowered a rope tied around a large cloth sack containing something very heavy and precious, until it rested carefully on the signature on the floor precisely at the moment that he ended his song.

Lower it as father orders,
Bring it, bring it, my nganga,
Bring nganga *step by step*

The old man continued to demonstrate in detail the ceremony of lowering the *macuto*, of preparing it, of returning everything to its place. Lorenzo understood now that his grandfather had tried to teach him the techniques passed down through the family since time immemorial, but he had been too young to learn it all properly.

He entered his room and threw himself on his bed. Where could he find something to identify the spirit of the *nganga*? The answer had to lie in the room above the fake ceiling. He had searched through everything there many times before, but he had to do it again: sort through those boxes full of faded photographs, relics, and trophies accumulated over the years by the Bantús; the small cask full of *cauris* from Africa, a strategic reserve for the generations-to-come of Bantús because they were no longer obtainable anywhere; the *piedra de imán* and the *piedra india*, used only in very special ceremonies; the copybooks in his childish handwriting of all of the secrets of *Palo*, dictated by his grandfather; the boxes of bones from the first and the second Lorenzo Bantús beside those of the third, his grandfather, that he, himself, had placed there. Some day, his own, those of the fourth Lorenzo Bantú, would also be kept there.

The bones of his grandmother, María de la Concepción, collected from the graveyard two years ago, were also there, in an urn of varnished mahogany made by the best cabinetmaker of Guanabacoa. Whenever he saw that ossuary, he always wondered if those bones should really be there, because she had been a fervent Catholic until the day of her death. On the other hand, how could he separate her from her husband if, in their lifetime, they had been inseparable?

He recalled the time that he had discovered the entrance to the space above his bedroom's fake ceiling. He had been away from home for several years, and had found it while looking for a place to hang himself after failing at everything in his life. He could think of no other decent and quiet place to end his life. It would be beneath his dignity to hang himself in a public bathroom or in a shoddy hotel. Neither could he choose a tree, which would have been the final offense to his grandfather who had always adored the *monte,* a term he had used for any place where grass and trees grew wild.

It was thus that he had decided to die in the only place that really belonged to him—his grandparents' house, to which he had hoped never to return. He had found the place intact despite the years it had stood closed, untouched after a thorough housecleaning by his aunts who had come from Matanzas to attend the burial of his grandfather. No one had dared enter it in all that time, much less steal from the house of the *Palero,* frightened by the stories repeated a thousand times by neighbors, who swore by the sacred sign of the cross made with the thumb and index finger over the lips that on nights of a waning moon, voices and noises could be heard coming from the house. Some whispered that the old Bantú wandered naked on the patio, as he had done when, already weak in the head, he somehow escaped the old woman's vigilance.

On those nights of sad moonlight, his grandfather, they said, came out of the room of the *nganga* accompanied by two other old, naked men. A kind of chant in a foreign language could be heard as they danced all night around the *ceiba* and the palm tree that had replaced the one destroyed by lightning. At the end of the dance, just before sunrise, the three old men urinated in an old bottomless copper pot at the foot of the palm tree amidst the patch of *monte* behind the house where no one ever dared to enter.

Searching for a rope to hang himself, he had entered his grandfather's room—now his room—and immediately found one ideal for his purpose, as if the old man had divined his need and left it there for him. Lorenzo threw himself face up on the bed to find the place where he could attach the rope. It wasn't going to be easy in the ceiling's polished woodwork. Then he remembered one of the three enigmas left by the old man for his grand-children: how to enter that space without breaking anything. He believed that his grandfather had invented those things to whet his interest in *Palo Monte*, because Lorenzo had never been drawn to witchcraft. "Grandpa, I'm going to be a doctor," he had always insisted when the old man tried to persuade him to follow in his footsteps.

Then he had detected a thicker strip of wood that seemed somehow out of place. That was the key to entering, he felt sure. And at that moment, facing death, with the firm decision to hang himself, he felt a twinge of curiosity about what was up there. His grandfather no longer inspired childish terror in him, nor did he any longer blame his grandfather for the rejection he had suffered from other children at school when they found out he was the grandson of the scary witch doctor.

The aromas from the various types of wood in the room evoked child-hood memories. He recalled the *Palo* fiestas: the interminable dancing and singing to the monorhythm of drums until late at night, and at times until dawn. He recalled the sweating dancers, and men and women falling into trances when the *nkisi* took possession of their bodies. He saw again the shining face of his grandfather with the lit end of a cigar inside his mouth, blowing clouds of smoke over the *nganga* and spraying it with mouthfuls of *chamba*, squeezing his lips tightly together as he blew so that the sacred liquor became a fine wet spray, charging the air with its sweet and spicy smell. And he heard again the invocations in that strange language that, without knowing its exact meaning, he had also understood.

He awoke with the rope in his hands. He had slept very deep, as he had not done in many years, the victim of a pernicious insomnia, broken at times by a restless sleep from which he awoke, perspiring, with shouts of terror and an accelerated pulse. It was already daylight. He looked up again at the ceiling, then climbed onto the head of the iron bed and moved the strip of wood that had caught his attention. The strip turned on a nail in the center, and the end of a board from the fake ceiling dropped onto the bed. On one side, the hanging board had perpendicular strips of wood fixed at regular intervals, forming a ladder. Grabbing it firmly, he climbed up to the secret room and promptly began to search through the things left by his grandfather, half expecting to find gold coins from the Spanish colonial period or family jewels. Disappointed, he climbed back down, bringing only the copybooks the old man had made him fill out years ago with the family's accumulated knowledge of *Palo Monte*. Glancing through them now, he realized that he could recite each of them by heart.

At that moment, he heard a loud knocking at the door of the *nganga* room. Surprised, he dressed quickly and went out, thinking that some neighbor must have seen a light and called the police. Instead, he found a thin black woman of indefinable age with a penetrating gaze and a small, very blond child by her side. The woman smelled of herbs and emitted a whistle as she spoke, caused by air passing through a gap in her teeth.

"Lorenzo Bantú. I've come to consult you."

He thought at first that he had never seen the woman before, but something in her savage gaze brought to mind a vague memory.

"Lorenzo Bantú died years ago. I'm his grandson," he said, dropping his eyes to the floor.

"Oh, yes, you're Lorenzo Bantú! Don't try to fool me!" the woman insisted, raising her voice, full of authority.

"I don't know how to work with the *nganga*," he said timidly.

"Yes, you do know how to work with it, Lorenzo Bantú. I'm your godmother . . . Don't you remember when you were initiated into *Palo* many years ago, when you were a boy? That *nganga* is yours. Don't try to fool me again, Lorenzo Bantú!"

The words struck him with an incredible force, a power he hadn't encountered since the times of his grandfather. He felt pulled toward the room of the *nganga* until he stood before the *nganga* itself. The woman followed him, leaving the little girl outside. Lorenzo was surprised to find the place completely clean, as it had been the day that his aunts returned to Matanzas. There was no dust and everything was in perfect order. A package of candles rested in its place next to a box of matches. The air was still, dry, and without odors. A bottle of *chamba* stood there as well, not on the right as his grandfather had kept it, but on the left, as if prepared for him to take it in his left hand, along with a cedar box of cigars.

He breathed deeply and looked at the woman, now almost invisible in the darkness of the room. He was fully aware that if he touched those objects, his grandfather would definitely have triumphed.

"The *nganga* hasn't worked for a long time."

"*Awaken it!*" Her voice was sharp.

He lit a cigar and took several expert puffs to make it burn evenly. Then he lit three candles. Although he had never done this before, he filled the room with smoke, following the style of his grandfather. Then he sprayed half of the bottle of *chamba* through the room with his mouth, awakening the old, familiar odor. From the corner of his eye, he noticed the seven shells that his grandfather had used waiting quietly on a dish beside the miniature replica of the *mpaca*.

From his throat, a strange chant burst forth. He, himself, was surprised to hear the voice of his grandfather rising from his own chest. His body from the waist up began to move in rhythm with the chant. With eyes closed, the woman responded to the chant.

Lorenzo Bantú reacted violently. What was he doing? What perverse enchantment was taking possession of him? Who was this dried-up woman who seemed to have arisen from the grave? He stopped his movements and stood rigidly. Firmly, he told the visitor: "It doesn't want to awaken. It hasn't been fed for a long time."

He felt the woman's look penetrating the back of his neck and a heat climbing upward to the base of his brain. Suddenly, she threw herself at him, offering him her hand, which was dripping blood. Trembling, the fourth Lorenzo Bantú took the woman's hand. Fascinated by the smell of the thick liquid, he let it drip over the extraordinary mix of objects in the pot of the *nganga*.

Peering into the mirror of the *mpaca mensu* where the *Palero* looks to make his divinations, he saw clearly the image of his grandfather with his large, white teeth, devilish grin, and small, round, lively eyes staring up at him. It was a much younger face, though—his own face! Effortlessly, almost absentmindedly, he began to throw the shells and tell the woman the oracle of her gods.

Now, many years after that life-altering experience, Lorenzo Bantú felt that something equally grandiose was about to happen. Something told him that he was on the threshold of a major change in his life. He had to identify the dead person who gave life to the *nganga*, and he felt sure that the answer was up there. He sensed that something was missing, and quickly realized that he had to remove his clothes. One lives naked in the jungle; his grandfather had walked about naked in his last days; he, himself, had been naked when he discovered the entrance to the secret room.

Once unencumbered by clothing, he stood on the head of the bed and repeated his movements to reproduce the original magic from the time he had first penetrated that place. He pulled down the hanging ladder and climbed up to the room.

In the darkness confronting him, something shone in a corner. Between the crooked boards of a box glowed a slight phosphorescence. He crawled to the box; it was the one containing the bones of the first Bantú. In the past he had observed it carefully; a deep and narrow chest made of a very hard and dense wood, cut by machete and adze. With great care, he climbed down the ladder with the box so that he could examine it more closely. The lid was held shut by a rusty nail that broke apart when he pulled gently. He moved the bones around without a clear notion of what, exactly, he was looking for. He turned the box upside down on the bed and a shiny black serpent escaped from among the bones. Unhurriedly, the *majá* slithered across the white sheet and up the bed's grillwork until it reached the ladder and disappeared into the darkness of the secret room.

The *killumba*—skull—and the phalanges of the little fingers and a tibia were missing! Overwhelmed by his discovery, the third heir to the *nganga* went out to the patio, opened the room of the *nganga*, and prostrated himself before it, wondering how to address it, realizing that it was now animated by the spirit of his great-great-grandfather. *The missing bones had to be inside that pot.* That explained the *nganga*'s strange behavior, refusing at times to obey him; its independence of judgement about many things; the strange solutions it frequently offered, characterized by a primitive and crude logic. He immediately regretted the times he had cursed it because of its apparent ineffectiveness.

He had to find a way to ask its forgiveness. After thinking awhile without finding a solution, he decided to pretend that nothing had happened. His ancestor could undoubtedly read his thoughts, so an explanation was unnecessary. But after several more moments, he decided to change his approach and present a question. "Old man, what advice can you give me about this business with Adrián? This is the greatest opportunity of my life, the only chance for the Bantús to become important, powerful, respected people. But that man is clever; he talks a lot and is very convincing. He has persuaded me to do things I've never done before but that appear in the copybooks dictated by my grandfather."

A thought suddenly came to him, as if someone had whispered it in his ear: "*The only way you can trust that man is by watching his every movement.*"

He awoke to his sister's voice calling him insistently. He opened his eyes. Sunlight was entering between the boards of the room. He had, unpardonably, fallen asleep naked before the *nganga*. He looked about hastily for something to cover himself with.

"Lorenzo!" his sister was calling. "Adrián's wife has been waiting for you for more than an hour. She wants to consult with you!"

That was the answer he had hoped for. The answer of the nganga! Again he prostrated himself before the *nganga* where the spirit of his great-great-grandfather rested, the Bantú who had been brought to Cuba as a slave at the end of the eighteenth century, the one who had already been *Tata Nkisi* in Africa.

THE HOBBLING OF A MAN

ANA HAD NEVER CONSULTED a *Palero*, despite having lived all of her twenty-six years in Guanabacoa. An Elégguá figure had never been placed behind the front door to protect her house, as in the houses of believers. Her mother was forever at war against the beliefs of "ignorant and superstitious blacks," and was horrified at seeing how they were penetrating the minds of her friends, displacing the only true faith, the Catholic religion of Jesus Christ, the Virgin Mary, and the innumerable saints, each one specializing in a particular type of miracle. Ana's mother knew them all.

Thus, in Ana's home they prayed to Saint Lucía for help with failing eyesight, to Saint Lazarus for orthopedic problems, venereal diseases, leprosy, and, lately, protection against AIDS. According to her grandmother, processions had been carried out in the past in times of drought in honor of the Virgin of the Cave and Saint Isidor, the farmer, to bring back sunlight.

Having noticed her interest in men beginning at age fifteen, Ana's mother had prayed to Saint Antonio for an early marriage, but without success. Ana had never told her mother that she need not lose sleep over this, since she had had an IUD in place since she was thirteen. She visited a gynecologist regularly, as did many of her friends, was terrified of AIDS, and demanded that her boyfriends always use condoms.

Soon after her mother died, Ana began feeling the need for a husband. She wanted to have children before it was too late, to have a home that she could manage, organizing things her own way, and to stop being a slave to a father and three younger brothers, none of whom had the remotest idea how to create order or beauty.

Who would have believed it? Despite such good grades in mathematics, she wound up as a maid! Although Ramón, her next-door neighbor, told everyone in the vicinity that she was a friend of Señor Camejo's widow, she could not fool herself. On her first visit to the old woman's residence, she had sworn to herself that she would never return, terrified by the vastness of the house, hidden in a grove of mango trees and overgrown weeds, and by the depressing demeanor of the old woman, who was partially bald, with reddened eyes, a heavily powdered face, and a sickly odor. Not to mention the high-ceilinged rooms, the enormous dark closets from which Count Dracula might emerge at night, and a legion of dogs barking constantly in defense of the premises.

But her mind was soon changed when, as she was leaving her house the next morning, Ramón grabbed her by the arm and said, "Look, Ana. That woman is too old to live alone. She needs the company of someone who will not rob her. You're the ideal person. When I thought of you, I told myself: In a few months she can win the confidence of Doña Elvira, who may even put her on her food-ration card. She may not last long—have you noticed her color?—and then you could earn the right to stay in the house. She might even leave you the house in her will. Her only relative is a nephew she's never seen."

The nephew arrived when least expected, soon after Ana had established official residence in the house. She had been caring for the old woman for over a year and had slowly become fond of her. She had even succeeded in making her bathe every day. The widow relied on her for everything. Her eyes looked better and her hair had improved. The dogs' tails swung wildly at the sight of Ana and could detect her a block away—she meant food for them! She now came almost every afternoon and frequently stayed overnight, since her father had retired, her brothers were in a boarding school, and bus transportation was undependable.

Adrián arrived with too much baggage for a short stay. As a kind of passport, he brought three boxes of family photographs. Surprised, Doña Elvira delighted in remembering herself as a young and beautiful woman, but her face hardened when she opened the second box, and she skipped quickly through the faded images in the third. She stood abruptly and went upstairs to her bedroom. Some very disagreeable memory had obviously been summoned by one of the old photos.

When Adrián began trying to ease tensions, the aunt blew up: "Insolent! He just arrived and already wants to start changing everything. Soon he'll be bossing us around—you'll see. Have you noticed the alcohol on his breath? He takes after his father, who died a horrible death from cirrhosis. And I see that he has a strain of African, he's a *jabao*. He must have got it from his damned father, since we have no black blood in our family." Camejo's widow made a gesture of disgust. "I don't know what my sister ever saw in that man."

But Ana was fascinated by Adrián. He was not only good looking, he had poise, was masculine and courteous, and was a great conversationalist. She had never met anyone like him. Her male friends had always been rude and vulgar. If she didn't stop them, they started treating her like another guy, which she couldn't stand. The more sensitive ones liked ballet and theater and were too feminine. Those who were masculine, polite, and interesting were invariably ugly—or married.

But it was different with Adrián. For the first time in her life, she was acting logically rather than impulsively. She was using her brains instead of following her sexual instincts. In doing so, she discovered a composure in herself that she didn't know she had. For the duration of this new situation, she would show extreme zealousness in her work and in the management of the house. No one knew where the relations between the aunt and her nephew might go, and she was, after all, the only one of them who could be easily evicted. She had already invested a lot of time and energy in this enterprise, so she couldn't act hastily.

The two women began to meet in the widow's room to criticize Adrián's faults: the time of day he went to bed and got up, his eating habits, his lack of consistency in shopping and taking out the garbage. For the first time in

Ana's presence, the widow reached down into her shrunken bosom for a golden key and opened a varnished cabinet just enough to stick her arm into it and grab a bottle of French wine, which she served in two tall, narrow glasses. Soon they were both laughing uproariously at Ana's imitations of Adrián.

These sessions became routine, and had Ana pushed a little further, Adrián would have been put out on the street. But she had conflicting feelings about him. Her romantic interests, for one thing. A prickling sensation—an adrenaline rush in his presence—led to erotic fantasies, stimulated all the more by her long period of sexual abstinence, due more to lack of opportunities than a shortage of eligible men.

Adrián had suddenly arrived, wooing her from the first moment, holding her hand at every opportunity, paying her frequent compliments, brushing lightly against her breasts in doorway crossings . . . On three separate occasions she had almost reached the point of surrender late at night. She would hear him moving outside her room and she would stand with her ear against the door, listening to his deep breathing on the other side and his soft pleas to her. He would knock gently a few minutes later and then go quickly to his room next to the kitchen, formerly the servant's quarters.

Sometimes she fooled herself into thinking that he was in love with her. Why not? She was young and attractive and had at least as much education as he did. The other woman that had been growing inside her warned that Adrián's sole intention was to establish permanent residence in the house. Men were abundant. What she needed most was a house—a roof and four walls. Her parents' house would have to be shared with her brothers, their women, and the children they would have. There just wasn't enough room for all of them.

Everything seemed to be unraveling when Adrián managed to get the family's 1958 Oldsmobile running. It had been resting on stilts since the '60s, when tires and batteries became scarce. Adrián arrived with a set of tires from God knows where, a new battery, two bottles of a green fluid, and a box of spare parts. He put on an olive-green mechanic's uniform from his time in the military and worked for three consecutive days, at the end of which a deafening roar filled the air and the car began to move. He drove it around the block and an awestruck Ana began to resign herself to the idea that Adrián was now a permanent resident with whom she would have to compete for the widow's house. But when she brought a mango juice without sugar to Doña Elvira, a diabetic, she found her in a fit of rage.

"I have never seen such impudence! With whose permission? Who let him touch the car? If I had cared, it would have been running a long time ago—and with a chauffeur! Tell him to leave it exactly as it was. And if he doesn't like that, he can go back to where he came from. In fact, he should just leave. Tell him that I never want to see him again!"

So everything was finally solved. Ana went to meet Adrián in the garage. It was essential that the young man not speak to his aunt, to avoid a change of plans, as had happened before. She had to carefully explain Doña Elvira's fury and her demands. The old lady could have an attack, the sugar in her blood might fluctuate, or something even worse.

Adrián arrived with a triumphant smile on his face and covered with grease. Ana, surprised at how underhanded she could be, told him with tears in her eyes and a faltering voice that the reward for all his work was eviction; that's how unfair life was. To show her solidarity with the young man, she cried bitterly and copiously, with an acting ability that was a revelation to her. Just like in the movies, he embraced her and kissed her on the forehead and eyes, smearing her with grease. Smiling, like a Hollywood hero in a desperate situation, he said: "Don't worry about me. I'll manage. Cheer up, you pretty girl." And he kissed her again, this time reaching down to her butt in his embrace.

Adrián retreated to his room, whistling. Ana, excited by the sensual contact, roamed the hall listening to the sound of him moving about in his room. Then a silence fell. What had happened? She went outside, walked around the house to his window, peeked through the Persian blinds, and saw him sleeping, completely naked, in front of the electric fan, with an erection.

She became very nervous. Now that Adrián was out of the battle for the house, it would be harmless, she thought, to have a brief romance with him before he left. She needed this to recover her emotional stability, which she had lost in recent weeks. Adrián was constantly on her mind, and having sex with him had become an obsession. She had to do it. She entered the room and began undressing. She was completely naked when he opened an eye.

That afternoon, in a final gesture of defiance, the nephew drove the car into town. When he returned, after nine o'clock, she was watching a Brazilian soap opera in the living room. Unsure how to handle the new situation, she opted to ignore their recent tryst, as if she had forgotten it, and pretended to be absorbed by the TV.

Adrián didn't say anything. He went to the kitchen and came back with a glass of milk in his hand. "I'm going to take this to my aunt. I won't argue with her. I'm just going to say farewell and will be leaving tomorrow morning very early for Cárdenas. A friend will pick me up with a truck at five a.m."

The following morning, Ana was puzzled by not hearing Doña Elvira moving about on the second floor. By the time Ana got up, the old woman would normally have already prepared coffee and would be watering her plants.

Alarmed, Ana went upstairs and knocked on Elvira's door. No answer. She then peered through the old woman's window by leaning out of the balcony next to her room and saw her on the floor with an open mouth, seemingly dead. She bolted down the stairway, shouting.

Adrián opened his door just as she reached the main floor.

"You're still here?" she asked, greatly surprised.

Elvira recovered from her hypoglycemic coma thanks to Adrián's knowledge of CPR. It became obvious that a man capable of carrying the old lady from the second floor to the car in the garage in the event of such an emergency was indispensable. Thus, Adrián became a permanent member of the household.

Following this event, the aunt changed her mind about her nephew. What she had seen as vices were now virtues; his blunders became smart decisions. His indelible flaw, that of being his father's son, remained, but she began to discover Arrinda family strengths in him without the genetic deficiencies of the accursed members of the Echenique family.

"Ana, we must find a good mate for Adrián. This running around with young women infected with AIDS must stop! He must settle down and he should not get trapped by some poverty-stricken woman. He needs a professional woman from a good family."

Ana was aghast. She knew the old woman well, and that reference to "some poverty-stricken woman" sounded like a veiled reference to her romance with Adrián. The damned woman *knew*. She must have spied on them! Adrián yelled too loud when he was in the throes of ecstasy. There was no way to avoid the creaking of the bed, and the mattress was too heavy to move onto the floor and put back up again every morning.

Adrián laughed at her apprehensions. He assured her that she was his woman for life. She was certainly a professional and a doctor *honoris causa* in bed, he said, a top-grade specialist in the phallic arts. That was far more important for keeping a man than a university degree. He would talk to the old woman. They would get married and move into one of the large, air-conditioned rooms upstairs.

Ana felt happy and safe, like never before. The old woman fully approved of Adrián now, so Ana didn't expect any opposition from her. But Adrián soon stopped talking about marriage and switching bedrooms. And their sex was losing its sense of urgency.

When she discovered that Adrián was seeing other women, Ana realized that she was at the point of losing everything—despite all these years working like a black slave, putting up with the sclerotic old woman, running two households with no one's help.

She now recognized her basic error. She had been too easy. She had always been too nice, and everyone had taken advantage of her, including her brothers and her father. She had also been too honest—and now she hadn't a penny or anything else to her name.

The month that she had resisted Adrián's courtship had been the best time of her life. She had lived a romance out of a novel or an old film. Having discovered the power of withheld sex, she had, for some time, played her role masterfully, inducing in Adrián a desire for true love—until she had surrendered.

He stopped her short at the first sign of jealousy. "I'm only conducting business. I'll tell you my system. I've had many women in my life, but only one at a time. The day you don't want to stay with me, simply tell me, and we will continue to be friends. The day I'm not happy with you, I'll tell you, and we'll each go our own way and remain good friends. That's my system. Jealousy kills love."

Despite his "declaration of principles," Ana was certain that Adrián was going out with other women. What was worse, he seemed to have switched to black women. Not light mulattas or nice-looking half-breeds. These were real, honest-to-God blacks, the kind that use witchcraft to keep a man forever.

That gave her an idea. She called on a big-bottomed mulatto manicurist whom she knew because he always had the best nail polish. Called "Nalgas," he was reputed to be an expert in matters of love. He brought up the subject himself, as if divining her thoughts, and told her about a client who had problems with her husband. "The man was too fast, a real rabbit. By the time she was beginning to get excited, he was finished and snoring. On the other hand, he was an excellent husband and a good provider. She didn't know whether to leave him or get herself a lover. I recommended a *Santera* who is an expert in these matters and she gave her a marvelous ointment."

Ana decided to explain her situation to him, pretending it was happening to a friend of hers.

Nalgas, half-closing his eyes with a supremely feminine expression, leaned toward her, overpowering her with the fragrance of his strong cologne—irresistible to men, according to him—and said: "Look, dear, in order to tie down that rich, white, handsome man you're involved with, you need the best *Palero* in Guanabacoa. Go see Lorenzo Bantú. Tell him I sent you. That nigger is tops in *bilongo*. If he prepares an *amarre* for you, you'll have this man sniffing your ass like a dog. But beware of that nigger; he likes tall white women with light eyes like yours."

The *Santera* with a white cloud in one eye who had been listening to Ana's predicament let out a loud laugh, poured her another cup of coffee, and went to get her brother.

PROFESSOR JACINTO

WAS THIS CHINAMAN a murderer or a thief?"
"No, although he was a real tough guy, a man of action in
his youth."

"A doctor? A nurse? Did he cure people in some way?"

"No."

"He wasn't a witch doctor, a mind reader, a medium, a spiritualist, or
even just religious?"

"Only a believer; he consulted with Li Chin until the day of his death."

"I ask you this because if he was someone special, somebody may have
wanted the body for a *nganga*. As you know, the majority of *ngangas* are
based on the bones of a dead person. The bones will impart to the *nganga*
the qualities the person had in his lifetime. The bones of murderers and
delinquents are very useful for *ngangas judías*, for harming someone, and
the bones of doctors are useful if you want to cure someone. You never
want to use the bones of an intellectual to create a *nganga*: They always
bring bad results because the *nganga* won't obey; it makes its own decisions.

"Don't laugh. This is all absolutely true. It has a magical logic. Listen:
The essence of *Palo Monte* is the pact made by the *Palero* with the spirit of
the dead person whose bones are in the *nganga*, which also has to include
carcasses of a *majá*, a *jutía*, some *mayimbe*—preferably buzzards—and owls
and bats that see well at night. It should also have the skull of a dog to protect and search, a scorpion to bite and poison, a *macao*, medicinal herbs,

and small branches from trees with different powers . . . All of this is under the guidance of the dead person's spirit, and the spirit must obey only its master, the owner of the *nganga*, because it has sealed a pact with the owner, who has paid with his blood and his money, which are also in the *nganga*. The *nganga* will respond according to the traits of the dead person in his lifetime, and to the other forces in the *nganga*.

"You have to remember that magic has three basic principles: first, like produces like; hence, tornadoes are 'cut' with scissors; a pin is driven into the 'heart' of a doll representing someone whose death is desired. Second, magic by contact or contagion: Things that have been in contact continue to influence each other; hence, a woman who wants to 'hobble' a man must use something that has belonged to him—hair or a piece of clothing. And third, in addition to these two principles originally postulated by James Frazer, you must add animism: Everything in the universe, not only human beings, has a soul, an animus—animals, objects, the stars, everything . . . Magic always rests, in one way or another, on these three principles."

"I don't think Cuan was anyone special or that any *Palero* wanted his body to create a *nganga*. Can you think of any other use for the body of a recently deceased old Chinaman?"

Seated on a small bench in front of an oak barrel from which he had just scooped a mug of homemade *aguardiente*, Jacinto pursed his lips in thought. He carefully poured the liquor into two smaller mugs. He set one of the mugs on the floor beside Alvaro, who had let his blond hair and beard grow since their last meeting and who was now looking out the window at the castle of the Tres Reyes del Morro and at the sea, which gave his eyes an even more intensely blue color.

This was part of the ritual of the visits from that man since the time, many years earlier, when he, Jacinto, had been arrested as an accessory to a homicide. He had been studying the divining system of an *oriaté* who employed methods of *Palo Monte* and *Regla de Osha* simultaneously. In that period, Jacinto was devoting all his time to the investigation of religions of African origin. One Sunday afternoon in February, while he was visiting the *oriaté*'s house, they heard a timid tapping at the front door. The day was very cold and, although the little house made of boards and tiles was completely shut, it felt like a refrigerator inside. A family member opened the door to find a man who was visibly upset and perspiring profusely and who asked for an immediate consultation. The *oriaté* told him to come back the following day because he was busy and, besides, he never worked on Sundays.

"My problem is very serious," the man said with an anguished expression in his eyes.

The *oriaté* decided to ask his *orishas* if he should allow the consultation, and they replied affirmatively. He realized that he could use the occasion to demonstrate his divining method to his visitor, the researcher. He would employ the *Diloggún* of *Regla de Osha* with its sixteen shells and continue according to what the shells indicated. The headletter in the strange *registro* was *Osa-Meyi*: seven shells facing upward on two consecutive throws.

"Friend kills friend," said the *oriaté*, reading the letter.

The man sat for a long while with his head bowed, then abruptly confessed to a double crime committed the night before when he returned home to find his wife in bed with his best friend. "What else could I do?" he asked. "I had to kill both of them." He wanted the advice of the *orishas* on how to elude punishment since "it isn't fair to spend the rest of my life in prison because of this."

The consultation continued with the cocos; the unanimous advice of the *orishas* was that he turn himself in to the police.

The man remained silent, doubtful. That was not the answer he had sought.

"Can't you do anything to prevent this from being discovered? I buried them in a place where no one is going to find them."

The diviner shook his head. His saints had spoken and he could do nothing to contradict their recommendations.

Resentful, the man left the *Santero's* house without paying. Shortly afterward, Jacinto also departed, astonished by the scene he had just witnessed.

Two weeks later, the police arrested the murderer, who confessed to his double crime, as well as his consultation. Jacinto and the *oriaté* were also arrested, accused of being accessories to a crime they knew about and had not reported to the police.

This was during the first years of the Revolution that had set out to change everything from the roots up. Young, inexperienced cops had replaced the police force of the Batista dictatorship, known for its sanguinary but effective methods.

The following morning, a very tall and blond young officer questioned the captives for several hours, showing a keen interest in divining practices and in Jacinto's strange studies, but without any mention of the crime of which they were accused. At the end of the interrogation, the officer's pleasant tone of voice dropped to a below-zero temperature when he said: "A jury could be persuaded to think of an *oriaté* like a Catholic priest. In that case, the *Santero* could have the right to protect a secret confession. But what about you?" he asked, turning to Jacinto. The researcher, not knowing how to respond, shook his head in dismay.

Those were difficult times, times of a fierce atheism. A scientific explanation could be found for *anything*. The new society had arrived conclusively with the liquidation of all class contradictions. The world was divided into two well-defined camps: that of the poor, the exploited, the good, led by true Marxist revolutionaries, armed with an infallible social science; and that of the evil, the rich, the exploiters, or, in the best of cases, the misguided, who didn't know what they were doing. To which camp did Jacinto belong?

The accused, perplexed, didn't know how to answer that question, either.

Jacinto had begun his research after his graduation as a sociologist from the University of Havana, very influenced by the work of Fernando Ortiz, Lydia Cabrera, and, later, that of Teodoro Díaz Favelo. Gradually, the mysticism of the Afro-Cuban religions had seduced him. In his neighborhood, he was considered apathetic toward the Revolution, and this was consistent with his class origin. Early in the century, his family had been the owners of half of the town of Casablanca, but had lost their fortune little by little. Now, Jacinto and four old aunts were the only relics of the Villalonga-Daussá family, famous for its wealth, for parties that lasted days on end, and for a certain dementia that ran through all of them to varying degrees.

Jacinto and his four aunts inherited the best residence in the area, now a ramshackle mansion that overlooked the rest of the town. During the first six decades of the century, the family had lived comfortably on rent collected from several warehouses and other port installations. These properties, but not the family home, were nationalized at the beginning of the '60s. The family was able to live, barely, on the indemnities that the government had paid them, corresponding to the value of the nationalized properties.

"According to the new law against vagrancy, since you don't work, you are, technically, a criminal, a person outside the law," the young officer told Jacinto.

At that point, Jacinto burst into tears. He felt hollow inside, as if part of his life had escaped him. The blond officer waited for a response, but since this was not forthcoming, he told the two men that they could go.

What? What did he say? That he could leave? Jacinto's scientific education rebelled against such inconsistency. He was firmly convinced that he was an accessory to a crime and also guilty of vagrancy—he was someone the new society should punish severely. Let them leave? This was more proof that the Revolution was in disarray and it confirmed his suspicion that power in the hands of the working class was a tremendous liability.

Months later, the trial of the murderer took place with no mention at all of Jacinto or the *oriaté*. However, the blond police officer continued to visit Jacinto, questioning him about his research and observing his lifestyle. Sometimes he spent hours at his house, examining his library.

Jacinto toyed with the idea of leaving the country and heading, naturally, to the United States, but he couldn't figure out how he would earn a living. Actually, the idea of exile terrified him—leaving his family home, the town and the country that, in his own way, he loved so much, and deserting the research that had consumed such a large part of his youth. He would be like a tooth yanked out by the roots, a dead object, a nothing. Besides, what would he do with his aunts?

At the same time, he could see no other solution to his situation, always in danger of being arrested for vagrancy. Then he learned that Lydia Cabrera, a highly respected authority on Afro-Cuban studies, was living a very humble existence in Miami. Apparently, the Cuban exile community in America had little use for experts in Afro-Cuban traditions.

Jacinto was astonished and delighted to one day receive a job offer from the municipal House of Culture; everything changed overnight. He began to work feverishly on the creation of a music and dance folklore group, and a wing of his house was soon converted into the group's general headquarters. The dark and rickety old mansion became a brightly lit and clamorous meeting place for townspeople to participate in or watch rehearsals. His life had suddenly become full of meaning and purpose. He began to feel as revolutionary as the next one, and he started to speak out in the meetings of his block committee for the defense of the Revolution, demanding more efficiency in the institutions of the municipality. Always, however, in the back of his mind, was the suspicion that the offer from the House of Culture was somehow related to that strange and unsought guardian angel.

It was in this heartening period that his first daughter was born, followed, later, by two more, each one by a different mother—women who passed through the folklore group, primitive ladies who quickly got bored with him, with dancing, and with their daughters, leaving them to his care. Meanwhile, his aunts, satisfied that their nephew was taken care of, died within a relatively short time, one after another.

The intrusive policeman continued to have an irresistible charm for Jacinto: He was an excellent listener, and Jacinto loved to talk. With time, his mistrust disappeared. The policeman always came dressed in civilian clothes and unarmed. He normally arrived when the house was alive with dancers and musicians. They would exchange greetings and the policeman would take refuge in an isolated room that was always locked because the key had been lost long ago. The room, once the family library, was filled with old books in complete disorder. The policeman would pick the lock of the library door and settle down to read or organize the books for hours at a time.

Jacinto found in the passing years that the officer was a valuable friend, able to do special favors for him. He couldn't ask for anything specific, but the mere mention of a problem often brought mysterious and unexpected results.

One day, the policeman arrived with a strange gift—a cot with a mattress and pillow. Jacinto set up the cot in the library next to the window. From then on, the visitor often read lying down, sometimes staying overnight.

Sitting atop a hill that served as a great backdrop to the town of Casablanca, the house had a wooden roof with Spanish tiles; over the years, the sea wind from the north had cured the woodwork, giving it a dull color and a dry, rough surface. The image of Jacinto performing his early-morning yoga exercises on a balcony slowly became a part of the local townscape. He was considered a person who lived beyond good or evil.

At a certain point, the policeman had started to take special notice of two of Jacinto's daughters. He was struck by their difficulty walking down the hill in tight skirts and high-heeled shoes, headed to the ferryboat that would carry them across the bay to Havana. Both were light-skinned, healthy-looking mulattas with an inexhaustible good humor. Although they looked around twenty, he couldn't remember if they were even sixteen yet.

The oldest of Jacinto's daughters, who was now almost twenty-five, was a strange woman who bore no physical resemblance to the other two. She had a silent and unsociable character, almost never left the house, and was very close to her father. She seemed to reject the policeman, perhaps because he monopolized Jacinto's time on his visits.

One day, Jacinto and the policeman were seated in one of the glass-enclosed porches looking down on the bay and the city. The voices of the three daughters carried out to them as they arrived home, and a soft breeze cooled the air.

Suddenly, the voice of the oldest sister reached them through an open door, rebuking the others. "So, are you off on one of your whoring sprees?"

"It's none of your business where we're going. Keep your nose to yourself! We know how to enjoy life a little, which is more than you can say."

They heard a door slam and the murmur of the argument continuing, the words now indistinguishable. Shortly afterward, the house grew silent and Jacinto began to peer fixedly toward the concrete steps leading down the hill. Almost at once, the two younger daughters appeared, heading toward the dock. Their father turned to Alvaro with eyes filled with pain.

"I'd like to ask you a favor."

The policeman looked out over the bay, eluding his friend's eyes.

"My two youngest girls are on a very dangerous path. They pick up foreign tourists, and I'm sure they sleep with them in exchange for taking them to good restaurants and cabarets and buying them fancy clothes. I'm terrified that they'll catch AIDS."

The policeman didn't answer. Jacinto waited a moment, uncomfortable, almost regretting he had spoken, then continued. "In a way, it's not their fault. They've grown up without a mother, and I guess I haven't been a very good substitute—"

The policeman interrupted him. "What do you want me to do?"

"Just scare them a little. Arrest them for a few hours on a charge of prostitution or drug possession. Something that will give them a good fright."

The policeman shook his head. "Neither you nor I have a right to do that."

"Why not?"

"Look, I don't agree with many things that are happening in this country. It's terrible that pretty young women sell themselves to foreigners. It's a shocking irony that one of the first and best things the Revolution did was to abolish prostitution. But those were different times and different prostitutes. Everything was solved by giving them new work and teaching them to read. Now, in the '90s, almost all of them have a good education. A lot of them come from respectable families. They don't sell their bodies because they have no other choice, as in the past. They aren't a majority, but there are too many of them. I don't know what to do, but throwing them in jail isn't the solution. And even if it were, I don't have the right to do it."

Jacinto was going to say something harsh, but restrained himself. The policeman never remained impassive in the face of any problem, but it didn't seem like he was planning to do anything about the situation.

The oldest daughter appeared and announced that dinner was ready.

When they entered the dining room, they saw that the table was set for just two people.

"Why doesn't she ever eat with us?" Alvaro asked.

"You frighten her. She says you always come and go like a ghost."

"I'll be more careful—or, rather, less careful."

"That's the way she is, always reading or studying. She's so timid. The other two are whores, but this one . . . I'd almost like to see her go out partying some night and return all bitten!"

The policeman didn't reply. He realized that Jacinto was more distraught than he had seen him in years.

"Come, *hija*, do me the favor of eating with us."

The young woman was watching television in the next room. She remained still a moment, as if weighing her options. Then she went to her room and returned almost immediately in a different set of clothes. She served the food she had set aside for herself in the kitchen and sat down at the table with them, avoiding the glance of the policeman.

"Narelys, I wonder if you could lend me a book I saw you reading four years ago, the last Friday of February. You were here in the dining room sitting in that chair. When I arrived, you went to get your father and left the book on the table. The title of the book was *Odyssey's World*. You were reading page twenty."

Surprised, the young woman nodded slowly, then began to rise from her chair. The policeman stopped her with a gesture. "There's no hurry."

He immediately regretted his words. He had seen her with the book a long time ago and, later, had bought a copy for himself. His capacity for remembering details made it easy for him to recall the scene vividly, but the girl would now realize that he had been observing her every move.

After coffee, Narelys brought the book from her room and laid it on the table beside the policeman.

"Thank you."

She smiled faintly.

Suddenly, Jacinto leapt to his feet, shouting, "Do you know what I just realized? That Chinaman was stolen for protection, a magic shield! All of the

Afro-Cuban practices consider Chinese magic the most powerful. No one can undo a Chinese curse, not even the person who made it. The old *Paleros* used to say that the cadaver of a Chinaman protects against anything; it's infallible. That must be what's going on."

"I've never read about anything like that."

"I'm talking about the remote past, when blacks were first stolen from Africa. Among them were African witch doctors, who for the first time in their life met Chinese people, who themselves had been brought here practically as slaves. My friend, I'm speaking about when all of this started. The cultural exchange had to have taken place on many different levels, and this knowledge of Chinese magic must have arisen at that time."

CAMILA

EAVING 41st AVENUE behind and letting his bicycle roll down Calle 16, he soon spotted his mother showing his "farm" to a woman with her back turned to him. Braking gradually to give himself time to recognize the visitor, he noticed only a pair of pretty legs and an attractive figure. He entered as quietly as possible through the open door of the garage and parked his "vehicle," but he knew that his mother had already seen him. A constant and silent communication existed between them. She almost always knew what he was thinking and where he was, regardless of the distance between them. Whenever he phoned, she would declare, "I knew it was you." Other times, she would say, "I've been expecting your call," as if he had postponed responding to a telepathic request from her.

He walked to a window in the dining room and drew the Persian blinds apart to get a better look at the visitor. He instantly recognized the profile of his colleague, Camila. Seeming to sense the scrutiny, she looked toward the house but failed to detect his gaze. He saw, nevertheless, his mother's slight smile, amused by his curiosity and happy for the visit, since she was always on the alert for women who might be able to give her grandchildren.

He took a cold shower to wash off the sweat from his one-hour bike ride from Casablanca across the bay to Miramar, facing the sun the whole way. He had a number of things to take care of in his garden, but to please his mother, he told himself, he dressed to greet the visitor.

As he went down the stairs, the aroma of freshly brewed coffee told him that his mother and Camila were in the kitchen. When he entered the room, the young police investigator left her cup and walked toward him, visibly nervous. "I have to beg your pardon. I wanted to take advantage of your authorization to call you in case of any difficulties, but I overstepped that a bit and decided to come straight to your house. I have a number of things to tell you."

His mother's beaming face as she brought him coffee expressed her approval of the young woman.

"I'm glad you're here, Camila. I imagine that my mother has already enlightened you as to my many virtues. I saw you in the garden, and look at me—I've even put on clean clothes!"

Camila smiled, surprised. Suddenly, as the mother-son game became clear to her, she felt inhibited, unsure of what to say. Then she remembered the reason for her visit.

"Thanks to you, we've been able to move quickly." Camila lifted her cup of coffee and followed Alvaro into the living room, where four comfortable, chintz-covered chairs were set around a bamboo table facing two large windows overlooking an enormous breadfruit tree and, in the distance, a stretch of the Almendares River.

Camila's mind flashed back to Alvaro's mother. Camila had spent almost two hours sharing the pleasant company and affectionate conversation of Dulce María, enjoying the charm of the home that the older woman showed off to her from top to bottom, as if offering it for a reasonable price. Almost without intending to, she had begun to consider her idol in criminal investigation as a possible father for her child. Nevertheless, Dulce María's excessive praise of her son, and the fact that he had been married twice already, had provoked a fleeting doubt: Could he be gay?

As they sat down, she forced her thoughts back to the business at hand. "The investigator from the national office is in full gear these days. Colonel Carrillo himself has presided over two meetings on the case, and it's clear now that the three trucks identified with the robberies come from the same transport base in Guanabacoa—something I would have discovered myself if I had more brains.

"Not all of the trucks spend the night at the base. We've found a cor-relation between the robberies in the last two months and the movements of six drivers who have taken days off due to 'unforeseen circumstances.' Starting tomorrow, a watch will be kept on all of the trucks outside of the base whose drivers have requested a day off, especially these six."

Alvaro nodded slightly but said nothing.

"Meanwhile, I visited the girl in the pharmacy—the one I saw flirting with the alleged bicycle messenger. She cooperated with me once she knew I was a police officer. At first, she thought I was the messenger's wife and denied that she knew him. I wanted to laugh, but after I identified myself, she told me that she hadn't seen him again after that day. I convinced her to make an oral portrait of him, and this is it . . ." She handed him the drawing of a blandly good-looking, blond-haired man.

Alvaro took the portrait and glanced perfunctorily at it but remained silent, as if his mind were occupied elsewhere. Camila suddenly realized that she had shared everything she had to tell him, and she now regretted having burst into his private life. She felt at the mercy of his steady scrutiny that seemed fixed on the slightest movement of her legs below her short skirt.

"So that's what I wanted to tell you," she said lamely, embarrassed.

He continued looking at her, apparently amused by her discomfort. "Don't you have any children?" he asked suddenly. "Why aren't you mar-ried? How old are you—thirty-five?"

"Thirty-one the seventeenth of next month," she answered sharply, resenting his calculation of her age. "I haven't married because I damn well didn't want to. The institution of marriage is in crisis nowadays; everything works against it. I'm going to have a child on my own, and I feel perfectly capable of giving it all of the love and protection it needs."

Alvaro looked surprised at her vehement response, and she felt annoyed with herself. Why had she reacted so strongly to his simple question? Something in her nature seemed to make her clash with almost every man she met. What a fool she was! She had to learn to make concessions. Alvaro was a fascinating man and he had helped her a great deal. Unfortunately, the milk was already spilled, she told herself.

Alvaro remained silent, looking at her fixedly, this time into her eyes, then said, "You may be absolutely right. It's a shame that you're so young." As he said this, he rose, indicating that the interview was over.

Camila remained perplexed by his last comment. When she left the house and walked down the sidewalk through the front yard, she felt, for some inexplicable reason, like crying. Why couldn't she be nicer to the men she liked? Alvaro, she thought, certainly deserved it. Still, the eternal fighting cock inside her advised, "*Oh well, Camila, to hell with Alvaro!*"

MILADYS PACHECO

COME IN, GODMOTHER. Sit down, please. You don't know how glad I am to see you! I have to tell you something terrible. It happened yesterday. I was on the verge of doing something insane. I almost . . . almost set your brother Lorenzo on fire . . . Yes, intentionally.

"I was going to set myself on fire, too. Today, I've calmed down enough to talk about it. I consulted Shangó with my shells and he told me to stay calm, so I've been on tilo decoction and grapefruit juice instead of water for the last twenty-four hours. And I took two cold baths to lower my blood pressure.

"Godmother, I know that you already know something. I heard that you've been asking questions, and I did get the message to go see you, but I'm going to be honest: If Lorenzo hadn't done what he did yesterday, I wouldn't have been able to tell you anything. Today, everything is different, and I have to talk to somebody or I'll explode. As his sister, you're the best person to get through to him. That's why I asked you to come; I didn't want to go to your house because if I see him I don't know what I might do . . .

"Yes, I'll explain. I don't know if you know Lorenzo's clients, Ana and Adrián. She's the maid in the house of Adrián's aunt, and, apparently, they're living there as husband and wife. But it seems that he's been sleeping around with a lot of other women and she's desperate. Someone told Ana she should have her man hobbled and recommended your brother as the best *Palero* for such work, so she went to see him last week. But Lorenzo is convinced that his *nganga* brought Ana to him because he had to know all of Adrián's movements. So Lorenzo sent her to me after her first consultation with him. He didn't want to keep working with her at his own house in case Adrián showed up. He asked me to prepare a 'husband-hobble.'

"She told me all about the consultation. She said that at first she'd been disappointed. She thought Lorenzo would tell her something spectacular, like the gypsies in the movies that tell you the day and hour you're going to die and the color of the eyes of the man you're going to marry. Or like the Indian fakirs that make a rope dance in the air. Instead, Lorenzo wrote her name on a piece of paper and put it under a glass of water and began asking her tons of questions—her age, if she was married, if she had children, if she was happy in her marriage. After each question, he threw the shells, and that went on for a long time.

"Ana said she was disgusted. But then, suddenly, Lorenzo told her: 'An old woman who is very fond of you will give you some old furniture when the moment comes to fire you. The man you are living with has many other women and if you don't hobble him immediately he'll leave you before the end of this year.' Ana said she was speechless. Then Lorenzo continued: 'Two women, a light-skinned mulatta and an older black woman, want to get you out of the way in order to take your husband. They have set three works in motion, two to hobble him and another one against you.'

"Ana said she almost fainted. She broke out in a cold sweat and her stomach began to heave. But that wasn't all. Lorenzo consulted the *nganga*, and she was really impressed. The *nganga* confirmed that the *bilongos* had been set in motion against her, and then a spirit appeared, begging God for Ana's happiness. It was a *delayed* spirit that hasn't yet found peace, Lorenzo told her. 'It's my mother!' she screamed, and began to sob. She couldn't stop crying and started to hiccup violently. Lorenzo gave her a half-glass of *aguardiente* and she relaxed after he passed the *mpaca* over her body.

"As you can imagine, she put herself completely in his hands. Lorenzo told her that if she followed his instructions, all her problems would go away. But he explained that it isn't easy to interrupt works that are already in progress.

"He also told her that it was necessary to begin at once. She must not tell anyone that she had consulted him, least of all her husband. It was important to make everything seem normal. From that moment on, she was supposed to keep me informed about everything Adrián did. Lorenzo told her I would do a husband-hobble, and he assured her that once everything was solved, she was going to have a daughter with green eyes. The old woman would then leave the house in her name, and her mother's wandering soul would rest in peace.

"So Ana began to come here every day, interrupting my other work. She lives in the old woman's house, but her family—her father and her two brothers—live three blocks from here, so she uses the excuse of visiting them every time she comes here. And that woman has told me everything about her husband, even what they do in bed! Sometimes I think she invents half of it.

"She told me that the husband-hobble was working like a charm. In just a few days, Adrián dropped the other women. He used to arrive home every night smelling of different women. He even arrived once all bitten up, as if he'd gone to bed with a bitch! You know Adrián, don't you? You must have noticed him—he consults with Lorenzo regularly. No woman, it seems, is safe around him.

"You have to have seen him. I met him once at your house, waiting to see Lorenzo. He immediately tried to strike up a conversation with me. And when I was walking home, he caught up with me and insisted on driving me home. Who wouldn't accept, the way public transportation is nowadays? But I cut him short when he invited me out, and I told him I'm engaged to Lorenzo.

"From what Ana has told me, Adrián must be involved in something illegal because he always has plenty of money, although no one knows anything about the work he does. Maybe he's found a way to get money out of the old lady, his aunt, who apparently has lots of things to sell. They live in a mansion guarded by dogs, and Ana says that the food those animals consume costs a fortune.

"After the work I did, Lorenzo decided to continue with the consultations himself, in my house. The first time went without any problems, although I realized that that nigger was excited by that whitey. When she'd gone, he took me to bed and finished very quickly. On the second visit, he sent me to the patio to get some of this and some of that, and when I returned, I found him stroking the woman's back with her shirt unbuttoned. I gave him a dirty look and, after Ana left, he immediately started fighting with me, saying I hadn't told him everything about Adrián. Ana had told him some very important things, he said, that I hadn't even mentioned. That's an old tactic of his. Every time I get angry about something, he immediately starts to defend himself by attacking me and putting me on the defensive.

"But, honestly, godmother, I don't know what to think about all of this— if it's all just a way to get Adrián's woman into bed with him, or if that man and Lorenzo are up to something strange together. The next day, he brought me a tape recorder and told me to tape everything Ana said because I was losing too much information about Adrián. Why this obsession? What are those two up to?

"Lorenzo and I have been together eight years, as you know. In all that time, he's never said a word about marriage. He's never taken me to a party or to the movies; he's never even taken me to the beach. He just comes here two or three times a week, spends an hour with me in bed, eats lunch, drinks coffee, and leaves. That's it. I've never asked him for a penny for the house, although he always gives me nice gifts. He's not stingy, but he has no obligations here. I'm still young; I'm not even twenty-six yet. Plenty of men pay attention to me. I've put up with this situation all this time because I've been sure that I was the only woman—the only one—that Lorenzo Bantú has been going to bed with.

"Yesterday, he came for another consultation with Ana and told me that I couldn't participate. He'd listened to all the recordings I gave him and had to speak with her about something very private. I pretended to understand, but since I can smell trouble from a block away, I had already prepared to watch secretly from the next room—Miladys Pacheco doesn't have a stupid hair on her head!

"He started the consultation with *chamalongo*, then he told her to take off her shirt. She immediately took it off and just sat there with her tits in the air, since she never wears a bra. At that point, Miladys Pacheco couldn't take anymore. In the almighty fight that followed, your brother came close to death because I threw a jar of alcohol all over him. He stood there staring at me, paralyzed, without even opening his mouth. It was a miracle that I didn't throw the match I'd lit.

"I still don't know how I stopped myself. Eight years of eating shit, without going out anywhere, stuck in this house waiting for him every day . . . I can't even look forward to having kids because Lorenzo says the Bantús only have them when they're old. All my nigger blood went to my head and something inside me screamed: 'Go ahead! Set him on fire! Burn him, burn him, burn him, *coño!*'"

PALERO

LORENZO BANTÚ STARED incredulously at Pedro. It wasn't possible that Mulo had been arrested. If that was true, then he had to find out immediately why the *chino* wasn't performing as he was supposed to. There might have been a minor mistake, easy to fix . . .

"Did you actually *see* the police arrest him?"

"Not exactly. But I saw when Mulo climbed into the truck and started it. Four policemen in plain clothes went after him. Mulo kicked one right out of the truck. The other three managed to pull him out, and there was a big brawl . . . Adrián and I were about a block away and as soon as we saw that, we ran away. I also noticed the policewoman who tried to arrest me the other day. She was there with her little pistol in hand, giving all the orders and talking on a cellular phone."

"You told me Mulo killed her with a karate blow."

Pedro shrugged his shoulders. Lorenzo Bantú shook his head disapprovingly and walked to the *ceiba*, as he always did when he needed to think. Pedro followed him. This time Lorenzo sat down on one of the big roots protruding from the soil and Pedro sat down on another a few feet away.

He had taught them with the greatest care. For weeks, he had instructed them how to do the *moyugba*, accompanied by the right body movements. He had made them practice the invocations in the Congolese language to avoid misunderstandings with the *mpungos* and the dead. He made sure they mastered the procedure so that nothing was left to chance. Everything had been done exactly as prescribed by his grandfather's teachings and by his *nganga*. Despite all of this, something had gone wrong and had to be remedied immediately. Something must be disturbing the spirit of the *chino*.

This was the first time he had used a *chino* as protection, and he had known in advance that it was full of risks. But the danger, he had thought, was more than offset by the impunity assured by his magic shield. "He who takes risks has the right to share in the profits," the lawyer who defended him in his first trial had said. This was one of the really true things he had learned in his life. "*He who shares in the profits must take risks.*" That was the corollary that he had deduced without the help of anyone—as true and profound as the first.

There was also the problem with Miladys to take into account. Miladys had gone completely nuts. She had tried to set him on fire. His sister had been sticking her wicked nose into everything, maybe she was to blame . . . What if Adrián had sent Ana to provoke him? Thinking about Ana, he realized he hadn't been in his right mind when he'd let himself be tempted by her. Some powerful force was behind all of this.

After some intense concentration, Lorenzo reached a conclusion: The *chino* was the only cause of what was happening. The *chino* had actually been sending him signals to rectify his work. The first one came when the police surprised Mulo and Pedro, and he had failed to consult his *nganga*. He hadn't thrown the *chamalongo* or looked at the *mpaca mensu* . . . The proof that the *chino* was behind everything was right before his eyes: Miladys had been ready to set fire to him at exactly the same time that Mulo was caught by the police!

Pleased with himself for unraveling the enigma, Lorenzo pointed a finger at Pedro and shouted: "I'm going to do a *registro*! I'm going to find out what's happening and who's responsible. *Carajo!* I'm going to make the ground tremble beneath your feet! You'll see! The guilty one pays! Nobody can play with me! Be here tonight at midnight and bring Adrián with you. I'm going to do a *registro*. If you two are clean, then I'm going to ask the *nganga* what's happening."

* * *

It was almost two in the morning, and they were still waiting for the right hour for the *registro*. Adrián was trying not to laugh. It had been hard to keep a straight face, seeing the look of fear in Pedro's eyes when he came to tell him that the *Nasakó* was demanding a *registro* to find out who was to blame for Mulo's capture. How could anyone, at the door of the twenty-first century, still believe in such crap—especially in Cuba, where so much effort had been devoted to combating all types of religious beliefs?

Anyway, he was starting to fall asleep. So much stupidity! Everything depended on shells and pieces of coconut, and on the interpretations dreamed up by the *Nasakó* from the soot stains left on a white dish by the flame of a candle. Well, maybe people who believed in those things were happier than others, but he doubted it.

Looking up, he saw that the branches of nearby trees were swaying in a strong breeze blowing seaward. That was the early-morning land breeze, the *terral*, that carried fishermen out to sea every day at dawn, as he had learned in his days on Shore Patrol. He recalled the time that he'd almost drowned when he was a new recruit. It was red snapper season, and he and a fellow recruit had gone fishing in a small boat borrowed from a fisherman. They'd gone farther out to sea than they had intended. Huge waves were suddenly generated by a summer squall that died as quickly as it had begun, leaving, in the exquisite afternoon, an overturned and half-sunk boat with two would-be fishermen clinging to it.

As the better swimmer of the two, Andrés left to seek help, while Adrián continued to hold onto the boat, watching for sharks. Night fell abruptly. The sea became rougher, moved by a high wind, the prelude to a new storm. He stayed as still as possible, trying to imitate another chunk of wood.

By midnight, the sea had calmed down. He was reaching the conclusion that this might be the last night of his life. Any small wave could finish him off. He had to take advantage of the moment of calm and swim as far as his strength would take him. The problem was—which direction to head? Scanning the relatively few patches of clear sky, he located the unmistakable Big Dipper and then spotted the North Star, which, by great luck, was clearly visible.

He removed his shoes and loosened his belt. As he swam, he shed his wide-bottomed sailor's pants, but only after he had salvaged a forty-cent coin from his pocket, a good-luck charm given to him years before by his father. He was no longer a part of a sinking boat; now he was slow-moving food for hungry sharks, totally unprotected within the immense liquid darkness.

At some point in space, his father's soul was surely watching over him; at that very moment, it was probably keeping sharks away from him. To survive, he would invoke the saints to whom his mother had prayed: the crucified Jesus Christ, the all-powerful God . . . even the *orishas*—why not? Human life couldn't be so meaningless. How absurd to end one's existence simply by encountering a hungry shark! There had to be a supreme order that governed the life of each individual.

He reacted suddenly with a sense of bitterness. Ah, how superstition overwhelms good sense in moments like these! All of this time swimming with that coin in his hand! "*It will bring you luck as long as you keep it,*" his father had said. He had reached adulthood with the coin in his pocket after having resisted many times the desire to spend it on candy, peanuts, or coffee. Now, in this moment of his supreme struggle to survive, the stupid coin obliged him to swim with a closed fist, hampering his strokes. Clearly, humanity hasn't advanced much; we are much closer to the caveman than we like to admit. How great if the world's problems could be solved by a mere talisman, or by a prayer! After death, the human body decomposes into the simple elements from which it is made, nothing more.

Energy is equal to mass multiplied by the velocity of light squared. Bodies in space attract one another with a force directly proportional to their mass and inversely proportional to the square of the distance between them. It was foolish to think of life after death, senseless to believe in things that defied the laws of physics. Everything in the universe was formed exclusively of mass in movement . . . mass and movement, mass and the infinite forms of movement . . . From that moment on, he wouldn't allow himself to think of anything outside of movement and mass, mass and movement, and the infinite forms of movement. He was mass in movement, and the sharks were also mass in movement, both moving in the same element at the same time. The probability of an encounter was perfectly calculable if one had all of the coordinates. He decided to drop the coin. He would rely solely on himself, his strength, his intelligence and knowledge. He would swim at a stable rhythm, without fear, to avoid emitting chemical substances that would attract savage animals. He had to assume the risk that his reason dictated.

At that very moment, the water gave way to rock under his hands. He kissed the sharp coral of the coast, much closer than he had dared to hope, and burst into tears. Could the storm have been pushing the boat south that whole time? How was such good luck possible? He felt obligated to express gratitude for his salvation: He would seek out the North Star each night and thank it so that it would continue to guide shipwrecked people on dark nights. Later, when he was calmer and felt solid ground under his feet, he realized that this was also silly superstition. The North Star would go on indicating the north for everyone, independent of anything he might do each night.

Andrés never reached the coast. Only some pieces of his clothing were found floating in the water. He had apparently crossed paths with a hungry shark.

When the door of the *nganga* room opened, Pedro jumped as if one of his testicles had been pinched. He was very worried, lighting one cigarette after another with trembling hands, much to the surprise of Adrián, who knew that Pedro was as tough as they came, as he'd shown many times in their prison days together.

"I'm clean!" Pedro shouted as he came out shortly afterward, as content as a child at his birthday party. "Your turn," he said.

Adrián was annoyed with himself for a mounting nervousness while waiting for his turn with the *Nasakó* and his stinking *nganga*. All he wanted was to finish this nonsense as quickly as possible. He entered the room and stood behind Lorenzo Bantú, who was busy *sahumando* the place with his cigar smoke and sprinkling the *prenda* with *chamba*. The witch doctor began chanting and swaying his body. He threw seven white seashells, each two inches in diameter. Five fell face down. He took one of the shells and hit the ones lying face down, then threw again. On the third throw, all of those shells fell face down. The *Nasakó* turned to Adrián with a furious gesture and thundered: "Imbecile! What has come out in every one of the *registros* for the last month? That you've been cheating on your wife. You know very well that you can't do that—that's what went wrong! Listen carefully, Adrián: If something happens to one of my warriors because of you, you'll pay dearly for it! Now get the hell out of here, *coño!*"

A NIGHT AT THE BEACH

ADRIÁN FLEW OUT of the room of the *nganga*. He felt humiliated and, at the same time, helpless, confused. He walked three blocks to the market where he had left his car in the care of a night watchman. The walk cooled him down a bit, but he needed to cruise around awhile until his anger died down. He couldn't go to bed like that.

He had been sleeping badly for some time now, tossing and turning all night. Why was he so worried lately? He had to be honest with himself. Everything had turned out almost exactly as planned; the only issue was his relationship with the *Nasakó*. At this point in the game, he should be the unquestioned chief, the leader. But that black man, incapable of matching colors in his clothing, dared to yell at him and threaten him—he, Adrián Echenique, the son of Manuel Echenique and Mariana Arrinda, who had never been second to anyone! He had always been first—in his school, in his neighborhood, with women, in his military service, even in prison. It was essential that he continue to lead the group; his plans had barely begun. The most important part was yet to come.

Suddenly, the perfect revenge occurred to him, and Adrián burst out laughing. The night watchman stiffened as he took the five-peso bill.

"Sorry. I'm not laughing at you."

"He who laughs alone may have much to atone, friend."

"Well said."

Adrián got into his aunt's Oldsmobile and drove for less than a mile. He stopped the car on a block where a single lightbulb burned at the entrance to a passageway. Four men seated at a card table were playing dominoes under the light while another two stood by, observing the game. Small piles of coins lay at each corner of the table.

"*Qué bolá?*" Adrián greeted as he passed.

No one answered. The players and onlookers ignored him completely. Adrián moved down the three-meter-wide passageway from which rows of rooms opened on both sides. A strong stench of acid, urine, and feces attacked his nostrils. He held his breath as much as possible and knocked hard on a door at the far end. A voice answered with a mixture of sleepiness and apprehension.

"Who is it?"

"Bonsai! It's Adrián. I need a bottle of the best rum you have."

The door opened partially, revealing a diminutive, fat mulatto in white underwear. Beyond him, in the darkness, a reclining figure covered herself with the corner of a sheet. The man already had the bottle in his hand. "Three *fula*," he said.

"Are you dreaming? Wake up!"

"Two and a half if you come at a human hour."

"Let me see." Adrián took the bottle and removed the three dollars from his pocket.

"I have marijuana. Want some?"

"Never touch grass."

"It's the best. From *my* territory, out there in Guantánamo."

Adrián shook his head and turned to leave.

"Something else. I know you're the top dog in Guanabacoa. You have the girlies like this . . ." The dwarf rubbed his fingers together. "But if you happen to've run short and want some pheasant for tonight, I have something special here for a client with class—fresh flesh just arrived from Baracoa. Take advantage of the occasion before she gets around and discovers Havana." The mulatto opened the door wider to give Adrián a glimpse of another woman's buttock visible on a cot in a corner of the tiny room.

Adrián again shook his head.

He almost had to stoop to pat the shoulder of the clandestine salesman, before quickly moving away.

"Remember, here you have El Bonsai, full twenty-four-hour service!" Adrián heard at his back.

As he reached the entrance of the passageway, one of the players, seeing the bottle of rum, asked with a wide grin, "*Qué bolá,* champ?"

This time, Adrián didn't answer. He got into his car and started off slowly to save gasoline, a luxury that was getting more and more scarce and expensive.

Miladys Pacheco lived nearby. The back of her house faced a quiet street with only one other house, inhabited by a deaf woman. The rest of the area was taken up by weeds and by a large carpentry shop of the Ministry of Construction. If he could awaken the mulatta, he felt sure she would come out with him. He knew her from the *Nasakó's* house, and on two occasions he had driven her home after meeting her "by chance" on the street. Although she was pretty, with very firm flesh and a figure that could excite even a cadaver, he had never taken her to bed because someone had told him that she was the exclusive terrain of the *Nasakó.* The black giant had been almost phobic about venereal diseases, especially AIDS, since the time in Angola when he became convinced he was going to lose his penis after a night of carousing in the brothels of Luanda. Given those circumstances, Adrián had made a strategic retreat from Miladys Pacheco; business definitely took precedence over pleasure. But now the situation was different. What was involved was more important even than business.

Miladys Pacheco slept in a room at the back of the house and was a light sleeper. She recognized Adrián's voice immediately, jumped out of bed, and parted her window shutters.

"It's something urgent. I need your help," Adrián said, hiding the bottle behind him. "I need you to go somewhere with me."

She looked at him without responding. Then, abruptly, she accepted. He went to get the car, and as he passed the carpentry shop, a black cat raced across his path, making him stumble. Bad omen! He slapped the wall of the shop in annoyance with himself. He had to get rid of all of those superstitions that had begun to crowd his mind. Tonight he would apply the best possible remedy: cheating on Ana against all prohibitions and, simultaneously, taking revenge on the *Nasakó* in the most delicious way possible.

Miladys Pacheco settled close to him on the wide front seat of the Oldsmobile. After starting the vehicle in the direction of the beaches east of Havana, Adrián rested his right hand on Miladys's solid thigh and began to make light conversation.

"What do you need my help for?" she asked.

"For something I don't like to do alone."

Miladys smiled. Adrián opened the bottle of rum and passed it to her, along with a plastic cup.

After she had taken her first sip, Adrián took the cup from her hand and drank the rest.

At the beach, they strolled away from Santa María del Mar, heading toward Guanabo, before reaching the wooden bridge. There, the dunes formed a promontory some five meters high between the highway and the water. Moving down the hill, they saw the immense silver sea lying before them as if asleep under the sad and fading light of the waning moon. Another bad omen! Adrián wanted to laugh, but didn't.

They took off their clothes and hid them in the shadows of a coconut palm. Miladys Pacheco set off running and, screaming from the chilly breeze coming from the sea, threw herself into the water. Adrián followed slowly. He pushed the bottle of rum into the moist sand near the edge of the water and set the plastic cup over the neck of the bottle. He walked into the sea up to his knees and waited for his blood to cool. Then he dove into the sea toward Miladys Pacheco, who waited a few meters away. He swam underwater until he reached her. He embraced her legs, then moved upward and stood behind her with his hands on her small breasts, harder now because of the cold water. The delightful curvature of her butt fit neatly against him.

"You're trembling," she said.

"I'm feeling a little cold. I'm going to get the rum." Adrián swam back to the shore and sat down to drink. She came after him and huddled close. Adrián put his arms around her and they sat, in close embrace, looking toward the horizon where the opaque moon seemed about to fall into the water.

Even at that moment, Adrián couldn't rid his mind of the *Nasakó*. He had to prove to himself that the man had no supernatural powers. Everything had to be pure suggestion. All the information Lorenzo had about him must have been obtained one way or another. Pedro or Mulo must have told Lorenzo about some of his recent affairs.

Two Shore Patrol soldiers appeared behind the coconut palms en route to Santa María del Mar. One was trying to restrain a dog on a leash that was advancing very purposefully toward them. Both recruits were very young. The one in the rear, seeing the nude pair, turned his head away and kept walking. The other, allowing the dog to pull him, came very close and stood staring at the woman even after the dog had lost interest.

"What's the matter, sonny? Haven't you ever seen a naked woman?"

"None like you." The boy was clearly under twenty and grinning wickedly as he spoke, a little scared by his own daring.

Recalling his days in olive-green, Adrián chuckled, thinking that they would have a good conversation topic for some time to come.

They found a perfect place for making love, a hollow in the shadow of several coconut palms, invisible from the beach and hidden from the highway by the dunes. Miladys Pacheco took the initiative at once, kissing him first on the forehead, then on his eyes, pausing pleasurably on his lips, before continuing to his neck and on down his body.

Daylight was approaching as they returned to the car. The mulatta laughed, showing her strong, white teeth. But Adrián was serious; his face reflected concern. "I swear it's the first time in my life it's failed me like that. I swear to God!"

CONSULTING A DEAD MAN

FTER ADRIÁN AND PEDRO left, the *Palero* removed his shoes and shirt, preparing to invoke his *nganga* dedicated to Zarabanda, the warrior god, master of keys, chains, prisons, and everything metal—weapons, above all—and the patron saint of farmers, soldiers, and engineers. Each generation of Bantús had enriched the *prenda* with something to add power to it. His great-grandfather had contributed the machete blade with which he had decapitated Spaniards in hand-to-hand combat, and the saber of a lieutenant colonel who he had killed in fair fight. The saber still bore traces of blood from his great-grandfather, wounded several times by the superior fencing of his opponent before he managed, with a ferocious lunge, to chop off the hand holding the saber, and then his opponent's head with a second swing of the machete. From the country's wars of independence, there was also a five-shot Biscayan revolver, now rusted.

His grandfather had been able to gather some earth from a cemetery discovered during the excavations of a former settlement of escaped slaves in the province of Matanzas, and added it to the *nganga*. Thirty-caliber bullets had been the tribute of a second cousin, who had been with Fidel in the Sierra Maestra. There was also a front paw of a lion, brought by Lorenzo from his military mission in Africa. The most recent addition had been an integrated circuit, contributed by a godson who was an electronics engineer and a professor at the University of Havana.

The *Palero* grabbed the bottle of *chamba* and sprayed his first mouthful over Pedro's *nganga*, which was gathering strength under the influence of the older and wiser *prenda*. The daughter-*nganga* had not yet been fed the blood of a black cock and a black goat, so it wasn't ready for use. The *Palero* then lit a cigar and puffed on it several times before putting it, burning end first, into his mouth and blowing the smoke through the room. Then, from the depths of his diaphragm, he brought on a voice used only for these occasions, so deep it seemed to emerge from a grave. He moved his bare torso from side to side to accompany his invocations:

> *Buena noche, buena noche,*
> *Buena noche, mi Lucerito*

Then he raised his voice:

> *Buena noche, mi Zarabanda* (Good evening, my Zarabanda)
> *Yo te invoco pa' preguntarte* (I invoke you to ask)
> *Por un criollo llamado Mulo* (About a Creole named Mulo)
> *Ya se lo lleva el cabo Ronda* (Arrested by the policeman Ronda)
> *Que cosa pasa, mi Zarabanda?* (What's going on, my Zarabanda?)

The *Nasakó* took four pieces of coconut shell and rubbed them between his hands before throwing them.

"*Oyékun!*" the *Palero* shouted, opening his eyes wide in astonishment when he saw the four shells face down. In a deeper tone, he added: "A dead person wants to speak." He stared in fascination at the mute shells as if the spirit of the dead person were likely to rise from them at any moment, demanding its right to speak. The *Palero* meditated an instant. What dead person could appear at this moment wanting to say something? It had to be the *chino*! He had not been expecting the *chino*, but, on second thought, it made perfect sense that he was there to complain about something that was interfering with his work.

Lorenzo's stupor lasted only a moment before he again took charge of the situation, speaking aloud to the dead man. "Let's see what you want.

Let's see what the honorable dead person wants." There was a faint tremor in the *Palero's* voice and a certain reticence in his hands as he took up the shells again and threw them onto the mat. He was glad now that Adrián and Pedro weren't there.

Recalling the food that Chinese families bring to their deceased, Lorenzo asked: "Do you want food? Do you want food, *chino?*"

This time, three shells fell face down and one face up.

"*Okana!*" exclaimed the *Palero* without disguising his fear. In a whisper, he added: "The worst letter!" Lorenzo Bantú turned around slowly three times in place, pulling on his earlobes. The letter could only be interpreted as a flat "no" and, furthermore, as a forecast of disaster.

He threw the shells again rapidly, anxious to unveil the wishes of that *chino* who had appeared here in the very room of the *nganga*. He felt totally unprepared for this situation; his copybooks made no mention of anything like this.

"Flowers? Do you want flowers?"

Again, a single shell fell face up. The fateful letter *Okana* again said "no!" The *Palero* turned around three more times, pulling on his earlobes. The two consecutive bad omens convinced him that he was facing a disaster of great proportions, but he had no choice but to continue trying to ascertain the spirit's desires. In a hushed voice, he asked: "A cross? Do you want a cross?"

Two shells fell face up and two face down. "*Eyife!*" the *Palero* shouted joyously. The dead man had responded with the strongest possible "yes!" *Eyife*, the clearest letter of the coco oracle, did not allow any other interpretation. Everything was finally explained. The absence of a cross on the Chinaman's tomb was apparently crucial. And now that the cause was known, the remedy was simple. He had to send a message to Pedro to tell Adrián to put a cross on the *chino's* grave immediately. But that wasn't all. Lorenzo took a deep breath and sat down to rest—during the entire ceremony, he had been standing barefoot on the tips of his toes with his knees bent.

Now Lorenzo realized that the cross would not solve everything. No, because *Okana* had also announced great misfortunes due to bad work, offerings not made—all of which was to be punished.

"I have to move quickly."

Lorenzo Bantú had to speak as soon as possible with the *Mokongo* of his Abakuá chapter. The *Mokongo* would certainly go to see Mulo the moment he learned about his arrest—he prided himself on the fact that his chapter never turned its back on a brother in trouble. But he would also find out the reason for Mulo's arrest, and Mulo would not be able to lie to the *Mokongo*. That flank had to be covered immediately and was something he should have done long ago, as Adrián had advised him many times.

A TATTOO ON A SHOULDER

WHAT'S THE SIGNIFICANCE of this design?" Alvaro showed Jacinto a photo of a tattoo on the shoulder of a person whose face couldn't be seen.

"It looks like an Abakuá sign. What did this man do? Kill someone?"

"No, he's in a gang of thieves."

Jacinto looked puzzled. "The Abakuá are not thieves. They're violent people with their own moral code, but they're not thieves. Although, naturally, there may be exceptions. Could there be a mistake?"

"No. His shoe prints match perfectly with those found in the houses that were robbed. He's a tall mulatto, strong, with big feet."

"What's his name?"

"We haven't identified him yet. He was arrested yesterday and they have been drilling him since, but he hasn't said a single word, not even his name, and he wasn't carrying any identification. His fingerprints aren't registered. All we have so far is the tattoo and these photos. What do you think?"

The policeman held out frontal and profile photos of the arrested man. Jacinto looked at them briefly and returned them with an almost brusque movement. "I prefer not to get involved in anything related to the Abakuá. Why don't we talk about something else?"

"I've always been very curious about the Abakuá Secret Society."

The policeman had come by bicycle, with a backpack over his shoulders.

He had removed six bottles from his backpack and placed them on the dining room table. His clothing was soaked in perspiration, his hair wind-tossed, his beard tangled, and his face red from facing the sun during the whole trip. His hair had been cut and his beard trimmed. It was a Friday morning in a summer with little rainfall and intense heat, after a rainy winter—climatic changes caused by the *Niño* current, according to the meteorologists. For the country, it meant difficulties with the sugar harvest following a poor winter harvest of vegetables.

"Let's take a look at what you brought," Jacinto said, to change the subject. "Aguardiente Bocoy!" he exclaimed, picking up two of the bottles to look at them more closely. "And sunflower and olive oil! I haven't seen these in a long time!" Pleasure lit up his eyes as he slid his hand over the bottle of *aguardiente* like he was caressing a woman's breast.

"The last time I came, you had to milk the bottom of your barrel. And I brought some oil to fry some *tostones* so we don't have to drink on an empty stomach. All of this was bought thanks to an uncle in Miami—one of the first to flee from communism. Who'd have thought the day would come when I'd accept his dollars, and with pure pleasure!"

"These are hard times," agreed Jacinto, detecting a note of anger, frustration, and bitterness in his friend's voice.

"For years, I pretended that the family abroad didn't exist, as if they'd all died. Now it turns out that the dead are enjoying excellent health and are sending us dollars."

Jacinto called out to his homebody daughter and asked her to bring two glasses. Then he went out to the patio, protected from the sea winds by the boomerang shape of the house following the contour of the hill. He returned with a small bunch of plantains, perhaps a bit too green, that he carried to the kitchen together with the bottles of cooking oil.

Jacinto downed a half-glass of *aguardiente* in one gulp, his favorite way to begin a day. He glanced at the photographs of the man with the tattoo and remained silent. It was clear to Alvaro that Jacinto feared getting into something that would have negative consequences.

"Ah, I forgot to say that it seems this guy was one of the people who stole the body of the Chinaman. Tracks from a big foot were found in the cemetery after the robbery—the same boots, slightly more worn on the left than on the right."

Jacinto peered again at the photograph of the tattoo. The policeman smiled, thinking that now Jacinto would be curious whether the Chinese cadaver had been used for protection, as he had suggested several days earlier. An Abakuá implicated in the case added another mystery and a new draw for Jacinto. The hook with good bait had been thrown into the water and the hungry fish had seen it. Now everything depended on the patience of the fisherman.

Narelys arrived with the first plateful of *tostones*. "You brought the oil?" she asked. He felt uncomfortable. A mere three years earlier, no one would have dreamed of making a gift of cooking oil. The food shortage currently confronting the country made it a treasure. He nodded politely.

"The olive oil has a wonderful smell. I'm going to keep it for salads. Thank you so much." The young woman backed slowly out of the room as she spoke, a strange habit the policeman had noticed before.

"I don't know what I'm going to do with her," Jacinto said, shaking his head. "The poor thing is tormented by that behind that God gave her. She never wants to go anywhere because men make comments about her butt. The other two take after me, flat as an ironing board—and they'd give anything for an ass like that, if only for one day of partying."

"I brought her a gift," the policeman replied, taking a package out of his backpack and handing it to Jacinto.

"What is it?"

"It's a set of six matching pairs of panties. I hope I chose the right size."

"Give them to her yourself."

"No, I can't. This is a gift from me to you. I have no reason to give her anything, much less panties. I thought of perfume, but the girl in the shop said the best gift for any woman nowadays is panties. It wasn't my idea." The policeman's explanation sounded clumsy.

"Well, I don't use panties," Jacinto said.

The policeman served himself a half-glass of *aguardiente*. He downed it quickly to catch up with his host, who was waiting to serve himself again.

"Narelys!" Jacinto called.

When the young woman appeared at the door, her father handed her the package. "It's a gift for you," he said, nodding toward the policeman, who looked down to avoid the girl's eyes. Now he regretted the gift. The perfume would have been better.

Surprised, the girl was about to say something, but Jacinto had already moved on to another topic.

"What do you want to know about the Abakuá?"

"Never mind, if you prefer not to discuss it."

"I can tell you what I know I can reveal without getting myself into trouble. Plenty of books have been written about the *ñáñigos*—Abakuás—revealing most of their secrets. What's left to discover is mostly about the rituals of each chapter."

"I've read quite a bit about it, but that was some time ago. I'd like your impressions of that world. How do those people think? What do they do now?"

"Do you want to know how it started?"

SIKÁN

THE GAZE OF Suwo Maniantó Eroró, *Iyamba* of Efór, followed the figure of his daughter as she walked with an earthen jar on her head in the direction of the Oddán River. He was surprised to see her alone. The other girls must have gone on ahead. Sikán was too prudent to go alone to the river, he told himself.

Sikán reached the foot of the palm tree that marked the best spot for getting water, set the jar down, and rested. Her eyes were immediately drawn to the other shore, the land of Efík, where her husband, Mokongo, was *Efiméremo*, or chief. Tonight the moon would complete a full cycle since her arrival to visit her parents and other relatives. Tomorrow morning she would have to return home, reluctantly. The *Efí* looked down on the impoverished Efó. They shared the same language, the same songs, the same dances . . . The only thing that apparently separated Efík and Efór was the river, but in reality, an immense sea of distrust existed between the two tribes. "The people of Efór are lazy and cowardly; they only care about drinking palm wine," her husband had said one day without knowing that she was hearing his words.

What could she do to unite the two peoples? Her marriage to Mokongo had improved the tense situation, but she had not been able to fulfill her father's hopes to resolve the precarious situation of his destitute tribe. She felt guilty about this. Worse still, she felt that the enchantment her beauty had awakened in her husband was beginning to fade.

Sikán approached the river's edge with great caution due to the croco-diles that preyed on other thirsty creatures. Everything seemed too still and silent. She was already regretting her impulsive decision to come ahead of the other young women in order to have more time to prepare for her departure tomorrow morning. Hastily, she lifted the jar of water onto her head and started her return trip. She suddenly felt a violent thrashing about inside the jar, and then heard a deep voice that shouted, *"Ékue!"*

Frightened, Sikán dropped the jar. Inside was a resplendent silver fish. Sikán stared at it, stupefied. The fish spoke and told her that its name was Tánze. At that moment, she heard the swishing of weeds behind her. She tried to run, but the serpent Erukurubén Ñangobió wrapped itself around her feet and she saw an enormous crocodile looming close.

Suddenly, a warrior with his bow already drawn appeared at the foot of the palm tree. The arrow whistled past Sikán's ear and pierced the heart of the crocodile, killing it instantly. Advancing with a smile, the warrior took the serpent by the tail, unwound it in a single movement from Sikán's feet, and threw it far away, into the middle of the river. Still smiling, the warrior made a slight bow to the princess and vanished slowly in the brilliant morn-ing sunlight. Sikán recognized the *íreme*, protector of the river.

"Abasí Eribagandó mutu chekéndeque! (My god Eribagandó is great!)" Sikán exclaimed.

She ran back to the village to tell her father the astonishing news. The *Iyamba,* as the highest-ranking member of the tribe, prepared to confront the situation without losing the calmness and dignity of his high post.

"I'm going to speak to that fish."

With a firm expression on his face, Suwo Maniantó gathered his weapons and set out, followed at a safe distance by his daughter. Suwo showed great caution as he approached the palm tree. The jar was still on the ground where it had fallen. Drawing near, the *Iyamba* heard Tánze declare himself to be the incarnation of the supreme god Abasí, who had chosen the *Efó* as the people to receive his revelations.

Suwo made Sikán swear to him she would never reveal that secret to anyone. Suwo then sent his daughter to bring the rest of the important chiefs of the tribe, the *obones.* Once alone, he obeyed the command of

Tánze and walked into the river with the jar containing the fish on his head, thus consecrating himself to it. He then hid the receptacle in a cave, behind three stones.

Suwo Mantantó Eroró initiated the other *Efó* chiefs in the secret on the banks of the Oddán River at the foot of the palm tree that had witnessed the tremendous events. Thus was formed the first Abakuá chapter. From that moment on, they would march unswervingly united, sworn to keep the secret at risk of death.

The *Efó* progressed rapidly, bolstered by a mysterious force that encouraged them to undertake important enterprises. In just one hundred working days, the *Efó* managed to build up the banks of the river to the point at which it had overflowed every year, ruining crops, flooding villages, and drowning cattle. With the river under control, the *Efó* prospered, and Suwo's fame spread, making him very powerful.

After some time, Tánze died. With his skin and wood from the palm tree under which he had revealed himself to Sikán, a marvelous drum was made that reproduced the voice of the fish. Thus was born the *Ékue*, the most sacred of drums. But with time, its voice grew weaker and weaker as the skin of the fish deteriorated.

The increasing well-being of the *Efó* aroused the suspicions of the *Efí*. Each time that Sikán approached her husband while he was in conversation with the notables of the tribe, everyone stopped talking, hiding their plans for war against her people. Soon she realized what was happening, however, especially after warlords from distant regions began arriving with their troops. An enormous army was being assembled to smash the *Efó*.

Sikán thought and thought about what she could do to avert the disaster. Then she made a supreme decision, knowing that she was risking her own life. She spoke with her husband Mokongo and his father Chaviaka, sharing the marvelous events that had taken place on the banks of the Oddán. She told them about the silver fish with the deep voice and the speaking drum made from its skin, and she assured them that the strength of the *Efó* was a direct result of the revelations made to her father by the supreme god Abasí.

For seven days the chiefs of the *Efí* met under the presidency of

Efiméremo Mokongo to decide what action to take. Present were Chaviaka, Moni-Bonkó, Morúa Yansa, Mosongo, and Encademo. On the eighth day, the *Efí* army set off, determined to drag out the secret of *Ékue* from the *Efó*. They advanced both by foot and by river on hundreds of boats with all of their weapons drawn and their faces and bodies covered with war paint, pausing only to make offerings to their gods with songs and dances favoring victory.

"You must not allow this killing, Mokongo, *Efiméremo* of the *Efí*! Tánze said: '*He who raises his lance against his brother will be punished by Abasí*,'" Sikán warned her husband.

Mokongo looked sadly at his wife. In his eyes she saw no trace of hatred or vengefulness but only the look of a man weighed down with the responsibility of his people's destiny.

"When they become a little stronger, nothing will stop them; they will take our land, our cattle, our women," her husband answered with a desolate expression on his face.

"Consider, my beloved husband, that Tánze's words apply to them, as well."

Mokongo made no reply though he was clearly impressed by Sikán's words. Sadly, he picked up his weapons and joined the river of warriors already moving toward the lands of the *Efó*.

Sikán passed quickly to her people's side of the river, where she turned herself in to her father, confessing her betrayal of the secret of *Ékue* and alerting him to the approaching danger. With a heavy heart, the *Iyamba* Maniantó communicated Sikán's treason to the seven *Efori* chiefs. Unable to restrain his tears, the old chief asked the Great Council to confirm the death sentence on his beloved daughter for betrayal of their most precious secret. The *Isué*, charged with the responsibility and power of their religion, affirmed the terrible sentence in silence. The *Nasakó*—in charge of curing diseases, communicating with the dead, coming to an understanding with the gods, and divining the future—also confirmed the sanction. Ekueñón, caretaker of the *Ékue*, followed suit. The great hunter Enkríkamo, who led the expeditions into the heart of the dark jungle in search of food, closed his eyes and nodded slowly, then looked off into the distance, trying to erase the sweet vision of the lovely Sikán. He had never approved of her marriage into the tribe of the arrogant *Efí* in exchange for hunting territory and other lesser advantages. It had always seemed to him that the treasure surrendered was much greater, and besides, according to hierarchy, Sikán should have been *his* wife. Now, circumstances obliged him to take part in the decision to sacrifice her. In some dark and unexplained way, the blame rested with the accursed *Efí*. It was high time to stop so much conferring and discussion. It was necessary to attack them by surprise at night. He, with only a handful of brave men, could slip into the tent of the coward Mokongo and bring back his head and that of his conniving father, Chaviaka, strung up together on his lance, and place them on this side of the river so that the *Efí* army would behold their chiefs killed by the *íremes* guarding the river. When no one seconded his plan, Enkríkamo emitted a shout of impotence and stalked out of the Council without authorization.

The *Isunekue*, assistant to the *Iyamba*, was given instructions to advise the tribe of the time and place from which the warriors would set out toward the final battle against the *Efí*, far superior in number and weapons. Before departing for the battle, the *Nasakó* ordered Ekueñón to hide the *Ékue* in the cave Acueberofie, near a palm tree, and to cover the entrance with the stone Asoga Itiaba, as Abasí had instructed.

The rival forces lined up along the opposite riverbank. Before ordering his warriors to attack, Mokongo announced their demands. They only wanted to share the secret of the *Ékue*. Were they not, after all, brother tribes? They too had a right to the divine revelations. In exchange, they would offer clothing, music, and spices.

The *Efó* deliberated long and heatedly. Finally, they neared a decision to accept the demands, but added other requirements to the offers of the *Efí*. Some, led by Enkríkamo, wouldn't agree, but after long negotiations, the conditions were eventually accepted. The *Efí* were baptized in the river, with the palm tree as witness. The *Efó* chiefs worshiped the sacred jar, washed their face and feet in the river, and heard the dying voice of the *Ékue*. The *Iyamba* presented the sacred jar, washing it seven times and repeating a prayer seven times: "*Dibo bacandibo.*" It was thus that the great agreements were reached that definitively united the two brother tribes.

In spite of the happy end to the threat of war, still pending was the death sentence dictated by the *Iyamba* himself against Sikán and confirmed by the Council of *Obones*. The *Iyamba* walked in deep distress by the side of the river, trying to figure out what to do. At that moment, a commission of notables from the village, headed by Enkríkamo, approached him, asking him to call the Council together immediately to discuss a matter of great importance. Once the Council was in session, the great hunter said: "We owe this victory to Sikán. It was she who put fear and the desire to share *Ékue* into the hearts of the *Efí* chiefs. She saved our tribe. How can we repay her by sacrificing her precious life?"

The *obones* were deeply perplexed by the problem now facing them. They debated the matter for three consecutive days without finding a solution. Then it was proposed that the *Iyamba* consult the dying voice of Tánze. The ancient chief of the *Efó* returned to the Oddán and, under the shade of the palm tree that had witnessed the miracle of Tánze, he cut a stalk of riverweed. Proceeding to the cave where the *Ékue* remained, he opened a gash in his arm and covered the stalk with his blood, which he then rubbed against the skin of the fish until he heard the sacred voice for the last time. Tánze revealed to him that the next sacred object could only be made with the skin of Sikán. The old father felt his heart falter. Then, with great effort, he rose and returned to the village.

Sikán's execution was announced by the Embákara under the *ceiba*. The father took his daughter to the fateful place and embraced her, sobbing.

"Father, do your duty. I will die happy because I did mine," Sikán said firmly, moving toward her executioner.

"You will live on as the voice of the *Ékue*; that is the will of Tánze," Suwo told his daughter just before her throat was cut.

Taking Sikán's head by the hair, the *Nasakó* rubbed her blood on the most sacred of drums. A new sacred drum was then made from the skin of the young princess. From the top of the palm tree, the bird Enkerepe Endobio flew off to tell others of Sikán's martyrdom.

It was thus that religious and political unity were achieved among the Carabalí, the four tribes that lived on the banks of the Calabar river: The people of Efór, Efík, Uró, and Bibí became a single nation.

ABAKUÁ

BUT THE MOST incredible thing is that this legend, woven around something that happened centuries ago in Africa, is very much alive in Cuba at the threshold of the twenty-first century," Jacinto explained. "You should see it. The Abakuá repeat the whole thing in their ceremonies. The *íreme* Aberiñán holds the leg of the sacred goat when they're going to sacrifice it, just like the first Aberiñán. The *Mokongo* of any chapter has to speak in Carabalí and repeat the words of Sikán's father. Even today, the words that the two tribes shouted to each other across the river are repeated in every ceremony: '*Efí focandó agoropá? Mo mi afocandó agoropá.* Do you agree? Yes, we agree.' It's been this way for two hundred years, since the first Cuban Abakuá chapter was founded in Regla."

As usual, Jacinto had delved into the depths of his knowledge at the slightest provocation from his friend. Jacinto attacked the remaining *tostones* and took a short sip of *aguardiente* before continuing. "You know, I've thought a great deal about Sikán, and I've tried to put myself in her place to figure out why she did what she did, and I think I've figured it out."

"What do you think?"

"James Frazer, in the prologue to his magnificent work, *The Golden Bough*, affirms that the fear of death has been the most powerful force in the inception of primitive religions. The human mind, even today, refuses to accept death as the end of everything. Religions have been denying it since the dawn of civilization. So it's natural that the primitive mind, one that believes every animal and every thing that exists has its own animus, considers that the dead, suddenly freed from all of the limitations of the living body, acquire higher powers. A man who has done extraordinary things in his lifetime or held a social position much higher than the rest must have still greater powers after death; that's the conclusion reached by magical logic. The *Regla de Osha* recognizes this in the phrase, 'The dead man makes the *orisha*,' and all or many of the *orishas* were kings, warriors, or notable people."

Jacinto paused again to eat another *tostón* and take a sip of *aguardiente*. "In my opinion," he said, gesturing with a *tostón*, "the legend of Sikán's death is based on something that really happened. Sikán was chosen by Abasí to receive Tánze. But since her actions were determined by Abasí, treason against her tribe was impossible. Otherwise, the magical logic would have been broken. That point always bothered me when I read the story or heard it told. I think the key to justifying Sikán's death must be sought in the greater meaning of the legend. She, the one chosen to receive Tánze, was the one who convinced the *Efí* to accept the *Efó* as brothers. It was her skin that was chosen by Abasí to give life to the new sacred drum. And she was chosen to die at the hands of those who loved her most. The significance of her death has to lie in the power that she acquired *after* death, which enabled her to protect her people eternally. And the greatest irony of all lies in the fact that a woman, Sikán, was the beginning and the center of the mystery of the world's most exclusively male society!

"The Abakuá Secret Society is essentially a mutual-aid group with a history of terrible internal violence. For a long time, they only admitted blacks, until the middle of the nineteenth century, when Andrés Petit, the *Isué* of the Bakoko chapter, founded the first *plante* to which whites were accepted. He was labeled a traitor and accused of selling the secret to whites for eighty ounces of gold. But, in fact, he used the money to free several Abakuá slaves. Andrés Petit was one of the most notable intellectuals of the nineteenth century in Cuba, a deeply religious man. He introduced whites because he thought it was the best way to preserve the Society, subject at that time to intense persecution by the colonial authorities. Without whites, the Society would undoubtedly have disappeared.

"For many years, and until recently, the word *ñáñigo*, which means Abakuá, sowed terror in the hearts of mothers because it was said that they stole children to sacrifice them in their fiestas and witchcraft."

The bottle of *aguardiente* suffered another attack with another plate of *tostones*. This time, Narelys entered with an embarrassed smile but avoided looking in the direction of the policeman, who, although attentive to the stories of Jacinto, followed the young woman out of the corner of his eye.

"When I was a boy, an Abakuá who lived on my block committed suicide. In that era, poor people held wakes for their family deaths in their homes or in the houses of neighbors. Funeral parlors were only for the well-to-do. At midnight, the Abakuás asked everyone to leave the house so that they could say farewell to their brother in their own way. I hid behind a door to see what was going to happen. Even then, I was interested in these things. They took the cadaver out of the coffin and tied him, standing up, to one of the posts in the patio, and all of the *moninas* lined up and each one slapped him across the face for having committed suicide! But that was a long time ago.

"No one can look at the ass of an Abakuá, not even his wife. And they can't wear those so-called athletic shorts because they look too much like women's underwear. They wear a kind of shorts with legs, and they don't take them off even to have sex. Neither can they wear any jewelry or clothing used by women. Of course, there's no such thing as a gay Abakuá."

They ate a late lunch. The main dish was hake, cooked with olive oil by Narelys. The fish was served with browned rice, a favorite of the policeman, and another dish of fried plantains. Jacinto continued talking about his favorite subject, without slowing his consumption of *aguardiente* in order not to lose the effect already achieved.

"Many of the practices of the Abakuá Secret Society mimic those of the Carabalí people, who were different in many respects from the other ethnic groups brought to Cuba as slaves. A traveler to Cuba in the nineteenth century described them as 'industrious, very hard-working, and thrifty, but they pardon no offenses.'"

Jacinto spoke of the contribution of the Abakuá to the island's carnival, both the dances and music. Then he rose to get his guitar. At first the policeman was delighted, but the slow ballads and Jacinto's rasping, monotonous voice made him sleepy. He managed to keep his eyes open until, finally, it was his host who fell asleep. The policeman and Narelys carried her father to his room. Upon removing his pants, they found that Jacinto was not wearing any underwear.

"As you can see, he's not an Abakuá," Narelys said with a mischievous laugh. During the struggle to take off his pants, Jacinto awoke several times and muttered random bits of songs until he fell back to sleep, embracing the guitar as if it were a woman.

It was growing dark and the policeman began a retreat back to the library where he slept when he stayed overnight. He walked carefully, holding onto anything at hand to maintain his balance. "You know, Narelys, this is the magic hour. The sun is already down but its light lingers on. During these months, night waits a long time before taking over, and the day no longer belongs to anyone, not even to the sun or the shadows of the night. This is the hour when all kinds of magic things happen, if you know how to look for them. See down there how quiet the bay is, and how everything that moves does so in slow motion? Wherever you look, if you really want it, a light appears. And all of that is there, at the reach of your hand. At this hour, things talk amongst themselves; listen to the siren from the little harbor pilot's launch, scolding the ship it's going to guide in."

Narelys laughed and shook his arm. "What crazy ideas you have! You're drunk, too!"

The policeman stared at her from top to bottom as if seeing her for the first time. She was very beautiful, he told himself, but not pretty. She had an incredible sexuality and, at the same time, a thoroughly innocent heart . . . quiet, but volatile. Over the years, the policeman had seen her maturing, along with her sisters, all of them reared by old and ugly women. Jacinto never spoke about the mothers of his daughters, and each time the matter arose, he changed the subject. The policeman, following deeply instilled principles of conduct, never asked about Jacinto's family. Jacinto was a friend, not a case.

Good sense told the policeman that he should avoid Narelys. That girl-woman could change his life in one second. But instinct was urging him to act otherwise, to unbutton her housecoat and take the nipples of her strong, round breasts into his mouth while his hands slid down to caress those powerful buttocks. An almost irresistible force tempted him to make love to her on the floor, with the bay and the seawall in the background and that blessed, ever-present breeze blowing over them.

"Not for lack of desire, my God!" he shouted, throwing his arms into the air. With that movement, he lost his balance and stumbled against a table in the hall.

"You see? You don't know what you're saying. You're very drunk. Come on, I'll help you walk."

The policeman let her help him. It was pleasurable to feel that arm across his chest, the contact with that firm breast, unhindered by a bra, pressed against his ribs, and that overwhelming female scent that he hadn't had so close for years.

They entered the library. The policeman freed himself and sat down on the cot. He removed his shoes and socks and felt the blissful coolness of the floor tiles against the soles of his feet. He pulled on his belt, which remained caught stubbornly on his trouser loops. Narelys observed him mockingly.

"I always sleep with my clothes on. Didn't you know that? A good policeman always sleeps dressed in case of an emergency in the middle of the night. Can you imagine a policeman in his underwear running down the street after a thief?"

"Do you want to see something?"

"What?"

"Something." Narelys suddenly let her housecoat fall and stood before him wearing only a pair of red panties. She made a slow turn. "How do they look on me?"

HE LISTENED RESPECTFULLY for three hours without the slightest indication of his feelings about the case. Each man expressed his own opinions, taking care not to offend any of the *moninas* because the reaction of the *Mokongo* could be explosive. The offender would be immediately expelled from the session, his rights suspended for six months or more. The *Mokongo* insisted on order.

His practice had been honed over twenty-five years of governing the Itiamo Beconsí Abakuá chapter. He had learned that people *always* want to express their opinion. It was essential that they do so in the presence of others, calmly, respectfully. Only thus were resentments and the isolation of the weak and the arrogant obviated and internal divisions, the worst of all poisons, avoided. The preceding head had brought on his own self-destruction by tolerating disputes among the members, many of them winding to conclusions at knifepoint. The new *Mokongo* had been chosen for his reputation as a strong and able arbiter at the Regla docks, where he had to deal with men from the coast, from inland, and from the open sea.

"Gattorno did what he had to do. He slit the ass of a troublemaker who tried to dance with his woman at a party; he served his time in the tank and came out with his own ass intact and fought in Angola. The Gato is a good worker, there's no doubt about that. There's no doubt that here, in the *plante*, he's always been a good *monina*."

The *Mokongo* cleared his throat. He paused to ascertain the consensus in the eyes of those present. Then he stood up to issue his judgement: "It is also clear that the Gato has not complied with his duties as a son. Is this the case?"

The *Mokongo* again let his eyes rove over those present. He made sure that each person assented with a nod.

"Then what the hell! If he's not a good son, the Abakuá rules are clear! Marcelo Gattorno cannot continue being a member of this chapter. No sir, those are the rules of this game, and they will be respected here as long as I'm in charge."

The *Mokongo* declared the session closed.

The *Nasakó* observed the *Mokongo*, who was preparing for consultations by the *Isué* and the *Empegó*, and doubted that this was the best moment to approach him. They had agreed that morning to meet after the trial, but he had estimated three hours of discussion, and it had taken several more. During the trial, differences of opinion had been evident between the old guard, those in favor of a strict orthodoxy, and the younger members, who were now the majority—even at the top—in favor of broader interpretations and of taking into account the particular conditions of each case. Without openly defying the old guard that night, the younger members had ceded ground only inch by inch, making strong arguments with their concessions, helped along by their higher level of education.

In the end, the *Mokongo* had imposed the dictates of the hardcore conservatives, employing his enormous prestige and personal authority, since the case was not an easy one. Gattorno's father was a hopeless alcoholic and his mother an uneducated woman who unburdened her problems, including the misfortune of having married Arcadio Gattorno, onto her children by beating them mercilessly . . . never showing signs of anything that resembled love.

Lorenzo Bantú figured that the *Mokongo* would be in no mood for more discussion after the strong showing from the young group. In truth, more than affirming his power, the *Mokongo's* decision had weakened it. Neither was the hour opportune, since it was already one-thirty in the morning and the *Mokongo*, who was more than seventy years old although he appeared younger, would have to get up at five-thirty to work at the docks. Over time, the *Mokongo* had become a difficult man to approach even in the most favorable of circumstances. But it was essential to talk with him immediately and negotiate some kind of agreement. If the *Mokongo* blocked their plan, everything would be lost. Adrián had insisted that the Abakuá chief be consulted as soon as possible, and the *Nasakó* had waited, perhaps too long.

"Shall we talk?" the *Mokongo* asked, appearing suddenly beside the wavering *Nasakó*.

"If you prefer, we can leave it until tomorrow."

"We agreed to meet after the trial. Isn't that what you asked? If you need to get home early or have another matter more important than your commitment with me, then we can leave it for another day. As far as I'm concerned, there's no problem. I have to leave for work around six, but between now and then, I think there's plenty of time to talk."

The *Nasakó* scratched his head. Things were getting off to a bad start.

"No, I don't have a problem."

"Let's go, then. I invite you to have a drink."

The *Mokongo* set off without waiting for a reply. He was curious about the matter raised by the *Nasakó* with so much mystery that morning on the telephone. For a long time now, he had wanted an opportunity to speak privately with the *Palero* to see if he could, finally, decipher him. After all his years in the *plante*, he was still an enigma. Many times he had judged him in one way or another, and each time he had been mistaken. He had been on the verge of vetoing his membership ten years before; he had not appreciated their first conversation. It had seemed to him that the young Bantú had all of the defects of the new generation without any of its virtues. Nonetheless, the old Abakuá nucleus had backed him one hundred percent. How could they reject the grandson of Don Lorenzo Bantú, one of the founders of the chapter, its first *Nasakó*? That would have violated unwritten but sacred principles. The following years had proved them right. Lorenzo lined up invariably beside the old guard and was always a force of equilibrium and an example for the new members; his conduct had been impeccable.

Years later, various influential members began to spread the same message: Lorenzo Bantú had the necessary qualities to become the next *Mokongo*. Lorenzo was one of the *pure ones* and he had an important influence on the new generation, young men who could be difficult to deal with because they didn't seem to respect tradition. Their reason for becoming Abakuás was often merely to flout their manhood.

The *Mokongo*, too, had begun to consider Lorenzo a possible successor. Why not? There were other candidates, including university-trained professionals with a certain social position in the city who would contribute prestige to the organization. But Lorenzo Bantú's advantage over them was the authority that emanated from his gigantic size, his serious and silent character, and his firm opinions, right or wrong. On the other hand, Lorenzo earned his living as a *Palero* and this was not viewed charitably by the more cultured members of the chapter who were always eager to erase the old *ñañigo* image.

The authorities would not be supportive, either. This was not a critical issue, but it was a strike against Lorenzo. When he was elected *Nasakó* of the chapter, the local police chief had come to see the *Mokongo* to tell him that at saints' fiestas at the Bantú home, overpriced beer and rum were sold, and sometimes even marijuana. "What does this have to do with me?" he had answered, to make it clear that he wasn't a man who could be pressured.

It annoyed him that the police wanted to control everything, even decisions about the top posts in a *potencia*. But the message was clear: They had their eyes on the Bantú and he, as the *Mokongo*, had to take this into account. Thus he abandoned the idea of Lorenzo as a successor, and he had let everyone know his opinion. To his surprise, Lorenzo was the first to accept the decision. On more than one occasion, he had affirmed in public that the next *Mokongo* had to be a man of culture, respected by the authorities. The *Mokongo* was greatly surprised by this retreat. He had suspected that the *Nasakó* was driving the campaign to promote himself. If the *Nasakó* wasn't creating a smoke screen, he really was a man worth his weight in gold. The young Bantú had always made him uncomfortable.

For some time now, Lorenzo had been involved in other activities. He had managed to recruit almost all of his godsons of *Palo Monte* into the *plante*, which gave him a greater influence in the *potencia*. He continued to court the old Abakuá nucleus, slowly thinning its ranks with the passing of aged members. The *Mokongo*, meanwhile, once again began to fear that Lorenzo was manipulating the new forces, seeking power and a change in policies; he reminded him of a *majá*, always gliding silently, always elusive. Tonight, for the first time, he would have a serious conversation with Lorenzo and find out, once and for all, what his game was.

They walked several blocks in silence. Then, as if continuing a conversation already begun, the *Mokongo* said: "Let's go to my house. It will do me good to have a drink and good conversation before going to bed. Have you ever heard so much useless discussion about something so clear-cut? 'Is he a bad son? Yes or no?' If he's a bad son, he can't be an Abakuá. In life, you have to have well-defined principles and guide yourself by them at all times. I always remember a Western movie called *Bewitched Town*. The sheriff was a real tough guy, and he had a rule that he never broke: If someone approached him with a revolver, he shot to kill. That's the way principles have to be. There's no other way to live in this world."

They walked another block in silence along a street lined with houses side by side on the sidewalk, in contrast to the preceding blocks, in which the houses had been set farther back from the street and had broad porches with mosaic floors, giving off an air of splendor that time had not yet totally erased.

The *Mokongo* opened the door of his modest home with a key attached to a thin chain that he had pulled from a small pocket in his pants. A heavyset woman was asleep with her head fallen backward before a blank television screen flashing small dots and hissing with white noise. The *Mokongo* cleared his throat and the woman immediately awakened, her round face producing a smile that displayed small and even white teeth.

"I fell asleep like an idiot with the TV on, wasting electricity." She turned it off hastily.

"Lorenzo, this is my wife, Marta."

The *Nasakó* noted the woman's faint moustache as they shook hands. She was much younger than the *Mokongo*; her wavy hair was long and black, her skin the color of coal, but her perfectly round face and slow movements made her seem older. The *Mokongo*, in contrast, was thin and agile, carried himself erect, and showed his age only in the numerous wrinkles that covered his face.

He invited the *Nasakó* to sit in one of the mahogany rocking chairs, remnants of the original living room furniture. The *Mokongo*'s wife withdrew, her leather slippers slapping against the tiled floor the length of the long hall leading to the rear of the house.

The *Mokongo*'s thoughts were still occupied with the evening's debate. "I'm worried about the new generation. They've grown up without knowing what it is to work. The Revolution made the mistake of giving them everything without their knowing where it came from. When they want something, they demand it as if they have a right to it. Otherwise, they steal it. Principles mean nothing to them . . . I don't know what's going to become of this country."

The *Nasakó* wasn't entirely in agreement, but said nothing. He was anxious to divert the conversation to other subjects.

The wife returned, carrying a tray with a bottle of rum, two glasses, two small plates, a dish of toasted peanuts, a bowl of ice cubes, and a pair of tongs. It was evident that she enjoyed attending to visitors and showing off her chinaware, probably kept in a glass-fronted sideboard for special occasions only.

"Take the ice away. How many times have I told you that men drink rum straight? It's very late, and you have to get up at five to prepare my breakfast. So go ahead. Are there more peanuts?"

The woman shook her head no as she picked up the ice cubes and tongs and left the room.

The *Mokongo* served rum into the two glasses.

"This rum is made by one of my daughters, a chemical engineer. You don't know how much money we save that way. I have two oak barrels that I got years ago in Santiago from a closed-down rum factory. How silly to close a rum factory in Cuba!" The *Mokongo* sipped his drink.

The moment had arrived. The *Nasakó* gulped down a long swallow. "For years," he began, "I've been thinking about an idea of yours."

The *Mokongo* raised his eyebrows. The *Nasakó* and Adrián had agreed that the key to their success was to compromise the *Mokongo* at the very beginning of the conversation.

"You've always said that we have to unify the Abakuá. Nowadays, every chapter is a world apart. Many *moninas* dishonor the name. Although the laws of the Society are the same for everybody, each chapter does as it likes."

"I would do anything to see that unity. I've spent years working in that direction, but I haven't figured out how to achieve it," the *Mokongo* admitted.

"Suppose that we relocated our *potencia* to an isolated place where no one from outside could watch us, but that is still near the town?"

"That would be excellent."

"We could make an Abakuá social circle, a restaurant where we can take our families and hold fiestas."

The *Mokongo* served more rum into the glasses, but Lorenzo felt that his attention was waning. He was not an imaginative person. Dreaming was not his style.

"We can let other *plantes* enter little by little, providing that they accept our rules and direction. Then we will create an Abakuá headquarters. You, of course, would be the supreme chief . . ."

The *Mokongo* suppressed a yawn. He began eating some of the peanuts, thinking that it was probably time to go to bed. The conversation was losing interest for him.

"I practically have my hands on the place, a fifteen-acre farm just outside the city on the way to the refinery. It's a good, big house for a social club with a restaurant and everything. There are old warehouses for the *cufones* of all the different chapters." The *Nasakó* stopped speaking. He helped himself to more rum, scooped a handful of peanuts, and began eating them quickly.

"And how are you going to get hold of all of that?"

"A godson is willing to donate it to the Society within eight months or so—maximum, a year."

The *Mokongo* remained silent, thinking. This sounded far too good to be true. There must be a trick somewhere in the *Nasakó's* proposal. "And why does this man want to give it all away?"

Adrián and Lorenzo had anticipated this question.

"The price is that I help him to set up a business by supplying him with reliable men who know how to keep a secret."

The *Nasakó* paused to observe the *Mokongo's* reaction, but saw only a wrinkled countenance and two glassy, opaque, and dead-looking eyes that told him nothing. Then he added carefully: "I've already done my part. The business is moving along very well. I'm not directly involved in it, nor would you be."

A long silence followed. The *Mokongo* went on sipping his rum and eating peanuts, one by one, while he gazed sidelong at Lorenzo Bantú. All this time, he had underestimated him. All this time, the man had been working silently, in the shadows.

The *Mokongo* stopped the rocking of Lorenzo's chair with the sole of his shoe and looked directly into his eyes. His left hand grasped the *Nasaskó's* wrist firmly. "And what do you get out of all of this?"

"Nothing. I'm not interested in filling my pockets."

"Answer my question. What do you get out of it?"

The *Nasakó* had never actually asked himself this question. He pulled his hand from the old man's grip, sustained his gaze, and answered without thinking. "To be somebody. *Coño*, to be somebody in this country!"

The *Mokongo* remained perfectly silent.

Then it was the *Nasakó* who blocked the rocking of the other man's chair. He grabbed his wrist and squeezed it as he spoke passionately. "We'll eliminate the weak ones. We'll create an army of warriors. Abakuá warriors would never utter a word if caught by the police. No one knows what's going to happen here. With this force at hand—you, as the supreme *Mokongo* and I, as the supreme *Nasakó*—they'll have to respect our *berocos* wherever we go. What do you think of your idea?"

THE MAJÁ

THE NASAKÓ HAD to make an enormous effort to open his eyes. The light entering from under the door burned his pupils like the slash of a razor blade. His mouth was filled with a thick phlegm and his heartbeat felt too slow. Was he dying? He grabbed the iron bars of his bed with both hands, pulling himself up, but his head felt like a huge ball of lead. Spasms of retching followed one after another, coming in waves from the depths of his innards like electroshocks, bringing up a bitter, green, sticky substance that smelled of acid weed.

He was left feeling empty and weak. He tried to decipher the meaning of several purple globs in the yellowish-green vomit on his sheet. Even more worrisome was the slowing beat of his heart. He tried to take his own pulse but was unable to find it. Then he attempted to call out for help, but no words came from his mouth. He shifted his gaze from the bilious liquid and looked toward the ceiling.

Why hadn't he thought of it before? This situation could be resolved with an appeal to the spirits of his ancestors. Their bones were up there, almost at hand's reach, and the spirit of the first Bantú was in the *nganga* in the next room. But in his confusion, he couldn't remember an appropriate invocation. He would have to plead in silence, in ordinary language but with great fervor, not to be abandoned now, precisely when he had so many important things to do. He tried to make his thoughts reach the *nganga* but felt that his message was not being received.

Then the chills and trembling started. What was happening to him? Was blood still circulating in his body? Then he recalled the afternoons in Africa when malaria had produced this same effect: the cold freezing him to the marrow.

The bed began to sway. He reached his arms down to the floor and the bed stopped moving, but the room immediately began to whirl faster and faster . . . Then he was no longer in the bed but sitting on the floor, watching everything turn.

The grandfather raised himself slightly, as if wanting to say something. He maintained an equilibrium for a moment, and fell back. Then he merely moved his fingers, calling him, calling him. He drew near slowly, controlling his fear. The grandfather looked at him with his ratlike eyes, dull and sunken now inside two great black holes, reminding him of the time that his sister made him look down into a deep well. Far below, he had seen a small light, shining, trembling, alive, at the bottom of the unfathomable darkness. That abyss had terrorized his dreams for years.

The old man tried to smile, and Lorenzo understood that he wanted to dispel his fear. The dying grandfather spoke in a rasping but strong voice, almost without moving his lips: "Careful . . . careful . . . She is bad, very bad."

"Who's bad, Grandpa? Who?"

"She's bad. Can't you hear her listening there behind the door?"

Lorenzo Bantú opened his eyes to avoid the vision of his grandfather in his agony. Everyone in the neighborhood said that his grandfather's work had turned against him, that the old man was paying for all the bad things he had done in his life, because the *Tatandi* Lorenzo Bantú had killed as well as cured, depending on the wishes of his clients.

It was strange that not a single cock had crowed all night. Why was everything so quiet? Was it time for the *majá* to come out? Why hadn't he thought of that? The *majá* would carry his message and explain everything up there in the secret room. Lorenzo began to laugh. What a fool he was! Giving so much importance to something with such a simple solution!

In the darkest and most quiet stretch of the night, the *majá* always emerged from the secret room to hunt in the woods beyond the patio, returning before sunrise. He heard it come out in his sleep. On its return, it always awakened him as it slithered over the tumbled sheets or over his face. It brought with it a smell of the forest; of cold rain and early-morning dew; of giant trees and damp weeds; of brilliantly red flowers; of dark, running water and the fish swimming in it; of humid, black earth covered with decomposing leaves and a faint smell of mold; of fresh air and night birds. These odors blessed the room and produced a freshness in the summer and warmth in the cold nights of February. The presence of the *majá* scared away rats and mice that had not dared to nest in any part of the house since the grandfather had died.

This night, the serpent delayed a long while before coming out. Perhaps it realized that he was ill and was trying to figure out what to do. Unlike other nights, it slid quickly down the iron bar of the bed to the cement floor and paused under the bed. Then, very slowly, it moved toward the door, avoiding the pools of vomit. Suddenly, the *majá* emitted a whistle, slithered swiftly back up through a small hole in one of the corners of the fake ceiling, and disappeared from sight.

Puzzled, Lorenzo looked toward the door and immediately saw what he most feared: the shadow of his sister's feet in the light under the door. Exasperated, he released his grip on the iron bars of the bed and let his heavy head drop onto the pillow. He imagined her standing there with her ear pressed to the door. He began to laugh, remembering that he had installed an extra lock on his door after he caught her spying on the work he was doing for Adrián. What would she do now?

Suddenly the door opened, and the silhouette of his sister was sharp against the light from the dining room. How did she get in?

"What's wrong? Do you feel ill, *hermanito*?"

Lorenzo wanted to reply, but the only sound from his throat was a strange croak, like the moo of a calf. His sister continued to look at him. She was dressed, he saw, in blue, the color of Yemayá. But as a godchild of Yewá, his sister always wore white clothing and shoes, with some detail in rose. Why the change?

Her voice was kind, without a trace of malice. But that was normal—she never showed what she was thinking. She was capable of driving a knife into one's back with one hand while offering a rich cup of coffee with the other. She never lost control before other people, never said a vulgar word, never did anything even remotely in bad taste. If a conversation became disagreeable in any way, she simply left the room; she did not allow anyone to speak badly of others in her presence.

"Are you nauseous? Do you have a headache or a fever?"

This time, he managed to answer yes to each of her questions with a nod. This was followed by a long silence filled only with that strange look from his sister's only seeing eye. Now, added to his trembling from the cold, his teeth began to chatter from fear, producing a ridiculous clicking sound.

"You've been caught, Lorenzo Bantú! You've been caught and you don't know it."

Her voice had become deep and masculine, as if coming from another person. Just like the voice of his grandfather in his agony! He felt himself trembling from head to foot, with a mortal cold invading his soul. He was dying. She stood looking at him without speaking. This time the silence seemed to have no end. Or was it that time had stopped for him?

"My godmother Margarita confirmed what I was already sure of." Now her tone of voice was again sweet and conciliatory.

Another long pause.

"An evil dead person has stolen your head, Lorenzo. You no longer know what you're doing." She made a gesture of infinite tenderness with her hands.

More silence.

"That's why you stuffed yourself with shrimp last night, knowing that this food is prohibited for you. I never let you touch it. He made you eat it. Do you realize that?"

The *Santera* walked to the side of the bed and bent over the helpless and trembling heap of her brother's body. In a low, honeyed tone, as if speaking to a child, she continued: "Don't you realize that the spirit of a dead person will make you do things that are harmful to you until he destroys you? That's how they are."

"Get out!" Lorenzo shouted in a hoarse, rasping voice that even he didn't recognize.

She lurched back as if frightened. Then she turned and left the room, closing the door quickly behind her, but remained on the other side, listening.

She heard the voice of another person she knew well speaking to her brother. "*You see? I told you. She's bad, very bad.*"

The total self-assurance suddenly abandoned her. The *Santera* leaned against the wall to recover her strength. There was no doubt, her brother was possessed by the spirit of their grandfather. She had heard them speaking moments before entering the room, and now she again heard their voices inside. She had to decide quickly what to do. Perhaps she would have no choice but to apply the most radical solution: *Muerto el perro se acabó la rabia*—Dead dogs don't transmit rabies.

PEDRO

LEAPING OVER THE WIRE fence, Pedro headed for the back door, brushing aside the two women who, initially surprised and frightened, tried to block his path but ended up following him, screaming like hens defending their nest. He dashed into the dining room, where the *Santera* was seated, cleaning rice. The two women also entered, stammering excuses for not having stopped the intruder.

Sweating profusely and panting, his hair tousled and his eyes red from lack of sleep, he sat down on one of the dining room stools and demanded to see Lorenzo Bantú at once.

Without slowing her work with the rice, the *Santera* replied in a low voice that Lorenzo was ill and could not be seen. In the same low, sweet tone, she told the women to return to their places; she would attend to the visitor. "It isn't your fault. When there is no man in the house to defend it, these things happen. Everyone knows that Lorenzo is in bed, helpless."

Pedro realized at once that his behavior could bring him serious problems with the *Nasakó* and, above all, with his Abakuá chapter, if the women complained about his aggressive actions. He had entered in such a belligerent way because Lorenzo Bantú's sister wasn't opening the front door for anyone and wouldn't admit anyone from the rear of the house, either. To avoid a run-in with the police, Pedro had been moving around the neighborhood through the labyrinth of interconnected patios. But common sense now counseled him to control his tone of voice and change the expression on his face to explain his urgency. The *Santera* listened in silence as she continued to clean the rice.

At the end of the visitor's explanation, a pleasant expression passed over the *Santera's* face. She looked at Pedro and repeated that her brother was indisposed. What could she do? She could not call him every time someone wanted to see him—unless, of course, it was of great importance. What was so important?

Pedro began to show signs of impatience. A raging violence was fermenting inside him with each new word from the *Santera*, with that oversweet, candied tone, as if he were a spoiled child refusing his food. What could be wrong with Lorenzo? If he were seriously ill, he would be in a hospital by now. Wasn't it enough that he had given his word of honor that it was a matter of urgent concern to the *Nasakó*? This was why he hated to deal with women; they always messed everything up, making the simplest things difficult.

With each progressive thought, Pedro's anger grew more intense, convinced that he was the victim of a malignant trap laid by the *Santera*. He stared with hatred into her seeing eye as he began to gesticulate violently, his fists closed, his face livid, his carotid veins inflamed, his voice labored.

She measured her opponent and opted for a tactical retreat. Pedro was a primitive person, capable of anything in the heat of anger. He had killed a man with his bare hands many years before and, even now, many of his arguments ended in bloodshed so that he was often in jail. His attacks of blind violence inspired respect in everyone. Even the Abakuá avoided disagreements with him. Besides, she reminded herself, Pedro worked with Adrián. She had seen them come together for their sessions with Lorenzo. She would do well, she told herself, to stay on good terms with the man and try to get as much information from him as possible.

"All right, Pedrito," she conceded with a smile that seemed friendly and sincere. "I'm going to make an exception in your case, but only for a little while. Promise me first that you won't tell anyone. Otherwise, the house will be filled with people. Come, follow me, and you'll see that Lorenzo's in no shape to receive anyone. I wouldn't do this for anyone but you."

* * *

Pedro was unsettled by the look of horror in the *Nasakó's* eyes, by the incessant movement of his head from side to side and the complaints issuing from his throat that sounded like the squeaking of mice. The *Nasakó* seemed to want to tell him something, but kept stopping and laying back with his mouth open, looking up at the ceiling.

"Godfather, the dead man has his cross now."

The *Nasakó* opened his eyes wider, this time staring at the buckle of Pedro's belt.

"Did you hear me, godfather? It's as pretty as can be. Adrián has a gift for these things. It looks just like the ones in the *chino* boneyard . . . Ah, I was forgettin' . . . Adrián says that Mulo will be out on bail in just a few days, but he don't want you or me to see him when he comes out. He's goin' to give him a vacation until he cools off."

Lorenzo seemed stupefied. Pedro raised his voice a little louder and repeated his message. The *Santera* drew near to the visitor, cautioning him to speak a little lower. Very worried, Pedro went on speaking to him: "I came to see you about the *ebbó* that you told me on the phone I had to do urgently."

Pedro gave up. The *Nasakó* was not receiving his messages, and even if he understood, he was in no condition to do anything about them.

"This man is really fucked up!" Pedro exclaimed, turning to the sister.

The woman laughed. "No. It's only indigestion. All men are cowards when it's their turn to be ill."

The patient suddenly freed a hand from under the sheet and grabbed Pedro by the shirt, pulling him down to say something into his ear. Pedro listened, then, straightening, remained for a few seconds looking back and forth, astonished, from the *Nasakó* to his sister.

"Has a doctor seen you? Do you want me to bring one?"

Lorenzo nodded weakly.

"I'll be right back."

Pedro dashed out without waiting for the sister's approval and returned a half-hour later. The doctor accompanying him was a young black woman, robust, energetic, and confident, with a very professional demeanor. She pressed her fingers against the patient's wrist for fifteen seconds while looking attentively at her watch, then took his blood pressure. She pulled down the lower lid of his left eye and leaned forward as if peering into a pit. While she did this, she listened to the description of the symptoms related by the *Santera*. After asking the *Santera* to remove the patient's pajamas in order to check his abdomen, she proceeded to probe with both hands over his liver and other organs. Finally, she cleaned her hands in a washbowl with soap and water and dried them on a towel handed to her by the *Santera*.

Although the doctor was new in the neighborhood, she was fully aware of the identity of the patient and his sister—witch doctors known to the whole town. Nevertheless, there they were, calling for a real doctor with the first sign of stomachache! She would have given a lot for all those who came seeking cures from these people to see them now, asking for help from science! Blacks like these gave a bad name to their race! And these were the worst of all, convincing others of absurd beliefs with the sole aim of living without working. When they fell ill, instead of taking their own brews and offering prayers and witchcraft to their saints, they rushed to the hospital for X-rays, medicines, and operations. At the slightest hint of a toothache, they were the first to visit a dentist. How grateful she was to her parents—who had never believed much in those things and had insisted that she study—and to the Revolution, that had made it possible for her to become a physician.

"His pulse is all right, just a little accelerated by the fever." She looked at the thermometer. "His temperature is one hundred one. His pressure is a little low, but within normal limits. His abdomen is flaccid. The liver is not swollen, and he has no pain or inflammation in his other organs." As she spoke, the doctor was filling out prescriptions and writing notes on her pad.

"It's probably a virus. If his condition doesn't improve, call me again, and we'll take him to the emergency room for an analysis. Here are the prescriptions."

As the doctor prepared to depart, the patient lifted a hand to attract her attention. She stopped and leaned toward him.

Although Lorenzo felt much relieved after hearing the physician's opinion, he opened his eyes wide and pronounced clearly, "I've been poisoned."

The doctor looked at the patient and then at the sister. The *Santera* smiled condescendingly and made a small gesture to the doctor. "Come, I'll explain."

The two women left the room, followed by Pedro.

Left alone, Lorenzo Bantú considered the implications of having accused his sister of poisoning him. He had to flee, to put himself beyond the reach of her powers, and he had to do it now. He imagined that after inventing some story to pacify the doctor, his sister would offer some coffee and they would chat for a while at the door before saying goodbye. In the end, she would hand the doctor a gift of some kind, charming her all the while with her sweetness.

"I'll come back this afternoon for a more complete examination," the doctor said as she left. She took two steps along the sidewalk, then turned. "If you notice any change at all, call me immediately. I'm here, just a block away, in the family doctor's office, you know."

The woman walked away rapidly. Pedro remained at the side of the *Santera*. With the doctor out of earshot, he pointed his index finger at Lorenzo's sister and said, with the greatest calm, "If anything happens to Lorenzo, I'll tear you apart!"

The *Santera* opened her mouth to respond, then changed her mind. She reentered the house, closing the door softly, resisting the impulse to slam it behind her. She smiled with satisfaction. Her work was beginning to cause tremendous damage in the ranks of the enemy. The other night, Adrián had left the consultation in a very bad mood and, later, her brother and Pedro had been drinking and laughing at Adrián's expense. That relationship was not going to last long. Now Mulo was in jail and the strange dealings of her brother with Adrián had been interrupted, although she couldn't understand what Pedro meant when he said, "The dead man has his cross," or why an *ebbó* had been needed. It was evident that Pedro, Mulo, and Adrián were involved in something important, but it couldn't be anything as simple as a theft. And Pedro's threat couldn't be underestimated; that beast never wasted his breath. She had to find a way of neutralizing him.

Lorenzo Bantú forced himself to sit up on his bed, covered now with a clean sheet spread by his sister. Then, leaning over, he searched for his shoes, unsuccessfully. She must have carried them away before the doctor came, while she was cleaning up the room and he was unconscious. He staggered barefoot to the door and opened it, looking up the hall toward the dining room and the kitchen of the silent house. He took several clumsy steps toward the back door, intending to reach the patio and, from there, the house of a godchild, who would surely help him.

The intense midday light entering through the back door stung his eyes cruelly, but he felt new life flooding into him with the wave of heat. Then, amidst the hallucinatory splendor of the light, two very thin, almost dried-up old women, covered with fine veins and dressed in white, obstructed his path.

"Lorencito, where do you think you're going? You're very ill. You don't know what you're doing. Go back to bed! Look at you . . . all naked like that!"

Peering down, Lorenzo realized with horror that what had been imped-ing his movement had been his loosened pajama trousers that by now had slid down to his ankles. Hastily, he pulled them up and, clutching them in one hand, humiliated, retraced his steps to his room. As he entered, he heard one of the patio guardians say to the other:

"Did you see that? Did you see the size of the *Nasakó's* thing?"

GUANABACOA

IT WAS SEVEN-THIRTY in the morning of September 7, the day of the Catholic Virgin of Regla, Yemayá, the queen of the sea in *Regla de Osha,* and preparations for the celebration were already underway in the city. Here and there, drumbeats burst out sporadically and immediately subsided—warm-up exercises for a long and very special Saturday. Alvaro had arrived in Guanabacoa in an automobile with a private license plate provided by Colonel Carrillo. To kill the half-hour remaining before his appointment, he bought a newspaper and sat reading it in the car.

Colonel García, the municipal chief of police, received him. He took the photos that Alvaro handed him and revealed an advanced degree of presbyopia by holding them out at arm's length to distinguish the features of the man with the Abakuá tattoo on his arm. Without speaking, García walked to the door of his office and asked someone in the adjacent room to bring coffee. Then, pointing to the photos still in his hand, he assured the visitor: "If this citizen is an Abakuá of Guanabacoa or of Regla, tomorrow morning, at the latest, we'll have his identification. He probably had this Abakuá tattoo made in order to look like a tough guy. Everybody's doing that. I'm even thinking of getting one."

"How many Abakuá are there in this municipality?"

"Over three thousand, counting the clandestine initiations."

"Clandestine initiations?"

"Each chapter is officially authorized to initiate twelve per year, but they arrange to initiate another twelve or so behind the scenes."

"Many problems with the Abakuá?"

"So-so. Fights, with killings now and then, and some public scandals. But it's very rare that you find an Abakuá involved in theft. Supposedly, each *monina* has to be honest, a good worker, a good son and good father, et cetera, et cetera."

"And in reality?"

"Well, this is a strict requirement in some chapters, but in others, no. Each chapter, *plante, potencia, tierra,* is a world apart. That's what makes working with them difficult. At least we've managed so far to have them select a board to represent all of them. Even though it isn't completely effective, the first fruit of that agreement has been law-and-order committees that they organize to control their fiestas. If things get out of hand, anyway, the police intervene, but only then. We used to have to set up a police cordon around all of their celebrations and intervene with billy clubs when fights broke out among them, and that created many more conflicts. So we've made some headway. Nevertheless, the basic problem is that they take justice into their own hands. Every once in a while, an Abakuá turns up here ready to go to jail for the rest of his life, confessing that he just killed some character for insulting him, or for touching his girlfriend's behind, or something of the sort."

At that moment, a young policewoman entered with a tray bearing two glasses of cold water and two aromatic cups of coffee topped by a layer of creamy froth. She deposited the tray on García's desk and departed without waiting for thanks, while her chief explained that the coffee had been prepared by mixing crushed brown sugar with several drops of coffee before combining it with strong coffee brewed in an Italian coffeemaker.

Colonel García figured that, with the pride-of-the-station coffee, he had fulfilled his duty to the special investigator sent by Colonel Carrillo. The matter he had brought seemed to be of little consequence, and he could see no reason to prolong the conversation. At the same time, he couldn't understand why Carrillo had taken the trouble to call and ask for his help in the mere identification of an alleged Abakuá caught in the act of attempted robbery. He stood up and led Alvaro to the office of Major Fonseca, chief of the station's undercover agents, who was expecting him.

Fonseca was about thirty years old, with rich brown skin, broad shoulders, a massive trunk, short extremities, and a mistrustful gaze.

"Good physique for infight boxing," observed the tall policeman, looking Fonseca over from head to foot.

Major Fonseca didn't appreciate the remark and would have gladly said something disagreeable about the uncommon height of the newcomer, but he contained himself, looking in a perplexed way at the man presented to him by the chief of the municipal police himself, an unusual treatment that Colonel García rarely gave to anyone. It was then that he realized that this was the same individual, now with longer hair and a beard, who several years ago had needed only two days to solve a homicide case in which they had been bogged down for months. At the time, someone had said that the tall blond policeman was an *abikú*, attributing supernatural powers to him, a habitual conclusion in that region about anything even slightly out of the ordinary. Alvaro handed the photos of Mulo to Fonseca without further comment.

"What's the problem with him?"

"Repeated robbery with forced entry."

"I don't think so."

"Do you know him?"

"His name is Pascual Wilson Cabrera. Everybody has called him Mulo since he learned kung fu." Fonseca returned the photos and, pointing at them with his forefinger, added, "If you told me that he killed someone with a kick in the groin because he got a dirty look or something like that, I'd believe it. Robbery?" He shook his head. "Never."

"Don't be too sure."

Fonseca decided not to argue.

"Besides identifying this man, we also need to capture his partners." Alvaro handed Fonseca the oral portraits of Pedro and Adrián.

"This face looks familiar to me," Fonseca said, tapping the likeness of Pedro. "I'll have my people check on it immediately. What do you want to do now?"

"Interrogate people who know this Mulo. Is that possible?"

"Yes, but I warn you: Don't tell anyone that he's a thief. If he hears of it, the day he gets out of prison, he'll look for you, even underground, and stick a knife down your throat. You can't even imagine how vengeful the Abakuás can be."

"I'm trembling."

Fonseca again felt an almost overwhelming desire to send the visitor to hell, but stayed calm. In an unusual philosophical insight, he told himself that the two of them were predestined to clash because they were opposites in every way. The visitor, too long, thin, blond, and hairy; he, very dark, short, stout, and hairless. He decided not to leave him alone for a moment in order to shorten his visit and see him out of his territory as soon as possible.

They drove first in Alvaro's car to visit Mulo's mother in a small house on the old highway entering Guanabacoa.

"*Mi vieja!*" Fonseca shouted, embracing the old woman affectionately. "I've come to let you know that Pascualito is perfectly okay. He had a little problem day before yesterday over in Havana. The police are holding him while they clear up a couple of things. Do you want to send him anything? Tomorrow I can take you to see him if you like."

The wife for many years of an Abakuá and the mother of another, she knew perfectly well the Abakuá golden rule: Never tell the police anything, under any circumstances. The immutable brightness of her eyes, the absence of questions or any sign of reaction in her voice or face, told the policemen what they needed to know.

Once in the car, Fonseca sank back in the seat and said, "Friend, there may be something in this, after all. The old lady didn't blink an eye. She already knew that Mulo was in the jug. Since the arrest was made far from here and we didn't even know about it, it means that his partners have advised the old lady. Don't you think?"

The blond policeman raised his eyebrows as Sherlock Holmes might have done when he said, "*Elemental, my dear Watson.*"

Fonseca turned to a subordinate who had come with them in the backseat of the car. "Find out who visited Mulo's old lady between yesterday morning and today. We have to figure out how the water enters this coconut."

Fonseca then took the visitor to talk to other people who knew Mulo. The last was the manager of the garage where Mulo washed cars. Their statements all confirmed Fonseca's opinion. Gradually, a consistent image of Mulo took shape: young, introverted, quiet, a good worker and a good son who struggled to escape the mediocrity imposed by his scarce education by trying to become a member of the national kung fu team. That would enable him to travel abroad, buy nicer clothes, eat better—and, by this almost unique path, be recognized as "somebody."

Mulo had a fiancée with whom he maintained relations in the style of half a century earlier: specific days and hours of visits each week, with the mother of the girl knitting at a discreet distance. Strict chaperones accompanied the couple on all of their outings. The girl was the daughter of an Abakuá who had no use for modernities. "They already have everything they need to marry," one friend said, and the blue-eyed policeman realized that he hadn't heard that expression since his childhood. Nowadays, couples considered themselves lucky to have a place to sleep, and many didn't even take the trouble to marry, although the ceremony was almost gratis and, in essence, implied no strong obligation.

Alvaro shook his head. Fonseca was right: Mulo didn't fit the image of a thief. What's more, he thought, he doesn't even fit in this epoch.

The two policemen returned to the station. It was past the lunch hour, but Fonseca's second-in-command had set aside some food for them. The officer placed the voluminous file on the table as they finished eating and stated solemnly, "We all agree that the oral portrait is Pedro Bermúdez. He and Mulo are inseparable. They even belong to the same Abakuá chapter. But nobody recognizes the other one."

"Who is the *Nasakó* of that chapter?" Alvaro asked.

Fonseca stared at him, surprised, and waited, as if expecting an explanation for the question.

Alvaro realized that he had made a mistake. "We'll discuss that later. Right now, I propose that we work on Pedro. Let's go to see Lieutenant Camila and show her the photos. If the identification is positive, we'll request a seek-and-capture order right there in Plaza municipality and go after the man with everything necessary."

Delighted with the proposal, Fonseca replied, "We're on our way!" Turning to his subordinate, he ordered: "Locate Pedro Bermúdez. You know who to take with you and who not . . . Just locate him. Do you copy me? So far, we still don't have anything against him."

The officer nodded and headed out, leaving them the thick dossier of Pedro Bermúdez.

Camila was surprised and clearly pleased by the visit from Alvaro, who introduced Fonseca and explained the purpose of their call. After mobilizing her mother to make coffee for them, Camila reviewed the photos in the dossier. The first dated from Pedro's days as an adolescent, but the final pages contained several full-face and profile photos. "Yes, this is the man! The one I caught with the recorder in his hands. I still have a clear recollection of him." Camila returned the file to Alvaro and stood with her arms crossed, smiling at him.

"Can you come with us for a seek-and-capture order for this municipality? We need to grab this character tonight in whatever 'bembé' he may be celebrating the fiesta of Yemayá," Alvaro told her.

Camila was delighted with any excuse to be near this man, whose air of helplessness and certain angelic manner would arouse a maternal instinct in any woman. But today he had a special look in his eyes, and his voice and his body movements were sure and commanding . . . or perhaps it was the pheromones in his perspiration that made him so attractive, she thought. On her way to get dressed, she passed closely by Alvaro and, casually, sniffed him again. At that very moment, she made a portentous decision.

Fonseca was certain by now about something he had merely suspected until then. That high-caliber investigator wasn't wasting his time trying to catch a miserable band of thieves—what's more, on a Saturday night—simply because of an overpowering dedication to work. He saw now that the man was probably trying to impress that little hen by grabbing the band of thieves that had beaten her up. And the little hen was giving clear signals of wanting to be mounted as soon as possible.

Catching Fonseca's libidinous glance moving from Camila to himself, Alvaro thought it might be best to reveal the true aim of their search. But after considering it for an instant, he decided to wait. He didn't want that information spread all over Guanabacoa. That would be disastrous. Better to let Fonseca think he was enchanted with Camila—which wasn't so far afield, anyway.

Fonseca was surprised that Alvaro wanted to return to Guanabacoa with him that same night to review the police files on the Itiamo Beconsí Abakuá chapter, to which both Mulo and Pedro belonged. Then he decided that the blond policeman was definitely nuts, and in his madness he was spoiling the weekend for him and for his subordinates. Any man who had his head screwed on right would stay there with Camila and return on Tuesday after getting the seek-and-capture order on Monday.

Fonseca's second-in-command was waiting for him at the door of the station and began to give his report immediately: "Pedro hasn't been in any of his usual haunts since last Thursday. Today, he was seen walking through some patios near the house of the Bantús. He must have gone to visit Lorenzo, who's sick in bed. Someone will tell me right away if he shows up there again . . . Look, boss, I'm sure that bird, who's a smart one, has flown the coop already. I'll bet anything. Right now, he must be drinking rum in Santiago de Cuba, where he has a daughter, or eating roast pork in Pinar del Río, where he has a pile of cousins."

Fonseca ignored the last comments, clearly intended to persuade him to suspend operations over the weekend. "Listen, you now have the seek-and-capture order for Pedro. Go after him with all of your people. Between today and tomorrow is the only chance we'll have to catch him hanging out at some friend's house here in Guanabacoa. We can be fairly sure he won't move from here in these two days. When you've located him, tell me—at any hour. Listen carefully! Pedro is almost certainly armed. He knows that if we capture him, he's going to be in the shade for at least five years. He'll try to escape by opening fire on anyone. Don't try to detain him with inexperienced agents under any circumstances. I don't want any national heroes or martyrs. That man will take anyone's head off without thinking twice!"

After leaving his blond visitor installed in an office with a stack of files and accompanied by one of his agents most knowledgeable about the Abakuás, Fonseca went to his own office to call Colonel García at home and report on the day's activities.

"Don't let that man out of your sight, and make sure he doesn't stir up a mess with the Abakuás," García ordered. "Remember, he'll go back to Havana, but we have to stay here."

Fonseca wondered whether he really had to stay at Alvaro's side, so he went to see him to help himself decide. Finding his charge still immersed in the study of the case files, Fonseca left to make sure there was no problem with the little hotel near the station where he had reserved the only room with a working air conditioner and a bathroom with water at least some of the time. He returned to the station and, calling the Abakuá expert aside, asked him not to leave Alvaro until he had him snoring in his hotel room.

Then he thought of a way to immobilize his visitor on the following day. "Alvaro, I invite you to lunch at my house tomorrow. I'll swing by the hotel at eleven o'clock to pick you up."

"I'll bring the beer."

"It's a deal!"

Alvaro was awakened at ten in the morning by a hotel employee knocking on his door. After showering, he went out to buy a twelve-pack of beer at a nearby dollar store that stayed open on Sunday mornings. At that hour, Guanabacoa was still recovering from the day before in order to begin new festivities in honor of the Virgen de la Caridad del Cobre, the Catholic patron saint of Cuba, who is also Oshún, the mischievous goddess of love of the *Regla de Osha*, who rules over all fresh waters and wealth.

A multitude had already gathered at Guanabacoa's largest church, where the procession to the virgin patroness of Cuba was about to begin. Alvaro contemplated the preparations briefly, then walked to the central park, where he bought a newspaper and sat down to read, killing time until he headed back to the hotel to wait for Fonseca.

Fonseca's house was modest but pleasant and set in an orchard of fruit trees with tall branches that provided a delicious coolness on the front porch that faced east, receiving the sea breeze. His wife welcomed Alvaro, then took the beer to put in the refrigerator.

On the patio of a house facing Fonseca's, a noisy fiesta celebrating Oshún was underway with music that set Alvaro's feet tapping. He suggested to his colleague that they go join the party for a few minutes while they waited for the beer to cool.

Fonseca declined the invitation. "You go ahead if you like. Not all of the black people in Guanabacoa are followers of those religions. Neither my family nor I have anything to do with them. I'm not going to give those people the satisfaction of swelling their numbers. The owners of that house are frauds and they take advantage of ignorant believers who fall into their hands. You can't imagine how commercialized that business has become. Nowadays, *hacerse el santo* costs a small fortune, equivalent to what a worker can earn in two or three years. These religions—not always, but many times—are merely instruments for delinquents and other antisocial characters. It's incredible that they have so much influence with all that the revolutionary government has invested in schools and in educating the people. If it were left up to me, I'd prohibit them. They're extremely primitive. But don't let me influence you. Here in the neighborhood, I'm considered an extremist . . . and, in this sense, I am."

After his third can of beer and in consideration of Fonseca's opinion about African religions, Alvaro decided to reveal his true mission in Guanabacoa.

"Look, Fonseca, the real job that brought me here is to find the cadaver of a Chinaman that Mulo and the others stole from the Chinese cemetery. There's no possible mistake: The footprints in the cemetery coincide with those of the boots Mulo was wearing the day he was arrested and with others from one of the houses that was robbed. Why would anyone want to steal a Chinese cadaver? Could it be to provide magic protection? That's why I asked about the witch doctor of that Abakuá chapter. Last night, I was reviewing the file on Lorenzo Bantú. What do you know about him?"

Fonseca scratched his head and finished his beer before answering. "Yes, Lorenzo might have recommended stealing the Chinaman, but you won't be able to prove it. In reality, you're not going to get what you want by arresting them; not one of those implicated will tell you where the Chinaman is. They're pure-breed Abakuás, and they won't tell the police anything. If we arrested Lorenzo Bantú, we would just waste our time and create more conflicts with the Abakuás."

The blue-eyed policeman remained thoughtful, sipping his beer. "I learned yesterday that a statement was given to the police by a doctor who treated Lorenzo."

"Yes, I heard about that. But the doctor said that she checked him and didn't find anything. What can we do? Those people fight among themselves like cats and dogs. Lorenzo and his sister are two of a kind."

They had eaten a heavy Sunday lunch and now the rest of the afternoon stretched out before them. Alvaro felt certain that his host would be happy to see him take off, leaving him free to take a Sunday-afternoon nap, though he wondered if the noise coming from the house across the street would let him sleep. The festivity seemed at its peak. Some two hundred people had accumulated on the patio and now it was impossible to see the dancers.

"What are you going to do now to find your Chinaman, eh?" Fonseca's eyes were shining from his six beers and from the frustration of the star investigator sent to his territory to solve the unsolvable.

The blond policeman finished his fourth can of beer, thanked Fonseca for the good lunch and his help, and left, feeling totally discouraged. From the beginning of this round of his investigation, he had felt that his work in Guanabacoa was not welcome. Even Fonseca couldn't hide his satisfaction with the failure of his mission.

CHAOS

ON SUNDAY, SEPTEMBER 8, José Miguel slept late because he had been celebrating all night. He woke up remembering that he needed to see the *Santera* to try to orient himself to the new situation. He brushed his teeth and sat down nude on the toilet. He remained there for almost half an hour, meditating on recent events. The most worrisome development was the sudden illness of the *Nasakó*. The pair, brother and sister, were forces in continual covert conflict, and the clash between them had reached a point of crisis. What role was the *Santera* playing in the new situation? Instinct advised him to make a pact with that dangerous woman so that the police wouldn't learn about his business with Adrián that was already rendering such good results. He rose from the toilet seat and contemplated his feces that had fallen in the shape of a question mark. Yes, unquestionably, the future was a big enigma.

"A tall, blond guy with a beard, a strange man, visited the police station yesterday. He looks like anything but a policeman, but apparently he is one, although his hands are covered with calluses and as hard as a farmer's. He went with Fonseca to Mulo's house to tell his old lady that Mulo is in jail, and now he's looking for Mulo's partners. According to the descriptions, the partners are Pedro and Adrián, though the oral portrait of Adrián doesn't look like him. This guy moves fast. He got an order for Pedro's arrest last night and they're looking for him everywhere."

The *Santera* remained silent. She hadn't looked at José Miguel the whole time, seemingly absorbed in examining the seams of a dress that she held in her hands. She had never been friendly toward José Miguel nor Pedro, and it was no surprise to her that the police were after Adrián. Yemayá Acuti was always very quick and effective in her work.

"Somebody talked?"

"I don't think Mulo said a word, but a police lieutenant recognized Pedro as the guy she found robbing a house. So he's really in hot water."

"Pedro robbing?" the *Santera* commented, surprised. "Well, anyway, all of that is their problem. They'll have to handle it with the police. Is that all you had to tell me?"

José Miguel resented her underestimation of his information, as if he had taken the trouble to come to see her with mere gossip. He made himself more comfortable, sliding down on his chair until his tailbone rested on the seat. "Last night, the blond policeman stayed late at the station reviewing the files on the Abakuá. He asked a lot of questions about Lorenzo."

This time the *Santera* stopped examining the dress in her hands and looked directly at the man seated before her.

"Why Lorenzo?"

"I don't know."

There was a long silence, and José Miguel began to feel in control of the situation. "In the police station, they showed him the report from your family doctor."

"What report?"

"Don't you know about the report?" José Miguel decided to light a cigar before going on, to aggravate that inscrutable woman eternally hidden behind a mask of sweetness. "The doctor—the one who was here the other day—reported that Lorenzo told her he had been poisoned. You don't have to be psychic to know he was referring to you. You're the only two living here."

José Miguel puffed on his cigar, shook his head, and took his time relighting the Lancero Cohiba that stubbornly refused to burn evenly, then continued. "That's what she told the police. She said that she hadn't given it much thought at first, since she hadn't found signs of poisoning. But when she tried to see Lorenzo later, you didn't let her in, making up excuses

both times she came by." José Miguel took two puffs on the cigar and deliberately blew the smoke in the direction of the *Santera*, who was listening
carefully, but had again stopped looking at him. "So the doctor wanted to
wash her hands of responsibility, just in case, and that's why she reported it."

The *Santera* remained silent a moment, then drew her eyes back to the
man who now avoided her gaze, as if in ecstasy with his cigar.

"Why did you think I knew about that report?" she asked.

"Miladys knows about it. One of her cousins is the policeman who took
the statement."

"That one . . ." Startled at what she had been about to say, she changed
her mind, but couldn't avoid a malicious smile. "She didn't tell me, but she
must have her reasons."

"I'm sure the police have an eye on both of you. That's why I came to
see you. Get rid of anything that could compromise you. Take it out
through the back patio. I don't think the neighbors across the street are
friends of yours." José Miguel stood up to leave, but the *Santera* took hold
of his arm.

"If you want to help Lorenzo, you have to rely on me. I need to know
who that policeman is . . . what he has against my brother. And if you know
something I don't know about Miladys, Mulo, Pedro, or Adrián, it would
also be wise to let me know about it. Tell me what business you are involved
in. I need to know everything."

José Miguel nodded slightly and left, feeling worried. He wasn't at all
pleased with the way things were going. Lorenzo was a man easy to decipher and to predict. One could work with him with absolute confidence—
but his sister was something else entirely. He had plenty to lose if the police
began to poke their nose into the affairs of Lorenzo Bantú and managed to
learn the identity of Adrián. He decided that his best course, for the time
being, was to cooperate with the one-eyed *Santera*.

The conversation left the *Santera* very worried. The work she had done to
set the police on Adrián's trail was beginning to endanger everything: Mulo
already in jail; Pedro moving like a madman through patios, threatening to
kill her, and now with a warrant out for his arrest. That strange policeman,

undoubtedly brought by her petition to Yemayá, had already somehow made a connection between Mulo, Pedro, Adrián, and her brother; and, thanks to the imbecile family doctor, she herself was now implicated. On top of everything else, Adrián must have some powerful protection because he seemed to have been swallowed up by the Earth and was the only one who, by all appearances, was not yet hobbled by the work she had performed against him.

By now, she knew all about Adrián's business. Ana's conversations, recorded by Miladys and by the *Nasakó* himself—that she had been able to listen to several times—described how Mulo and Pedro arrived with trucks full of things that they unloaded at night at one of the old warehouses. Every two or three days, José Miguel arrived with his truck, taking away some of the stolen goods. Since his truck was much smaller than the one used by Mulo and Pedro, there had to be a hiding place somewhere on the grounds of Doña Elvira's estate where the rest of the stolen items were kept. Following the instructions of the *Nasakó*, Ana searched the grounds, particularly the ramshackle warehouses, when Adrián wasn't around, but found nothing.

Mulo would never confess to the police, she could be sure of that. If Pedro was captured, he wouldn't reveal anything, either. Adrián was safe with those two. The only way to implicate him would be if the stolen merchandise was found on his premises. But José Miguel would then be implicated as well, and perhaps Lorenzo, because Adrián was not an Abakuá and he would probably confess everything in order to get off with the lightest sentence possible. To destroy Adrián, the police had to find the secret hiding place and the stolen goods at his house.

THE CLUES TO THE CITY

AFTER LEAVING FONSECA'S house, he wandered around the rest of the afternoon and all night in long strides through Guanabacoa's narrow and dark streets, obsessed with his failure: He had found all the threads, but none that would take him to the center of the skein. He decided there was no point in seeing Fonseca again, to keep asking questions with no answers. No police hunt would make this city reveal the whereabouts of a Chinese corpse stolen precisely as a protection against the police. The investigation in Guanabacoa was absurd. Fonseca was absolutely right.

The problem here is the complicity of the city, he told himself. Since his arrival, all of his movements had been anticipated. He had been expected in each place he decided to go. Those he interrogated seemed to be waiting for him. Their answers were airtight, and it was obvious that they had been prepared in advance for outsiders who would never understand how things functioned in Guanabacoa, where everything was joined together by invisible connections like the blood vessels of a living organism. And the police were a part of that schema, of that intricate web of relations.

To confirm this, he only had to observe what was happening right around him at that very moment. It was the day of the Catholic Virgen de la Caridad del Cobre, who had been found floating on the Bay of Nipe by two astonished Indians and a black slave boy who were looking for salt, apparently a scarce commodity by the early seventeenth century. A wooden figure of a virgin with the infant Jesus on her left arm and a golden cross in her right hand was floating on a board with the inscription: "*Yo soy la Virgen de la Caridad.*" Because of the Virgin's innumerable pious works over three centuries, Pope Benedict XV declared her the patron saint of Cuba in 1916. Although she was originally recognized as the Virgin Mary, images of her are found everywhere nowadays as a mulatta or black Virgin with a perfectly white infant Jesus on her left arm and the Christian cross in her right hand.

Under this same mantle and at the very same moment, devotion was being paid to Oshún, the goddess of fresh water, of love, and of fortune, the patron saint of whores and queers in *Regla de Osha*. Which of the two were they really celebrating—Christian charity or pagan love? But it was not that simple. Oshún splits into different enigmas according to each of her paths: Oshún Yeyé Moró, young, beautiful, playful, eternally flirting; Oshún Yumú, weaver of fishermen's nets and baskets, old and deaf, severe and serious, rocking in a chair on the bottom of a river when she isn't digging graves in a cemetery; the good Oshún Akuara, gay and a good dancer, always refusing to cast spells; the wise Oshún Funké, a teacher; and perhaps the sinister Oshún Kolé-Kolé, who lives in the mud in the greatest poverty, eating whatever the buzzard, with whom she occasionally flies, brings her.

In other fiestas Alvaro visited that night, the *orisha* worshiped was Chola, the primitive goddess of fertility, of sex, and of carnal love in the *Reglas de Palo*, *Mayombe*, *Brillumbe*, and *Kimbisa*.

His feet and body were keeping time to the music at one of the fiestas he had found on his way back to his hotel. Only the initiated, those who had their saint *asentado* and had been presented to the *batá* drums, had the right to dance in those fiestas. The observers, like him, had to follow the music fixed in their places. Suddenly, one of the dancers fell into a trance, abandoned the dance area, and began to wander about like a madwoman. "Oshún mounted her," someone commented, upon hearing the shrill little laugh characteristic of the goddess. At that moment, the possessed woman came running from behind Alvaro, grabbed the tips of his shirt collar to pull his head down, and whispered in his ear: "*Who do you believe in? Who?*"

He left, horrified at hearing his own question said aloud.

It was past five A.M. by the time his long strides carried him to the Parque Central, nearly empty at that hour. A chorus of drunken voices was intoning a *guaguancó*, accompanied by the tapping of coins on two empty bottles and the percussion of hands on an empty wooden box. Several men, perhaps inebriated, slept on benches. A couple was making love noisily in the darkest corner of the park. The policeman climbed up onto an empty bench to get a slightly broader view of his surroundings and asked the city in a low voice, because he had learned there was no need to shout, "In whom do *you* really believe?"

As a ray of sunlight fell across his face, everything was suddenly clear: He had found the clue he had been seeking. He turned his steps in the direction of the only place where he could find the solution to the problem that had brought him here. He had begun approaching this conclusion earlier in the night, when, for the first time, he lent an ear to what the city had to say, danced to the beat of its music, and felt the breath of its gods very near. He had finally started to interpret its signs.

DILOGGÚN

A TALL, BLOND MAN entered and sat down in the low chair facing her. He crossed his long legs in one direction, then in the other, unable to find a comfortable position. She stared at him, startled and fascinated. He wore a sweaty and smelly shirt and had dark circles under his eyes, shadows that accentuated the intense, brilliant blue of his eyes, like two living crystals. There before her was the policeman sent by Yemayá Acutí in response to her work.

She turned her back to give the visitor the impression that she was busy arranging some things on the floor, but placed her hand on her chest and felt the fast beating of her heart. She had been aware of both an anxious curiosity about the special investigator who had come to Guanabacoa in answer to her call to destroy Adrián and, at the same time, a vague fear. She had asked the cocos about him several times and, invariably, two cocos with the faces upward and two with the faces downward had appeared—the letter *Eyife*, announcing certainty, a definitive "yes." *He was her responsibility now, for better or for worse.*

"Have you ever had a consultation with the *Diloggún* before?"

"Never."

"Uncross your legs, please."

Before her on a small table covered with a white cloth, he counted sixteen small seashells, filed down at the back, and, apart, two whole shells. Five other small objects lay on the table: the head of a small doll, a dark seed, a vertebra of some small animal, a round black stone, and a white ball.

She began by pouring three tiny streams of water on the spot where she was going to throw the shells. "*Chubú meta di omituto, ilekun mi dabobó, ilé tutu, orí tuto, okán tuto, aché tutu, omó tutu, omí tutu gbobbo wadi ilé tutu awó aikú Babá wá*" (To speak, three bits of fresh water, so that the door is cool, my whole house cool, my head cool, my heart cool, the guardian angel cool, the one consulting cool, cool in registering all secrets and revealing that there is no death, Obatalá).

Still speaking in the Lucumí language, she then asked for the blessing of the *orishas*, beginning with Elégguá, and of her ancestors, for their help in impeding the dark spirits of the dead. She ended by greeting her godparents. All under the avid gaze of her first client of the day.

"First, I'll do the opening throw, the one that presides over the consultation. Then I will give you this small black stone, *otá*, and this small white ball made of eggshell, *efún*. Without me seeing them, you will take one in each hand, and I will ask for the left or the right according to whether a larger or a smaller *odu* comes out in the next throw. If you give me the *otá*, it means that the throw came by *osobbo*, by the unfortunate path; if it's *efún*, it means that it comes by *iré*, the good path. Do you understand?"

"*Otá* for a bad path and *efún* for a good path," the man repeated.

"The same thing can take place for good or for evil. If the shells announce a trip by *iré*, it will be successful, with a happy result; if it's by *osobbo*, it's because something bad is going to come from that trip. If it announces death by *iré*, someone will die and it will bring you a benefit— for example, the death of an enemy. Do you understand now?"

The man, still staring fixedly at the *Santera*, nodded. "What happened to you?" he asked, concentrating his gaze on her lifeless eye, revealing the curiosity of a three-year-old child and addressing her with a familiarity that not even those who had known her all her life dared to express.

She again felt surprised, this time by his indiscretion wrapped in such an ingenuous manner. She was sure that she hadn't moved a single muscle or let her eyes drop before his penetrating gaze, as he scrutinized the one place on her entire body that no one should notice. It caused her physical pain to see anyone looking at her bad eye. He must have done it to destabilize her, like a devil in angel's clothing. Or was it purely innocent? Soon, the shells would tell her on which side he was playing.

"Now I'm going to make the initial throw," she said, ignoring his question.

The *Santera* spread eggshell powder over her hands, then collected the sixteen shells with the backs filed down. She rested her hands against the forehead of her client, who inclined slightly. "With the permission of your guardian angel." She then brushed her clasped hands filled with the shells over his shoulders, chest, and knees, and implored: "*Kosi ikú, kosi aro, kosi ofó, kosi oyé*" (That there not be a death, that there not be illness, that there not be losses).

She threw the shells onto the table. They all fell face up. "*Meridilogún!*" She explained the *súyer* that accompanied the letter: "Born to be wise; he hears no advice."

For the third straight time, she was surprised, now by her own shells. The *Iyalosha* lowered her eyes a second, trying to control the irregular rhythm of her heart and the subsequent quiver in her voice. The game was decided.

"The shells say that you are a direct son of Olofí, the supreme god. We *Santeros* can only read as far as the twelfth letter, *Eyinla*, twelve shells face up. The thirteenth to the sixteenth must be interpreted by Itá, by a *babalawo*. But I can tell you now that you should receive Olokun immediately, do the *Kari Osha* . . . and *asentarse* all of the *orishas*."

"Olokun?"

"When Olofí created the world, everything gave off vapor and fire. Then he changed the vapor into clouds and the rain put out the fire. From the enormous holes between the rocks, he made Olokun. Yemayá, the sea, was born in that hole with water. Olokun lives in the deepest part of the sea, together with a gigantic serpent that comes out when there is a full moon. Olokun once wanted to destroy the world, and Obatalá had to tie him down with seven chains. You should learn the science of divining of Orula and the secrets of Osaín, master of all herbs, so that you can learn to direct that enormous *aché* that you have for doing good, as is predestined for you."

For the first time, the visitor seemed disconcerted. The intense blue of his eyes softened, and for a second the *Santera* thought she was seeing the eyes of Adrián in a moment of sadness. Her heart again pounded.

"What happened to your eye?" he asked in a compassionate tone.

For the first time in her life, she spoke of her defect without embarrassment. "A traumatic cataract caused by a blow from my grandfather."

"Can't it be operated on?"

"I haven't wanted to do it."

The policeman took the *Santera's* face in his left hand. He turned her head to a profile, then in the opposite direction. "Do it. Have that eye operated on. You have a very pretty face, a perfect oval. You're the most beautiful Negress I've ever seen in my life. Only that eye detracts from your beauty."

She began to feel very nervous with the contact of the extraordinary man's hand, something she would not have accepted from anyone else. Then, without thinking, she began the *moyugba* to Yemayá.

"*Yenya orisha obinrin dudukueke re maye avaya mi re oyu ayaba ano rigba iki mi Iya oga ni gbogbo . . .*"

The man's blue eyes clouded over. Slowly his eyelids drooped and his head began nodding. For a second, it seemed that he was falling asleep, but he immediately opened his eyes wide, struggling against the hypnotic prayer that he couldn't understand.

"*. . . okin yeye omo eya lojun oyina . . .*" Without stopping, the *Iyalosha* continued to search for protection against that unknown force, "*. . . ni reta gbogbo okin nibe iwo ni re elewo nitosi re omo teiba modupue Iyaré mi.*"

"I've scarcely slept for the last three days," he said, excusing himself for his distraction.

"You see, I can't help you. You should go to a *babalawo.*"

"How much do I owe you?"

"I can't charge you anything. Because of what that throw says, it is prohibited for me to charge you."

The policeman remained seated, silent, thinking. Then: "Mulo, Pedro, and someone else stole the body of a Chinaman from a cemetery." As if begging a favor, he added, "I have come looking for that body. That's all I want. Nothing else."

The *Iyalosha* breathed deeply, like she had just heard an astonishing revelation. She stared at him closely. "What day was that?"

"Last July 17th."

The policeman noticed the woman shiver slightly.

"Give me two days. Come in two days, two hours before sunset. I will do a work that will allow you to find that dead man."

When the visitor had gone, she spoke in a low voice. "Yes, I know where the corpse is. Find a cross near where Adrián spends his nights and the body will be near it. It's the cross and the dead man that Pedro spoke to Lorenzo about."

JOSÉ MIGUEL

HE HAD NO DIFFICULTY determining that the brain behind their operation was Adrián, despite efforts to break the work up and keep him occupied with the sale of the stolen goods. Neither was it difficult to conclude that Adrián's safety was vital for his own. Only Adrián had proof of the sale of the stolen objects. If Adrián, who was not an Abakuá, were arrested, he wouldn't hesitate to exchange information for a substantially reduced sentence. Since the most important thing for the police was the recovery of the goods, in the end, he, José Miguel, would be their principal suspect. And that could mean four or five years behind bars.

The capture of Mulo, the seek-and-arrest order against Pedro, the suspicious illness of Lorenzo Bantú, and—above all—the arrival in Guanabacoa of the strange and tireless policeman, were clear signs of the danger hanging over him. He therefore advised Adrián, by means of Ana, that he had a table reserved for lunch for the two of them at Bodeguita del Medio at noon on Monday. He needed to clarify several things with Adrián, and knowing his weakness for good food, José Miguel felt sure he would come.

Adrián wasn't surprised by the invitation. It was one more positive sign from the man who might become the chief of counterintelligence in the new *íremes* army being formed. At the moment, he was in charge of the sales network. His talent for collecting information had flowered early in their association. José Miguel had taken advantage of his long-standing connections in the black market to establish personal relationships with clients and suppliers. He had an impressive memory and was extremely resourceful. Although the sale of the stolen booty was an indispensable part of this first stage of the project, in the following stage, José Miguel should pass to the General Staff . . . perhaps even as his natural replacement when the time came, because José Miguel was a part of the scene, a fish swimming in a school of fish, a pig wallowing in the mud among the herd of swine, one more buzzard circling at three thousand feet. José Miguel only lacked imagination. He had read once, years ago, that Albert Einstein considered imagination more important than knowledge. Since then, rather than repress his own fantasies, he had begun to encourage them. His imagination had become the principal source of his pleasures, as well as all of his troubles.

José Miguel arrived at the restaurant's bar a half-hour in advance. Even though he had already conducted a thorough investigation of Adrián's life on behalf of Lorenzo, his direct dealings with him had always been brief and limited to very specific matters. When José Miguel had proposed the risky talcum business, the younger man, with an infallible instinct for self-preservation, had quickly identified the shortcomings of the proposal. José Miguel considered their present arrangement very good business, although it had the drawback that everything was recorded and that Adrián held all the evidence: "requests for merchandise," the invoices listing the goods received, and the payments he received for his commission on sales.

Adrián strolled up in a pale blue guayabera, hand-embroidered and perfectly cut, combined with dark blue trousers, blue-tinted sunglasses, and black shoes and socks. The most notable thing about him, however, was his unusual and subtle perfume.

The headwaiter seated them at a table near the kitchen, from which a maddening smell of roast pork drifted, overwhelming Adrián's perfume. They ordered their lunch and were immediately served almost-frozen Hatuey beer. After a quick sip, Adrián seemed ready to listen to José Miguel.

"I'm going to give you some information. Then I'll ask you an important question. I need to be sure that when the time comes I'm not going to be left holding the bag."

"Shoot."

"The other day, a policeman from Havana arrived in Guanabacoa. He brought a photo of Mulo to find out who he is and identify two of his accomplices. Mulo is being held in Havana and the police are looking for Pedro. The policeman also had a description and oral portrait of someone who doesn't look much like you, but they say he chews on a matchstick the same way you do." José Miguel scrutinized Adrián's face closely as he spoke, but didn't detect the slightest change. "This policeman supposedly came to investigate the band of thieves that Mulo belongs to, but there's something that doesn't jibe."

"What doesn't jibe?"

"I've learned on very good authority that this man never devotes himself to these minor cases. They pull him off the bench only when they have to win a zero-to-one game in the final inning, when they are the home team and the rival team is at bat with the bases full and no outs. Then they bring in this monster to pitch and win the game. They use him only for important crimes, big robberies, et cetera. He's been asking a thousand questions about the Abakuá since he arrived and also about Lorenzo Bantú and his sister. And listen to this: He acts like a crazy man half of the time, walking the streets all night, observing saints' fiestas . . . This guy must have come on another mission that they aren't talking about yet. Unless he's burnt out and they've sent him over to Guanabacoa to finish going nuts. But I don't think he's nuts by any means, because in three days he's already found out too much."

"What do you think has really brought him here?"

"That's precisely the question I wanted to ask you."

Adrián set aside his beer and remained thoughtful, but when no answer came, José Miguel went on.

"What's he looking for? What are we heading into? Since I'm involved up to here," José Miguel touched his throat, "I want to know what's going on. What's the picture? Why do the police have cannons turned on simple sparrows?"

Adrián briefly considered telling him about the theft of the Chinaman, but decided not to.

José Miguel finished his beer. Adrián, he was sure, knew something but wasn't talking. He decided to continue offering bits of information until Adrián opened up.

"That policeman consulted with Lorenzo's sister early this morning."

"Consulted . . . how?"

"With the shells, but I don't know what she told him. All I know is that the one-eyed bitch is a real devil. She gave the *Nasakó* something that has him lying in bed like a rag doll and talking nonsense. He even went out into the patio naked. All the neighbors saw him. There are real problems between the *Nasakó* and his sister, real problems! What is sure is that she has him tied up good, and I don't know what's going to happen next between them."

Adrián already knew through Miladys, all of whose cousins were policemen, of Lorenzo's illness and the visit by the family doctor, but he had given little weight to the information. It seemed unlikely that the sister would try to poison Lorenzo.

José Miguel decided to open fire from another flank. "For some time now, the Bantús have been monitoring you. Did you know that?"

"Monitoring me?"

"Through Ana."

"Ana?"

"Yes, yes, through Ana."

"How . . . through Ana?"

"Through Miladys Pacheco, Lorenzo's woman."

"What's Ana got to do with Miladys?" Adrián was frowning, incredulous.

"Ana consulted with Miladys. Then Miladys told everything to Lorenzo."

Adrián's face clouded over. José Miguel attacked his roast pork and fried plantain *tostones* that the waiter had just put before them. Sensing that José Miguel still had important things to tell him, Adrián remained silent, waiting.

"The *Nasakó* also gave consultations to Ana in Miladys's house, until Miladys broke up with him."

Adrián's tension was obvious, and small drops of perspiration appeared on his face. He would have liked to ask more questions, but didn't want to reveal the intense macho jealousy that had suddenly arisen in him. This extraordinary information about Ana, Miladys, and Lorenzo had him reeling, and for the first time he felt insecure. He began to eat a little of his food and finished his first beer. Then he told José Miguel: "The police are after us because of a big problem that I'll explain to you later. I don't think you have to worry yet."

"How can I contact you? Do I have to call Ana?"

"You can call me on the telephone at home at any time the hands of the clock coincide. Call, let the phone ring twice, hang up, then call back. I'll imitate my aunt's voice because she never answers the telephone. Ana won't answer either. When things cool off a little, I'll bring you up to date on everything. I have a lucrative proposition for you that you won't want to turn down."

José Miguel was astonished. "You're going to stay at home?"

"No. But don't worry. Nobody will know where I am or where the merchandise is. If you need a safe place to hide, call me and say that you need a pair of shoes, then go to the address that I give you at night, reversing the number of the house."

There seemed little else to say, and the two men finished eating in silence. The waiter brought a third bottle of beer for José Miguel. As they waited for coffee, José Miguel brought out a bulky package from his shoulder bag.

"This is for you. Lorenzo's sister asked me to give it to you personally. I don't know what's in it, but if I were you, I'd dump it in a trash can."

Adrián raised his eyebrows and took the package. "It feels like something made out of cloth and something else loose—maybe even jewelry."

José Miguel paid the bill and left first. Adrián stayed with his coffee. It wasn't wise for them to be seen on the street together.

As he stirred his coffee, Adrián felt ten years older. In less than two hours, his world had changed fundamentally. The general had discovered that the enemy was deep in his territory and had been entrenched there for some time. Of everything José Miguel had told him, probably the least important fact was that Ana had been consulting the *Nasakó*—but the news hurt him almost physically. It wasn't only Ana's flagrant betrayal of him, but the possibility that their meetings had led to other things. The rational part of his mind told him that this was practically unimaginable in Miladys's own house, but his imagination tormented him anyway. Was Ana the reason Miladys had broken off her long relationship with Lorenzo?

TRANSFERRING A SPIRIT

THE BLUE-EYED POLICEMAN sent by Yemayá had revealed the last piece of information she needed to make everything clear. She now recalled the night that she had witnessed her brother's activity in the room of the *nganga*. On his own, behind her back, Lorenzo had been doing an important work for Adrián, Pedro, and Mulo that required the sacrifice of a four-legged animal. She fully understood now what she had seen that night. Lorenzo had made a final consultation with the *nganga,* and, before her eyes, had conducted a ceremony facilitating the theft of the Chinese corpse. That same night the spirit of the Chinaman had entered their house, and its presence had not let her sleep. The spirit, profoundly offended, had taken possession of her brother's head. That was the meaning of *Itawa* in the opening throw in Margarita's consultation; the hidden enemy that she had never been able to identify. And in the throws by *apere,* Oyá had warned her clearly: death, disintegration, return, paid debt. It all referred to the Chinaman, and it was necessary to return the corpse that was decomposing, disintegrating, to pay that debt. Her *orishas* were counseling her right; it was absolutely necessary to help the police find the Chinese cadaver. She had no time to lose. Now was the moment to act against that terrible spirit that had taken possession of her poor brother's head and his will. How naïve her brother had been to think that his magic could prevail over the spirit of a Chinaman! How had he dared to perform such a work without consulting her? There was only one way to solve the problem.

* * *

The taxi arrived at exactly eleven P.M. The driver waited a half-hour while she let the minutes pass so that they would enter the temple precisely at twelve midnight, the exact moment to begin the ceremony. The trip was short, but on the way they had to pick up Teodora, the legendary Mamá Nkquisa in *Palo Monte*, who had initiated Lorenzo in *Palo* when he was barely eight years old.

Everyone was waiting at the temple when they arrived, to witness and take part in the ceremony. Lorenzo Bantú entered the church under his own power, but stumbling, with his sister and another black man as tall and strong-looking as he, known to everyone as Despaigne, holding him on either side. Despaigne had left his job in agriculture some time ago to devote himself to the occupation of transferring spirits and was considered the best in the country in his field.

The only light in the church came from several candles on the main altar. In spite of the late hour and the careful selection of those whose presence was necessary, the *Santera* counted twenty-one people, almost twice the number agreed on. Perhaps they had included the choir at the last moment, she thought, or was twenty-one the required number?

The *Padre Maestro* and the First and Second *Capacitados* of the Santo Cristo del Buen Viaje church were waiting at the main altar. There were also the venerable *Tatandis*, Armenteros and O'Farrill, invited along in case of any unexpected phenomenon that required their science. The *Padre Maestro*, losing no time, made the sign of the cross, blessing Lorenzo and those who were going to participate in the ceremony.

"Creature of God, I cure you and bless you in the name of the Holy Trinity, Father, Son, Holy Ghost, three people, and a true belief, and of Our Lady, the Virgin Mary, conceived without stain or original sin . . ."

As he recited the prayer three times, he hit Lorenzo and Despaigne with branches of sweet basil. The pungent aroma of the herb immediately saturated the room. The assistants removed Lorenzo's shoes and belt. Despaigne also stood barefoot and shirtless.

"I cure you and bless you. Jesus Christ, our Redeemer, blesses you and may His Divine will be done in everything. Amen, Jesus. *Consumatum est.* Amen."

While the *Padre Maestro* was blessing them, the First and Second *Capacitados* "tied" the four corners of the temple—to avoid the interference of the police—with dirt, bits of *pata de gallina* herb, and traces of earth from the main *nganga* of the temple and the *nganga* of Zarabanda. These ingredients were placed between two cornstalks in the form of a cross and sprayed with *chamba*. Each one was then tied securely, forming the *nkagues*, while three "Ave Marías" were sung. The *Capacitados* stamped on the floor with both feet three times and stepped on the *nkagues* with their left feet before the little bundles were placed strategically in each corner. The ceremony of tying up the corners of the temple ended with the burning of seven small piles of gunpowder, which indicated that everything was in good order and would be successful.

With the preparations concluded, a prayer was begun on behalf of everyone present in order to convoke all the necessary forces:

> *Sala maleko maleko nsala*
> *Sambia y Doña María que encubre a Sambia*
> *Con licencia San Pedro, San Roque,*
> *San Sebastian, Cachimba, Mamá Canasta,*
> *Kiyumba, Cuatro Esquinas, Guardiero Nganga*
> *No hay mundele que me nkangue,*
> *Con licencia mi Padre Nganga*
> *Abri kutu wirindinga*
> *Quien debe pena pague nfinda.*
> I, Saint Peter, at your feet,
> Please give me power to succeed.

Complete silence followed. In the darkness, those present began making a circle around the protagonists of the drama. Despaigne held Lorenzo by the hands, helping him maintain his balance. In the center of a chalk signature rested the *Fundamento*, the principal *nganga*. A large chalk circle demarcated the area in which the decisive ceremony would take place. The

Second Father placed a candleholder with a thick candle at one edge of the circle. The candleholder, the *Fundamento*, Lorenzo, and Despaigne were now standing in a straight line.

The *Padre Maestro* exchanged glances with the First and Second *Capacitados* to make sure everything was ready, then extended his arms. His strong, clear voice again sounded in the small temple, asking for silence.

An assistant lit the candle in the candleholder. The choir sang the following mambo, this time to frighten away Satan, *Lugambé*:

> *Lugambé* loves no one
> *Lugambé* killed his mother
> *Lugambé* killed his father
> *Lugambé* doesn't have a friend
> *Lugambé* is a *gangulero*
> *Lugambé los Malos Palos*
> *Lugambé los Tronco Ceiba*
> *Lugambé los Tata Nfungue . . .*

"Lorenzo Bantú, as your clothing is torn, let any work that anyone has done on you be torn!" shouted the trio of Fathers furiously.

A group of assistants began to grab and tear Lorenzo's clothing. In deference to Abakuá custom, Lorenzo could not be left totally nude, so a loincloth had been tied around his waist to hide his buttocks and genitals.

The *Padre Maestro* drew near with a cross in his hand and his voice rang out: "Just as your clothing is ripped apart, so be any kind of work done on you. I command in the name of this *Fundamento nganga* descended from Mamá Lola, the glorious *nganga* of the brother Andrés Facundo Cristo de los Dolores Petit, founder of the *Regla Kimbisa,* Santo Cristo del Buen Viaje church."

The last bits of shirt fell to the floor, and one of the assistants carried a bundle of Lorenzo's clothing out of the temple. Then Despaigne gripped Lorenzo's hands firmly, interlacing his fingers with those of the giant. The arms of both men were raised, forming a great arc.

The choir sang:

Good night, holy night,
With permission of the Holy Father *Um Um Um*
Good night to all *Indiambo* (dead)
Good night to all *moane* (people)
With permission of the *ntoto* (Earth)
Good *lumbo*, good *lumbo* (health)
Don't be snatched by any *Indiambo* (dead person).

Suddenly, a great ball of fire flew from the candle over the *Fundamento* and broke apart on the back of Lorenzo, who shuddered where he stood, immobilized by Despaigne. In the instant that the flame illuminated the place, the physical pain of the two men whose gigantic statures magnified the gravity of the ceremony was plainly visible. The air filled with the acrid odor of burnt hair. The face of Teodora was like a mask of intensely black wrinkles floating in the air, the rest of her body invisible in the darkness. Out of that darkness appeared a bottle of liquid from which Teodora took a large mouthful. Her cheeks puffed out, making her wrinkles disappear. With incredible strength, the old woman expelled the liquid over the candle. Another great ball of fire reached Lorenzo, who shuddered still more and remained trembling as if with fever.

"*Now!*" commanded a voice that seemed to come from another world.

At the third ball of fire, Despaigne cried out and leapt backward as if repelled by a powerful force. Falling to the floor, he rolled over several times and continued to convulse, foam bubbling from his mouth. Lorenzo, lacking Despaigne's support, swayed, and was not aided until the *Padre Maestro* shouted: "Catch him! The evil spirit has left him."

They dressed Lorenzo in new clothing. Despaigne was carried to the *nganga* devoted to Zarabanda at the other end of the temple. The First *Capacitado*, along with several assistants, began to work with him to pass the spirit of the Chinaman, which now possessed him, to the *nganga*, where it would reside until a decision was made as to its final destination.

Lorenzo was given a drink of *aguardiente* and then the assistants began the general cleaning required of people who have been possessed by a dead person's spirit. Cotton balls were dipped in a mixture of coco water and holy water from a Catholic church. With that water and Castille soap, they washed Lorenzo's hair. His head and feet were lightly bathed with a mixture of roasted corn, young onion, cacao butter, grated coconut, eggshell, and other secret, powerful ingredients brought by Armenteros and O'Farrill. Lorenzo's head was covered with a white handkerchief for several minutes while two white doves were passed over his body.

Throughout the cleaning, the choir sang and moved their bodies to the rhythm of ordinary mambos:

> *Mari Wanga*
> *Mari Wanga yaribán*
> *Kereré é bongué*
> *Mari Wanga*
> *Baluande bó Baluande bó*
> *Baluande toki la kuenda*
> *Mamá Kasimba ko Kasimba*
> *Kasimba ko*
> *Mamá Kengue Mamá Kengue*
> *Como llueve ba é.*

The purification ceremonies for Lorenzo and Despaigne continued all night. They ended at daybreak with songs honoring the *Fundamento*, Zarabanda, all the Catholic saints, and the *orishas* that had been so cooperative. Then Lorenzo, his sister, Teodora, and the ill-treated Despaigne got into the taxi that had spent the night waiting for them.

As they left the church, a neighbor from across the street opened the window of her bedroom on the second floor and called out: "You've kept me awake all night! Anyone can see that none of you niggers work!"

THE SACRED HIDING PLACE

TIRED OF PLAYING CARDS, Pedro and Adrián were drinking beer and watching television. They had been in their hiding place for less than a week, but the cloistering was already destroying Pedro's tenuous equilibrium. Since his last stretch in prison, he had sworn that the police would never again catch him alive, convinced that he could not bear being enclosed. Now, this place was giving him the sensation of being locked up again. Adrián was trying to keep him entertained or asleep while he sought solutions to this new problem. He couldn't let Pedro leave the hiding place—although Pedro would never tell the police anything, he would keep no secrets from the *Nasakó*.

Adrián stared at the package from the *Santera*. Since José Miguel had handed it to him at Bodeguita del Medio he had been resisting the impulse to open it, even though he realized that knowing its contents might somehow be urgent.

"Why don't you open it? You spend the whole day looking at it," Pedro commented for the third time.

"The right moment hasn't arrived yet."

Pedro scratched his head, surprised at some people's strange behavior.

The place was big and, to a certain extent, comfortable; it had been the cistern of an old soft-drink factory that had originally drawn water from several small springs before the Revolution. A large reservoir had eventually been necessary to store all of the water that flowed in on non-working days.

Those springs made the El Perico soft drinks and mineral water famous, displacing many competitors. The image of water pouring from greenish rocks, forming a natural and crystalline blue pool before disappearing into the countryside, displayed in photographs and films, captured the public imagination as a symbol of purity. This illusion was maintained in advertisements long after the springs had ceased to flow.

As years passed, the demand for water in the area surrounding the factory grew and wells were drilled indiscriminately. The water level dropped until most springs ran dry, resuscitated only in years of frequent storms. Before that happened, however, Doña Elvira's prudent husband had contracted the drilling of four deep wells and installed vertical pumps in each to extract the liquid from underground in the quantities needed. To avoid public knowledge of the catastrophe that had reduced the factory to the same level as its competitors, a huge concrete dome was built over the dry cistern. The dome, "erected for hygienic reasons," hid the reservoir and its nonexistent springs from view.

Another threat arose with the growth of the city. The land surrounding the factory was used to build shacks, all with latrines that emptied into the formerly virginal subterranean stratum. The feared contamination of the water was verified. The competition surreptitiously paid for analyses of the water purity, the colibacilli count, and the chlorination level. Inspectors from the Ministry of Health followed, and then the drop in sales.

The excessively comfortable lifestyle of the owners declined rapidly. Illness, weak business, and, finally, the death of Don Cosme brought El Perico to ruin. All of the functioning machinery was sold off at bargain prices, but the offers for the land and the building had not satisfied Doña Elvira.

Shortly after the triumph of the Revolution, the state took over all kinds of businesses. But the government passed by Doña Elvira's property upon finding only rusted ruins, flourishing mango trees, and a pack of formerly pedigreed dogs degenerated by plebian blood from sexual contact with other dogs in the neighborhood.

Adrián had discovered the empty cistern and its main entrance by accident. Indirect questions to Agustín, Doña Elvira, and some of the oldest neighbors allowed him to reconstruct the history of the place. Another discovery facilitated his plans: All of the underground electric and telephone wires were in perfect condition. A pleasant atmosphere prevailed, fed by a current of air entering between the rocks through the fissures and caverns by which water had once flowed in.

Three places existed by which one could enter and leave the cistern. The first was a big manhole, covered by a steel lid, in what was formerly the principal warehouse of the now-collapsed factory. A second was the public entrance to the springs from the early days. That entrance was now obstructed by weeds, old pieces of metal, and a fallen section of the roof of the main warehouse. Finally, the cistern had a water outlet in its lowest point that led to a deep ravine, the original path by which the current from the springs had run out. The outlet was a concrete tube with a twenty-four-inch steel core, one hundred feet long, capped at the end by an enormous valve manipulated both electrically and manually. Holding onto a rope, Adrián had traversed the entire length of the outlet. This had brought him near the house where crystalline waters had once flowed.

Wild growth enclosed the whole factory, surrounded now by the mango grove. The army of dogs kept out curious intruders, who had to content themselves with peering through the fence at the Hayden and Super-Hayden mangos ripening to paradisiacal colors.

Adrián had considered the cistern at first as a perfect place to situate the bunker from which he would one day direct the operations of his emporium. The project called for an illegal preliminary stage in order to accumulate the large quantities of money required for respectability and power in the capitalist system that, he was confident, would be restored in the country in the near future. Directing his steps to that aim, he had surreptitiously installed a network of secret microphones around the ruins, permitting him to detect external noise. He later installed a standard alarm system on the perimetric fence, designed to prevent surprises, but left completion of the security system with closed-circuit TV cameras for the future.

For a time, he was able to keep the hideout a complete secret, using it as a place to read, sleep, and listen in on telephone calls, trying to discover any infidelities by Ana. The needs of the organization that he was forging, however, soon required the utilization of the refuge. The growing booty from the house robberies quickly overtook the sales capacity of José Miguel, leading them to use the cistern as a warehouse. It had thus been necessary to share his secret with Pedro and, to a certain extent, with José Miguel and Mulo.

Adrián had prepared a corner of the locale with two refrigerators, chairs, a table, beds, and enough food to withstand a long siege should the occasion ever arise. He kept secret two of the points of access, only using the one with the steel cover, situated at one end of the principal warehouse still standing. Beside the lid he had piled some twenty sacks of charcoal and prepared a mechanism attached to a cord in the cistern by which, at any given moment, the contents of a sack of charcoal could be dumped onto the lid of the entrance, hiding it. Only Pedro knew of this entrance.

In one of his visions during a *consulta*, the *Nasakó* "discovered" the existence of the hiding place, before the awed Pedro, who, months later, was still talking about the miracle of the discovery. This sealed the role of the place as a sanctuary for storing the assets for financing the first part of the great strategy, known in detail by Adrián and the *Nasakó* and only guessed at by Mulo and Pedro, the other members of the General Staff.

The moment had eventually come in which the accumulated treasures were of such a magnitude that the spirit in the *nganga* affirmed that a special protection was needed. This was the first time the spirit had shown such an initiative, having been satisfied until that moment merely to opine in response to the questions posed by the *Nasakó*. This time, the spirit ordered the use of one of its strategic weapons—an infallible ally, a recently buried Chinaman— to protect the "sacred place of refuge," as the spirit of the *nganga* insisted on calling the hiding place. In view of the intense enthusiasm of Pedro and Mulo for this "special protection," Adrián, against his better judgement, had gone along with the idea of finding and stealing a recently buried Chinese corpse.

Now his dreams, finally beginning to materialize, had come up against their first serious problem, and it seemed clear that the cause of it was precisely the stolen Chinese cadaver. The essential danger was the meeting between the *Santera* and the policeman who had recently arrived in Guanabacoa. Why would that policeman consult her? Another riddle to unravel was the strange package she had sent him. That woman was turning out to be a great enigma. At first, his idea had been to take her to bed and thereby gain acceptance in the Bantú house. He had been held back by something strange in her, a mixture of ardent desire followed by absolute withdrawal and remorse. As he gradually became acquainted with other people who frequently visited the house, he noted the aura of great respect for her and her reputation of extreme rectitude, gentleness, and impenetrable chastity. All of this inhibited him. Had he been mistaken in his estimation of the *Santera's* feelings about him? For a time, it had seemed that the connection between them was advancing inexorably, but he had then decided that possessing her would be a serious mistake, and he had begun to avoid her. In his future association with the *Nasakó*, he had thought, such a relationship would be an obstacle rather than a help.

Later, as he got to know her better, fear entered the picture. He was afraid of taking an irreversible step, of finding himself trapped forever in the magic of her strange attraction. What prevailed finally was his instinct for self-preservation; the possibility of unleashing an uncontrollable force led him to reject her that night when she had apparently decided to give herself. And for an instant, a fleeting moment, he had seen in her one good eye a look of hatred. He understood now that he had hurt her beyond any possibility of forgiveness. He had made her a lifetime enemy, as hatred replaced the passion she had felt for him in her heart. What could be the meaning of that gift she had sent with José Miguel?

"Pedro, do me a favor. Open that package and let's see what's in it."

Glad to have something to do, and to satisfy his own curiosity, Pedro took out his Sevillian knife and cut the string and tape, taking care not to touch the contents. With the tip of his knife, he withdrew a long, multicolored dress from the package. At that moment, something fell to the floor, making a peculiar sound. Pedro stared at the necklace on the floor, astonished. "It's a dress, some sandals, braids of hair . . . and a necklace of Oyá!"

"What does it mean, Pedro?"

"There's a *pataki*—a legend—that tells how Oyá saved Shangó after he sought refuge in her home, while fleeing from Oggún, who then surrounded the house with his troops. Each night the goddess left her home for a while and came back. Then, one night, she cut her hair and helped Shangó disguise himself with her clothes, necklace, and braids, and thus walk away free, outwitting Oggún."

A SIMPLE SOLUTION

AFTER A FULL NIGHT'S SLEEP, Alvaro felt like a new man. Those eyes that had looked so terrible had a different blue color today, and he seemed much younger. The *Santera* was also relaxed when she received him. She had slept almost all day, recovering from the ceremonies of *Rompimiento de Trabajo* and *Recogimiento de Muerto*, leaving her goddaughters to take care of everything. She was dressed entirely in white except for a necklace of blue beads.

After she had made the required invocations, she threw four pieces of coco onto the small table where she worked, then smiled, pleased. "You asked me to help you find the cadaver of a Chinaman, no?"

The policeman assented with a slight nod.

"The work is very simple and is going to depend exclusively on you."

The *Santera* rose, walked to another small table that held the telephone, took the cord, and tied it around the apparatus. Then she remained still, looking at her visitor. "The work is done. This work will lead you to a place where you have to find three things. Do you understand?"

The eyes of the policeman flashed in the semidarkness of the room. He again nodded in affirmation.

"You have to find a secret place where a man is hiding. That man will tell you everything you want to know. You will find a cross, and near the cross, the corpse of the Chinaman."

Alvaro rose and started to move toward the door when, behind his back, he heard a brief prayer followed by a cascade of dry sounds on the small table. He again heard the rattling of shells being thrown, then the voice of the *Santera* began to tell his oracle.

"There are three women in your path. Next year, you will have three children—all of them boys."

He froze for a second as he grasped the meaning of the oracle. At the door, he turned toward the *Santera*, winked, and made a slight sign by opening his right hand as if to show something. "All by *iré*," he said.

With the departure of the policeman, the *Santera* felt a shiver run through her body, a sign that some *orisha* was calling her attention. She made a quick mental check to assure herself that she was proceeding correctly. She had invoked Yemayá for work against Adrián, and the all-powerful goddess of the sea had responded by sending her that inexplicable man who had knocked at her door precisely to ask for her help in carrying out the work that she had requested of Yemayá—to set the police on Adrián's trail. Several factors obliged her to offer that help, the most important being the need to restore the Chinese cadaver to its rightful place, thus eliminating that locus of tension, that occult enemy so full of tricks. Only thus could she rest easy. Another extremely important mission was to neutralize the cause of all the strange events that had been happening in the house of the Bantús. Everything was poised for the final move to destroy Adrián, identified by Yemayá as an enemy.

But if everything was in order, why this uneasiness? She felt another shiver—this time, it seemed to her, related to the blond policeman. But what else could she have done? She had no other option. That man, clearly sent by Yemayá, was a direct son of Olofí, and she could not, for a moment, forget that.

She looked to the altar governed by a doll dressed in blue; the eyes of Yemayá, made of a brilliant black material, stared at her fixedly. Then she felt several more shivers, one after another, each more intense. She couldn't meet the penetrating gaze of the doll, as if it wanted to tell her not to console herself with the pretense that she was acting under the express command of the gods. Yemayá had sent her that man so that *she* would decide if she wanted to destroy Adrián or not. The choice was entirely hers. Once again, the *orishas* returned to her the responsibility for her own actions. Had her gods abandoned her to her own resources, denying her advice?

The *Santera* straightened her back. Yes, her decision was to carry on with what had been planned—to guide the police to the hiding place where Adrián must be hidden. And to do that, there was only one route, whatever its cost might be.

SETTLING ACCOUNTS

LORENZO SPENT THE DAY after the ceremony of *Rompimiento de Trabajo* and *Recogimiento de Muerto* in a state of lethargy. Now and then, he opened his eyes in his warm, dark room in which he couldn't distinguish day from night; not even the eternal strip of light under the door was visible. He knew that something inside him had changed.

He awoke with an aching body. All of his muscles felt as if they had been pounded by a meat hammer. But the heaviness in his head was gone, as were the horrible nightmares, the bad taste in his mouth, and the weakness of his legs. For the first time in many days, he felt hungry, very hungry, extremely hungry; every part of his body was demanding food, as if the acids in his stomach, that raging boiler, were rapidly consuming the rest of him. He rose to go to the bathroom and found the light turned on in the hallway. In the dining room, food was served, its wonderful aroma drawing him like a powerful magnet. With a frantic pleasure, he ate a platter of pork chops, a full bowl of white rice with crunchy *raspas,* and a plateful of fried ripe plantains.

Returning to bed proved to be a mistake. His full stomach swelled with gases. The bad taste returned to the base of his tongue and he began to belch with the repugnant taste of pork fat. His dreams bordered on nightmares in which the sound of drums predominated—the drum was his heart, pounding with fear. He was abruptly awakened by his sister's hand striking a hard, dry blow on his nude stomach that resounded like a *bongó* drum.

"Let's talk, Lorenzo Bantú! We have a lot to talk about!"

By the tone of her voice, the hardness of her glare, and the stiffness of her posture, he understood that the conversation was not going to be pleasant. In a way, he had played against her and lost. The settling of accounts was now inevitable, but his mind was still clouded and he felt incapable of reasoning clearly.

"Do you know what happened last night?" The *Santera* paused, waiting for an answer, then continued. "They removed the Chinaman from your body. He almost finished you off!"

His memory was slowly returning, reflected in his sleepy face.

"How could anyone with half a brain think of fucking around with a dead Chinaman? To show off, by doing strange work for Adrián, you got yourself in over your head!"

Lorenzo understood now. Everything was rapidly falling into place.

"It's about that bastard Adrián that I want to talk to you. He pretended to be your friend, but he came here to destroy this house. I've found this in every throw I've made."

Lorenzo was now fully awake, and alarmed. Ever since his sister adopted *Regla de Osha*, she had avoided using vulgar language and an aggressive tone of voice. But what he was seeing now was the frightening woman he remembered from his childhood, the one who little by little had come to dominate their grandfather, constantly showering him with insults.

Implacable, the *Santera* approached him, shouting, "Adrián has two-timed you with Miladys! Did you know that? You must have known! He stabbed you in the back by putting horns on you!"

Lorenzo leapt from the bed. He grabbed his sister by the shoulders and shook her hard. "You can't play with that! That can cost a man his life!" She reacted immediately, digging her strong, sharp fingernails into his chest.

Lorenzo let go, surprised by the quickness and violence of her reaction, the fury in her seeing eye, and the lacerating pain of the bleeding scratches she had made.

"How do you know that?" he demanded.

"It came out first in a consultation with my godmother. Very clear: one coco face up, a female; on another coco, face down—the betrayal of a man by a woman. It could only be her. Later, I confirmed it with the cocos here in the house. There's an explanation. Miladys was furious with you because of Ana; it was normal that she wanted to get even. Any woman with blood in her veins would have done the same. I'd tumble with the *macho* of any woman who put horns on me. An eye for an eye and a tooth for a tooth! . . . Besides, Miladys already had her eye on Adrián. She rode in his car twice. Did she tell you that? Well, she told me, your sister! You should have heard her talking about how handsome Adrián is!"

The *Santera* returned to her calm voice, adding with a certain condescension, "Well, you lost her after she tried that whitey. She hasn't even called to ask about you, and she had to know that you've been ill. If you doubt my word, José Miguel told me the same. Naturally, he asked me not to tell you because he knows you're crazy about that fat-assed slut."

Lorenzo started to move. He was suddenly compelled to do something for which he had been preparing mentally all of his life, but something for which one is never really prepared: to kill for the first time in cold blood.

He left the room and went to consult his *nganga*. He removed his shirt and shoes and tied the purple rag around his forehead before prostrating himself before the *prenda*.

Ever since he had discovered that the spirit in the *nganga* was that of his great-great-grandfather, he had held mental conversations with him without any preceding liturgy. He merely closed his eyes until the figure of a black man almost exactly like his grandfather appeared in his mind. He greeted him always in the same way, with confidence and respect: "*Buenos días, mi taita. Cómo está, mi taita?*" His great-great-grandfather would raise his head slightly, indicating that he was well and, without smiling, move his head again, this time downward, giving his blessing. Only then would Lorenzo ask his questions, one by one, and the answers would appear at once in his mind.

This time, the great-great-grandfather frowned upon learning of Adrián's betrayal and ordered Lorenzo to take the saber in the *nganga* that was still smeared with almost-century-old blood. With that weapon, he would be invincible. Zarabanda in person would accompany him. He had to kill with cold steel.

The *Santera* called José Miguel from the telephone in her bedroom. The night before, she had alerted him to wait for her call the following day, not to leave his house for any reason, and to follow her instructions to the letter. "José Miguel, Lorenzo is going to come see you to find out where Adrián is. Take him there. This is very important for both of you. Don't let them fight; remember, there's a woman between them. I hold you responsible for not letting anything happen. Do you know Adrián's telephone number?" The *Santera* gave him the number twice, repeating it slowly.

After hanging up, the *Santera* collapsed onto a chair. She had delivered the final blow in the plan that she had been contemplating for so long. If it failed, the consequences would be incalculable.

Seeing her looking faint, Euridice hurried to the dining room and returned with a cup of coffee. "Godmother, you work too much. Rest a little. Lie down and I'll prepare dinner."

Feeling somewhat restored, she moved to change the votive candle before Yewá. Seeing that it still had about a half-inch to burn, however, she decided to wait awhile, since she had to save candles as much as possible. She threw herself onto the bed to think everything over.

Lorenzo, she was sure, would find Adrián—thus guiding the police. She could think of no other way to reach the devil. José Miguel knew exactly where he was hiding and was his link to the outside world, but the presumptuous brute would only tell Lorenzo. Adrián had to be hiding in a spot protected by the cadaver of the Chinaman—probably someplace among the ruins of the former soft-drink factory that Ana was never able to find. But the Chinese corpse no longer had any power: Its spirit was firmly enclosed in one of the *nganga*s of the temple, pending her decision about what to do with it. Now that the magic protection of the place had been annulled, her brother could go directly to Adrián. The policeman with the intelligent blue eyes sent by Yemayá would do what he had to do. Nothing should fail. Adrián was now entirely at the mercy of his father Shangó. If the *orisha* decided to save him, he would let him know what to do, and against Shangó's will, no one could act. She rested her head briefly on her pillow and dozed.

The room was suddenly filled with a maddening perfume. Adrián took her face in his left hand and turned it from one side to the other. "You're the most beautiful Negress I've ever seen in my life," he said.

ILL OMEN

HANGING UP after the call from Lorenzo's sister, José Miguel lit a cigar, stretched out on the sofa, and began to ponder. Today was Friday; he hadn't slept well and had gotten up earlier than usual, tense, with a strange sensation in his stomach. When he examined his excrement—as he did every morning looking for clues about what was going to happen that day—they were much darker than usual and formed a cross, both undoubtedly bad signs. The *Santera* had called him again to repeat almost exactly what she had said last night. She had told him not to move from his house in order to wait for her call. Since then, he had been trying to decide what her game could be. The whole thing seemed like a plan conceived with the strange policeman.

On the other hand, Lorenzo's recovery from his illness, whatever it had been, was good news. The *Santera*, he figured, must have been scared by what he had told her about the doctor's statement to the police. Perhaps she had then given Lorenzo an antidote. But the policeman's second consultation with the *Santera* promised nothing good. Since that man's first visit to the *Santera*, José Miguel had had the foresight to monitor him, and had made his three boys trail the cop on their bicycles at all times. But they had lost him the night before. Another bad omen.

Now, suddenly, Lorenzo wanted to see Adrián, and things didn't exactly seem to be harmonious between them. The most elementary prudence suggested that he avoid that encounter, but with the little information he had, it was impossible to know what was really going on. If he didn't do as the *Santera* had asked, or if he tried to fool Lorenzo, he ran the risk of losing Lorenzo's friendship and confidence, and of arousing the animosity of the *Santera*. Lorenzo was a man of very rudimentary thought and action in some situations. On the other hand, if the *Santera* had decided to cooperate with the police, everything was lost. It seemed to him that he had no choice but to follow events as they arose.

When Lorenzo arrived, his cold greeting let José Miguel know that the *Nasakó* was prejudiced against him, although he could think of nothing that he had done to deserve that treatment. This was not the way Lorenzo Bantú would normally greet him after two weeks without seeing each other. The *Palero* was considerably thinner, but looked better without the belly that had begun to grow on him. He carried a long package wrapped in newspaper.

"Let's go. Take me to see Adrián."

"We have to call him first. It is almost three o'clock. We have to wait a few minutes until the hands of the watch are one on top of the other, about three-fifteen."

At a signal from José Miguel, a young woman, round of face and figure and wrapped in a red housecoat, brought two cold beers and two mugs that José Miguel had brought from East Germany after finishing two years of work in that country.

"Lorenzo, Ina, my *compañera*."

The young woman blushed and nodded.

Lorenzo Bantú drank his beer quickly. The young woman immediately brought him another and, in a few minutes, another. Lorenzo's eyes were glued to the hands of his wristwatch. José Miguel sipped his first beer slowly—calm and on guard—while he observed the *Nasakó* closely.

"Tell me something, José Miguel, what do you know about Miladys?" Lorenzo burst out, unable to contain himself any longer.

The question and the tone of his voice alarmed José Miguel. Evidently, Miladys had broken off relations with the *Nasakó*. She hadn't visited him during his illness and Lorenzo wanted to find out why. José Miguel's modus operandi was to never intervene between a man and his woman, following the wise old rule: *Entre marido y mujer nadie se debe meter.*

"I haven't seen her for quite a while."

"So you don't know anything about Miladys?"

José Miguel realized that he was already too involved. "If you're going to call, call now. Now's the time. Remember: two rings, hang up, and punch the number again." José Miguel handed the wireless telephone to Lorenzo, who, unacquainted with this type of apparatus, stared at it, perplexed. José Miguel took the phone, punched in the phone number, paused, hung up, dialed again, then returned it after he heard Adrián's voice, imitating his aunt.

"Listen, I want to see you right now."

Lorenzo frowned upon hearing the response.

"Don't give me that crap, Adrián! What do you think you're doing, talking to me like an old lady! I'm on my way. I have something urgent to settle with you."

The *Nasakó* put the phone down and stood up. "Let's go. Take me in your truck."

José Miguel nodded. He finished his beer and glanced at the woman who was quietly removing the glasses. The two men left the house and climbed into a 1955 Chevrolet truck—better now than when it was new, José Miguel always said, once he had changed its motor for a German-made diesel.

THE TRAP

THE "VILLA OF THE DOGS" was invaded silently by the Special Police Brigade without drawing the attention of the neighbors, who were taking their siesta, lulled to drowsiness by the extremely hot afternoon. The dogs, neutralized one by one by trained personnel, slept the sleep of the just, scattered under the shade of the mango trees. A hole had been cut at a strategic point in the fence, through which a group of uniformed men in red berets passed. In minutes, the brigade spread across the grounds to converge on the house like cutter ants around a citrus tree as they searched the earth inch by inch, leaving guards at designated points—perspiring and happy to be putting into practice skills so long rehearsed.

Adrián hung up the telephone and remained pensive. His gaze took in the vastness of the refuge, then paused to observe the infantile expression on the face of Pedro, absorbed in the tribulations of Donald Duck. He walked to the far end of the locale, following a path through the enormous variety of stolen objects. He began to urinate—in a latrine perforated by Pedro and him with a sledgehammer and chisel in the concrete cistern floor and the green rock that lay below it—while he contemplated why Lorenzo's voice had been so furious and threatening. The *Palero* had never visited his house, and it had been clearly established between them that their only direct contact would be in the *Palero's* house, outside of his regular consulting hours and the sight of his regular clients. If there was anything on which he could rely, it was the word of Lorenzo, who always complied strictly with their agreements. What was more, he was extremely disciplined with the security measures they had established. This new development implied a problem of considerable magnitude. He finished urinating and returned, still puzzled by the telephone call.

By the hour and the method used to call, it was clear that José Miguel had told Lorenzo how to communicate with him, and now he was undoubtedly on his way here, guided by José Miguel—but neither of them knew the exact location. Or did they? Had Pedro talked? Or Ana? Could she have spied on them in spite of his warning never to go to the back of the property?

Why did Lorenzo need to see him so urgently? Shaking his head, he decided not to waste neurons trying to guess. It could be anything—something revealed by a throw of the shells, some gossip about him offered by the spirit of the *nganga*, or any other stupidity of the sort. His whole relationship with the *Nasakó* had become an unholy mess. How the devil was it possible that he, who thought himself so intelligent, had fallen into this morass?

Carrillo, notified of the operation by the chief of police of Guanabacoa, dropped everything to be present at the finale. He decided to go dressed in civilian clothing, in a car with a private license plate, just in case the *coup de grâce* turned out to be a fiasco. It had been difficult to keep this bizarre operation under control. For three weeks, he had resisted all of the complaints about his star investigator—the first because of his unorthodox method of questioning the grave digger from the Chinese cemetery, who, frightened by the visit, had called the police; that in turn had set off a full-scale investigation to locate the strange visitor.

Alvaro, by pure instinct, had realized from the beginning that part of the investigation in the Chinese quarter had been kept from him and that Lin and his collaborators were only the visible tip of a very large iceberg. As payback, he had managed to infuriate the most methodical, patient, and organized officer under Carrillo's command. Carrillo, on the other hand, had stayed on top of all developments with the idea of a full disclosure with his eccentric friend when the right moment came or, perhaps, of simply sending him back home to his vegetable crops.

Meanwhile, the police of Guanabacoa, after initial reticence, were now well impressed. Without knowing what the whole business was about, they felt confident that the strange investigator was probing into a major problem incubating in the interior of the Abakuá world. So far, it was only a subterranean rumor, a noise from the deep, but, in any event, clear, unmistakable signals that a volcanic eruption was threatening. Carrillo hadn't understood at first who they were talking about when they referred with such enthusiasm to the *abikú*, a term that recalled tales meant to frighten children under the age of five. The physique of the policeman, so much taller than the average Cuban, his extraordinary devotion to work once he became interested, and his peculiar way of reasoning through the unreasonable, had already made this man, whatever else happened, a legend in that territory.

The chief of police of Guanabacoa, obliged by the mandate of Carrillo, although perplexed by the importance being given the case, took command of the troops that would carry out the final assault. He appeared at the house of Adrián's aunt and had a brief conversation with Ana, who, freshly bathed, opened the door dressed in shorts and a strapless pullover. The policeman maintained an official attitude, but when Ana opened the door wide to let him in and turned to move into the interior of the house, swinging her hips and butt in erotic synchronization, he rolled his eyes heavenward and sighed deeply.

He was followed at regular intervals into the house by Carrillo, Fonseca, and, finally, by a tall blond man who had removed a spare tire and hydraulic jack from the trunk of the car he was using. When Alvaro arrived in the living room, the explanations had already been given and Ana, dressed now in a long housecoat closed at the throat, was sitting in an armchair, waiting. Carrillo and the chief of police were whispering to each other and barking orders into a cell phone.

"Which is Adrián's room?"

Ana guided the policeman with the tired blue eyes to the room, trying to think of anything compromising that might be there that she could quickly hide. The policeman observed the air conditioner, perhaps checking for secret hiding places, Ana thought.

"Does it work?"

She moved quickly to turn it on. The policeman put a hand before the current of cool air and nodded. "If you have no objection, I'm going to lie down here awhile."

For Adrián, the silencing of the dogs' barking was confirmation that the property was being taken over by assault troops. Through the system of listening devices installed outside, strange sounds had begun to reach the cistern. These developments had occurred only after an alarm notified him that the fence had probably been cut at some point. There wasn't much to do. He looked at his watch. Full darkness wouldn't fall yet for almost three hours. He put on a cassette of piano music, turned down very low so that it couldn't be heard from outside. For the moment, it was the best he could do.

As soon as Pedro realized what was going on, he decided he had to leave at any cost. He whispered anxiously to Adrián after each sound they heard, until he finally exploded like a furious madman. "I'm not going to wait for them to trap me in here like a rabbit! I'm getting out! No one's going to take me alive! They'll have to nail me with a shot in the back!"

Adrián had anticipated this reaction. He showed Pedro the old entrance to the springs, obstructed now by vegetation and debris. If Pedro was careful, he could clear his way little by little, hiding among the tall weeds until nightfall, then slip out of the grounds without being detected.

"Are you staying?" Pedro asked.

"Yes, I'm going to run the risk. I'll use the time to listen to the orchestral music that I know you don't like."

Pedro grinned despite himself. Adrián showed him the exit and helped him to move debris aside and place it behind them, until the return to the interior of the refuge began to be almost too closed. The exit was dark except for a few spots that indicated that it was still light outside the tunnel. The two friends embraced each other. The absence of light prevented Adrián from seeing the tears in Pedro's eyes.

"You know this is a military organization," Adrián whispered.

Pedro, surprised, paused an instant before replying. "Yeah, sure."

"You know I'm the chief. I've never given you an order. This whole time, we've only shared the work. Now I'm going to give you my first order. I don't want you to disobey it under any circumstance."

"You're my brother, Adrián."

"Besides your brother, I'm your chief. Give me your pistol!"

Pedro was stunned and delayed a few seconds before slowly, reluctantly, like a man finally deciding to cut off his leg to save the rest of his body, handing the weapon to Adrián. Immediately, he turned and tore vigorously into the remaining debris, taking care not to make too much noise or to uproot more than absolutely necessary the vegetation growing in every direction in that immense tangle of obstacles.

The general at war understood that the enemy would soon arrive at the doors of the bunker. Undoubtedly, the police had followed the *Nasakó* there. Now he understood the meaning of his call, his surprising anger, demanding to see him immediately. Slowly, it dawned on him who had to be behind everything that was happening, as well as the meaning of that dress and those ornaments, sent to him by a woman terribly wounded but, in her sorrow, madly in love.

BETRAYAL

FAR FROM COOLING the air, the shower had drawn the heat from the streets, walls, and roofs of houses, throwing a steaming vapor into the faces of the few passersby. José Miguel got out of the truck and walked resolutely to the wide metallic gate, sealed with an enormous lock of Chinese make. He glanced casually up and down the street before opening the lock, pushing the heavy gate open, and stepping aside to let the *Nasakó* enter before closing it.

José Miguel again took the lead among the mangos and high weeds. He was surprised and suspicious not to encounter a single dog. He always brought food for the beasts to ensure their friendship and to avoid the loud barking and aggressiveness that he had found on his first visits. Now the canines knew the sound of the truck from far away and normally waited for him, wagging their tails behind the gate and pushing each other aside to lick his hands. Where were they?

The atmosphere changed completely, as if they had entered another country. On the estate, the temperature was several degrees cooler than in the surrounding city. The air was light and smelled pleasantly of herbs, flowers, and general humidity. The green tones and the silence began to dilute his tension and sense of alarm. Nevertheless, José Miguel moved ahead cautiously, hiding behind trees and weeds, using war tactics learned in the jungles of Cabinda in Angola, until they reached a spot near one of the ruined warehouses. "Here is where Pedro always waits for me with the merchandise from the warehouse. I never see Adrián."

Lorenzo began to search for something in the grass. José Miguel confronted him. "What's going on? Give it to me straight. Ever since you arrived at my place, you've had a snout a yard long. You hardly even greeted me. What're you looking for? This fiesta could be very dangerous."

"I must find Adrián. I have men's matters to settle with him. The entrance to the 'sacred hiding place' has to be around here somewhere. Adrián must be hiding there like a rat, and you see that he hasn't come out to meet us. You have to know where the entrance is, but you don't want to tell me. My sister warned me about this."

"I don't know what you're talking about or what the hell your sister has told you about me."

The *Nasakó* began to walk among the trees. José Miguel sat down to get accustomed to the idea of spending a long time in jail. Since entering through the gate, he'd had the distinct sense that he was walking into a trap. Now he felt certain that the sinister hand of the *Santera* was behind everything. When she couldn't get rid of her brother by witchcraft, she had laid this trap with the police in order to send Lorenzo to prison, along with Adrián and him. Everything was going to end terribly, and he had no way of avoiding it. Any attempt at flight was useless. If this were the case, the game was already lost and a false move could cost him a shot to the head.

Soon, José Miguel heard the *Nasakó* calling him. He walked over to where Lorenzo stood looking up at a strange cross nailed to a mango tree. "The entrance to the hiding place has to be near here. The Chinaman himself asked me for that cross. I ordered it put up."

The *Nasakó* continued to search the area. He had no choice, he finally told himself, but to resort to his magic faculties. At moments like this, he always let himself be guided by impulses from his innermost being—sometimes confused and incomplete, but always reliable. He tore away the newspaper covering and raised the Zarabanda saber that José Miguel had seen many times in the *Nasakó's nganga*. The *Palero* took off his shirt, undershirt, shoes, and socks and tied his undershirt around his head. Then, with the

saber gripped tight in his two hands before him like a divining rod, very sure
of what he was doing, Lorenzo Bantú began to sway and chant each verse
in a low voice, raising his volume as he tested each spot:

> Search, Zarabanda, search!
> Search, Zarabanda, search!
> Search, my sword, search!
> Search, my steel, search!
> Kill, my steel, kill!

In this way, he explored all around, awaiting some sign of the hiding
place of his enemy.

"Adrián," he shouted, "I'm going to find you, no matter what! You know
I'm going to find you!" And singing louder, he continued his chant:

> Search, Zarabanda, search!
> Search, Zarabanda, search!
> Search, my sword, search!
> Search, my steel, search!
> Kill, my steel, kill!

José Miguel decided to intervene, but as always when the *Nasakó* was
practicing a religious ritual, he spoke to him with great respect and deference.
"*Nasakó*. Will you permit me? You always said this place is protected by a
Chinaman that they got out of the Chinese cemetery. With that magic shield,
nobody is ever going to find the sacred hiding place. And that includes us."

Lorenzo stopped, paralyzed for a moment by the logic. His features contracted, furious at his impotence. But his expression changed immediately
as the demolishing reply swept into his mind from the depths of his ancestral knowledge: "Don't give me that shit, José Miguel. You don't know what
you're talking about. This is the saber of Zarabanda!"

Then, stretching to his full height, inflating his chest and the veins of his
neck, Lorenzo shouted: "I am Zarabanda!" As if startled by what he had
just said, he repeated in a low voice: "*I am Zarabanda!*"

Sure now of his new powers, Lorenzo walked toward José Miguel with the saber raised high and, as he drew near, pointed the blade at his neck. José Miguel stared at him, alarmed.

"What the hell can a dead Chinaman do against Zarabanda?" Lorenzo asked, and then immediately repeated, shouting: "Tell me, what the hell can a dead Chinaman do against Zarabanda?"

José Miguel didn't respond. He was tense, glancing at the saber blade and calculating the movement he would need to make in case it dropped suddenly. *The Nasakó is completely out of his mind, and no one can argue with a madman*, he told himself.

Lorenzo lowered the saber, turned away, and continued his search, shouting back at him, "Stupid fool!"

José Miguel felt the insult almost like a saber blow. No man could treat him like that, even the *Nasakó*, nutty as a fruit cake. Who the hell did Lorenzo think he was? No one could insult José Miguel Ochoa and get away with it. And if the *Nasakó* was too stupid to realize it, that was his problem. He decided to counterattack in his own way. "Lorenzo," he said, "I'm going to tell you something. Your sister is working with the police. On Monday, she talked with a special investigator sent from Havana—a tall blond guy. Yesterday afternoon, she saw him again, in your own house. And I can assure you that your sister, who has always wanted to get you out of the way, made a deal with him. Look around you, the whole place has been taken over. There isn't a single dog! Anytime someone tries to come in here, those devils tear him apart. There're some fifteen dogs here, and where are they?"

Perplexed, Lorenzo raised his hands to his head. Always intense in his sentiments, the revelation of his sister's betrayal suddenly unleashed a volcano of ideas that froze his actions. Here was José Miguel, a lifelong friend and Abakuá brother, confirming his own suspicions. His sister was working against him. This meant that her advice was intended for his harm. Everything was becoming more and more confused, but he immediately saw the truth very clearly: He was alone; everyone had turned against him.

By the wild expression on the *Palero's* face, it was evident that the surprise had been great. José Miguel now felt that he was brandishing a more powerful sword than that of the *Palero*.

"Shut up!" Lorenzo shouted. "I don't trust her, but I don't trust you, either. You knew that Miladys was two-timing me with Adrián and you didn't tell me anything." The *Nasakó* again raised the saber menacingly and approached José Miguel. "Today, Zarabanda is going to settle many accounts!"

From among the tall weeds, a German shepherd suddenly appeared, followed by a sturdy young man in a police uniform with a maroon beret on one side of his head. The dog immediately began to dig energetically under the cross.

"There, didn't I tell you, Lorenzo? There's the proof. The *fiana* have taken over the whole place."

The *Nasakó* advanced toward the intruder with his saber raised high. "I am Zarabanda. Nobody can mess with Zarabanda, boy!" He had been convinced from the start that he would have to overcome the guardians of the hiding place. It had never occurred to him that they might take the shape of police, but it was all the same to him now that he felt invincible. He made a turn to let the enormous red afternoon sun blind his opponent. The young man in the maroon beret—a good trophy for his *nganga*—stared at the strange figure before him with a childish smile on his beardless face, as if he were watching a circus act.

Lorenzo took his last precaution. He quickly slipped out of his trousers and, wearing only the loincloth used in the *Rompimiento de Trabajo* and *Recogimiento de Muerto*, he directed his ferocious gaze to hypnotize the astonished cop, who, serene and unafraid, was unaware that death was only a few paces away.

The *Nasakó* suddenly lunged forward with the saber raised, letting out a terrifying shout. The young policeman leapt back and to the side, but was unable to prevent a nasty cut on his left arm. He drew his pistol and placed a bullet in the barrel with surprising dexterity. He pointed his weapon at the enormous and furious black man, who prepared to attack again.

"Drop that machete, citizen Zarabanda!" the young man shouted, supporting his wounded arm with difficulty on the leash that held the dog now eager to enter into combat.

In the quiet of the afternoon, the bloodthirsty war cry of the African *mpungo* was again heard, followed by a shot that cut the war cry short. The sound immediately faded amongst the trees and the scent of ripe mangos, and the place was again submerged in silence. Then the boom of something heavy striking the ground, as if a great tree trunk had been felled.

Suddenly, the Iyaré Margarita *appeared again, throwing the cocos at the end of her consultation. In front of her and very near, a coco had fallen with the white meat on top of another below it, indicating the betrayal of a man by a woman. "What is the meaning of that throw, godmother?" she heard her own voice asking. Margarita collected the obís and, without looking at her, responded: "It speaks only to the* Iyaré."

The *Santera* awoke with a cry from her brief sleep. She heard the rapid steps of one of her goddaughters coming to see what was happening. She sat up in her bed, frightened. At that instant, the votive candle in front of Yewá's little house went out, an unmistakable sign of bad luck. She felt sure that at that exact moment the betrayal of a man by a woman had been consummated: *her* betrayal. And again she saw the *Iyaré* Margarita remaining pensive for a second before relaying the meaning of her first coco throw. Then, spoken in a loud rasping voice, the *súyer* that accompanies *Itawa*: *"Everything in life has its opposite, all things cast a shadow. There is no first without a second, there is no second without a first. You must lure your enemy to your side to increase your own power; if you destroy your enemy, it will not encumber you, but this will diminish your prestige."*

Lorenzo fell to his knees before the hole excavated by the dog in the soft ground where the edge of a coffin had appeared, wrapped in a gray cloth stained with the ochre of the red earth. José Miguel ran to the wounded man and kneeled at his side. Very pale, the young policeman, like a child who has broken a window, pulled at José Miguel's sleeve and spoke loudly, trying to tell him something at the same time that the *Nasakó* whispered in his ear.

"You were a witness. If I hadn't shot, he would've cut my head off with that sword."

"José Miguel, my brother. Did you realize?"

"What else could I do? I had to defend myself."

"That's why the chino *asked me for a cross."*

"Look at the cut on my arm!"

"He asked for the cross to let the police know where he was buried."

"Anyone else would have shot him when he first attacked me."

"What a bastard, that chino! *He really fucked me up. He's finished me."*

"You are my witness, citizen. Tell the truth. I had to defend myself. If I hadn't, that man would've killed me."

The *Nasakó* closed his eyes to the sleepiness and the cold invading his body, the Angolan cold of malarial fevers, the same cold feeling of his sister's powders, the heavy drowsiness of his childhood when he slept next to his mother.

José Miguel, who almost always wore a smile of disbelief, was now very serious, thinking about other things—about the absurd way the *Nasakó* had sought his own death, brandishing the saber of Zarabanda, clad in a loincloth like his ancestors in the jungle; thinking that perhaps, with time, he would become an *orisha*, since all saints had first been men who had died with great powers before their spirits were transformed. Then José Miguel realized that there was nothing strange about the behavior of Lorenzo, since he had nothing else to live for, knowing the betrayal of his sister and knowing that Miladys was no longer his.

José Miguel shook himself. He had to think of other, more mundane things. "Don't worry, son. I'm a witness that you shot in self-defense. But let's see how you take care of me and get me out of this mess, because, if not, it might occur to me to testify to something else."

Suddenly, they were surrounded by police officers, guns in hand, approaching from all directions.

THE NIGHT OF OYÁ

WITH THE COMPLICITY of a sky filled with clouds impregnated with rain, darkness fell suddenly, blanketing everything. A typical tropical storm was threatening but hadn't yet unleashed its fury, making the heat and humidity more oppressive. The strange, blue-eyed policeman, who had spent a couple of hours sleeping in Adrián's bed until the sound of a shot woke him, drew near to Ana and told her that he would make sure that no one bothered her when she was going to leave. She needn't worry about the safety of the old lady or the house, because everything was being carefully watched.

Recalling his words a half-hour later, she realized that she needed to let Miladys know what had happened. Someone had to tell her that the *Nasakó* had been shot in the middle of the chest and that he might already be dead. She could, of course, call her on the telephone, but news like that should be conveyed in person. And maybe Miladys knew how to contact Adrián to let him know that the house and grounds had been taken over by an army of policemen. She needed to let Adrián know that he had to leave Guanabacoa and Havana fast. Then Ana asked herself how the policeman had known that she wanted to go out on a night like this.

She went quickly to collect her raincoat and an umbrella. Judging by the volume of the thunder, the storm was going to break at any moment. What would Doña Elvira do when she came down to make coffee in the morning and found the house full of policemen? She had closed herself up in her room when she heard strange voices and she hadn't yet reappeared. Ana decided to write her a note and slip it under her door. Then she made sure that everything was in order in the house before she informed the blue-eyed policeman that she was leaving.

The guard at the entrance gate looked at her, perplexed. She hastened to explain.

"I'm Ana. I live here. A very tall, blue-eyed policeman, white, and another one, black and short, told me I could leave whenever I like."

"And who was the woman that left just a minute ago?" the policeman asked. "I thought it was you."

"What woman?"

"A tall one with green eyes, wearing a kerchief on her head, and braids. She had on a big, colorful dress."

Ana was confused a moment. Who else had green eyes? "Oh! What a dunce I am! That's my sister. Which way did she go?"

The policeman indicated the direction and Ana started off, walking slowly while she was still within sight of the policeman. Then she broke into a desperate run, wanting to call out to Adrián, but not daring to shout his name.

THE EXHUMATION

THE CADAVER of Rafael Cuan was exhumed under the strict supervision of specialists with municipal and provincial judges brought in hastily as witnesses. The decision was made to transfer the cadaver to the Institute of Legal Medicine to carry out a major forensic study with a view to determining the cause of death. A careful toxicological examination and analysis was ordered, including a test for any nonconventional poisonous substances.

Alvaro, Carrillo, and the chief of police of Guanabacoa were present at the first inspection by the coroner. The cadaver was well conserved with no sign of foul play.

Carrillo seemed disappointed. Upon departing, he shook Alvaro's hand and embraced him. He turned to the others present and said, "Here before all of you, I want to congratulate a retired officer who we asked to take charge of this investigation because of the difficulties it presented. It is to him, beyond any doubt, that we owe this important success." He again embraced Alvaro and walked a few steps with him toward the door, then issued a combination order-request: "It would be a good idea if you stayed here until they take the cadaver away."

"And with that, my responsibility in the case ends?"

Carrillo again shook his hand and patted his shoulder as a sign that his work had indeed concluded.

Alvaro was going to say something, but decided against it. He had observed a detail that seemed important to him, but kept silent, his pride a little wounded.

He would have liked to participate in the thorough examination of the cadaver and the coffin at the Institute of Legal Medicine. Carrillo had dismissed him with the pettiest of excuses: The police of Guanabacoa and the Special Brigade would be sufficient for what remained to be done. He was now convinced that the real reason for the search was to try to find something on the cadaver or in the coffin itself—although he had no idea what that might be.

Returning home later, he told himself that he was being too imaginative. Why not accept the official explanation? Why did there have to be some secret purpose beyond what he already knew? Perhaps the detail he had noted had no importance whatsoever. *But why wasn't the dead man wearing his old belt, the one his daughter had told him Cuan asked to be buried with?*

MAYULÍ

DESPITE HIS SUCCESS finding the missing corpse, Alvaro was frustrated about Carrillo terminating his participation. Why? Lack of confidence in him . . . ? He decided to shut his mind to the case.

He looked at himself in the mirror and saw that he wasn't that old. Carrillo was right, he should get married a third time. He needed the equilibrium that only a woman can give. Three was a lucky number. This last thought made him recall the voice of the *Santera* as he headed out the door: *"There are three women in your path . . ."*

Who were those women? Surely Narelys was one, but he couldn't face her father after they'd been found like Adam and Eve sleeping on the floor in the library. Jacinto had expelled him in such a scandalous way . . .

Camila could be number two. She was a very smart and attractive woman, but his instinct for self-preservation started beeping every time his mother mentioned her.

Who was the third woman in his path? Mayulí? That was impossible. Even though she was in her late twenties, she looked much younger. If there was a third female in his path, he should start looking for her. Besides, Mayulí hadn't shown any special interest in him. He had given her his phone number, but she hadn't called . . . Although maybe she *had* called and his mother hadn't mentioned it!

* * *

This time Alvaro couldn't surprise the young woman, who spotted him at a distance. She stood at the door of the hospital, watching him with a smile, then ran toward him, embracing him affectionately. "How lovely to see you! I lured you here with my thoughts." Mayulí held onto his hands as she stepped back to look intently into his face.

"The case is over for me. This is a purely social visit."

"Colonel Carrillo called last night to tell us the good news. He said they're going to conduct some forensic investigations, and that it will take some time. Afterwards, I suppose we'll have to bury my father again, but we'll make sure we use one of the cemetery chapels with locks and a burglar alarm."

Alvaro took her arm. "I'll see you home, this time in style, in a car. I borrowed it from my mother. I'm too tired to ride the bicycle today, but I wanted to see you . . . very much."

Mayulí smiled. "A car? Good, we're making progress. I invite you to have dinner with us, if you have some time to spare."

"All the time in the world."

Seated in the only chair in the room, Alvaro again contemplated the checkerboard of rooftops visible from the open window of Mayulí's room. Today, the sky was clear and he could see the intense blue of the sea through the narrow spaces between the roofs. Calle Zanja was quiet, with almost no traffic or pedestrians. What had brought him here again? He questioned himself, not sure that this visit was a good idea.

As she entered, Mayulí again filled the room with the fragrance of a recent bath. She carried a tray with a bottle, glasses, and small plates with food. "Dinner will be ready in a little while, so I brought this as a snack." She set the tray on a small bureau, then walked to the door and slid the bolt, locking it. The last time he had been there, she had left the door wide open. Now, she served him rum from an amber bottle, then sat down on her bed, facing him. Alvaro wondered if his imagination was playing tricks on him or if Mayulí was actually insinuating something. The possibility produced a strange sensation of unease. He hadn't expected this. He had planned on having an informal chat with her about her father. He also hoped to see some of the old photos of Cuan she had shown him before.

Instead, everything seemed to be heading in an entirely different direction. He reminded himself that there was an age difference of almost twenty years between them, so he could reject the crazy notion that this lovely creature was interested in him romantically.

"It's strange the way we can be around a person our whole life and never really know them. Yet with others, after only a brief encounter, we feel as if we've always known them."

He nodded but remained silent, wondering where she was going with this.

"Do you believe in love at first sight?"

Alvaro leaned his head to one side, suggesting doubt.

"I think there is also friendship at first sight. Ever since I met you, I've found your company very enjoyable. Whenever I think about the last time you were here, I remember how I liked listening to you and seeing you laugh . . . I like older men. The guys my own age . . . they seem to me so . . . I don't know . . ."

He definitely wasn't prepared to be this intimate with her. She was wearing a lightweight kimono, clearly revealing the perfect roundness of her medium-sized breasts that would fit neatly into his hands. Each position that the young woman adopted seemed to disclose a tiny bit more of those enticing thighs. What could explain this behavior? Was she trying to buy him off? That would mean that she had something to hide. Perhaps she thought that with the discovery of her father's cadaver, something incriminating had turned up and his unannounced visit frightened her . . . Perhaps the fact that there had been no belt on her father's corpse.

As he had learned in his military career, the best defense was a strong offense, so he began to question her. "Although, as I told you, I'm off the case now, I'm curious to know more about your father—an interesting man who lived through turbulent times."

Mayulí stayed silent, as if nervous about the path he was following.

"Who was Ming, really? What did your father tell you about him?"

Mayulí seemed to freeze. She immediately assumed a defensive attitude, and her tone of voice changed radically. She repeated the same words she had said to him before. "Ming appeared out of the blue about two months before my father died. Papá was very surprised by his visit. Ming began to come to the house almost every afternoon. He always left around five o'clock after talking for about two hours in Chinese and drinking green tea. Since his arrival coincided with my father's illness, I chatted with Ming on the days when I was taking care of my father. I spoke with him in my very poor English."

"Did your father tell you anything unusual about Ming?"

"Just that they had been friends when they were young, nothing more."

Alvaro swirled the liquor in his glass as if he were dissatisfied with her answers. Now Mayulí pulled her kimono close around her.

"You told me that your father wanted to be buried with his old belt. When he was exhumed, he wasn't wearing the belt. Where is it now?"

Mayulí stood up. She went to the bureau and put her almost-untouched glass on the tray. She turned toward Alvaro and said scornfully, "Ah! For a moment I thought it was true that your work with the police was over and that you were here on a social visit. I even thought that you might be courting me!" She gave a short, forced laugh. "How silly of me!" Two tears filled her bright eyes and she hid them behind her hands.

He again had before him the young woman who had so impressed him on his previous visit. Deciding that he had committed a gross error, he remained in his seat, trying to figure out what to do next. "Forgive me. I've been rude. I'm honestly sorry. I'm very clumsy and always end up hurting the people I care for most." Alvaro then stood up with the idea of leaving, disgusted with himself, but he didn't take a step.

Crying, she managed to explain: "I wanted to see you so badly and talk with you about everything that's happening. I was so glad when you said you'd finished with the investigation and had come to see me . . . I felt relieved . . ." Deep sobs interrupted her words. Then, "Of all the people I know, you're the only one I thought could help me. It seemed like a miracle when you said you'd come just for me . . . And then you start asking the same questions as all the others, as if I . . ." Suddenly her face hardened, then she moved to the closet and aggressively yanked the door open. She unhooked a hanger with two belts and threw it at Alvaro's feet.

"These are the only belts I've ever known my father to have. Take them with you and go away."

Mayulí walked quickly to the door and left the room.

* * *

Alvaro stayed alone for a few minutes, staring out at the sea of roofs. Then he too left, feeling foolish, old, and defeated. When he reached the street, he started to search for his bike, then saw his mother's car and remembered. Slowly, he opened the driver's door, sat down, and started off with no destination in mind.

Half an hour later, he was back. He parked the car in the same place as before, ran up the stairs to Mayulí's apartment, and rang the doorbell twice.

Mayulí's mother opened the door and stared with wide eyes at Alvaro, who now held a bouquet of roses in his hand.

"I want to marry your daughter. Will you accept me?"

A smile spread across her face as she lifted her shoulders. "You have to ask her. She's in her room."

The door to Mayulí's room was open. She was lying on the bed with her head beneath a pillow. He tiptoed to the one chair in the room and sat down.

"Go away. I don't want to see you again," she said, but her voice lacked conviction.

"I came back to marry you."

"You're too old."

Alvaro went to the bed and sat down beside her. She began to cry silently, a deep sob escaping every once in a while. Alvaro guided his hand to the girl's head below the pillow and began to caress her hair. He kissed her on her shoulder and then let his head rest on her back. She slowly went silent as if she had fallen asleep.

The waning light gave way to a quiet evening. She turned face up on her bed. He took the pillow away, but she kept her eyes closed. He lay down beside her and she made room for him. Alvaro embraced her and pulled her tightly to him. Little by little, they stretched out on the bed, looking deep into each other's eyes, and they both began to scold themselves for the misunderstanding. Finally, she started giving him small kisses on his hands and arms and, gradually, turned her mouth to his. In the process, the kimono opened and he felt her breasts brushing against him with each of her movements. He kept passing his hands over her face and hair, kissing her desperately. A moment later, Alvaro saw the kimono flying toward the chair.

THE BIRTH OF AN ORISHA

SAW IT ALL! *I was right there in the middle of the battle the whole time.*" The narrator lit a cigar while his audience pressed closer around him in order to catch every word. They had been pestering him for information for several hours and he had finally relented. "Listen carefully, because this is the one and only time in my life that I'm going to tell it.

"He came to my house, looking for me, and said, 'Let's go! Today's the day!' I made a gesture like this with my hands, asking where we were going, but he didn't answer. He went out the door, crossed the street, and climbed into my truck. It was then that I saw the long object wrapped in newspaper in his left hand. I got a strange feeling, like an electric current, that made me follow him just as I was, without a shirt or shoes. I jumped into the truck, started the motor, and warmed it up a bit. He pointed his finger to tell me to turn at the next corner. That way, with him pointing, we made a bunch of turns and I couldn't tell where we were going.

"Any other day, I'd have protested like hell, but the day before yesterday, I didn't dare even speak to him. He was tense and seemed to be listening, as if someone was whispering instructions in his ear. All of a sudden, we reached a tall green gate at the back of the *finca de los perros,* that place at the edge of town with the dogs.

"He hit the floor of the truck with the long object that he was holding in both hands. Then, with his eyes staring ahead like this, he yelled, 'This is it!'

"I braked and stopped the truck. He just sat there like he was in a trance.

I didn't dare move. After what seemed like a century, that man got out of the truck as calm as a fish. I got out as fast as I could and followed him. When he reached the heavy gate with a Chinese padlock this big, he pulled the Zarabanda saber out of the newspaper . . ." The narrator stood up and looked around at his growing group of listeners.

José Miguel took his time relighting the extinguished cigar and puffed on it several times, seemingly absorbed in his reminiscences. He then gestured for the group to step back, making room. "Lorenzo raised the saber." José Miguel lifted his arms like he was brandishing the weapon. "And in one stroke, he cut the padlock!" He lowered his hands as if they were still grasping the imaginary saber and sat down on his chair.

"Lorenzo walked ahead briskly into the grounds while I waited, expecting some twenty attack dogs to appear. *They're going to eat us alive*, I thought, but the most incredible thing happened. Those ferocious, fearless dogs did appear, but they immediately turned tail and ran, and we didn't see hide nor hair of them again all afternoon. The *Nasakó* started into the orchard, walking straight ahead like he knew exactly where he was going. I had a hard time following him through all the tall grass. Then, suddenly, a young *fiana* appeared and ordered us to halt. He was with a dog that was busy digging, trying to uncover something. It kept on digging the whole time without paying attention to anything else.

"The *Nasakó* told the young policeman, 'Don't point that gun at me. You will regret it!' and he then stripped down to nothing but a loincloth. Almost naked like that and with the sun shining directly in his face, he looked like one of the African gods. The policeman stood there, pointing his rifle at him."

The narrator stood up and signaled for the crowd to move back again. His spectators obeyed, leaving a circle about three steps in diameter. "Lorenzo moved over to me and said, '*Hermano*, Zarabanda has sent for me. I have to die fighting without hurting anyone.'" José Miguel looked around him, surprised by the multitude that had gathered. It was three o'clock in the morning and the funeral parlor seemed to be overflowing. The word had spread and mourners from other wakes had joined the crowd to hear the fantastic story of the *Nasakó's* demise. The narrator began to walk through a narrow path that opened among the listeners until he reached

Lorenzo's coffin. Pointing to it, he continued, "He leapt toward the policeman and knocked the rifle out of his hands with the saber. Then three more *fianas* appeared with two dogs, this big, that looked ready to attack, but when he looked at them, the dogs slunk away as if they'd seen the devil. Then Lorenzo attacked the other policemen and it looked like there was going to be a bloody battle. But it was only a matter of seconds. The policemen ended up on the ground without their rifles, but that gave the first cop time to draw his pistol. Lorenzo ran toward him shouting, with the saber raised. The young policeman had no choice but to shoot him in the chest. *And that was just what Lorenzo wanted.*"

Lorenzo Bantú's funeral was a major event in Guanabacoa. Many factors contributed to the spectacle: the nature of the crime that he had been accused of; the circumstances of the combat in which he had died, practically on top of the coffin of the *chino* whose spirit had taken possession of him, and, according to people knowledgable in these matters, had taken revenge on the *Nasakó* for the theft of his body; the lopsided battle against four highly trained members of the Special Police Brigade; and the way Lorenzo had ultimately let himself be killed. All of this—in addition to his miraculous works as a *Palero* and his impeccable reputation as the *Nasakó* of one of Guanabacoa's most prestigious Abakuá chapters—explained the enormous multitude that accompanied his coffin to its place of burial. Furthermore, a mobilization of police was ordered by the municipal, provincial, and national authorities to prevent any violence. Undoubtedly, the first-hand testimony from an exceptional witness, who was also an Abakuá, was a great help in ensuring that nothing untoward occurred during the funeral.

One last incident marked the burial. Lorenzo Bantú's wake lasted three days instead of the one day that was customary in Cuba because of the indecisiveness of the Abakuás, who had to figure out where he would be buried and who would deliver the funeral oration, along with other important details of the Abakuá funeral rites.

At the exact hour set for the burial, a severe storm with unusually intense lightning, thunder, wind, and rain erupted and lasted until Lorenzo was buried.

JOSEPH MING

CARRILLO STOPPED his automobile before a tall gate in a stone wall some eight feet high, beyond which could be seen the upper floors of an enormous mansion. The gate opened, revealing a complex of buildings that occupied almost an entire block, isolated from the neighboring houses by the wall that resembled a barricade more than a simple division. None of the people at the gate, working in the gardens, or entering and leaving the buildings were dressed in military uniforms, but their body language and the nature of the complex revealed that they were members of one of the country's special security corps.

Carrillo drove up to the entrance of the main house and left the car with the keys in the ignition. A young man appeared and drove it away. Awaiting Carrillo at the top of five wide steps stood a middle-aged woman with dyed black hair tinted red, whose makeup seemed excessive for someone her age. Without saying a word, she turned to show him the way. They entered through a large door into what had obviously been the entrance hall of the home of a very rich family before the Revolution. Two pink-marble staircases rose from the hall in a semicircle to the upper floor where the bedrooms and other private areas of the original owners had been.

They walked down a long central hall on the upper floor with doors on each side. The woman opened one and ushered him into a former bedroom, converted now to a conference room with a long table and five chairs on each side. Another chair was placed at the head of the table beside a wide window through which too much sunlight was entering. The woman went directly to the window to adjust the curtains, then sat down near the head of the table and indicated to Carrillo to take the chair opposite her. "General Gonzalo will be here very soon," she said.

A moment later, a tall, heavyset man, probably in his sixties, with abundant iron-gray hair and pink, recently shaved skin, entered carrying a thick blue folder in his hand. He was wearing a cream-colored guayabera and smelled strongly of cologne. Carrillo rose and saluted. The general laid a hand on Carrillo's shoulder, inviting him with the gesture to sit back down, while he himself sat at the head of the table, placing the file before him. The general leaned slightly toward his visitor. "Carrillo, I'm going to give you a brief synopsis of the case, although you already know a lot about it. I want you to be able to focus clearly on all our objectives."

Carrillo nodded.

"When we began investigating the disappearance of the cadaver of Rafael Cuan, we immediately started looking for Joseph Ming, a foreigner who visited Cuan often in his last weeks. After three days, we located him in a private home in Miramar, where he had rented a room. Upon interrogation, we learned that he had a Canadian passport in the name of Alfred J. Khan, with a tourist visa to enter the country dated four months earlier. We placed him under preventive arrest on the grounds that his visa had expired a month before. In checking on his identity, we found that, although the passport was valid, the real Alfred J. Khan was in Sarasota, Florida, where he has been living since his retirement several years ago. We therefore had sufficient grounds for charging Ming with illegal entry into the country and deporting him to Canada, where he would have to answer to charges of assuming a false identity.

"We then sent his fingerprints to INTERPOL and learned of yet another identity and of an old detention order from 1952 for international drug trafficking. Since then, we've collected more information from many sources. Ming's real name is John Gabriel Rawlings. His father, John Sebastian Rawlings, an Englishman, worked as a representative of several American and British firms in China and Hong Kong during the 1920s. In

1925, he married a young Chinese woman. John Gabriel was born in Shanghai in 1926. In 1937, when the Japanese launched their great offensive in China, Rawlings took his family to the United States and settled in San Francisco, where he continued to work for the same companies. After the Second World War, he returned with his family to China to work in the same capacity as before. Rawlings's son, who we know as Ming, was then twenty, and spoke perfect Chinese and English.

"In 1949, Chiang Kai-shek's army was defeated in Yunan by the Red Army under Mao Tse Dong and fled from China. Li Mi, an intelligence officer in charge of twelve thousand soldiers, managed to escape from Yunan and pass to the northeastern corner of Burma, the famous 'Golden Triangle,' with the intention of controlling the production of opium in that region. General Pao, chief of police in Thailand, took charge of opening channels for drugs that had formerly passed through China.

"Burma had just won its independence in 1948 after almost seventy years under British colonial domination. The country's national interests were further complicated by a new factor: the beginning of the Korean War in 1950. With Burma as a military base, the CIA was planning to employ Li Mi's troops in an invasion of China as part of the American strategy in the war against North Korea, which quickly degenerated into a conflict with the Chinese as well. Li Mi's army remained in Burma until 1961. We gathered all this information from CIA sources made public long ago.

"According to unconfirmed reports, Li Mi was the brother of Rawlings's mother, and he took his young nephew with him to Burma after the boy's father died and his mother returned to California in 1950. In the first half of the 1950s, a powerful drug empire emerged based in Thailand and Singapore. In 1960, Rawlings-Ming was detained in San Francisco on four criminal charges related to drug trafficking as part of a huge scandal brought on by the death in 1957 of a ship captain, a hero of World War II, and two sailors on the beach of Malibu, California. The criminal proceedings lasted several months, and the record of the prosecuting attorney's deposition said . . ." General Gonzalo thumbed through the papers before him, "that since the defendant was the nephew of Li Mi, with triple nationality—Chinese, U.S., and British—and had connections with and knowledge of the drug business, the young Rawlings had been the ideal man for reorganizing the post–World War II international network of the Golden Triangle opium and heroin trade. In 1962, Rawlings was sentenced to fifteen years in prison for tax evasion. None of the other charges could be proved. He was let out in December of 1975, and from that point on, we don't have a single piece of information on him until he appeared in Cuba. Undoubtedly, he was not traveling for pleasure.

"When we told him about the information we had on him and that we were preparing to deport him to Canada, Rawlings-Ming told us the story of the secret society of the *Seven Dragons*. He said that he had come to Cuba to establish contact with the Green Dragon, who had been thought dead. He succeeded in finding the lost Dragon, who then died while Rawlings-Ming was in Cuba.

"He told us that the Chinese government wanted to send a coffin adorned in jade and precious stones for the repatriation of Cuan's cadaver. This was confirmed when Chinese authorities requested our help in the repatriation of the cadaver, with the consent of his family here, of course." The general paused briefly, then added, "The coffin and a refrigerated container for transferring the cadaver arrived—and are quite impressive, by the way.

"We tried to get the name of at least one of the other Dragons from Ming—or, rather, Rawlings—but he said he didn't have authorization to give us the information. Meanwhile, the game continued. We told him we had no alternative but to return him to Canada. Then he proposed the following deal: He would trade information related to the security of our country for our declaring him dead and keeping him under arrest for five years in a comfortable and isolated safe house. He offered to cover all the expenses, including rent for the safe house, the custodians, and all the necessary security measures. Based on some of Rawlings's limited disclosure, we knew that much of his information might in fact be extremely valuable.

"Without committing ourselves to any deal, we went ahead and made an 'error': A cadaver of a drowned man was found on one of the beaches east of Havana and 'among his belongings was a Canadian passport in the name of Alfred Khan. The police are investigating.' That report was made public.

"Rawlings was very pleased. He promised to hand over all the information on Cuan. I would like you to participate in the interrogation from this point forward. Ask as many questions as you think are necessary. The whole thing will be recorded."

"Excellent," Carrillo said.

"If at any moment he stops cooperating, I'll signal you by tapping my finger on the table, and then you can set off the bomb we have up our sleeve for him . . . If you have no questions, we can begin."

Carrillo nodded and stood up.

The woman again led the way along the central hall, this time to a small elevator that was completely packed once they stepped inside. They rose slowly, then the elevator opened, revealing a hall and another door guarded by two uniformed policemen holding rifles. The guards saluted the general, who reciprocated, then turned to open the door with a key. They entered a spacious room furnished with two sofas, several armchairs, a television set, and a center table. Two plainclothes guards stood rigidly at attention and saluted the general. A thin man of some sixty years of age and of medium height, with slightly Asian features, rose from an armchair and bowed his head formally three times to the general, who introduced Carrillo.

Carrillo cast a quick glance around at what had presumably been the private sitting room of the original owners. At the far right of the room there was an ample pantry-bar with a table and two chairs. At the other end was a desk with a chair, a filing cabinet, and a bookcase. A bedroom opened off either side of the sitting room. The one facing east was painted a very light blue and the other a pale pink, undoubtedly the main sleeping chambers of the house's former inhabitants. All of the windows were protected by elaborate iron grillwork that had allowed the owners to sleep without fear of intruders. Now they served to prevent the departure of a captive guest.

Carrillo whispered to the general, "Gonzalo, when my vacation is due, can you do me the favor of detaining me here for a couple of weeks? How's the food?"

Gonzalo smiled. "For you, exquisite and low in cholesterol."

The guards inside the room retired to one of the bedrooms but remained standing in the doorway, watching the group.

The interrogation began. "Mr. Rawlings, will you kindly explain again and in full detail what relation you had to Cuan?" Gonzalo asked.

Rawlings-Ming started to speak in English, with the woman translating. "In 1950, I began to work under Cuan's orders organizing an international network for selling drugs produced in the Golden Triangle. Cuan controlled a strong organization of ships with well-trained crews that transported valuable contraband merchandise—mainly diamonds from Angola, emeralds from Colombia, and gold from South Africa. He never lost a single shipment. He also controlled locations where the merchandise was unloaded and distributed to large retailers. Cuan's whole organization was maintained with maximum discipline. Each crew became a combat unit when necessary. Each man, in addition to his role on the ship, had many other obligations. At that point, we were trying to increase the number of ships and trained personnel.

"In a relatively short time, using several of Cuan's crews, we put together a new and independent organization. I was in charge of operating that fleet, always under Cuan's orders."

"Who was heading the whole operation . . . Li Mi?" Gonzalo asked.

"I can't comment on that."

There was a moment of silence. Gonzalo nodded and the prisoner continued.

"During the years I worked under Cuan's orders, we met only three times. The first meeting lasted three days, the second, one day, and the third, a few hours. In each case, a ship picked me up at night—the first time in Veracruz, the other two times in Nassau. I was closed into an inside cabin. I always heard Cuan arrive in a fast launch and settle into the cabin next to mine. Then we talked by direct telephone, and he could see me by closed-circuit television, but not vice versa. I'm sure that everything I said and did was recorded on film. It was a way of keeping me at his mercy. At the end of our last meeting, he came to my cabin to greet me. I felt very moved at meeting him personally."

The general began to show signs of impatience. That was old information, perhaps of interest to Carrillo, but not to him. He raised a hand and said, "In 1957, three men were murdered on the beach at Malibu, in California, triggering a big investigation by the DEA and the FBI. You were involved. Tell us what that was about."

"That would be part of the deal I've proposed," the detained man said.

The general slapped the blue file closed and his pink face turned red. "Look, Mr. Rawlings, just as we have proven our willingness to negotiate, we can also show you our claws, if that's what you prefer. We are here because of your promise to tell us everything related to this case. Everything!"

"You asked me about something that happened a long time ago," Rawlings protested.

"But you know very well that it is linked directly to your trip to Cuba," Carrillo insisted in a soft voice, "and to the murder of Rafael Cuan."

"As far as I know, he died a natural death. His daughter told me so at the funeral—"

"We have proof that you poisoned him," Carrillo interrupted.

"I came here to make a pact with him, not to kill him."

"So what happened? Cuan refused to accept the pact, leaving you with no choice but to poison him. Wasn't that the scenario?" Carrillo insisted.

"I didn't poison him."

"You're wasting our time," the general replied. "We found traces of a special poison in your luggage that has been identified by the coroner as the cause of Cuan's death. Furthermore, you had a motive. This is enough evidence for any court in the world to convict you."

Rawlings remained silent, looking out the window. Then he turned to his interrogators and said slowly, "Sometimes the simplest things are inexplicable because life is in a constant state of flux. Nothing stays the same. Many years ago, Cuan came to America on a mission that he fulfilled brilliantly with an unorthodox but very effective course of action. Tainted money has been the basis for almost all of the world's great undertakings. The gold of America, stolen by the Spaniards, gave birth to capitalism in Europe. Drugs continue to fund respectable businesses every day and provide honest employment for many people. When China was struggling alone against Japan, Cuan didn't hesitate to seek money by any means, and with that money the members of the *Seven Dragons* performed incredible feats that would have been impossible otherwise, enabling them to play a decisive role in the history of modern China.

"With time, however, the struggle changed completely. There was no longer a need to fight against the Japanese. The problem was how to carry out the great socioeconomic changes that China needed. In 1957, only eight years after the triumph of the Communist Revolution, cereal production in China rose to 200 million tons, after having grown eight percent per year over the previous seven years, while the rest of the world considered itself lucky to achieve three percent growth. The 'Great Leap Forward' concentrated over 500 million peasants into 24,000 people's communes. Nevertheless, one of the Dragons felt strongly that this was not the path that China should follow.

"This Dragon decided that it was imperative that Cuan stop sending money to the Society, in order to neutralize the power of some of the other members. But it was impossible for him to stop Cuan.

"In 1957, I, myself, plotted and carried out his murder. But I would find out only later that he was more astute than I. He had managed to fool me and other very talented people. We tried to create the impression that his death and that of some of his men had been the result of a war to dominate the drug trade. If it had been revealed at that time that it was an internal job, it would have certainly meant our own destruction.

"According to some very confidential information that we had, Cuan had moved between several of his impregnable safe houses in Central America and Mexico. He used two or three doubles, all under the identity of Donald W. Chang. To be sure which of the Donald Changs he really was, I identified him from photos taken surreptitiously, since I had a very clear recollection of the man from our meeting on the ship several years before. As it turns out, he'd totally fooled me, because the man who had greeted me on the ship was not, in fact, Cuan.

"The whole time, I thought that I had delivered a master blow. Now, in some ways I still think I did, since although we didn't manage to kill the Green Dragon, he did disappear completely from the scene. The money ceased to flow and our enemies lost a great deal of power. New ideas flourished and, with them, China's path again changed course. Our former adversaries are now friends and allies. When we eventually learned that Cuan was alive, a very important person still considered him a great threat. It became essential to reach an agreement with Cuan."

"How did you discover the Green Dragon was alive?"

"He revealed it himself. Not long ago, a Beijing bank received a check for five million dollars to build a monument-tomb for the eternal rest of the founders of the *Seven Dragons* secret society. The check was accompanied by a note naming the three surviving Dragons in China as trustees to jointly manage the account. It was clear to them that the only person who could have made that donation was the Green Dragon, thought dead, a supposed victim of the war with Colombian drug lords.

"My boss, one of the Dragons, assigned me the mission of finding him and convincing him to remain silent, but with 'no violence under any circumstances.' He told me: 'My fate is linked to that of Cuan. If he listens to you, he may pardon me and remain silent. If he makes an accusation, I will state my case to justify the earlier betrayal and ask for clemency. If you kill him, my honor and my life will be lost. There will be no possible defense for me.'"

A long silence followed, in which Carrillo and General Gonzalo tried to interpret Rawlings's words. Carrillo asked the translator to repeat his last statement.

Then Rawlings resumed his narration. "Before coming to Cuba, I thought a great deal about why Cuan had chosen to remain silent for so long. Why hadn't he struck back after the assassination attempt? He had enough patience to wait for an opportune moment, and he had the intelligence to figure out who had ordered his death. He could probably have crushed us. If he had done so, he would be one of the most powerful men in our country today. Why did he choose to do nothing? Did he fear for his life and the safety of his family? No, Cuan was not afraid of anything. The only explanation is that he was actually in agreement with the political and economic objectives we were pursuing and simply accepted his *Tao*, his destiny. And we figured that his place of hiding had to be Cuba because it turned out after the hit that Donald Chang had his family in Santiago de

Cuba and his son lived here. I just followed that thread until I found him. He was waiting for me.

"The first thing I told him was, 'You have been wise to understand that we were acting correctly and bravely to accept your *Tao*.' Cuan looked at me, smiled, and replied: 'Betrayal is never pardonable.'

"In the last three weeks before his death, we talked about many things. He laughed a great deal—like a child laughing at his own pranks—when I mentioned his having fooled me the last time we supposedly met on the boat, and the certainty I had felt in identifying the photos of the 'real' Donald Chang. 'I knew that you might betray me at some point,' he told me. But our talks were very friendly. He asked me about Beijing and the places he had known when he was young. He introduced me to his daughter.

"When he died, I thought everything had actually ended in the most convenient way. His death under the name of Rafael Cuan said nothing to anyone. His corpse could be sent to China to rest forever in the *Seven Dragons'* tomb. It was only the theft of his cadaver that aroused the attention of the police and the Chinese community in Havana, and his true identity was soon revealed. Now you tell me that he died of poisoning and that some of the poison was found in my luggage. Then I can only think that he poisoned himself to make it appear that I had done it. Cuan has defeated me again—and, again, it was my own fault. I didn't pay close enough attention when he told me that *betrayal is never pardonable*."

Carrillo and General Gonzalo ate lunch in a small dining room on the ground floor.

"Unlike you, I don't doubt that there are very high-up people involved in this case in China," said the general, who had already finished his frugal lunch and now waited for his guest, who ate much more than he. "This case has a longer tail than the dragon of the Chinese *comparsa*. We have to handle it from now on with silk gloves. I have to make a report and wait for orders."

Carrillo finished chewing a piece of meat before he answered. "I can't help thinking that Rafael Cuan must have a fortune stashed away somewhere. He sent five million dollars for that tomb. There must be plenty left."

"It's possible," agreed the general, more concerned with the political impli-cations of the case than with a hypothetical fortune. "Or perhaps the money he sent was all that was left. Cuan might have understood that, in reality, it didn't belong to him." As usual, the general was taking a position contrary to Carrillo's, a method he often used to extract information from others—in defending their opinions, they inevitably "burned up" further information.

Carrillo speared the last piece of pork with his fork and raised it to his mouth, but held it there while he spoke. "I strongly believe that his real intention was to get hold of Cuan's money—at least, some of it. They nego-tiated, and perhaps Rawlings threatened Cuan and his family. Cuan didn't yield, so Rawlings poisoned him."

"It's possible," Gonzalo conceded.

"Following this hypothesis, his objective would have been to obtain the codes to all or some of the secret accounts where Cuan kept the money. Maybe the codes were in that old belt of Cuan's. His daughter told Alvaro that he was buried with the belt, but he wasn't wearing it when he was exhumed. Perhaps someone got to him ahead of us. That might have been why the Dragons were so interested in recovering Cuan's cadaver and why they sent that fancy coffin. That's why Ming stayed in Cuba after Cuan's death."

Gonzalo remained silent.

"But why would Rawlings then make a deal with us to declare him dead and stay in Cuba as a prisoner?" asked Carrillo.

"It's his best option. Apparently, if we deport him to Canada, he's going to be arrested for usurping Alfred Khan's identity—and who knows for what else. Here, if he's tried for poisoning Cuan, it would be very difficult to keep the whole story a secret, and the last thing the people behind Rawlings want is for all of this to be made public. It would certainly embar-rass some very important people, even if Rawlings were absolved."

"Absolved?" Carrillo said.

"It seems to me that if his objective was to eliminate Cuan, it doesn't make sense that he would spend two or three weeks meeting with his victim before finally murdering him. He could have eliminated him several other ways, leaving Cuba in haste. Why hang around Havana after Cuan's death like he did? For now, the most logical explanation is the one Rawlings presents."

General Gonzalo concentrated on the coffee they had just been served and seemed to lose interest in his visitor's hypothesizing, but Carrillo continued. "I wouldn't be surprised if Rawlings's whole story about the *Seven Dragons* intervening in politics for the good of China is simply an invention of his and of his associates, whoever they are. In my opinion, the attempt to assassinate Cuan was merely aimed at taking over the drug-distribution network that he controlled. The *Seven Dragons* society must be one of the Far East's drug cartels. Cuan knew too much, and he had to be eliminated. Do you have any proof that Cuan sent that money to build a monument? Have you been able to check this story with the Chinese government?" Carrillo moved his chair back from the table and paid close attention to General Gonzalo, who appeared surprised by his question.

The general could barely conceal his irritation at the direction the conversation had taken, invading his sacred territory. His voice had a slightly sarcastic edge as he replied, "Frankly, the only tangible pieces of evidence we have are that coffin, which looks like it was intended for an Egyptian Pharaoh, and an official note from the Chinese government requesting our collaboration in repatriating the corpse of the Chinese citizen Rafael Cuan to his native country. Naturally, we have not begun to question anyone: 'Your Excellency, are you the Yellow Dragon? Marshal So-and-So, we suspect that you are the Black Dragon . . .'"

"I still think the whole operation could have been organized by a drug cartel," Carrillo insisted.

"Of course it *could* have been, my friend. And now I must leave. I have an important meeting, but finish your dessert and coffee in peace." The general stood up. He shook hands with Carrillo and started to leave, then turned back. "Wasn't it Alejo Carpentier who said that the history of America was a chronicle of the marvelously real? *Anything* is possible under our tropical sun."

As soon as Carrillo got back to his office, he had his aide place a call to Colonel Pablo Chang in his house in Santiago de Cuba. Several minutes later, the army colonel was on the line.

"Hello, Pablo, how are you doing?"

"Oh, business as usual. What's new?"

"A few days ago, we found Rafael Cuan's coffin with the body inside, intact, buried on a farm near Guanabacoa. It seems some *Palero* recommended to a band of thieves that they steal the corpse of a Chinese man as protection against the police. The autopsy and the forensic investigation revealed that poison was the cause of Cuan's death. I thought you might be interested."

"Thanks. Listen, I'd like to have a word with you. This time, I'll come meet you there. I'll try to catch a plane tonight or tomorrow morning. I'll call you as soon as I get there."

General Gonzalo rang Carrillo early the next morning before leaving for his office. He had made a full report to his superiors the previous evening and now he needed to share a piece of urgent news.

"Ming was found dead this morning."

"So Rawlings—"

"Listen to me, Carrillo. Ming committed suicide. The case is closed," the general said, speaking very slowly. He immediately hung up.

H E BECAME AWARE of a ceaseless ringing in the hall. He lifted the receiver and heard Jacinto's angry voice. "*Son of a bitch, did you know that Narelys is having twins?*" He woke up startled and jumped from his bed.

The nightmare had been his conscience working on him, he told himself, but thank God it had only been a dream! For one thing, not enough time had passed for Narelys to know if he had left her pregnant, much less if she were carrying twins. He smiled, recalling their lusty lovemaking on the floor, since the cot had been too narrow for the two of them. Since then, however, he had cursed himself for the millionth time for having gotten involved with Jacinto's daughter.

His mother had breakfast waiting for him on the table, a clear sign that she wanted to talk to her elusive son.

"Camila was here yesterday all afternoon and started helping me while she waited for you. What a good worker! She eventually had to leave, but she asked for you to call her. I know she's anxious to see you. She told me that you're so shy, she has to take the initiative."

He ate fast with the combined force of hunger and a desire to escape the conversation. He needed to get to the garden to examine the havoc created by the goat, who had started breaking loose recently. The two times he had slept at home in the last week, he had found her calmly chewing the damaged vegetables with a seemingly smug look on her face.

Suddenly, the phone rang. His mother answered and brought the wireless phone to him at the table. "It's for you," she said, touching his shoulder with two fingers, indicating the stars on the shoulders of a uniform—Carrillo was on the line.

"We have the results of the autopsy. Cuan was poisoned, after all. And there are some other important facts that I have to share with you. This has become a real jigsaw puzzle. I need a fresh mind on it . . . I want you back on the case immediately."

"I can't."

"Let's not start this again. What I'm saying is that you'll have all the information in your hands—all of it."

"I shouldn't get involved in the case now . . . I'd have a tremendous conflict of interest. It happens that Mayulí and I . . . well, we're having an affair. I should explain that it started after I was already off the case. I'm going to get married again. She doesn't mind the age difference."

"Are you talking about Cuan's daughter?" Silence. "What's going on with you? Are you becoming the faun who has to fornicate with all of the nymphs in the forest?" Carrillo paused. Alvaro then recalled that his chief was well aware of his fling with Narelys, and he had also mentioned informally his mother's attempt to hook him up with the young policewoman, Camila.

"It must be the beard," Carrillo muttered to himself. "I knew you should have shaved that beard. All this is happening because of the beard. You have to shave it."

"No, not the beard," Alvaro replied, raising a hand protectively to his face, then hung up.

The next day, Carrillo called at about seven A.M. and told him to get ready—they were going to meet a very important person. Once again, he told himself, he had no choice but to let his garden go to pot. He had been working for over an hour and was sweating profusely. He went into the garage, changed out of his work clothes, and climbed up to his room barefoot, wearing only his boxer shorts. He showered and dressed in one of his best guayaberas, white drill trousers, and black and white pointed-toe shoes inherited from his father.

Carrillo arrived in his car at eight wearing a white sweater, blue jeans without a belt, and an old pair of tennis shoes. Accustomed to asking no questions of his superiors, Alvaro simply commented on the beauty of Havana at this early hour of a Sunday morning. From his house in the Kohly area, they followed Calle 10 to Quinta Avenue, the lovely heart of Miramar, one of Havana's most beautiful neighborhoods since before the Revolution. As they neared the former Havana Yacht Club, now a club for construction workers, Carrillo began to talk. "I don't think there's any conflict of interest. Your relationship with Cuan's daughter doesn't matter. She isn't a suspect in her father's poisoning. We know who did it."

Alvaro remained pensive a moment. "Ming?"

"We have irrefutable proof that it had to be either Ming or Cuan, himself, committing suicide while also framing Ming by putting poison on his clothing. Either way, we consider that chapter of the case closed. So, the idea of Chinese vengeance may not have been far off track, after all."

Alvaro again remained thoughtful, vaguely surprised by the news. He heard Carrillo's voice guessing his thoughts: "Ming was detained, not dead. We needed to send a signal to a certain place. It wasn't our intention to misinform you with the case records reporting his death."

"*Vaya!*" Alvaro exclaimed.

"But Ming is dead now. He killed himself last night."

Alvaro pursed his lips. "Well, let's hope he decides to stay dead this time."

"Yesterday I had a meeting with Ming in the safe house where he was being kept. A fascinating story was unveiled. I'll tell you all about it when we finish this meeting."

Carrillo took a left turn at the intersection with La Estrella, entering Siboney, another of Havana's most exclusive neighborhoods in a previous era. "We're going to meet Colonel Pablo Chang. Now, just listen to what he says and observe him closely. After you pointed out that it was important to investigate Cuan's reasons for calling Pablo Chang before he died, I personally visited him in Santiago de Cuba. I wanted to keep any questions off the record because of his rank—due to be promoted to brigadier general soon. When we met, he explained to me that Cuan had worked for an accounting firm in the Chinese quarter of Havana that handled the legal affairs of his father's business. His father was Donald W. Chang, a rich industrialist from Santiago de Cuba who died in an airplane accident in 1957, when Pablo was still a boy. Cuan had been very helpful in managing the affairs of his mother's inheritance, and, over the years, they became friends. That was all. Chang was very concise in answering my questions, perhaps because of his military training, although I had the impression that he could have told me more. Yesterday, I called him at his house in Santiago to tell him the result of Cuan's autopsy, without offering any details. Then he said he wanted to talk with me and said that it was his turn to come to Havana, so we're meeting in a house his family has here in Siboney."

Carrillo slowed the car before a ranch-style home with a red-tiled roof. An open gate gave access to three large wooden doors in a hollow of the terrain that the architect had used for building a garage and other service areas. The vehicle rolled down the entrance road and stopped before one of the doors. A man with Asian features and very straight black hair, who appeared to be about forty-five years old, came out of the house to greet them. His muscular frame of medium height was clothed in a pale blue polo shirt, Bermuda shorts, and Nike tennis shoes. Alvaro felt uncomfortable in his long-sleeved guayabera and wished Carrillo had told him to dress informally.

Carrillo and Chang exchanged salutes, then Carrillo introduced Alvaro. Chang led them to a patio where several rattan chairs were placed beneath some mango and avocado trees near an empty swimming pool and a small bar. "I think we can talk here," he said, bringing a bottle of *añejo* rum, ice, and glasses from the bar.

"Carrillo, when we met in Santiago some weeks ago, I decided not to tell you anything about what I'm now going to say, because I believed it had no bearing on what had happened. The poison found in the autopsy changes everything." Chang poured a shot of rum into each glass and drank a sip of his.

"I'm going to begin with my father's death in October 1957. We lived in Vista Alegre in Santiago de Cuba. Papá traveled almost all the time, but every time he came home—when we least expected him—he brought me many gifts and played with me a lot. Several times, he took me up in the airplane that he piloted himself.

"When he wasn't there, our house was filled with my mother's relatives. Imagine, nine brothers and sisters, over thirty nephews and nieces, my maternal grandparents, and even one great-grandmother. They were all very poor and came to my house to eat things they had never tasted before in their life. My mother had been my father's laundress before they married, so that was like Cinderella's wedding. What Papá didn't know was that he had married a tribe. But whenever he arrived, everything always quieted right down, as if by magic.

"I was twelve years old when they told us that a light plane carrying my father had disappeared over the jungles of Honduras and Guatemala. I remember my mother sitting hour after hour by the telephone, hoping for good news. A week later, they told us that the plane had crashed and my father and the pilot were dead.

"The first time that death had touched our family, as far as I knew, was several months before my father's accident. The Batista police had murdered one of my cousins, just sixteen years old. We held his wake in our house. I'll never forget that night, with all of the women in the family suffering nervous breakdowns, sobbing and cursing the government, hitting their heads against the walls. The men talked in low voices among themselves, swearing revenge. Half of Santiago de Cuba turned out the next day for his funeral. It all impressed me very deeply.

"At the time of my father's accident, the war against Batista had reached a high point, and three of my uncles and several cousins were with the rebel troops in the Sierra Maestra. News of deaths reached us constantly, but I never managed to assimilate the idea that my father was dead. I suppose that was partly because we didn't have a cadaver to mourn, only a small wooden box with his ashes. Mamá also protected me as much as possible. She kept his burial service very simple, with only a handful of people at the cemetery. In a certain way, I still half-thought of him as living, and dreamed often that he had arrived with stacks of gifts and taken me up in his plane.

"Shortly after that, my mother brought me on a trip to Havana and we spent several days here. Havana showed few signs of the civil war that was growing more intense every day. It felt almost like a different country. Mamá was very pleased because the office of Antonio Choy that handled my father's business accounts had all the records of the properties very organized, with her and me named as his only heirs. When we returned to Santiago, the struggle was even more intense and everyone was talking about an offensive by Batista's army to wipe out the rebels.

"When the Revolution finally triumphed on January 1, 1959, everything seemed to return to normal, but very soon the economic situation of the country worsened. Then there was the Agrarian Reform, the invasion at the Bay of Pigs, and the guerrilla war in the Escambray Mountains. Between 1960 and 1964, my father's properties were all expropriated, and the family fortune disappeared. The only thing that remained was our house in Santiago and this one in Havana. When the missile crisis came in October 1962, I joined the army, and I was never concerned with the family business—my mother handled that. Finally, I don't really know how, Choy's office began to send us a monthly check that more than covered the expenses of the house. I never knew what funds provided that income, but they seemed to have no end.

"In February 1974, I brought my mother to Havana to the Oncological Hospital, where they had to remove one of her breasts. The accounting office no longer existed, but Choy sent us a car with a driver that was at our service for almost a month. In August of that same year, I was in Havana again on my way to the Soviet Union, where I spent five years in a military academy. Before leaving, I had to attend several meetings at Army Headquarters, and I also wanted to thank Choy for everything he had done for my mother and me. Between one thing and another, Choy was left for the last minute. The day of my departure, I called him and he told me not to bother coming to see him. He was going to send the man who had always taken care of my father's matters in his office, and that it was him who I should thank. That was how I met Cuan. He came to pick me up and took me to a very nice Chinese restaurant that had just opened in Old Havana. I don't remember the name."

"La Torre de Marfil?" Carrillo said.

"That's it. And he offered to drive me to the airport after our lunch. Cuan reminded me very much of my father, but shorter, though his manner was very courteous and inhibited, whereas my father had been a lively, joking type of person. We said farewell at the airport and he gave me a big hug. I saw to my surprise that he had tears in his eyes. Then he hugged me again and, this time, he was actually crying. I returned his embrace and for an instant I felt like he really was my father. During my stay in the Soviet Union, I tried to erase that idea from my mind as impossible. I came home twice on vacation and once more for my mother's funeral a few months before my graduation. On all of those trips, I went directly to Santiago and returned to Havana with only enough time to catch my plane for Moscow.

"But since a tiny doubt lurked in the back of my mind, I began to research the accident that had cost my father's life. I got copies of practically every report that had anything to do with the accident. I was able to arrange for a group of specialists from the armed forces to analyze the material. They reached the conclusion that an explosion might have torn off the right wing of the plane that then fell about five hundred yards before the fuselage and the other wing dropped. Without being able to inspect the remains of the plane, they could not be certain that there had been sabotage, but it was a possibility. I also had forensic specialists review the autopsy and identification records of the cadavers. Apparently, there was no doubt that one of the cadavers corresponded to the description and dental records of Donald W. Chang, born in San Diego, California. That settled the matter. My father was really dead—period.

"When I returned from the Soviet Union, I spent six years working here in the western provinces. Cuan began to invite me to eat with him almost every month. It's hard to describe those first lunches. At first, we both felt uncomfortable, until one day he told me, crying, that he was my father. He very humbly begged my forgiveness. I didn't know what to say, since I had proof that he was not my father.

"As if guessing what I was thinking, he began to recite details that only my father and I could know. For example, he said, 'Do you remember when we were flying over the Gran Piedra and I told you the story about the Frenchman who had a coffee plantation there, and you asked me to fly over it again?' I finally told him the results of my investigation and asked, 'If the real Donald Chang died in that accident, who is my real father?'

"'That's a long story that I'll share with you little by little,' he said. He began telling me about an organization he belonged to whose aim was to struggle on behalf of China in whatever circumstance its members found themselves. He left China in 1937 to fulfill a mission: to find money by any means to help finance the activities of the other heads of the organization, who acted independently in very diverse locations. Everything functioned perfectly during the war against Japan. Afterwards, it became much more complicated. The Communist Revolution under Mao triumphed in China in 1949, but an antagonistic state was formed on the island of Taiwan by the remnants of Chiang Kai-shek's army. Some of the members of the secret organization were in China and others in Taipei. Meanwhile, the internal struggles within the Chinese Communist Party lasted for decades. Some of the members of the secret organization had diverging ideas and had joined opposing power groups.

"One day, my father put his hand on his heart and said, 'I more than fulfilled my mission. I sent large amounts of money to the secret bank accounts of each of the other members of the organization. But then someone very powerful mandated a death sentence against me. I don't know who or why. I was able to survive because I had always taken many measures to hide my true identity, even from my children, who are the people most dear to me in this world.' Then he explained why he had adopted the name Donald W. Chang. In 1944, he bought a house in Santiago de Cuba in order to enact the security plan he had devised. He started to laugh and told me that the plan had failed before it could really begin because he couldn't resist the charms of his laundress. And to complicate matters further, I arrived unexpectedly.

"His idea was to use Donald W. Chang, a man of his age and similar physical characteristics who already took care of some of the business within his organization, as a front man. He would be the visible head of the enterprise, the man who appeared at many of the transactions, with an identity relatively easy to uncover. Another man would use the same name and identity of Donald Chang, but would only take part in very special occasions; he would allegedly be the *real* top chief, and his secret residence would be in Santiago de Cuba. A thorough investigation would lead to this second and false Donald Chang, and it would be thought that he was the true head of the organization, while my father's actual residence would be in Havana under yet another identity.

"When he ended up marrying my mother in Santiago and having a son, he launched another security plan, with several safe houses in Mexico and Central America, where his decoy and his double would move, constantly protected by security forces. Since the house in Santiago de Cuba and other things, including me, were already in the name of *Chang*, he decided to temporarily leave things as they were. This obliged him to use the name Chang and take extra care when he visited Santiago.

"At the same time as the plane crash, a captain of one of his ships, who was a key link with the rest of his organization, along with his two body-guards, were murdered in Malibu Beach in California. It seemed obvious to him that the whole thing was an inside plot to take over his organization. He made a complete withdrawal and stayed very quiet because he didn't know who had ordered the deaths. A year later, the Revolution triumphed in Cuba and everything was greatly facilitated. For many years, the country practically closed in on itself. Foreign tourism virtually disappeared. Anyone visiting the country came for very specific reasons and was thoroughly investigated.

"At first, I believed everything he told me without question. The bottom line of his story was that he had done everything on behalf of his homeland, China. But in each of our meetings, his stories became more dramatic and difficult to believe. A moment finally arrived when I told myself, 'Coño, this is all a big lie!' I became convinced, much to my dismay and contrary to my childhood dreams, that I was watching a pathetic old man who had made a fortune by fraudulent means and was trying to hide from the Mafia. In the process, he had made the decision, or had no choice but to make the decision, to abandon his wife and son, leaving his fortune to them in order to convince everyone that he was really dead. And after all those years, to maintain the respect of that son, he was inventing stories to justify the unjustifiable. Those legends were only a way of seeking forgiveness and, in a way, absolution before his own conscience."

Chang offered more rum to his guests; Alvaro accepted, but Carrillo declined with the excuse that he would be driving. Chang joined Alvaro.

"To the saints!" Alvaro said, letting some drops of rum fall on the grass, imitating what he had seen in Guanabacoa.

"To the memory of my father," said Chang, clinking glasses with his visitor. The conversation then turned to other topics for a few minutes until, at Carrillo's request, Chang continued his narrative. "One day, the old man told me very solemnly that he had a lot of money in many bank accounts, but using the money before his death would be very dangerous for him and for his family. Once he had died, no one would even guess where it had come from. I considered the possibility that he had managed to stash some away somewhere: maybe that was why he had been sentenced to death. Meanwhile, he had remarried after my mother's death and had a new daughter. But I only had to look at where and how he lived to realize that all of his big talk was merely the dream of a man who might have once had everything but now had nothing.

"When he started to speak about millions and millions of dollars, I realized he had gone totally wacky." Pablo Chang smiled and remained silent for a moment before continuing.

"I was surprised at the direction his stories were taking. I had thought that, after fantasizing a bit, he would move on to other subjects, but he seemed to have become obsessed with that supposed fortune deposited in various banks. In this last year, he entered a phase of delirious dementia. He asked me to secretly communicate to the top authorities of the country that he wanted to make an important donation to take effect after his death, a fifty-million-dollar grant to begin with . . ." Chang threw back his head and burst into a loud laugh and, by contagion and the effects of the rum, Carrillo and Alvaro laughed with him.

"Listen to this. He gave me precise instructions for negotiating with the commander in chief. He said he wanted the millions that he was donating to be used for productive investments and that only the profits could be touched, not the principal. With that, he began to lay down a series of conditions. With my face as straight as possible, I explained that I am subject to military regulations, and that I would have to request an interview with the head of the army to explain the matter to him. In that way, I managed to keep him quiet for a bit.

"I spoke with a specialist and he told me that it could be senile dementia. He said that some old people suffer from psychoses that are very difficult to diagnose because in many aspects, they function normally. I had to resign myself to inventing something new each time he called, until he became angry with me and began to curse my superiors. He couldn't understand how they could postpone their acceptance of such a significant donation.

"One day, he told me that he had decided to alert the surviving members of the secret society to the possibility that he might be alive. Following the absurd logic of everything else he had told me, I said, 'But Papá, if the bastard that ordered your death is still alive, he'll come after your head again.' As if he was making a great decision, he said: 'That's exactly what I want, son. I have to resolve this situation while I'm still alive.' I started to feel really sorry for him.

"After I was stationed again in Guantánamo, he called me one day at the military base under my command, very excited. 'Time is running out,' he told me. 'You have to come now, something very important has come up. My plan worked. I need to tell you something.'

"I was worried. It seemed like we were going to have to put him into an asylum. I spoke a little later with his wife and she assured me that Rafael— as she always called him—was very well and that she had just heard him laughing, something that she hadn't heard for a long time. He was with a visitor—an old Chinese friend. She said he had a good appetite and had just eaten a bowl of shark-fin soup that he had taught her to make, and had asked for more.

"I thought about going to Havana and making up another story, but it was impossible because I was tending to some problems at the naval base occupied by the *Americanos*. Soon afterward, I was told that he had died. I managed to get to Havana that evening and return to Santiago the next morning. At least I was able to spend a few hours at the wake. Then, incredibly, as you informed me, his body was stolen from the cemetery."

Chang turned to Carrillo and said, "Colonel, when you came to see me in Santiago, I was tempted to tell you all of this, but it seemed like it would just complicate matters. If you are now asking for my conclusion about the whole thing, I can tell you I'm still not sure whether or not he was my father, but I am sure he began to live out the intrigues that he, himself, had invented, and that he wound up crazy as a loon."

DID YOU KNOW that Camila is an excellent pianist? This morning, she played Lecuona's 'Comparsita' for me over the telephone. Such a talented and hardworking girl!"

Alvaro's mother couldn't accept the idea of her son marrying anyone other than Camila. She didn't care to hear about "the other one," as she had baptized Mayulí. Every day, she held long phone conversations with the young policewoman—in her view, the perfect prospective daughter-in-law—and every day she discovered new and marvelous things about her.

"Are you sure you weren't hearing a recording? Mamá, listen, pay attention to me. Mayulí is the sweetest woman I've ever met. And I'm in love with her, as gaga as a thirteen-year-old. I have decided I'm going to marry Mayulí on the seventeenth of this coming month, and you're going to have to accept it once and for all."

Dulce María collapsed into an armchair, looking so pale that her son ran to get her a glass of water, which she gulped down as if it were a miraculous medicine.

"But this time you have to get married in the church. That's the only thing I'm going to ask of you. You're my only son, and I've held onto this illusion my whole life."

Alvaro sighed with relief. A church wedding to please his mother was something he could live with. Now he had to have a final conversation with Camila, who seemed dead-set on getting his semen one way or another.

In their last phone conversation, she had hinted that she could blackmail him by telling the whole police force that he was afraid of going to bed with her, and everybody would think that he was a homosexual—the worst catastrophe that could befall a policeman in Cuba. Camila was very confident of her ultimate triumph because of his mother's support. Certainly, the two women were a deadly combination that he had to somehow break apart.

"Mamá, I need your help. I have to figure out how we're going to manage all of our expenses. I already have a buyer for my mountain bike and the Walkman for a hundred dollars. I've collected everything I have made of gold, which I plan to sell to the gold shop, although I don't think it will be worth much. On top of that, my savings for the last ten years amount to 9,362 pesos, almost twenty percent of what I earned. That's about 375 dollars. Imagine! We have to pay for a civil wedding, a church wedding, a reception of some sort, then a honeymoon. And, after that, the baby clothes, baby food, baby soap, and baby powder . . .

"I'm going to talk to Mayulí today and see how we can reduce our wedding expenses to a minimum. I hate to talk to her about this because it's her first marriage—and, I hope, her last. But she's so young, and all young women dream about having a beautiful wedding."

"I have some savings from what my brothers send me from the United States. When I tell them you're getting married, I'm sure they'll want to contribute something. Let's make a list of the things we'll need. You'll see that everything will be all right."

Alvaro, as always, got depressed at the mention of money from the United States, although he was well aware that it had been crucial in providing the two of them with adequate food over the past few years, as well as house maintenance and the replacement of home appliances that, one by one, had become obsolete after years of good use.

That afternoon, Alvaro decided to go on foot to Mayulí's house to figure out the best walking route. He would soon have to give up his bicycle, and although he hoped to persuade Mayulí to come live with him and his mother, if he failed to convince her, he would have to walk between the two houses thousands of times. With a map, he estimated the distance at slightly over three miles. He could probably cover the distance in around forty-five minutes. He started out at five P.M., taking advantage, wherever possible, of the shady side of the street and moderating his pace to avoid breaking a sweat. Shortly before six o'clock, Mayulí was in his arms and smiling happily up at him.

"You're the loveliest thing that has ever happened to me. Every minute I'm with you is like a gift. But, my precious one, we have to analyze our finances and figure out where we're going to live. My mother's waiting for you with open arms. We have almost too much space in that house, but it will be great for children. If I snore, you can have your own room next to mine. If you don't want to see so much of my mother, we have our own wing of the house complete with a kitchen and separate entrance."

Observing the worried look on his face, Mayulí remained silent, and he continued. "You say you would prefer that I move in here, but I have to tend to the garden that is going to be our economic salvation. I've figured it out. Look, here are the figures. What that garden produces will be more than enough for us, and almost half will be left over to sell. We'll also have my pension, plus whatever else you earn in case you want to go back to work after the children are a little grown . . . That will be up to you. Right now, we need to calculate the cost of the wedding and other immediate expenses such as providing for a child. I'd like to go over it all with you."

Every time he had tried to talk about expenses thus far, Mayulí would make a gesture of resignation. She would try to pay attention for a little while, but then always managed to distract him and change the subject. This time he was determined to be firm about important matters such as renting rather than buying wedding clothes, deciding how many people each of them should invite to the wedding, what food and drinks they should offer at the reception, if a reception was absolutely necessary, et cetera, et cetera. For the first time in his life, he was sleepless thinking about money, money, money. And he had suddenly realized the seriousness of marriage and the decision to have a child.

Mayulí's eyes danced with impish amusement. "But you talk about children as if they were just around the corner. You seem to think I'm pregnant, although we've barely been together three weeks. How can you be so sure? You've been influenced by that *Santera's* prediction, so you think all the women you're with will get pregnant, as if you have a magic wand there!" Mayulí laughed and, as always when she wanted to change the subject, smothered his protests with kisses. She understood, nevertheless, that this time the big blond man who had won her heart so completely was truly anguished about his financial situation and would not stop worrying about it until they discussed what they were going to do.

She drew him to the bed to sit down beside her. "Look, let's make everything simple. We'll have a civil wedding at the Wedding Palace. Then we'll have a very simple reception here with our closest relatives and no one else. Then we'll go for three days on our honeymoon to whatever hotel we are assigned by the government, and that's that. We really don't need a big party to be happy."

Mayulí lowered her head a moment, then raised it sharply, as if she had made an important decision. "But darling, there's something else I need to talk to you about. Today was a special day for my father and me. I have to start doing something I promised him, and I would like your help."

"What is it?"

She shook her head. "I'll tell you about it later, after dinner."

Mayulí's mother was tireless in demonstrating her affection for her future son-in-law and in offering him food all the time, convinced that he needed to gain weight quickly. That evening, she had prepared several of his favorite dishes in abundance. She encouraged him throughout the entire meal to eat everything, which he did with pleasure, though he was sure he would not gain an ounce.

After the meal, the three of them watched television in the living room until Mayulí rose, kissed her mother good-night, and gave a signal to Alvaro. Once in her bedroom, Mayulí opened her closet and handed him a pair of old tennis shoes he had brought the week before when he painted her room. "Wear these shoes. Where we're going, we can't make any noise."

Alvaro put on the shoes, looking at her questioningly, but Mayulí offered no further explanation. She collected several items and went into the bathroom, then returned, dressed in black pants and a black sweater with a black kerchief on her head. She swung a small backpack, also black, over her shoulders, walked to the bedroom door, and turned the key. Returning to her closet, she dropped to her knees, looked up at Alvaro, and said quietly: "Follow me, but don't say a word!"

As she disappeared into the closet, Alvaro, perplexed, followed her in this strange ceremony, fascinated by the movement of her butt before him as she crawled inside. Moving like that in such a cramped space was difficult for him. Reaching what seemed to be the wall, she shifted something and continued, promptly swallowed up by total darkness. They passed through a narrow tunnel until his head suddenly struck Mayulí's leg. She took his arm and helped him stand, then squeezed his hand as if asking him to trust her.

He saw an electric panel on the wall with small green and red lights that lit up and went out as she pressed buttons on the lower part. She continued at the panel for several seconds before closing the box, leaving them again in complete darkness. Alvaro felt one of her hands grasping his belt and followed her docilely until they reached a place marked by green phosphorescent paint. Mayulí raised a metal lid on the floor and disappeared down a ladder, also phosphorescent. After descending what he calculated to be around twenty feet, they walked upright along another narrow passageway until they reached a door, also marked with phosphorescent paint. Mayulí opened it with a key. She closed the door behind him and said, "Now we can talk." Alvaro heard a click and had to close his eyes against the sudden intensity of the light. They were in a large L-shaped room.

Alvaro walked around slowly. On the right side of the room, four armchairs were grouped around a low table; a television set sat on a stand embedded in the wall, and a small door gave access to a bathroom. At the end of the opposite side were a large bed, a night table, a wardrobe, and a bookcase. A wooden partition separated this area from an electric stove, a cabinet with drawers, a table, and a sink. The central section had an enormous desk flanked by two large bookcases. But the most noteworthy items were the Chinese-landscape wall paintings. The upper part of one wall bore an ornate sign: *"Kingdom of the GD&D."*

"What does that mean?"

"When I was little, I used to play right there. My father built me a small playhouse shaped like a castle that was filled with my toys. He called it the Kingdom of the Green Dragon and the Dragoness."

Mayulí sat down at the desk and pulled a laptop out of a drawer. She moved her fingers over the keyboard with the dexterity of an expert. From her backpack, she produced a CD that she slipped into the computer, and Alvaro could see on the screen that it was loading files.

"This is going to take awhile. Would you like to make us some tea?"

Alvaro went to the kitchen area and returned shortly with two cups of green tea without sugar, a beverage he had learned to enjoy in Mayulí's company.

Mayulí interrupted what she was doing and drank a sip of the tea. "Let me explain where we are. This apartment house was built in the '40s in a spot where many shacks and two good houses already stood. The shacks were demolished and the two houses were integrated into the new building. The lower floors became garages. The basement of one of the houses, way below the floor of the garages, was totally isolated and unused. It was going to be filled up with earth, but my father figured out a way to connect it by corridors and a stairway to our apartment. He made an agreement with the owner, a man named Chang who he knew quite well. Papá furnished the room and ventilated it through our apartment. He then took the liberty of 'borrowing' telephone lines from several offices on the upper floors. Two of them have Internet access that nobody uses at night. So much time has passed since then that nobody even knows about this place.

"My father loved mysteries. I'm the only one in the family who knows about this place. I've spent many hours of my life here with him."

Mayulí moved over, sat down on Alvaro's lap, and continued sharing her memories of her father. "As you know, my dad worked for years as a humble accountant in Choy's office. When that work stopped after the Revolution closed all private businesses in the early 1960s, he began to translate news from Cuban newspapers and magazines and sell the translations to news agencies. He kept doing that until the very end. At first, he worked with a typewriter and sent his translations by shortwave radio; later he sent them by telex, after that by e-mail, and more recently by Internet.

"When I was small, he brought me here with him. While he worked, I watched television or played with my dolls or did my homework. Every now and then, he stopped what he was doing and played with me like he was another child. He invented songs and stories about dragons and princesses. As I grew older, I spent more and more time here, completely removed from the world, following my father's rigorous training program, learning what he wanted me to know, although he never did convince me to study economics at the university.

"To interest me in that field, he invented a game. We were supposed to be millionaires who had to take care of our money. To start off the game, each of us opened an investment portfolio with the same amount of money. The winner was the one who could make the initial capital grow more. Using newspapers and magazines, and later the Internet, we tracked the value of our stocks, the rates of foreign-currency exchange, the interest rates at the banks in which we supposedly held our money, and other related investment information.

"I loved risky investments, like gold mines in Tasmania, oil explorations in the Caribbean, new Internet companies, satellite and communication firms . . . He, on the other hand, was very conservative in his investments. When my assets lost money, I got depressed, and I got incredibly happy when they increased in value. We loved playing this game and it took up a lot of our time."

Mayulí got up and kept talking. "Usually I consulted my father on when to buy and when to sell. And on what information I needed to best evaluate a given investment. He gave me long and thoughtful recommendations with full explanations. Most of my father's knowledge about modern finances came from his days working for a very rich man named Donald Chang, a client of Choy's accounting office, the same man who owned the building. My father and Chang were the same age, and became close friends. They used to go out together a lot to enjoy Havana's '50s nightlife, he told me."

Mayulí went back to her cup of tea. The expression on her face became somber. "The problem was that little by little he began to confuse the game with reality." Mayulí's voice sounded like she was about to cry. "Little by little he actually *became* the millionaire Donald W. Chang, who at that point had been dead for years . . . He started to talk about investing in tourism development in Cuba, with the profits put into children's health care and other good causes. Seeing him like that was very painful for me at first. As time went on, he seemed so happy in his fantasy world that I became convinced it was better for him than facing the harsh reality of our lives. I decided to help him with his dreams, and I myself dreamed some, too. Why not?

"Before he died, he left me in charge of carrying out the project exactly as we had conceived it, without breaking any of its strict rules. He made me swear to it many times. I know it must sound crazy to you . . ." Mayulí looked at Alvaro. She took his hands and asked, "Are you willing to help me with this game? It really is fascinating, but it takes time, attention, and lots of knowledge and imagination. We'll start with something that was very close to my father's heart—a company that is making an initial investment of fifty million dollars in Cuba, using the profits to cover the expenses at a children's hospital."

"Just one hospital?"

"Do you have any idea of how much it costs to run a 400-bed children's hospital? If fifty million dollars is invested well and yields an annual profit of eight percent, it would only cover about thirty dollars a day per patient for food, electricity, medicine, X-rays, medical equipment, uniforms, cleaning supplies . . ."

As Mayulí kept describing the project down to the last detail, Alvaro's mind wandered in another direction. Suddenly, the whole case had become crystal clear to him. Cuan, like millions of other immigrants for half a millennium, had abandoned his real world of hunger, war, hate, and oppression to come to a new and remote world seeking food, peace, freedom, love, and wealth. After many years of relentless work without getting anywhere, Cuan had met Donald Chang, a man who had accomplished all his dreams. When Chang died, Cuan had become obsessed with the idea of *being* Chang. In that game, he found everything he had ever wanted, including a fortune as big as he could imagine . . . But he'd also inherited all the fears of the dead man, and had to hide for much of his life in that hole. When he tried to resurrect the dead man, he met death himself.

His detective self had many questions. Nevertheless, he would ask nothing. He was not there as a policeman but as a man who had finally found his soul mate, someone who needed his love, his absolute confidence, and, above all, his protection. When Mayulí finished her explanation, he looked into her eyes and squeezed her hands.

"You can count me in," he whispered.

For the first time, Alvaro saw Mayulí in her true dimension, a mistress of arcane knowledge, and he recalled Camila's intellect—perhaps both were members of a superior sex.

CLOSING COMMENTS

THESE ARE SOME of the closing comments in the final report we just finished preparing. I'll read you some select parts to get your opinion before I submit this to the minister." General Gonzalo opened a thick file to a page marked with a strip of paper and read: "*The customized coffin and its refrigerated container, which were supposed to carry Cuan's remains to his native Beijing, were withdrawn by Chinese authorities. The ambassador himself called to apologize for the 'error.'*"

"Why isn't Cuan's corpse being returned to China? Why did 'Chinese authorities' change their mind about this?" Carrillo asked.

"Hold on, let me find our explanation for that," Gonzalo said with a faint smirk on his face, while opening the report on another page. "To answer your question, I'll read you a statement by an informant who managed to participate in a very private gathering. He wrote:

. . . The reunion was called for the inauguration of a monument on the outskirts of Beijing on a piece of property belonging to the descendents of a famous university professor murdered by the Japanese in 1936. There was a crypt in the center of the gardens with seven compartments, each a different color, five of them occupied with marble coffins of corresponding colors. At the beginning of the ceremony, the speaker stated that according to the rules of the Seven Dragons society, the names of members should never be mentioned. He then explained that the remains of four of the Dragons were there in the coffins—White, Blue, Maroon, and Black—and, referring to the

empty green coffin, he said: "The Green Dragon is believed to have been killed by the Japanese, but his body was never found."

"In other words, they don't admit that Cuan was the Green Dragon. Why?"

Gonzalo flipped to another part of the report. "Here are the reasons we found for this change:

An announcement by the Cuban police stated that the body of a drowned man had been found with the Canadian passport Ming was using. The Chinese authorities must have opened their own investigation to figure out why Cuan's corpse had disappeared, and stumbled onto Ming. They must have found out who Ming really was. They probably learned that the money sent by the Green Dragon was dirty. Any news tarnishing the honor of these important men after such a long time was unwelcome.

"That's a reasonable explanation. Who witnessed the inauguration? Someone from the Cuban embassy in Beijing?" Carrillo asked.

"The source of the statement is very curious. It was sent to the Second Secretary of the Cuban Embassy signed by 'A *good friend of Cuba.*' We think that note must have come from China's intelligence service, as a move to stop Cuban inquiries into a national secret. They gave us enough information so we can 'close' our case. And because of the way they did it, they want to keep this matter completely unofficial."

"That sounds reasonable, too," said Carrillo. After a moment, he asked, "Did you say four Dragons were buried there?"

"Yes, another Dragon has died since we started. Thanks to this 'good friend of Cuba' we can guess who this Dragon is and why he's dead." Gonzalo again flipped through the report. "In addition to the statement describing the inauguration of the monument, we received copies of a letter that Cuan sent to each of the three surviving Dragons in China. It starts by saying, '*I'm sending this letter to you because you're the only surviving Dragon I trust.*' After that, the letter goes into a lengthy explanation of what happened in the past and why Cuan considered the attempt to murder him to be treason, committed by one of the other surviving Dragons. The closing line of the letter is, 'Whoever *did this had to be profiting somehow by my death*.'" Gonzalo put the report aside and continued his explanations.

"The intent of Cuan's letters is clear—it leaves the culprit no choice but to come out into the open and try to silence him again. When Ming appeared, Cuan knew his nemesis had arrived and that his real enemy, Ming's boss, would be revealed." Gonzalo stood up. "The new corpse in the monument has to be the traitor's. Treason is never pardonable, we have learned."

Carrillo understood that his time had now ended and stood up to shake the hand Gonzalo was offering. "It sounds reasonable," Carrillo conceded. "Cuan wanted to erase any possible menace to his children, and at the same time get revenge *à la* Chinese."

"Don't move, coffee and sweets are coming," Gonzalo said. "That's one of the reasons I'm running away. I can't bear the sight of sweets without devouring them."

Carrillo laughed and sat down again, watching Gonzalo leave the room as a pretty girl in uniform brought him a snack.

"The case is closed, there's a reasonable explanation for everything. Chiefs are happy, bureaucrats are happy, everybody is happy. How wonderful life would be if it were really like that," Carrillo said, admiring the beautiful girl. She smiled at Carrillo, not understanding a thing and showing a missing tooth.

CONFLICTING INTERESTS

LIFE SLOWLY FELL into new routines. Mayulí visited Alvaro's home for the first time to meet her future mother-in-law. She was enchanted by the beautiful house overlooking the Almendares River and the coastline; the spacious rooms and the exquisite gardens on the large property. She began to stay there twice a week while she and her mother-in-law got to know each other, with the immediate result that the original plans were altered to include a church wedding. With Alvaro's work renewed, and with the help of the dry season—good for growing vegetables—his agricultural project began to reward his efforts. Several days a week he walked to Mayulí's house after working in his garden all day. There he had dinner, began to learn about computers, and tried to help out with the strange work she did in the hidden room. But every night he visited, a heavy drowsiness blocked all his efforts to learn and be a good helper. Invariably, he fell into a deep sleep by ten o'clock.

A week before their wedding, Alvaro received a call from Jacinto. The voice of his old friend sounded polite but cold. Both were aware that nothing would ever be the same between them again.

After the usual greetings, Jacinto revealed, "I shouldn't be calling you, but Narelys begged me to do it."

Alvaro froze. He felt his hand shaking and his heartbeat accelerate, remembering Jacinto's call in his nightmare.

"She is inviting you to her wedding this coming Sunday. I don't think you should come. It would be better if you didn't see her for a long time."

Alvaro heard the telephone click at the other end of the line. The *Santera's* oracle flashed in his mind. He smiled, thinking how much he'd worried about the three women in his path, and the three children he was going to have, and all the money he was going to need for food and clothing. In the end, happily for him, the three women had shrunk to one. And, though he had repeatedly asked Mayulí about a possible pregnancy, her response was always a Mona Lisa smile.

As the wedding day grew closer, the two mothers-in-laws and Mayulí started to hold daily conferences, reviewing every detail. Two days before the wedding, Alvaro worked in his garden longer than usual since he was going to be away for over a week. He hired a neighbor and spent the whole afternoon explaining the chores he should do in his absence.

When Alvaro met Mayulí at her home that day, she was talking with her mother, who left them alone as soon as he arrived. Mayulí took him to their room and made him sit down and listen to what she had to say.

"I have news for you. This is the eighth week we've been together. Today I went to see a doctor to have an ultrasound test. The answer is yes, yes, and yes."

Alvaro jumped out of the chair and hugged her. "We're having a baby!"

"No. You don't understand what I said."

"No?"

"We're having three babies—triplets."

Alvaro collapsed back into the chair.

The wedding of Mayulí and Alvaro was a major social event in the Chinese quarter. It began with a civil ceremony in the Vedado Wedding Palace, chosen by the bride. From there, a procession of ten automobiles, two of them enormous limousines rented for the families and some close friends, drove to the Catholic church, Santa Rita de Casia, on 5th Avenue and Calle 28 in the heart of Miramar, chosen by the groom's mother for the religious ceremony. Finally, a reception was held in the house of the Casino Chung Wah, a Chinese society in the heart of the neighborhood where the bride lived. The guests numbered roughly two hundred, of which Alvaro knew scarcely a dozen. These included Colonel Carrillo and the recently promoted Brigadier General Pablo Chang, who had retired so he could head a multi-million-dollar project in the tourism industry, half-financed by the army and half-financed by a Swiss bank on behalf of a foreign finance company.

The wedding gifts were exhibited in a room off the main hall and included seven dragons in diverse colors coiled on a five-foot-high porcelain jar with their fiery mouths open to those who approached to admire the monumental work of art sent by General Gonzalo. An orchestra played music appropriate for the occasion, beginning at seven that evening. A new car, adorned with balloons and a *"Just Married"* sign, waited for the bride and groom to take them to Varadero Beach, where they would spend their honeymoon at a guest house owned by the Chung Wah society.

When Carrillo arrived at the area where Alvaro, Mayulí, and the two mothers-in-laws were greeting guests, the two friends moved away, each carrying a glass of champagne.

"What do you think of this shindig? The whole thing must have cost around five thousand dollars."

"Where did you get the money?" Carrillo asked.

"The whole caboodle is being paid for by Choy. Mayulí says it was a promise Choy made to her father when she was born. The old boy has a good memory, though I'd have preferred getting the cash. We could have had a modest wedding and still had a few thousand left over. This is a big waste of money."

"Oh well, let the rich spend their money however they choose . . . I have some surprising news for you." Carrillo's face was serious. "You were right all along. There must be a powerful drug cartel involved in this Cuan matter." The police chief finished off the glass of champagne Alvaro had given him, and almost hissed: "They're trying to bribe the two of us, you and me."

"What?" Alvaro gasped.

"Listen to this. They've opened an account with a quarter of a million dollars in a London bank in your and my names as an initial 'donation' for the purpose of 'expanding the use of computers by the Cuban police.' If the donation yields good results, more donations will be forthcoming in the next two years. Get that!"

"This has to be a hoax."

"No, I researched it. There is a branch of the bank here in Havana. The manager told me on the phone that the money is waiting for us."

Alvaro remained silent, staring at Carrillo, who continued with his news. "What's more, you're supposed to go to Madrid for a three-month course in computing, all expenses paid. When you return, it will be my turn!"

Alvaro, his arms crossed, stared in silence, while Carrillo went on. "The whole thing is more transparent than water. We don't have to be very clever to understand what's meant by 'if the donation yields good results, more donations will be forthcoming.' In other words, if you and I accept the bribe. I already made a report on all of this."

"Who's making the donation?"

"A so-called GD&D Foundation. Nobody knows what the organization does or where it's based."

"Excuse me, Carrillo, I'll be back."

Alvaro walked quickly over to his wife and gently pulled her away from a group of women in a corner of the hall. Carrillo, bewildered by his friend's move, observed the newlyweds' first fight with amusement. He decided to find something to eat and get another glass of champagne. This time he had been smart and had brought a chauffeur.

The newly married couple decided to make an early exit. Their argument was attracting the attention of many in the room. Nevertheless, Alvaro decided, this matter had to be fully discussed before their life together could follow a normal course. They left the gathering.

As soon as Mayulí reached the street and saw that nobody else was around, she said: "There was no possible way I could get you out of your damn garden. I had to do something."

Alvaro's silence was more ominous than anything he could have said.

"I couldn't do all that work by myself. Even if I've already quit my job."

"Why didn't you tell me? Why?"

"I trust you, but there are some things . . . you don't understand. You're still a policeman."

"That's not true."

"Why were you so interested in my father's old belt?"

Alvaro suddenly felt embarrassed and considered lying, but he told himself that she didn't deserve that. "I thought I might find Chinese codes written in it related to fabulous sums of money kept in the world's leading banks. I thought that was why Carrillo was so interested in locating the body—to find a treasure that could help solve at least some of the great economic problems now facing this country."

Mayulí shook her head. "Ay, such ignorance, my God!" She leaned in and kissed him. "One CD can hold six hundred novels and still have space left over. You can encode the number of a bank account so that even the most sophisticated hacking technique would take years to figure it out."

Mayulí looked at Alvaro as if he were an abandoned Third World child. "I was planning to tell you little by little. I want to help bring you up to date about the world we live in. I really need your help. I've spent half my life in that hole and there are lots of things I know nothing about. You don't realize it, but there's a hell of a lot of work to do. We have to invest more than $500 million, and it keeps growing every day."

THE SMELL OF HUMID EARTH and chicken droppings greeted the man from the city as he opened the door. Several clucking hens followed him through the door and began wandering around the room where four people were waiting. A countryman of about forty was standing against a window that looked out on a nearby cornfield and, further away, dark summer clouds. Next to him, a younger woman sat on a bench with a sleepy three- or four-year-old child in her arms. Facing them was a very thin old woman. The new arrival sat on one of the two empty benches and looked the place over. The room was built with badly cut, unpainted wooden planks, and roofed by zinc sheeting, with an earthen floor. The construction leaned against a wall of an old masonry house through which a hole had been opened and embedded with a frame and a door.

A couple of the hens slipped under the seats to scratch the earth and defecate, ignoring the humans. The old woman eventually got up, chased them out of the room, and closed the door, making the place suddenly dark. After a while, the door connected to the house opened and an old man with a straw hat in his hand appeared. The old woman stood up and joined the old man, leaving the room. The countryman then rose and was followed through the same door by the woman with the child in her arms.

Once alone, the man from the city switched seats to look through the window at the faraway clouds. A soft, cool, humid breeze blew in with a fresh smell. A half-hour later, the countryman and his family came out and the city man went through the door into a dark room. When his eyes adjusted to the darkness, he saw the shirtless *Palero* blowing smoke on his *nganga*. The visitor stood a few steps away from the man, who turned to attend to his new client. The *Palero* took off a white cap, revealing a shaved head, a white face with thick, black eyebrows, a very black moustache, and a bushy goatee that was beginning to gray.

The newcomer moved two steps toward the *Palero*, took off his hat and glasses, and shouted: "This is exactly how I wanted to catch you, you son of a bitch, Pedro Bermúdez!"

The *Palero* was briefly paralyzed by surprise, but leapt up and cried: "Adrián Arrinda himself!"

They joyfully embraced each other, then Pedro went to get something to drink and they sat down on two very low benches, almost at floor level, to reminisce about old times.

"I escaped by a miracle, and I owe it to you," Adrián explained. "If I had kept the gun, I would have tried shooting my way out and the Special Brigade would have drilled me with bullets! I left like I had nothing to do with it, right in front of the guards."

"Impossible!"

"Dressed like a woman, with the dress, the braids, the necklace, and the sandals."

"You're joking! If I had known you were going to do that I would have stayed to flirt with you."

They both laughed and looked keenly at each other.

"How are you doing?" Adrián asked.

"Not bad. The difficult part was starting in this place, the armpit of the world. Now I have a good clientele, because that"—Pedro pointed at the *nganga*—"is 'hot.' Guess who I have in there!"

Adrián thought for a moment, staring at the iron container he had so often seen near Lorenzo's *nganga*. "No. It can't be . . ."

"Yes, yes, that's who it is. Lorenzo Bantú himself! Where better could he be than with a friend? If I hadn't done it, somebody else would have stolen his bones from the cemetery. That skull is worth a million, don't you think?"

Adrián nodded, stood up, and moved near the *nganga*, watching it carefully.

"And that's nothing," Pedro continued. "I recovered his Zarabanda, too. I paid a hundred *fullas* to one of the Special Brigade men who knew what was going on and picked it up in the confusion and then hid it. So now I have Lorenzo and his saber, and nothing can stop him. Have you heard anything about Mulo? What happened to José Miguel?"

"Mulo is still in the tank. José Miguel—he's a smart *guajiro*. He was commended by the police chief for calming everybody down and explaining how the police were not to blame for Lorenzo's death."

"Now tell me, Adrián, how did you manage to stay in the same place, as if nothing happened. That's incredible!"

"Simple. They were looking for the Chinaman. The rest of it was none of their business, and they had nothing on me. No one knew about the secret refuge, so no one looked for it. It's still full of stuff. That's why I came to see you. I have a proposition that you can't refuse."

"*Coño*, Adrián, that's unbelievable." Pedro sat quietly for a moment, then his face lit up with an amazing realization. "That proves that Lorenzo was right! *A dead Chinaman is infallible protection!*"

GLOSSARY

African-rooted religious beliefs in Cuba

During the four centuries of Spanish colonial rule, hundreds of thousands of Africans from many different ethnic groups were forced to come to Cuba as slaves. They brought with them their religious beliefs and practices—which included divination, music, and dancing. Their beliefs interacted with and were influenced by the Catholic religion of the ruling Spaniards. Over time, the following religious practices were born: *Regla de Osha*—commonly called *Santería*—with Yoruba roots from Western Africa; and *Regla Mayombe*—usually called *Palo Monte*—with Bantú origin from Central Africa. Natives from the Calabar River basin founded the Abakuá Secret Society, which is based on a religious legend. Since early times, these beliefs—still alive, with many followers of all races and educational levels—have influenced the Cuban people in many ways.

The author knew that a novel like this could not be written unless he acquired a detailed knowledge of these religions and firsthand information on the ways they affect the lives of their followers. A complete list of the author's information sources would be out of place, so included here are only the most fundamental ones: Lydia Cabrera's *El Monte* and *La Sociedad Secreta Abakuá*; Enrique Sosa's *Abakuá: Una Secta Secreta*; Natalia Bolívar's *Los Orishas en Cuba*; and the Guanabacoa Museum. The work of Teodoro Díaz Favelo was also quite helpful for a deeper understanding.

Gods and deities of Regla de Osha/Santería mentioned in the novel:

Aggayú Solá. Giant father of Shangó.

Babalú Ayé. Protects against leprosy, venereal diseases, and other ailments, including AIDS.

Elégguá. The *orisha* who opens and closes all paths, who determines the destiny, life, and death of human beings.

Eshú. Elégguá's dark side.

Inlé. The doctor in *Regla de Osha*. Also patron of fisheries and hunters.

Iroko. A minor *orisha* who lives in the *ceiba* tree.

Los Ibedji. The Twins, minor *orishas*, offspring of Shangó and Oshún. They protect children.

Naná Burukú. A minor *orisha*. Mother of Babalú Ayé.

Obatalá. Creator of men. Ruler of all human heads, controller of dreams and ideas.

Obbá. Minor *orisha*. One of the wives of Shangó. Lives in the cemetery where she guards the tombs.

Ochosi. Hunter par excellence.

Oggún. Rules over all things made of iron.

Olofi. The supreme god who distributed his powers among the *orishas* (gods).

Olokun. Owner of the ocean's depth.

Orishaoko. God of agriculture, patron of farmers.

Orula. Ruler of divination. His sons are the only ones who may become *babalawos*, the highest priests in *Regla de Osha*.

Osaín. *Orisha* that represents nature itself. Owner of all herbs and trees with magical powers.

Oshún. Goddess of love and riches. Ruler of all sweet waters. Yemayá's sister.

Osún. Companion of Elégguá. Messenger of Obatalá and Olofí. Represents life itself.

Oyá. One of the goddesses that rule over the cemeteries. Master of lightning.

Shangó. Master of thunder, fire, and war. This *orisha* has insatiable virility.

Yemayá. Queen of the sea. Patroness of fishermen and sailors.

Yewá Binoyé. Queen of the dead. One of the *orishas* who rule over the cemeteries.

Gods and deities of Regla Mayombe/Palo Monte mentioned in the novel:

Chola. Goddess of love. Same as Oshún in *Regla de Osha*.

Zarabanda. A very powerful god, ruler of all the things made of iron. Same as Oggún in *Regla de Osha*.

Gods and deities of the Abakuá Secret Society mentioned in the novel:

Abasí. Supreme god of the Abakuás.

Tánze. The sacred fish that revealed the secret of the *Ékue* to the *Efó* tribe.

Common Words:

The author has explained the meaning of most of the foreign words as they are introduced. This glossary may be helpful with some key words that are used several times throughout the novel.

Abakuá. Member of the Abakuá Secret Society or of that origin.

Abikú. A child who cannot have brothers and sisters, supposed to be hexed. A person with magical powers.

Alafia. See *Coconut oracle*.

Aché. Inner power, virtue, grace.

Agogó. Instrument used to call the attention of Obatalá.

Aguardiente. In Cuba, an alcoholic beverage made from sugar cane molasses. Rum can also be made from *aguardiente*.

Aleyos. (*Regla de Osha*) A person who has not been fully initiated, but has received "The Warriors" (Elégguá, Oggún, Ochosi, Osún).

Amarre. Hobbling, to put a hex on a man or a woman so he or she cannot leave.

Añejo. Old. Any rum that has been aged for several years in oak barrels.

Babalawos, Babaloshas. (*Regla de Osha*) Highest priests. Sons of the *orisha* Orula.

Berocos. (Abakuá) Testicles.

Bilongo. A hex, curse.

Bohío. In Cuba, a poor country house made of lumber with a thatched roof.

Brujo de nación. (*Regla Mayombe*) A person who was already a priest in Africa before being enslaved.

Calle. (Spanish) Street.

Caurís. A marine shell found in Africa, used by the *Diloggún* oracle.

Ceiba. A big tree similar to the African baobab, sacred to all Afro-Cuban religious beliefs in Cuba.

Chamalongo. (*Regla Mayombe*) A divining method.

Chamba. (Regla Mayombe) Very powerful beverage made with *aguardiente*, gunpowder, and other ingredients, including powder rasped from the human bones that might be in the *nganga*.

Chequerés. (Regla de Osha) Instruments used to call the attention of the *orishas*.

Chino. A person of Chinese origin.

Coconut oracle. (Regla de Osha) This oracle uses four pieces of coconut meat. Four pieces of coconut shell or four seashells can also be used. The four pieces can fall in five different ways in response to a question asked after the proper prayers. Each of the five ways is a "letter" and each "letter" has a different interpretation, which can be very complex. A simple interpretation of each "letter" follows:

- *Alafia.* All four pieces of coconut with the meat up. It means yes, all is well, but it is not a conclusive letter.
- *Eyife.* Two pieces with the meat up, two facing down. This letter means a definite yes.
- *Itawa.* Three pieces with the meat up, one facing down. It means yes, but there is a difficulty to overcome.
- *Okana.* Three pieces with the meat down, one facing up. It means no, and it is a bad omen.
- *Oyékun.* Four pieces with the meat down. It means that a dead person or an *orisha* that rules over the dead wants to speak.

Comparsa. Organized group of dancers in a carnival.

Consulta. A divining session. Also, *Registro*.

Cufón. (Abakuá) The site of a chapter. Plural: *cufones*.

Diloggún. (Regla de Osha) Oracle that uses eighteen shells. Two shells are kept by the priest; sixteen are thrown.

Ebbó. Offering.

Eleda. (Regla de Osha) Guardian angel.

Empegó. (Abakuá) One of the high officers of a chapter.

Entre marido y mujer nadie se debe meter. (Spanish) Nobody should meddle between a man and his woman.

Eyife. See *Coconut oracle*.

Fiana. Police (slang).

Fundamento. (Spanish) The foundation, the basic components of something.

Guaguancó. A song with a dance.

Guajiro. A man who lives in the country and works the land.

Guanabacoa. Town across Havana Bay. Stronghold of all Afro-Cuban religious beliefs.

Hacerse el santo, or *asentarse el santo. (Regla de Osha)* To be initiated.

Ilé Osha. (Regla de Osha) Room where the *orishas* and their attributes are kept.

Íreme. (Abakuá) The spirit of a dead warrior.

Isué. (Abakuá) One of the high officers of a chapter.

Itawa. See *Coconut oracle.*

Iyalosha. (Regla de Osha) A woman initiated in this religion, a woman priest.

Iyamba. (Abakuá) Chief.

Iyaré. (Regla de Osha) High woman priest.

Jagüey. A gigantic tree.

Jutía. A large edible rodent that lives in trees.

Kari Osha. (Regla de Osha) The ceremony of initiation, lasts a week.

Killumba. (Regla Mayombe) Skull.

Kindambazo. (Regla Mayombe) A strike or hex.

Macao. Mollusk.

Macuto. Bundle. In the old days, the *nganga* was kept in a sack. That *"macuto"* could be carried by the owner—so *"nganga"* is often referred to as *"macuto."*

Majá. Snake.

Mayimbe. (Abakuá) Buzzard.

Mokongo. (Abakuá) Head of a chapter.

Monina. (Abakuá) Member of the Abakuá Secret Society.

Monte. In Spanish, a forest or large number of trees growing wild. In *Regla de Osha,* any place where vegetation grows.

Moyugba. (Regla de Osha) Prayer.

Mpaca. (Regla Mayombe) A bull's horn charged with magic substances.

Mpaca mensu. (Regla Mayombe) An *mpaca* with a mirror at its base, used for divination.

Mpungo. (Regla Mayombe) God, goddess, also the spirit who lives in the *nganga.*

Mumanso. (Regla Mayombe) Room where the *nganga* is kept.

Ñáñigos. Abakuás.

Nasakó. (Abakuá) High priest of a chapter, usually a *Regla Mayombe* priest.

Nfumbe mayor. (Regla Mayombe) A very important dead person. *Nfumbe:* dead man in the *nganga. Mayor:* bigger, important.

Nganga. (*Regla Mayombe*) Usually, an iron pot where the skull, bones, and the spirit of a dead person reside, along with other magic ingredients. The *Regla Mayombe* priest makes a pact with this spirit, who thereafter obeys him.

Nkisi. (*Regla Mayombe*) Dead person.

Obís. Coconut pieces used in the coco oracle.

Obones. (Abakuá) The higher officers of a chapter.

Okana. See *Coconut oracle.*

Oriaté. (*Regla de Osha*) Priest.

Orisha. (*Regla de Osha*) God, goddess.

Otá. (*Regla de Osha*) Stone.

Oyékun. See *Coconut oracle.*

Palero. (*Regla Mayombe*) Priest initiated in *Regla Mayombe.*

Plante. (Abakuá) Chapter.

Potencia. (Abakuá) Chapter. In Spanish, *potencia* means *power.*

Prenda. (*Regla Mayombe*) Nganga. In Spanish, *prenda* means ornament, jewel.

Raspas. Hard core of rice at the bottom of a cooking pot.

Registro de Itá. (*Regla de Osha*) Divination ceremony performed by four *babalawos* that takes place once in the lifetime of a person, during the initiation to *Regla de Osha.*

Registro. A divining session. Also, *Consulta.*

Rogación de cabeza. A ceremony performed to strengthen a person's guardian angel.

Rompimiento de Trabajo and *Recogimiento de Muerto.* A ceremony by which a hex on a person is broken and the spirit of a dead person is taken away from that person.

Sahumando. Applying smoke, mainly tobacco smoke, to rid something of bad influences.

Santero/a. (*Regla de Osha*) Priest.

Súyer. Usually the complex meaning of a "letter" in the divination methods.

Tata Nkisi. (*Regla Mayombe*) High priest.

Tatandi. (*Regla Mayombe*) Old and venerated priest.

Tierra. (Abakuá) Chapter. In Spanish, *tierra* means earth.

Tostones. Fried pieces of green plantains. Singular: *tostón.*

More Crime Fiction from *Akashic Books*

Spy's Fate by Arnaldo Correa
305 pages, hardcover, ISBN: 1-888451-28-9, $24.95

"A captivating thriller based on the murky U.S.-Cuban spy wars. Correa deftly paints the history of Castro's Cuban intelligence service and the changing face of the Miami exile community . . . The insightful sociopolitical picture, the nasty maneuverings of both services, and the credible spy plot make this a fascinating read." —*Publishers Weekly*

Adios Muchachos by Daniel Chavarría
Winner a 2001 Edgar Award!
245 pages, paperback, ISBN: 1-888451-16-5, $13.95

". . . a zesty Cuban paella of a novel that's impossible to put down. This is a great read, recommended for public libraries." —*Library Journal*

"Full of humor and wit, Chavarría turns this basic story of survival into an erotic, fast-paced thriller. Times are hard, but who said they had to be dull?" —*Village Voice*

The Eye of Cybele by Daniel Chavarría
450 pages, hardcover, ISBN: 1-888451-25-4, $27.00

Akashic Books' second release by highly acclaimed Uruguayan mystery novelist Daniel Chavarría, *The Eye of Cybele* is equal parts historical epic, whodunnit-style thriller, highbrow erotica and philosophical discourse. Set in the fifth century B.C.—during the reign of Pericles—the novel fictionally recreates the behind-the-scenes scandals and political intrigues that occupied the Athenian home front at the height of the Peloponessian War.

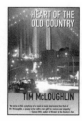

Heart of the Old Country by Tim McLoughlin
A selection of the Barnes & Noble Discover Great New Writers Program
216 pages, trade paperback, ISBN: 1-888451-15-7, $14.95

"Set in a crummy corner of present-day Bay Ridge, Brooklyn, this sweet, sardonic and by turns hilarious and tragic first novel opens with a no-hoper named Michael going through his motions . . . The novel's greatest achievement is its tender depiction of Michael as a would-be tough guy, trying to follow his father's dictum of 'Give them nothing,' while undergoing a painful education in the real world." —*Publishers Weekly*